I0685054

S'GAR

(Just say 'Es gar')
A novel by Jack Darnell
Author of Sticky and Rags

J & S Publications
jacsher@aol.com
Belmont

ISBN 978-0-9819507-4-7
First Printing

Books by Jack Darnell
Rags
Sticky
Gracefully Grasping for Dignity
Toby's Tales
Why Not Forever

Proudly printed in the United States of America

Acknowledgements

I want to thank my lovely wife for all her support and advice. This lady has followed me all over the world and supported me in my many endeavors. We have two sons. Much of the time she was alone with the boys, while I was chasing some dream. I would like to thank her also for calling a halt to my wild idea to sail around the world. Instead she suggested we replace it with her dream to hike the world's most famous foot path, the Appalachian Trail. And so it was. I followed her from Springer Mountain in Georgia to Franconia Gap in New Hampshire, approx 1850 miles. An adventure and thrill we will never forget. There is still a dream to hike the remainder of the Trail through the White Mountains and Maine, the parts we skipped to reach Mt. Katahdin, in Baxter State Park, Maine. We did climb Mt. Katahdin, what a spectacular view from the summit.

Sherry and I have appeared and taught from Cuba to Canada. Working from one organization, Church, BSA function and Senior group to the next. We have taught for a week at a time in Youth camps and traveled hours for one performance. The attendees have been from as few as three to as many as a few thousand. We have met many wonderful friends while living full time in our motor home. Now we realize the world has grown, I have tried to advance with it. Sherry and I have some wonderful internet friends who give support through our Journal the 'Shipslog'at http://shipslog-jack.blogspot.com/. The internet friends are from many walks of life and many states and countries.

****

About the book **S'gar**

This is a work of fiction. Any similarity to person's living or dead is coincidental. I say over and over, fiction is fun, a way to escape for a short period from the reality we know.

****

Praise for the authors books:

(Rags) .... Anna Mae said, "I Loved the book and couldn't put it down"!! (Retired in New York)

(Sticky) I loved this book. I got it yesterday and other than sleeping, I spent the last 24 hours reading it. It was a great mystery, plus a romance and gave a lot of information about new technology and even some history of the last frontier! (Alaska) I will reread again. It is definitely worth reading! L. Mitchell, Kansas City, Missouri

***** (Sticky) I found this book to be a good read, it held my interest throughout the whole story; it was written in a concise clear way easy to understand and follow, and it included reference to God and faith of not only John but his wife, Hattie, who he loves very much. I would highly recommend this book for anyone who is looking for a mystery story to read. B. Wooten, Southern, CA.
*****

When I received my copy of "Sticky" I thought that I would just scan a little bit of it and read it later. I could not put it down and read half of it that evening and finished it the next morning before I did anything else. It was an exciting story that kept me glued to the pages. Ken Herron, International Consultant, Author of "Amos" and Newspaper Columnist.
******

"Sticky" was a wonderful book. Once I started reading I couldn't put it down. It kept me wondering how Sticky was going to prove his innocence, very interesting reading.

Shirl, Secretary Belmont, NC

****** **"Jack Darnell drew on a wealth of life experience in his creation of "STICKY". A riveting story of a son's love for his parents and the principles they endowed him with will keep you enthralled to the final page". -- Glenda Hulbert Okeechobee, FL**
*****

Jack Darnell is veteran, and a man who believes in his country and practices what he preaches, he is also a great story teller. Jack and his wife live full time in their motor home and travel is their passion. They love the outdoors, people and places. Jack wrote a book called "Sticky", Sticky earns his nickname because he finishes the jobs he is given by sticking to them until there done. Sticky is great reading as it combines intrigue, compassion, true friendship, crime and some hard nose tactics and in the end, justice.

4

As a retired Police officer for me it was a book that was hard to put down, and my wife and I had to take turns sharing in the reading...Woody, New York
****

An intriguing epic woven from a web of corruption, deception, and intimidation: Where innocence prevails. Debbie E. .... Kentucky.
******

I have read an advance copy of Rags, outstanding book of adults and youth, enjoying life. I loved Louise, my kinda gal. I like an unorthodox Chief of Police also. But Rags, the man was my favorite. You have to love that guy. You don't want to miss this book.
S. Lucille..,. Wildwood, Florida
Sticky and Rags are available through the internet or at the authors BLOG
http://shipslog-jack.blogspot.com/

I also wanted to thank you for the book. I have read every one of Tom Clancy's and John Grisham's books. Your book was just as spellbinding if not more so. I do want to purchase the new book. Of course, I will want a signed copy...... Nathan, PLS Mountains of North Carolina

About the book:
Gracefully Grasping for Dignity
Hello Jack old buddy. I got your book and its good. I believe you have found your calling. I consider a good writer one who is down to earth and is easy to understand. Very good book. Thank you very much.

Jim

Hey Jack....I read the book...."Gracefully etc"...and found it very informative....I would recommend it to any family who find themselves in the place of having to make a decision one way or the other about their parents welfare....or spouses....or children!!! Ora, Kentucky

Why Not Forever

I loved your book "Why Not Forever" which I finished last night!! It's most unusual for me to finish a book that quickly - but it was such interesting reading. Love the way you laid out the advice on sex, dropping little hints early, and using it to tantalize the reader to keep reading....The chapter or section which was most meaningful to me had to do with your advice to seniors about the old question of re-marriage after the death of the spouse.

Bishop Fred Brannen, Missions Administrator, former missionary

All the authors books are available through Internet or at the author's BLOG

http://shipslog-jack.blogspot.com/

Contact the Author at: jacsher@aol.com

Foreword
The birth of S'gar and his history (Late 1950's)

"Dallas, you'd have to put yourself in my shoes to understand my position. When I left Duke I was at my peak in the medical profession. It was good but I was missing something from life. I had been coddled from my youth through the time I left my position at Duke; it seemed I had been in school all my life. Then I had allowed my (or my dad's) ambition to take me to the top in administration. It was not hard to drop that great job when the CIA came by to offer me those secret thrills and adventures. Excitement I never knew existed. I became THE DOC on all the 'black ops'. During an operation my adrenalin flow was max. Then after my experience with 'B', I just lost it. I realized it was not some game but innocent lives were at stake. When I departed Washington no one knew where I was, except you. That time in the woods alone with a dog, salvaged my life. Now I find that I have finances beyond my wildest dreams, thanks to you. I again want the anonymity I had in the woods. But this time I have another dream I plan to assist some down trodden folk. I want some of these people to be happy. At least I would like to assist them in gaining better lives."

"Okay Jerry, I can understand that, and it is very noble. But why the name change for heaven's sake? Changing your name is no problem. I can change your name to Fido if you want. I know a friend who changed her name to Rain. Shucks, you can make it FDR or Elvis. I am very curious why S'GAR? Also there is a problem with pronouncing it; you said it is pronounced something like ES'gar, with an s, right?"

Jerry Wiley, heir to Wiley Industries, had lived a strange and secretive life in the last few years. The latter part of his life was completely opposite from his early life. In his early years the biggest thing was losing his mother while he was in high school. His father never remarried and submerged himself into his company. He also was determined that his son would become an Icon in the world of science and medicine. In the process Jerry accepted his father's dreams and took his school studies seriously. He had a high IQ and was always top in his class.

He did not spend his time chasing girls, but chasing the formulas and answers to questions that plagued his mind. He honed his inquisitive engineering mind and set records for grades and attendance at his High School. He was proud of Taylor's 'Dragon' and the green and white of the school. His father was a proponent of public education, although private schools beckoned, he remained in public high school.

It wasn't only his mind that his father insisted stay in top shape, but also his body. He was not allowed to participate in contact sports for fear of injury to his head or hands. But he was constantly in the school gym or working out at his father's private gym at home. He was successful in convincing his father that Judo and Karate were necessary for self defense and that it also kept the decision processes sharp. He excelled in the martial arts and held two black belts by his junior year. His was a normal high school experience except for the opposite sex. His extreme focus on health and academics precluded much more that a speaking relationship.

He entered Duke on full scholarships. He had prepared himself so well he was already ahead of his freshmen counterparts. Very early he established his position as head of the class and remained there all the way through to his Doctorate.

Upon receiving his doctorate, he was offered, and accepted the position of first assistant to the head of University. Within a couple years he was the youngest head of Duke Medical School. At this point there were still no women in his life, nothing for him except a push for excellence.

Then he received a very confidential communication via a friend, 'the CIA wants to talk'. The intrigue of the request got Jerry's attention. The meeting was set up, and to his own astonishment he agreed to come and work for the CIA. Jerry Wiley, for reasons unknown to the public, resigned his post at Duke and disappeared from public view, but not from his father's wrath. Unable to understand or fathom his son's actions, the senior Wiley, practically disowned his son. Jerry could not explain to his father that he had to leave or suffocate. Communications were dissolved for a couple years.

The father's business was sinking and his health was going. Jerry had a couple close encounters with death himself and decided he should try to reconcile with his father. To his surprise it was not hard. After that life was better for both.

When Mr. Wiley passed away the business, which was in a downward spiral, fell to Jerry. Obligations to the 'Company' (CIA), kept Jerry away from the helm.   Then there was a 'Situation'. The US President's nephew and two children were kidnapped and ended up in Columbia, South America. Jerry was on the team to extricate them. In the process one of the children, labeled 'B', died. The death started Jerry on a downward spiral. He flew to Pittsburgh and turned the Corporation over to the Corporation's Attorney, R.D. (Dallas) Fletcher. Jerry asked only that Dallas send him an allowance of $100 monthly. He said, "I will be in touch" and then he disappeared. The CIA put out a search for him with no luck. Once Jerry settled, he notified Dallas where to send his $100. As a cash money order, general delivery to a small town in North Carolina called Mount Bell. The envelope used was to have no return address. Jerry's life changed drastically during that time frame.

****

Years passed and now with his attorney sitting across from him they are discussing, of all things, a name change. Jerry Wiley, famous surgeon, is changing his name to S'GAR. To be pronounced ES'gar. "You ask why, Dallas? I have a reason, but mainly because I like it. I like having one name and that name is going to be S'gar."

"Fine Boss, if you want to be called ES'gar or Cigar, then that's what it will be, but can I still call you Jerry?"

"Sure, when nobody is around," laughed S'gar. "Dallas you can call me anything you want, you are the one who saved this business and made it what it is today." This was not boss and employee, it was just two good friends talking.

"Dal, I am calling the new organization 'The MVA'.

"That's cool boss, are you going to tell me what it stands for?"

"The Modern Vigilante Association."

"No Jerry, don't go crazy on me now, we just got you back!"

"Just think of it as a supplement to law enforcement, because that is what it is going to be, and it is going to be healthy."

"Boss, you can't fix all the ills in this world. I said earlier, it is a noble thought, but impossible."

"I am not going to get them all Dallas, but I am going to fix a few, one at a time."

"The MVA, huh?" Attorney R.D. Fletcher says, shaking his head, while the newly born S'gar smiled.

Chapter One
(1995)

"I will what?"

The dark stretch limo with darkened windows sits on the side of a lonely county road near Charlotte, North Carolina. Inside are four men. Three of the men are aft in the luxurious leather seats; the driver, Corey, is speaking to the business suit. There is a large muscular man named Rick on one side and a trim stately senior on the other. There between them in his business suit is the president of a local bank.

"You will never hit your wife again and you will never threaten her. We will know if you harm her in any way, and we will be back to visit you. At the present this is just friendly advice. Believe me the next visit will not be so friendly and you can rest assured you will not enjoy it one bit." The man in the front seat of the limousine was speaking over his shoulder.

"Now, Mr. Hazelton, I will go over this one more time to be sure we are on the same page. Do you love your wife?" asked the man called Rick.

"Certainly I love my wife and I would never harm her, whoever has told you that I do is lying. I know she would never say anything like that." Hazelton said defiantly.

"I don't intend to tell you how we know, but we know. I also believe she would never say anything about your abuse. Didn't you tell her the last time that you would kill her if she ever said anything? I would say she has good reason to believe you would do exactly that. Now, I don't care if you are in denial that you are abusive. That is honestly not relevant, because man, WE KNOW you are. We also know your wife cannot protect herself, so we are volunteering to do that. She doesn't know anything about us or that we are visiting you this evening. We called your

11

house to say you would be late for dinner; a very important client had called. Now as to our goal, it is the same as yours should be, to make your wife a very happy person, the one she used to be. We have no other agenda."

"I can't believe this is happening. You are obviously crazy or have the wrong guy."

The older man spoke, "Son, you get only one chance at this. So listen well. First, the penalty for ANY abuse of that sweet lady from this minute on will result in permanent damage to YOUR body. You do understand permanent, like in forever. WE will determine whether you ever use your arms or your legs again. I would take this very serious. You should take it more serious than you, as a banker, would take a million dollar loan, with no collateral. We have no interest except that your wife is safe. If you love her we want you and her to live happily ever after, and we mean that in all sincerity. You have never heard of our organization, and hopefully never will. The man, who formed this company years ago, has searched for, and found many people who needed help. He has helped hundreds of people live better lives. I will be very candid, since this conversation will never see the light of day; we could simply drive on out of this state with you and put you in a vat of acid. That way your wife may not be happy, but she would be safe. WE are giving you another option. Here is an envelope with some instructions and suggestions. Everything is for your wife's own good, if you are helped in the mean time that is great. Now don't start denying, because that shiner your wife had last week was enough. Her medical records of broken bones and bruises, all from falling and similar accidents smells to high heaven. Her doctors must be suspicious, as well. We assume if you were a man of less stature in the community, they would already have reported it. Before you ask or claim that her doctor informed, you are wrong. We can retrieve any information we want. When you look inside the envelope you will probably believe me. I know that was a mouthful I have just said, but do you understand?"

"Yes."

"Good, I think you can read well enough in here, remove the contents of the envelope, and look over the documents. There is one document that you must sign. The rest are instructions and several therapists' names. You can pick the one you want, but you will pick one. You will make appointments; none will be cancelled or missed." Ben paused for a moment, and then he continued. "You can tell your wife you found Jesus, or just want to straighten out your life. I would bet she will be relieved and happy to accompany you to the therapist."

During the next fifteen minutes Mr. R.C. Hazelton read information that he was sure that only he knew. He saw his bank balance, his savings, and all the stocks he owned. His secret account at a friend's bank was there and his driving record with a DUI that he had paid well to have expunged. Then at the end he read a document that made him squirm. It was an admission of abuse. He was ashamed of his actions. For some reason he could not control them and he hated himself for it. But he would not; he could not sign a document admitting it.

He recognized several names on the list of therapists that he knew, 'Lord, I cannot go to any of them' he thought. Then he saw the list of injuries. 'Did I do all that? Am I an animal? Yes, I did this to my wife. God I do need help'.

"Okay I have read this material and I see that you have broken several laws to get it, but you know that, don't you?"

"Mister, you are a banker not an attorney! For your information only, we are from the MVA, which is the Modern Vigilante Association. We choose to deal in relativity. Let me see if you can understand this. You are six feet three inches tall and in pretty good shape. You weigh two hundred ten pounds. Your wife is five feet four and weighs one hundred fifteen pounds. You have HIT this woman, you have BROKEN her arm, you have BROKEN two of her fingers and she came close to losing the sight in one eye. You, sir, are a bully and an abuser. Did you break the law?"

"But.."

"No buts Mister Hazelton, did I just tell the truth?"

"Yes, you did, and I am ashamed, so ashamed. I do not know what makes me do that."

"We don't either Mr. Hazelton, and we do not prefer the tactics we are forced to use here. But please make no mistake; we will not hesitate to do exactly what we have promised if you do not follow the instructions to the letter. Here is a pen. Sign the confession. You will never see us again. You will never see this document again unless your lovely wife is harmed. Then you will see it on the front page of the local paper. That is correct Mr. Hazelton, think of the headlines. Local bank president confesses to spousal abuse. This is not intended for court, but to expose you for what you are."

"I can't sign that!"

"Oh yes you can, it is a very simple decision. Think this over about a minute. Rick over there is six foot six. The boy is ex-army and ex-navy. He weighs two fifty five. He is an expert in several phases of the martial arts. Normally it takes less than three minutes to convince someone to sign. Besides we prefer not to rough you up before you go home for dinner. Now, are we on the same page Mr. Hazelton?"

Lamely, Hazelton took the pen and signed the confession. The rest of the documents and information was returned to the envelope. "Mr. Banker, you deal in percentages every day. Our organization has a ninety percent success rate, think of that. You have a great chance to become a better person, one YOU can even like. It is your chance to be a good husband. The percentages are in your favor. Mister, believe me, you do not want to know about the losing ten per cent," the older man nodded to Rick and then leaned back in his seat.

"As you heard, I am Rick, Mr. Hazelton, and I don't like men who hit women. Now for my boss's satisfaction I hope this ends with his approval, because he pays me very well and I love my work. I hope your wife is happy ever after. But, I just like to get intimately acquainted with a potential adversary." Before Hazelton knew what was happening, Rick reached for the banker's right shoulder. It was the worst pain he had ever experienced and he screamed involuntarily as his right arm went limp. "Now, you know me as a real person. A person, who, if told to will really hurt you. I have reached out and touched you, Hazelton. Your arm will be back in service in two or three minutes, but it will be numb for an hour. So in that time you plan on following any instructions the MVA has given."

The limo headed for Mr. Hazelton's home where his lovely wife was waiting. As the trip progressed he learned he would be observed until the MVA was satisfied that he was serious and wanted to mend his ways and love his wife as a husband should. They were dropping him at his door. His wife would take him to get his car in the morning.

"I have one final suggestion that will make your life much better. In our research we found that you at one time attended the same church your wife attends. You were active and your family appeared to be happy. Perhaps you should give that some serious thought. Your wife would appreciate it," as the senior man finished the driver closed the door. Quietly the limo drove away.

"Ben, do you think Mr. Hazelton can take a hint?" asked Rick.

"I really think so, Rick. I think all he needed was someone to make him face reality. These guys who abuse have no self control, but they can learn it. That has been proven. Do you agree Corey?"

"Yeah, Ben, I do. We all have to learn self control. That was one of the main points made clear in both the SBI and the FBI," said Corey as he made his way to the next appointment.

"Abe will be in town for awhile and monitor Mr. Hazelton's progress. We have two more assignments here in Charlotte. Then we head back to Pittsburgh."

"WE have a car dealer who loves to take advantage of folks who have no choice except to bend to his demands after he has them hooked. The dealership is called 'The Walking Man's Friend'. The slogan is, 'Walk in with a frown, drive out with a smile'. Seems the smile hasn't lasted as long as it should. There have been way too many unhappy customers. As a matter of fact, there are no happy ones."

"What about the other case?"

After giving driving directions, Ben, the senior spoke, "It figures to be short and quick. Both messages will be delivered by our local friendly biker gang. It is a group of bikers who are as law abiding as we are. They hate injustice, but today they will appear to be this perpetrator's worst nightmare, the 'Hell's Angels'. S'gar has met and worked with them on several other situations. He has donated to the charities they support as well as to their own kitty. We will meet up with them, sit in the background and observe. We have several customers who will be there personally. We have a list of the rest. The bank account has been checked, he can afford to refund, at eighty percent, the amount paid by each customer. The bikers have a list of check amounts and payees. In my years with S'gar and MVA, I have grown to enjoy seeing 'justice' prevail."

As the stretch pulled into a crowded lot, the bikers made room. The owner was standing with Ox, the leader. Ox raised his hands up; he held several phones, indicating they were in control. Then Corey flashed his lights twice. In this situation there was no way for the dealer to communicate with the outside world. Bike engines were being raced. A couple riders were doing doughnuts in the lot. The bikers walked over to an Oldsmobile, surrounded it and picked it up. The owner's eyes got big and he was looking very uneasy. The Olds was carried to the center of the lot. One of the owner's metal ramps was pulled out from under the building. The hood was raised on the Olds, the ramp inserted and the hood lowered. It was obvious someone was going to jump the car on a motorcycle.

Shouts and yells of encouragement went up as a big bike eased up the ramp a couple feet to test it. Then he backed down, spun a doughnut and headed to the far end of the yard. Everyone gave way allowing a path for the run. Not a word had been said to the owner. Two burley guys walked up on the porch and escorted him out to the Olds. They first put him under the small ramp. Shook their heads, retrieved him and took him to the trunk on the Olds. Not too gently they threw him up on the trunk lid, close to the rear window. There was one guy holding his feet the other holding his arms. One of them nodded to the jumper, who raced his engine, dropped the clutch and headed toward the ramp. He veered at the last minute and slid sideways past the car. He revved the engine, said something unintelligible to the holders and headed back for another run. He got set, revved the engine, and headed for the ramp. This time he went up the ramp and coming down with his rear tire burning the paint just past the terrified owner, and finished the perfect jump.

Ox held his hands high for quiet, and walked over to the terrified owner, but he spoke to the jumper. "Buck, I thought you could spin the buttons off his shirt. You missed by four inches. The cleats on the tire will make a nice track on Mr. Sleaze here." The owner was looking, terrified at the burned paint still smoking, from the spinning wheel.

"Ox, I was hoping to do it again. Y'all hold him there while I make another run. I know I can do better." He was making a move to kick start the bike, when the owner finally got his voice.

"Men, what do you want from me, I will give you anything, just tell me the problem."

"The problem is simple; you have cheated the last person in this town that you are going to cheat. That means you will cheat no one else in this town. I would like to think you would get religion, but I doubt that. So you will do the next best thing. I have a list here of everyone concerned and the amount you are going to pay them. Some of your good customers have been invited here to accept their pay in person, the others we will deliver, with your regrets for what you have done. Are we getting together in our thinking yet? Just so you will understand, this is only half of our bikers. The rest are going to be mad they weren't invited, so they will want any excuse to come back. We are just glad you picked a location this far out of town so we can enjoy this without interruption."

"Man I can't write that many checks they will bounce."

"Nah, do you see that pretty stretch there? Inside are representatives of the MVA. You will be notified later what the MVA is. They gave me this printout of your bank account. They totaled the list, and you can cover it. If you think my guys are a little rough, you have no idea who is in that vehicle; or why they are so upset at you. I would just write the checks and not incur any more of their wrath. You definitely cannot afford that," Ox spoke low but was staring intensely into the eyes of the auto dealer. "Are we in agreement here?"

"Yeah, I know when I have a losing hand. Let's go into the office."

In the office Ox spoke to him once again as the dealer was writing the checks. "In case you are thinking about stopping the payment on ANY of the checks, I would advise very strongly against it. First of all, every penny of your insurance has been cancelled, and will not be renewed. The man out there in the car can do that, and has. Also, tomorrow you will find your permits are pulled to operate a used car lot. Yes, he can do that and he has. He does not like cheating, lying crooks and he has decided you are exactly that. You don't like it, but his organization, the MVA or the Modern Vigilante Association, holds all the cards. We are just hired hands to do whatever it takes. Son, the Man pays well, so we don't mind coming back. We really don't mind following you to any part of the country. Keep that in mind and finish writing the checks. In case it hasn't occurred to you yet, you are finished. You are out of business."

As Ox talked, another biker gathered every key in the office. He removed all the ID tags from them and then they were shaken together in a can. Holding the keys the biker went out to one of the cars and locked them inside. Everyone had cleared the lot. The limo was gone. Ox handed out the checks to the ones waiting; he stuffed the remaining checks in his pocket. Then he straddled his bike and rode, smiling, out the gate. The last biker locked the gate, and threw the key over in the weeds, waved toward the office and rode off himself.

The owner was still sitting behind the desk shaking, seeing his house of cards falling around him. He thought, 'I definitely made the wrong person mad in this town, I guess I should consider myself lucky, and that is an understatement'.

****

Over on a dead end street about five miles from the car lot, a bewildered man stood on his porch. His young son was beside him. Both wore dungarees and old tank top undershirts. Trash was in the yard, and the house was unpainted. Beer cans and a few liquor bottles were scattered over the yard. They were listening to fifteen motorcycles idle, as the bikers occasionally raced an engine. They simply sat there staring at the house, ignoring the occupants. After about thirty minutes, another group of bikers rode slowly down the road. They appeared to be escorting a dark stretch limousine. The parked bikers parted to make room for the stretch to ease to the very end of the road. The two on the porch were so intense on the coming procession; they never saw the four bikers move in from both sides of the house. As the stretch stopped, both man and boy found themselves lifted off the porch and carried toward the limo. Struggling done no good, it was much like a cat and mouse, no contest.

Slowly, the side window on the stretch glided down. They could now see inside the Limo. Ben spoke, "Mr. Smith, I represent the Modern Vigilante Association, the MVA. I am delivering a very important message. All you have to do, to remain alive, is learn to keep your filthy mouth shut. You will need to make an attitude adjustment and quit threatening and harassing the folks that work under you. They are tired of it Mr. Smith. If anyone is fired or another act of mistreatment occurs, I will not be back, but my friends will. Do we understand each other?"

"Yes sir."

"Correct answer. I also believe you mean it. Now, that is not the only reason I am here. You, Mr. Smith, have raised an intolerable bully for a son. He is a bore, nasty and in general not a very nice person. If he continues on his present path he will spend his life in prison. I expect you to make some changes in that direction." Turning his attention to the son, Ben continued. "Now, Tommy boy, I have a list of classmates and others, whom you seem to enjoy bullying. If any of these children are abused, either with your mouth or your fists, your father will receive a visit from these gentlemen. That will happen only one time. After that you may go for a motorcycle ride yourself. These guys do not like little smart mouths either. Do you understand Tommy?"

"Y-yes sir."

"Correct answer also. Your teachers say you are a bright kid. They say you have potential to make something good of yourself. According to the records, when you apply yourself, you can be a mathematical genius. You have a very high IQ. So I would suggest you change directions, make friends and you will be proud of yourself. Then your father will also be proud. Your father did not have the opportunity at an education that you have. He too, could have been more than he is, but he settled for being able to push and bully people. Think about it. I shouldn't have to spell that out anymore now should I? So take a look at school work as a way to get out of this trash pile, and be someone in this world. Make some friends; they are more fun than enemies. Do you think you can do that? Both of you can straighten up this trash dump. Take some pride in yourselves and yours, for heaven's sake."

"Yes sir."

"Then I don't think we will have to come back. If I had a silver bullet I would give it to you Tommy. Maybe your daddy will take time to explain the masked man and the silver bullet, after we leave. Good bye, I hope I never see you again. Let me rephrase that, the next time I see you I hope you are receiving some award in high school or in college. We will keep track. We always do. There can be rewards. " After a moment of complete silence he finished with, "Neither of you will speak of the MVA, it is not wise."

The window rose slowly and the limo backed up the street.

****

"That is the way it went sir," Ben was finishing his report to S'gar.

"So how do you rate the possibilities of success in the three episodes, Ben?"

"I believe the possibility of success is very good. All three examples are common situations you have faced here at the MVA since the beginning. That is, as far as I can tell, reading over the history. In each case you have a typically misguided individual who needed a nudge in the

19

right direction. I think our psychiatrists hit these on the head. They reacted exactly as predicted.

This is a conversation S'gar has had hundreds of times since his creation of the MVA. The feeling of satisfaction cannot be measured. It is nice to know you are doing something that will enhance lives. He keeps remembering the philosophy he learned from an old preacher in Mt. Bell. His philosophy was: you can accomplish a lot, if you do not care who receives the credit. S'gar never cared who got the credit, just so the job got done.

The MVA had been successful in helping over nine thousand individuals in the forty years of its existence. Most were individuals like the ones Ben had just faced. They were people who had started in the wrong direction in their lives and did not know how to change course. The MVA had taken that opportunity to help them make the necessary change. Over the years they had reached into the Senate twice and in the House of Representatives eight times. It was spread equally between Democrats and Republicans.

The present concern is a huge red flag, being ferreted out by the intricate warning systems set in place by the MVA. It appears there is a conspiracy among judges, of all things. There is a lot of circumstantial evidence that points to the fact that the judges are accepting payment to dispense justice. Their sentences seem to only affect two select groups, youths from underprivileged homes and the mentally challenged. There is no concern for the damage being done to the citizens of this great country. It is an area were special expertise will be required. S'gar knows exactly who to call on at a time like this. This will require the services of some of his first truly prize pupils in the area of investigation and stealth. The kids he came in contact with when he was on his 'sabbatical'. The boys were only in junior high at the time. It had been a truly wonderfully serene time in his life and one that brought on his change or his epiphany. During that period the seed was planted for the MVA, a benevolent foundation, one that supplements enforcement of our basic freedoms and the American way of life.

Chapter Two
(The Past..1962)
Player #1…. 'J' The Dreamer

J Leon, also known as J Leon Jr. but from the first grade preferred to be called J Leon. He had enjoyed an interesting childhood. Early in the small town of Mt. Bell he had met some boys who had become lifelong friends. They all graduated from High School in the early 1960's and went their separate ways. Each one knew if there was a problem, they could call on the others. There were four of them. The three and a half musketeers, he had been the half. It was a joke they all enjoyed. Everyone knew J was just a little more on the wild side. There were times when folks were not sure what side of the law he would end up on.

Just after school he was awarded $1250 for his part in recovering the evidence that sealed the FBI's case on two bank robbers. He had been about twelve or thirteen years old when they found the evidence. It was on an overnight camping trip on an island out in the Catawba River. That night they had found the weapons used in two bank robberies. It had been exciting back then. Working with Chief Harris and meeting Bill Muse, a real FBI agent, had been a thrill. They got to ride in the Gaston County Sheriff's boat as they took them back to the island. The reward was five thousand dollars. The four boys split it equally. That had been their motto, all for one and one for all. Due to their youth it was held in trust until they were eighteen. The interest had made it total up to $1325. He took his money and immediately bought a beautiful black 1953 Ford Crestline Victoria. He was interested in making some money fast. After saying goodbye to his friends he was heading toward Las Vegas. He had heard stories of the fame and fortune waiting there. He loved the TV program 'Route 66' and could not wait to buy a Corvette and just travel with the money he was going to win.

At the cross roads he picked up a dozen donuts at the Donut Dinette. Across the road he stopped at Lewis's station to fill up. He picked up a map and asked around if anyone had driven to Las Vegas. No one had, so with the map on the hood of his car he drew out a route west, to Vegas. His last goodbyes were to Joe and Charlie at the station. As he left toward Gastonia he burned a little rubber in low and got a squeal out of second. He was thinking 'good bye to Mt. Bell, you little cotton mill town, hello Vegas and the big time'. He turned the radio up took out a donut. Life was great. Old Gurney of WCGC was playing 'Moonlight Gambler' by Frankie Lane. By the time he passed the radio station on Wilkinson Boulevard, he was blowing his horn and waving, while old Jerry Lee was singing, 'Whole Lot of Shakin' Goin' On'.

****

J's dream was shattered like most dreams of instant riches. It didn't take long for him to blow the rest of his reward money at the slot machines. This is impossible he thought, but there he was in Las Vegas, Nevada broke and about out of gas. Mt. Bell was nearly two thousand miles away, and he had no friends here. He could hear the gang say, 'come on J, man use your head!'

He was able to land a job parking cars as a valet attendant at the Empire Casino. It paid one dollar twenty five an hour. At least that was better than the eighty cents back in a cotton mill. He met a lot of folks parking cars. He was able to find a few dollars and some chips by checking the crevasses in the seat cushions. It was a habit he had learned as a kid. Every house they moved into he headed for the chairs and sofa, looking for lost change. He did the same with every used car his dad had bought. Now the habit was paying off a little. He was warned about stealing from the cars, but the lost money the owners would not miss. Once he found a diamond ring and sold it on the street for a hundred dollars. His logic on the slots was: if I put enough in the slot machines, eventually one will pay off big. So, after gas and food the rest went to the slots. He slept in his car and bathed in the casino bath rooms. He remained perpetually broke.

It wasn't long until he made friends with Stanley. Stan was cool; he drove a Vette, dressed slick and tipped well. He invited J to come up to his apartment a couple times for a beer. J was no drinker, didn't even like the taste. But Stan was so cool and to please him J would nurse one beer and watch TV or listen to music. About the third trip, Stan said he had a business proposition for J. It was just a simple little job, but it would pay big. The job only entailed driving a van. If J handled it well, there would be more. "I will tell you about it tomorrow around noon, if you are interested." Hey, how could he not be interested, this is why he came to Vegas wasn't it? He would return to Mt. Bell in style. The deal was all he could think of. It was hard to wait for the meeting, finally it arrived.

"Hey J, my man, meet Houser. Houser, J."

They were in a casino parking lot. Stan walked them over to a van. It was a paneled van with the 'stick on' lettering that read, 'Emergency Service'. Stan slid the side door open and motioned everyone inside. "J, this is the deal. A man owes me a lot of money and refuses to pay. I can't allow that, gives me a bad name. So this afternoon we are going to collect it. It will be simple but his boys are gonna be mad at first. That is why I want to leave fast. It ain't a big deal. Later, I am gonna call the man and explain. That is all there is to it. I will pay you eight hundred to get us away, once we collect. Here, take two now. You can drop us and the money off at my car. Then you can drive on and park the van at the Sunset Theatre. We will pick you up there and go back to the Casino; does that sound like something you can do?"

"Sure Stan, sounds simple enough to me. When does this go down?"

"Okay, listen close here, because the timing is important. Let me see your watch. Okay, we are the same. At exactly two forty five you pull this van right past that corner over there to the hot spot, which is over there where the red cones are." Stan was pointing to two cones he had placed there earlier. "I want you to go past the first one and pull up so your driver's door is just beside the other one. Open the sliding door just a crack then get back behind the wheel and pretend you are reading this newspaper," Stan handed him a paper "Leave the van idling, I will get in

23

the van just after you park, when I say go you follow the map that is in the paper. You know Vegas pretty well by now, so study the map while you wait. You have about a half hour."

Stan and Houser got out of the van. Now J was alone and was thinking. 'Man this is cool; I bet nobody in Vegas messes with Stan after this.' J started studying the map. It was fairly simple but a lot of turns. Wonder why that is? He could see Stan had drawn an X and wrote 'drop here to get my car'. Then the route went on to the theatre. 'Do this right J and you can become the wheel man like Mickey Rooney in 'Drive a Crooked Road''. In just a few minutes he had the route down pat. Then at exactly 2:45 by his watch, he pulled into the hot spot.

J eased the van into the hot spot as directed. Pulled the brake, put the shift out of gear and cracked the sliding door. He sat back at the wheel and held the paper. He was beginning to be a little nervous now. A few minutes later Stan slid quietly into the van, "Put it in gear and be ready, do not look back, eyes on the road, when I say go, you burn rubber." J nodded and slipped it into low gear, held his foot on the clutch and waited. A few minutes later Stan slid the door open and eased back into the shadow of the rear.

Through the mirrors he saw a couple guys round the corner; the first thing he noticed was one was carrying a brief case with a chain to his wrist. Second was that the big man following just behind, held a pistol down by his leg. Next he saw Houser appear behind the guard and put a gun to his head. At the same time Stan reached out and yanked the front man's upper body inside the van. "Easy and nobody gets hurt. Lay your pistol here on the floor Dub. Take these bolt cutters and relieve Mouse of the case."

For the first time J realized both Stan and Houser had ski masks on, here he was naked. He also was not expecting guns. He realized he was shaking. Houser hit Dub over the head and Stan using Dub's gun hit Mouse and pushed him out of the van. As Houser swung in, Stan yelled "GO!"

J dropped the clutch and spun out onto the street. He checked his mirror and saw the two rubbing their heads and running toward a black car. He was following the route perfectly when he realized the black car was behind them about a block back. He heard Stan say, "Man we made a haul." J looked back and saw the brief case open and it was full of bundles of cash. Looking back at the road he hit the brakes and swerved to miss a taxi. Stan, Houser and case came forward, the cash all over the floor.

"Man, I thought you could drive?" They were snatching the cash trying to get it all back in the case.

"Those two guys you hit are behind us in a black car, Stan."

"Lose them for heaven's sake, are you stupid?" Stan and Houser tried to look out the right side mirror.

"It will be pretty hard to lose them in a van with emergency service written all over the side, but hold on."

J ran a red light and took an alley to the right. Drove some of the back places to get close to the place where Stan's car was parked. "I will be at your car in about a minute. Are you bailing or riding in the van?"

"Hey stupid, if they ain't behind, drop us fast, otherwise I shoot you and drive myself. My mama drives better."

"Here we are," J slid the van to a stop.

As the passengers got out, Stan slapped him hard and said, "Get going you idiot. That two hundred I gave you is all you get. That is over paying you, and I don't want to ever see you again!"

J had already made up his mind he would never see Stan again. This was stupid, and way out of his league. He had been naïve, but now he knew he had just been part of a robbery pure and simple. Well, not too simple. There was no way he was headed toward the theatre. He would go get his car and split. He did smile a little; Stan had paid more than two hundred. Under his shoe were two packs of bills. He slid them to the side when his passengers had frantically looked out the mirrors to see the black car that was following. Now he reached down and retrieved the packets and stuffed them inside his shirt. He rolled them up inside his undershirt and buttoned his shirt. At that time he spotted the black car, shoot! Now what? The accelerator went to the floor while he headed for a favorite road of his; it was dusty with a lot of curves. It also had one small cliff with a wooden barrier, just after a sharp turn. He thought, 'James Dean'.

Okay, here we go plenty of dust behind to slow them down. This had better work or I am dead. I watched 'Rebel Without a Cause' with James Dean three times. I used to dream of practicing his rolling out of that car. Well James, it better work. J went into the last turn about thirty, and pressed the accelerator a little and headed for the wooden barrier. When he was about a couple hundred feet from the barrier, he put the van out of gear let it slow some, opened the door and rolled out. He hit the ground with a slap and a scrape. Man that dirt hurt but it had worked. He came to a stop in the dust and could not see anything. He felt around him and found a low spot and crawled into it. He heard the van crashing down the slope. As the dust settled a little more he saw a large rock close by and crawled to it. He felt for the money and it was gone. Oh man, he thought, all this for nothing. He didn't have much time to think because the black car slid to a stop about fifty feet ahead of him. Both men jumped out in the dust cloud and ran to the broken barrier.

"The idiot went over the side. I hope they are all dead," yelled Mouse. "The driver was the new kid at the Empire. If he ain't dead he will be." J could tell that both guys had guns, must have had extra ones in the car, dang the luck. "Dub, go down and see what is going on." Mouse had walked all the way to the ledge. J recognized the car. He had parked the car many times. 'I hope the keys are in it', he thought. He did not have far to go to get to the car, but he was still shook up from the jump. He tried to be quiet, but that was impossible. "Hey, stop," Mouse had heard his feet scraping the dirt. He yelled as he fired at the running target.

Feeling an impact in his side he thought, 'I'm hit' and he almost fell. He was still running. 'Please Lord, let the keys be in the ignition!' They were. He started the car, threw it in reverse and did a backwards slide around then yanked it into first gear. He was throwing up a cloud of dust when he heard the rear window pop and a sting in his shoulder but he was in the clear and around the corner. He headed for Vegas and his old car. As he drove he felt his side for the blood he knew was there but to his surprise what he felt was the money. It had moved to his side in the rollout and Mouse had hit the money, "Whoopi!" J yelled as loud as he could. His shoulder was not even bleeding, but his shirt was torn. Most of the damage was from the rollout he had done before the cliff.

At the Empire he pulled up to the Valet spot. One of the guys in uniform popped out, "Yes sir, what?... J? What in the world happened to you? What are you doing with the Mouse's wheels?"

"Long story Tommy, don't have time. But here is a hundred. Mouse is out on Back Road Five and he is pretty mad. Would you get someone to take the car to him? Tell him he is looking for Stan and Houser. They hired me to drive for eight bills, but did not pay. I didn't know what I was getting into. I'm headed home to Texas. I have had enough of Vegas. Take care of yourself, nice knowing you." J was running for his car. Mouse might get another ride; he was not staying to find out. Boy was he glad he decided to tell everyone he was from Texas. He had enjoyed being a cowboy. Now, it might have paid off.

He looked at the gas gauge; he had half a tank, great. He had nothing better to do so he would go north to Salt Lake City. He planned to drive as long as he could stay awake, get some coffee and keep on going. He would not really rest until he reached somewhere in Colorado. He could buy some clothes and then get a tourist cabin and rest. While driving he had plenty of time to think. 'You got fast money okay J, but you nearly got killed in the process. It is for sure I won't try to get rich gambling again. That was stupid. Buddy's daddy always said gambling was wrong, and only the crooks running the games won. He was probably right. I definitely saw more losers than winners and I certainly was a loser'.

With the car headed north he kept a look out for any car that might be following him. He also watched his speed. He didn't want to get stopped for speeding and have to explain why he was so scratched and beat up. He took out one pack of the money and tried to guess how much he had. The stacks had different denominations. The smallest was twenty, some fifties and a few hundreds. It would definitely get him across country.

He was glad to see the Nevada/Utah border. He breathed a sigh of relief, but was he clear? How would he know? Questions flooded his mind. It was time to stop for gas and a snack. He stopped at the tanks of a small country station and a kid came out, "Filler up with regular and check under the hood please." J. reached into the back seat and pulled out another shirt and headed for the men's room. He used the old shirt as a wash cloth to wash up as well as he could, then put on the other shirt. He combed his hair, set his duck's tail, felt better and headed for the Pepsi box. He opened the bottle and took a big swallow. He gathered up several snacks and a couple candy bars and took them to the register. The kid totaled the gas and food, J gave him a twenty, "take out for the bottle deposit, I am taking it."

The kid looked at the bill, wrinkled his freckled nose and said, "This bill has a hole in it."

"Yeah, I just got paid in Vegas; every bill had a hole in it. Sorta looks like someone stuck a pencil through it."

"Or shot it," said the kid.

"That too," returned J as he smiled and took his change, "good bye."

"Amigo," called the kid and J turned, "Watch the road going north. The North Carolina tag sticks out and the sheriff, he gets a lot of out of state cars in the next county."

"I'll keep it down, and thanks for the warning, me amigo." J saluted and left.

As he drove north smiling to himself, the car began to skip. "What now?" J thought as the car just died and started coasting, he steered off the road as far as he could. After it rolled to a stop, he got out and raised the hood. The international sign, which says, 'something is wrong and I probably have no idea what'.

As he looked under the hood, a truck pulled in ahead of him. A tall red headed man in an Air Force uniform got out and walked back. "What is the problem friend?"

"Howdy there, I'm J Leon, leaving Vegas after running out of luck. Now it seems like I have run even further out of luck." J looked back down the road. He was constantly wondering if someone would guess he had intentionally misled them and would head north.

"Well, J, I am Dick Workman. I know a little about these cars, maybe it is something simple. What did it do?"

"Hey Dick, it just started skipping and died."

Dick stretched his lanky frame under the hood. "I think you may be in luck, J. It looks like your distributer wire just fell out. At least, it is lying there disconnected." Dick reached in and replaced the wire into the distributer. "Jump in and see if it will start."

To J's relief, the engine started with one turn of the starter. He let it idle. He was not about to turn it off, after hearing it start. He put it out of gear and got out. "Dick, what do I owe you? I am learning, but I don't know much about engines yet."

"You don't owe me anything, I would like to stick around and chat but I haven't been married long and Joan get's upset if I am late. Have a good trip through Utah. She shouldn't give you any more problems," before leaving Dick quickly explained the distributer wire, distributer and spark plug wires. Dick stuck out his hand, they shook, and Dick was gone.

J thought to himself, 'I should have known that. I have changed points and plugs before, just never messed with the distributer'. The remainder of the trip through Utah was uneventful. He was able to get some western clothes and a new pair of boots. His 'pay' had totaled a little over three thousand dollars. He figured that was not enough bait for Mouse or his bosses to come after. He supposed they would be after Stan and Houser much more than himself. After all he was just an idiot, as his good friend Stan had so succinctly put it. Well, at least I got paid for being his idiot. I'll bet they will find it pretty hot to know the ski masks didn't save face.

He spent a couple days in the edge of Colorado at a small tourist court in Glenwood Springs. This was real Mountain country. He had always loved the Smokies and thought they were big. But after seeing the Rockies, he was in awe. They were absolutely stunning to him. Yes, they were inspiring and beautiful. He met some wonderful folks; they were friendly and very accommodating. The cooking was good and the stay was relaxing. One evening some of the boys at the Tourist Camp invited him to join in a friendly game of poker. J just smiled and said, "I don't gamble anymore. My career, as a gambler, was short and costly." They all understood and laughed.

After two days he threw his new clothes in the back seat, waved good bye and headed for Denver. Driving gave him time to remember his childhood, home town and friends. Buddy's daddy was their pastor for a few years. He always said you could never build a life on gambling, it was too easy to lose. The pastor had said once, "Do you think they build all those big beautiful buildings in Las Vegas by making other people rich? No sir, they build them by making other people broke." I think I just grew a notch, but it sure was costly. It is amazing how you can get side tracked by dreaming of quick money. Boy, it almost got me killed.

J stopped in Denver and spent part of a day just looking around. He bought another western shirt at a big department store. He was looking for something to take back to his mama. He could not come up with a good idea. J was also learning that motels were less expensive farther away from the big cities, so he headed east to find a good inexpensive motel. He took US36 going toward a town on the map called Stasburg. He did not find a tourist cabin or a place to stay until he came to the Stasburg Hotel. He got a room for three dollars a night. The room was clean and smelled fresh. There was a nice restaurant on the ground floor; this was pretty far away from Vegas and he was beginning to relax some. He began to feel like a traveler. He had a duffel bag now; he took his clothes out and hung them up. Took a bath, relaxed and listened to the radio.

Supper time came, so he headed for the restaurant. As he walked into the restaurant, a pretty girl just a little older than he was, brushed past him. After the little bump, she apologized. It was apparent she had been crying. J went in, took a table and reached for a worn menu. As he was looking, he failed to see the waitress walk up just behind him. "You don't need the menu, son. Just order the special. It is country style steak, green beans, mashed potatoes and gravy. It comes with tea and a homemade roll for a dollar and a quarter. How is that?"

J looked around and up to see the friendly face of Anna the waitress, she was popping her gum as she chewed noisily, "That is just what I was going to order," J said laughing.

"I always get 'em right, son. It will be coming right out." She was wearing a big name tag on a checkered shirt and tight jeans.

'She is a pretty lady, for an old woman. She is probably thirty or thirty five years old', thought J.

The two men at the table just ahead of his were in the middle of a serious conversation. He couldn't help but hear. The man with his back to him was saying, "She will come around when she realizes it is a lost cause. She don't really want to live out there anyway, it is her old man."

"You told her if she fixed the fences and come up with the eight hundred dollars next week, you would consider it square. Ain't that pushing it a little close?"

"Nah, where is she going to get a hand and eight hundred dollars around here? Ever-body knows they had better not help her. I hold most of the mortgages in these parts. Don't nobody want to cross me son."

"Yeah, I know you are right, but why do you want the broken down place anyway? It has been a pain for years. Ain't but fifty acres, you must own eight thousand your ownself."

"I can see you don't pay much attention son, no man has enough land, besides the total is now eight thousand five hundred and thirty-five acres."

J was caught up in the conversation and didn't notice Anna putting his tea down in front of him. Sheepishly he looked up at her and she just slightly shook her head slowly left and right and cut her eyes toward the men. Then she walked over to the two men, "Can I get you anything else Mr. Drover?"

"No Anna, but the offer to come home with me is still open," the man called Drover said. He had sort of a lecherous smile. J could see his face as he turned to look up at Anna.

"Huh uh, Mrs. Drover would be very upset, and so would Thomas back there cooking. You know he expects to marry me as soon as this place makes a million," Anna said as she picked up some dishes and headed back to the kitchen. J's attention was drawn back to the men.

"Anyway, I got to get back out to the ranch, Johnson. I will see you in a week or so."

"Right Mr. Drover, I'll be looking for you." Both men took a toothpick from the little jar on the table, left some money on the table and walked out the door.

When Anna brought his supper out he asked, "Who were the two men that just left."

"They are the local powers that be. Mr. Drover owns the elevators over yonder, the hardware, and most the buildings in town. He also owns most of the land as far as you can see. Mr. Johnson runs the 'Locomotive Shop', and invests in some real estate. I just told you that, 'cause you were hearing the conversation. You being a young man, I was afraid you might get it in your mind to be a Robin Hood or one of the Three Musketeers."

"Well for your information I was half of one," J said smiling.

"Half of one what?"

"When I was a kid I joined up with three real cool dudes that were called the Three Musketeers. They didn't want to change the name of the group to Four Musketeers, so they made me a half musketeer. So we were the three and a half musketeers. For some reason it made more sense when I was a kid," he said smiling. "But who was the girl that left just as I came in?"

"That was Maria, she and her dad 'about own' a very small spread on farther east on Thirty Five. I couldn't get the whole story but she is over a barrel. Mr. Drover claims his fence is damaged. He will have the whole place for pennies on the dollar unless she finds a miracle, but that ain't likely around here. That is not your problem. Enjoy the meal, Thomas is a good cook. He used to drive a chuck wagon with the cattle drives, really." Anna smiled and walked toward the kitchen popping her gum.

He was surprised. The meal was delicious, and a lot of it. The conversation he had overheard was really none of his business. That is a local affair, and I should be on my way in the morning. This is a nice little place. It is even smaller than Mt. Bell. Just thinking the name took him back to his childhood. Sunday school was as regular as public school. You weren't supposed to miss either one. J did not always want to go to Sunday school, but most of the time it was fun. The stories were good. For some reason that little song they used to sing, now how did that go?

> Zacheaus was a wee little man and a wee little man was he,
>   He climbed up in a sycamore tree for the Lord he wanted to see.
> And as the Savior passed that way He looked up in the tree,
> And He said, 'Zach come down out of that tree,
> Because I'm going to your house for tea.......

Anyway the way the teacher told it, Zach was little and people made fun of him, but Jesus had liked him. He was the underdog. It was something like that. If the Musketeers were here, we would go help the maiden in distress. That was always fun to think about; they used to talk about really helping somebody who was the underdog. But the guys aren't here; are they? He finished his meal, and leaned the straight chair back on the two legs. Just enjoying the meal he had finished.

"Well do you want pie? We have peach and apple, twenty cents a slice. It is good too."

"You sold me, I like apple," answered J.

"Want coffee or milk?"

"I think I will have a glass of milk. That sounds like a winner."

"Coming up," Anna said smiling and walked off again.

J finished and paid his bill. Before walking out he was looking at the candy display. Anna walked behind the counter. "Don't tell me there is room for candy."

"No, but I was thinking, what time is breakfast?"

"We start serving at five thirty."

"You here at five thirty?"

"Every morning except Sunday."

"Pretty long day."

"Son, all days on the prairie are long. You will find out."

"Not me Miss Anna, I am heading east and home. Good night, see you in the morning."

J climbed the stairs. He had always wanted to be a cowboy. This trip had allowed him to see the prairies and the Rocky Mountains. These are things that the average boy from Mt. Bell would never see. Most boys there either saw the cotton mills or Detroit. Neither of those had interested J Leon. Back in the room he checked to make sure both windows were open, got undressed and lay in his underwear and listened to station XERF on the radio. It wasn't long until he drifted off into a deep peaceful sleep.

******

The noise from the restaurant caused J to stir. He got up, packed his things and headed down to breakfast. In the breezeway he recognized the girl he remembered from yesterday. She was talking to two cowboys. J caught part of the conversation of one of the cowboys. He couldn't help but overhear it as he went into the restaurant. What he heard was just, "Maria, you know we can't help you. Drover would either kill us or we would never find work in this town again. Both of us want to, we just can't."

The door shut and the conversation was behind him, he thought. Then he heard Anna, "Well good morning traveler, have a seat. I will be right with you."

J took a seat and picked up the menu, and Anna walked up. J looked at her, smiled and said, "Okay, no need to look at the menu, what do I want?"

"I'd say you want two eggs over medium, hash browns and you look like a ham man to me. Is that okay?"

"Why ask if it is okay? You said you know such things."

"Okay, do you want sour dough biscuits with that?" Anna was smiling.

"Biscuits are good. Do you have molasses?"

"Will honey do?"

"Yep, I prefer molasses, but I like honey too." Anna smiled, nodded and headed for the kitchen. The place was filled with locals, getting ready for work it appeared. The girl, Maria, had walked inside and he watched her go to several tables to talk to workers. They all shook their heads negative. The woman named Maria left the restaurant. J turned his attention back to the worn menu. He was looking at it, but his mind was not on that frayed paper. It was on Zacheaus, the underdog.

His breakfast came. It was fit for a king. Loaded with butter and beautifully browned hash browns. There were three large eggs and a giant slice of ham. Anna smiled down at him. "I figured you need a working man's meal before you head out."

"Miss Anna, I am driving, not working. But this looks and smells delicious. I don't think I have ever seen a better looking breakfast," J automatically bowed his head and asked a silent blessing. Something his mother had always said. You should be thankful for all you receive.

"It appears you are a well bred young man. We Westerners like that. We like respect for God and country. If you need any more biscuits or coffee before I get back, just yell."

The breakfast was wonderful. He almost hated to leave. But there was nothing for him here. He enjoyed his breakfast. Anna refilled his coffee a couple times. He just leaned back on the back two legs of the strait chair and smiled. That breakfast was as close to his moms as he had ever had. Of course his mom did not do hash browns. He was raised on grits.

J left a fifty cent tip and paid his bill at the register. Anna had said good bye and wished him a safe trip. He was at the door when Anna called. "Wait up traveler!" She came running to the door. "I need a favor. Thomas made lunch for Maria and her dad. I hate to ask, but I know it is on your way. Would you drop it off for me?"

"Anna, I don't know where they live."

"You can't miss it. Turn off to the south at the first mail box east of town. The old man has a giant anchor holding the mail box. That gets most folks attention, an anchor out here on the prairie. It is about twenty miles I think. I just don't have time and we missed her, she left crying again." Anna looked very worried.

"Sure, I will give it a try since it is on my way, I am not in that big a hurry anyway."

"Me and Thomas will appreciate that. Your next meal is on the house when you are in again."

"You and Thomas will have that million dollars and five kids by that time," laughed J. "But you can bet I will keep that in mind." He took the heavy sack, grabbed his duffel bag and headed toward his car.

The car started good. He had been apprehensive, since it died on the road back in Utah. J Leon headed out of Strasburg. He checked his odometer so he would know when twenty miles was near. He had been nearly twenty miles when he spotted the large anchor with a mail box welded to the top. He slowed down and turned into the worn drive. He seemed to drive forever until he came to a beautiful valley. There was a log house with flowers surrounding it. The place looked peaceful.

He parked and opened the door. As he sat foot on the ground he heard a loud 'BANG'. Something in J said that is a rifle. A voice followed. "Get back in the car ye land lubber, and set sail out of here. You can tell, Drover, the place ain't gonna be given away today!" J could not see anyone to match the voice.

Just as he was about to close the door a horse and rider rounded the house at a run. The rider, whom he recognized as the girl, Maria, from the hotel, pulled up sharply. Quickly she surveyed the situation, "Dad, hold your fire, he ain't one of them!" She dismounted, just like he had seen many times in the movies. She pulled her hat off and dusted her pants as she approached the car. She smiled and said, "Sorry about the reception, but the Chief is trigger happy today. Are you lost?"

"No mam, I am just trying to deliver something. Anna sent this lunch out here for you and your dad. You left in a hurry and she missed you. So she asked me to bring it since I would be passing by," J was reaching across the seat to pick up the paper bag when he caught sight of a figure moving in the shadow of the house. When he saw the rifle he froze. "Are you sure this is safe?"

Maria smiled and nodded her head then yelled, "Dad don't shoot this tin horn, he might bleed all over your lunch," she turned to J and continued speaking, "I'm really sorry about this, I am Maria. Please get out and I will make some coffee."

"If it is all the same to you mam, I will skip the coffee. I have been shot at and hit and shot at and missed already on this trip west, and that is enough."

"Really? You are serious aren't you?"

"Yep, I was shot at and hit in Las Vegas. Fortunately he hit something in my shirt that stopped the bullet, or I would be dead. So I have had my fill of guns for one trip."

"I didn't get your name, and thanks for coming by. We seldom get visitors; I would love to hear your story over coffee. I would also like to make up for daddy's ill temper."

The man with the rifle that J assumed was daddy came over towards the car. J spoke to Maria. "I'm just plain J, like the letter J. I am lately from Las Vegas headed back to North Carolina and the quiet sedate life in a cotton mill town."

Maria addressed her daddy, "Daddy come on over here and apologize, if your ego will let you. This is J. J this is my daddy, retired Chief Wayne Hodge, formerly of the United States Navy."

"Sorry about firing over your bow there mate, but we have some pirates running loose here on the prairie. I just mistook you for one of those mislead miscreants." He held out his hand as J got out of the car, "I do apologize. If Maria vouches for you, you gotta be good as a rain locker in a drought."

J grasped a handgrip for which he was not prepared; this old geezer was one strong dude. "That is all right chief, as long as the shot was across my bow." Both were smiling.

"Please come in and I will make us a pot of Navy coffee. Daddy's favorite past time is drinking strong coffee." The three headed for the house.

"You know this is weird, my dad is a retired Navy chief. I am a Navy brat also."

Chief Hodge and J talked while Maria put on the coffee. The Hodges had been stationed in Guantanamo Bay and J's family had also, but at different times. They talked about fishing there. Chief Hodge had worked at NSD, the Naval Supply Depot while J's Dad was with the FTG, the Fleet Training Group. The tours over lapped, so J and Maria had actually attended the same school, but Maria was two grades ahead of J. There were common families they knew. Everyone knew the Campbell's and the Perez's. Maria came to the table and joined the conversation. They all remembered the Mardi Gras celebration. J had won the best decorated bicycle in the parade the year Chief Hodge and family had left. Talking about all this was fun.

The coffee smelled good. Maria asked, "Now I am dying to know J, were you serious about being shot?"

"Yes, and it was no fun, I was scared out of my skin."

Maria was getting up, "Wait just a minute and I will get the coffee. I don't won't to miss any of this story." As Maria got up she brushed against J. Something electric went through J. He couldn't remember ever feeling like that around a girl. Her smell was exhilarating. He was confused, but it was a very pleasant feeling.

After Maria brought the coffee, J related the story. Both the Chief and Maria were spell bound as he told the story. He did not mention how much money had stopped the bullet.

"I like the cut of your jib boy; you should stick around and fight the Pirates. We are gonna win, you can bet your skivvies on it." Chief Hodge got up and reached for his rifle, he checked the chamber for a shell and continued, "Gotta get back on watch, never know what will sail in." Chief Hodge stood ram rod straight as he practically marched out.

"J, dad is not as crazy as he sounds. He is a good guy. In the Navy he was a Data Processor or a DPC. He produced all the payrolls for Gitmo, both civilian and military. Now, for some reason, he wants to tell everyone he was a Bosun's mate Chief."

"Maria, my dad was an ENC, or an engineman. He was referred to as a 'snipe'. Dad retired and now works in Mt. Bell, North Carolina. He took a job in management in a cotton mill, which is where his family had worked," commented J. "The coffee is good Maria, but I have to ask you a question."

"Sure J, what is it?"

Why did her voice sound like music, and why was he light headed? J got hold of himself and continued, "I saw you twice in the last two days. I know you were crying once. And the second time, I could tell you were on the verge of crying. What is the problem?"

"J, dad bought this land when he retired. He financed the land through Drover who is really a con-man. Something has come up every time the land was near pay off. This time it is damage to Drover's fences. We know we are responsible for some of the damage but not all of it. We have no way to prove it. Even if we tried, the deadline would pass while we tried. As you can see, dad's only answer is to shoot the fools if they come out here."

"Maria, I am just a kid out of high school. I went to Vegas to get rich like a fool. I know nothing about legal things, but I overheard Drover after you left. He said you needed eight hundred dollars. Has your dad got it now?"

"No, he hasn't. We spent the money on cattle, mainly for feed and molasses licks. If everything goes well from here on out, dad will make a profit for the first time since he started on this piece of land."

"For some reason, Drover does not want that, if I understood the conversation I overheard."

"I have no idea why he is pushing for this property. It does have water, but so does most of his property."

"Well as I overheard it, a man never gets enough land, to quote Mr. Drover," J said.

"Dad wants to fight him, so I am trying to repair a quarter mile of fence by myself while dad keeps watch. No one in town will dare work against Drover. Besides that, they would have to work on the credit, because we couldn't pay them. Everybody needs the money now, to make their land payments to Mr. Drover."

"Well, can you repair the fence?"

Maria looked at him and smiled, "Not by myself. Of course I told daddy I could, but it is impossible. He knows it, but he is becoming delusional or something." Maria said and started to take J's cup for a refill. As she did their hands touched.

J had started to speak, but the same feelings flooded his being. He looked directly at Maria. For the first time, he realized this was the most beautiful woman he had ever seen, including the center folds of that new Playguy magazine. He just could not speak. Her eyes met his. They moved toward each other and their lips touched lightly. Lightening went through J's young body. Maria jerked away quickly taking the coffee cup, she went into the kitchen.

Inside the kitchen Maria was trying to sort out her feelings. She stood there with the pot in her hand. It began to tremble. She sat it down and said to herself, 'he is a kid, this cannot be happening. Take the coffee in. He will forget it'.

When she entered the room she knew she was lying to herself. This was love, no matter how young he was. She sat the coffee down in front of him.

"M-Maria," J stuttered, "I don't know a thing about fences, but I don't mind work. Pay don't mean nothing, I have all I want. I am not on a schedule, so I can stick around awhile. Can I help?"

"Oh, all I need is another pair of hands around me, I-I mean around here to help." She had embarrassed herself.

"Maria, I think I…" J could not bring himself to say 'I love you'. This was too soon. "I think I will stay and help if you will let me."

"I can't think of anything I would like more. I have never known anyone from North Carolina and you can tell me about a cotton mill town."

"Okay, if you will teach me about this wild country out here."

For a few minutes, they just sipped the coffee and starred at each other. Their thoughts were their own. When the second cup was finished Maria said, "Okay cowboy, let's teach you to repair a fence."

"We will have to ride double, if you don't mind. Poker don't mind since we are both little." She laughed.

Maria swung up into the saddle, J swung up behind the saddle as she had directed, "put your arms around me. Poker is very gentle, but you never know when something will spook her. Snakes and rabbits startle her sometimes."

J placed his arms around Maria, and it was all he could do to hold his peace. He wanted to yell to the top of his voice, 'I love you Maria'. He was awash in all those strange feelings. Never had he felt so wonderful.

It was a short ride to the fence. They both dismounted. J looked at Maria. Maria looked at J. J took a minute to arrange his thoughts into some kind of order and said, "Please do not think I am a stupid kid Maria, but do you believe in love at first sight?"

"Not until today…. never until today, but today? Yes, I do."

"Never in my entire life have I met someone as beautiful as you. Never have I felt like I could fly to the moon and back, until I felt your touch. Maria, I am in love with you."

J took Maria into his arms, he felt the electricity again. Emotions were reached that had never in his young life been stirred. He realized he was taller than she. He looked down into her eyes. Maria spoke but it came out a whisper, "I don't know you, but I love you J-man. I know I love you." Their lips met, she folded into his arms and they held the kiss for an eternity. Love had found a place to live. They kissed and their eyes spoke. When their lips parted and she laid her head on his shoulder, they did not have to speak. They were both happy. For a few minutes they were transported out of this world into a world of their own. Two people who had known each other less than two hours were committed for life. Neither of them had known such joy.

J spoke first, "I hate to break up the most wonderful time of my entire life, but don't we have a fence to fix?"

"You bet, my prince, just follow me," said Maria smiling happily.

In the next little while, between kisses, J learned what he had to do. Maria told him there was nearly a quarter mile of fence down. After setting five posts, and going forty feet, J knew the job would be impossible using the present tactics. By supper time they had gone one hundred feet. Wearily, they climbed aboard Poker and headed home.

At the back porch J was taken back a hundred years. There was a wash basin on a makeshift shelf and on a post was a broken piece of mirror. There actually was a dinner triangle hanging there. "We'd better wash up for supper 'cause the chief will have it warmed up," said Maria.

J dried his face and hands on the clean but ragged towel hanging on a nail. They opened the screen door and went into the kitchen. It was a real 'old west' kitchen. There was the smell of burning wood, and a cozy warmness. The chief was standing at the old wood stove with his back to them, but he spoke anyway, "Well did you get finished, or have you been lolly gagging leaving me here to tangle with Drover. He never come today, by the way, but he will tonight or tomorrow, you can bet our skivvies on that mates."

Mixed with the smell of oak burning, the smell of food attacked J's taste buds. He was instantly starved; they had not eaten since breakfast. The chief spread the food out on the table, along with some Indian fried potatoes rolled in some kind of herbs. They chatted and passed food around. The chief asked the blessing and they started to devour the food. It was getting pretty dark outside.

"Chief, does that old Ford 9N tractor run you got out yonder?" asked J.

"What does a city boy know about a tractor? Yeah, but it needs the points set and plugs cleaned. Why'd you ask?"

"Oh a buddy of mine had an Uncle Howard back in Mt. Bell that had an old 9N. I saw him digging post holes once and he explained how it worked. You wouldn't happen to have a post hole auger with that thing would you?"

"Now, I don't know mate, but out in the tack shop there is some stuff. Seems like there may be an auger looking thing there. All that junk came with the ranch. I just use the tractor to haul hay to the cattle every once't in a while when we have a drought. What you got on your mind?"

"Well, if we could punch the holes with an auger, we could do one every ten minutes I guess. The auger attaches to the power take off on the 9N. It may take some getting used to. But it might just work."

"Hot dang, you might be right mate. After supper we will take a lantern out and look around."

The rest of the supper time was taken up with small talk, and a lot of smiles and eye contact between J and Maria. The chief then took out a big apple pie. J said, "Pardon my language at the table but I am as full as a tick, but I know I can make room for that apple pie," and he did.

"I will clean up Chief while you and J go out and see if you can find an auger," said Maria. She was all smiles at the prospects of the hole-digger, praying that there was one in the shed.

Out at the tack shed, the chief sat the lantern on an anvil. J looked on curiously. The chief picked an axe handle that was leaning against the shed. He turned quickly toward J and drew back the handle, showing he was ready to swing at J's head, then he whispered, "Son I don't know what your game is, I am not as dense as I would appear to most of the world. I see the eyes my gal is flashing you, did you touch that girl out on the prairie?"

Taken aback and not knowing exactly how to answer to keep from getting brained, he stuttered, "I-I uh, exactly what are you asking me Chief."

"Now who is dense? You are a city boy, been to Vegas played around and slept around, probably acted like you were on liberty in Tijuana. Now you find an innocent gal on the prairie and think you can have your way with her using some land lubber sweet talk. It ain't gonna work. You understand me?"

"Chief, don't swing that stick, let me explain something. First, Mt. Bell is not close to a city. It is a cotton mill town. One more thing, I was raised in the Navy by Christian standards. I was taught you do not sleep around until after you are married. Now you are making me mad. Maria is a wonderful girl. The loveliest one I have ever met. I can't believe you don't trust her to take care of herself."

"Oh, I trust her alright; it is slick landlubbers I have a problem with."

"No you don't, you think she would mess around with someone she just met, and fall for some sweet talk. She is more grownup than that. She is a sweet wise person who is trying to keep you from losing this prize piece of land here. She went into town begging men to come out and work. They all turned her down, but she tried. Here you are doing nothing but playing guard duty while she works. You are acting as hard headed as some of the Bosuns dad worked with in the Navy, you should have been one."

"I ain't out here for no lecture from a kid still wet behind the ears. Think I believed that wild story about the robbery and shoot out in Vegas? Ha. That was as much a lie as you are. Now, I will ask you once more, did you touch my gal while you were out on the prairie with her?"

"As a matter of fact, he did, daddy," Maria stepped from the shadows and walked up beside J. She reached over and pecked him on the cheek. "I know you will not believe it right now, but we fell in love. And he has never touched me inappropriately but he did kiss me, and I loved it. You know what? I think we are going to be married and it is not going to be a shot gun wedding. What do you think J?"

"I think you are insightful. I was trying to figure how to ask you to marry me. And I don't even know how to go about it. But I want you more than anything I have ever wanted in my life. Just being around you makes me feel like a king. I hope you will marry me, after we get the fence fixed, and this ranch belongs to the hard headed chief here."

The axe handle slowly fell to an unthreatening position, and Chief Hodge leaned it back up against the shed. "Neither one of you whippersnappers has any idea what you are doing or saying. But contrary to your opinion son, I trust this girl more than you will know. I am not ignorant of the fact she is holding this ranch together. So let's see if there is an auger in here that works."

Entering the shed and holding the lantern high they looked around. The chief hung the lantern on a nail and started moving some of the plows and equipment around. "That looks like one," yelled J excitedly, "let me dig it out." He pulled several things off it and stood it up. It had the appearance of a corkscrew and was rusty. "I think it will work if we soak it in coal oil or kerosene, do you have any?"

"Yeah, I got five gallons of kerosene, drag that sucker on out of the shed. I will be right back." The chief disappeared into the dark.

"I heard the nice things you said about me J that was sweet."

"No it was the truth," he took her in his arms again and tasted her tender lips. He was starting to welcome the feelings he had when he held Maria. To himself, the only expression that fit was 'WOW'. "You just can't believe how I feel when I hold you, it is like a thousand volts, and the peace of a slow moving river at the same time. I know I love you. Were you serious about marriage?"

"Si, Yes, Oui, I am very serious, no boy or man has ever made me feel this way. I am sure I know how you feel because I feel the same. It is wonderful isn't it?"

"Si, Oui, Yes it is, you are a doll. When we get the fence fixed, we will find a jewelry store."

"No, that won't be necessary J. Before mama died, she gave me her rings, if you do not mind; I would prefer to wear them."

The chief came back carrying a five gallon can and a couple burlap sacks. They wrapped the joints with the burlap, and soaked the burlap in kerosene. It looks like that is about it for tonight. Let's go back to the house," remarked the chief as he walked off carrying the lantern. "Come on in after you get through with all that mushy stuff. I am not so old that I do not know how you feel. BUT both of you just better mean it, you hear?"

"Yes sir," they answered in unison.

As their eyes adjusted to the dark J looked up into the night sky, no night had ever been so beautiful. He took his new love in his arms and held her tight and all was right with the world. Somehow heaven was near and his heart was singing. They both looked at the big western sky. As they looked a beautiful shooting star lit up the sky. He held his new love and wished upon a star, for a long life, and growing old with this marvelous woman named Maria. Again his mind said, 'WOW'. "I Love you Maria with all my heart. I know this is true love. I have never felt this way before."

As she stood close drinking in the night, the warmth and a love that was pulsating, she said, "More than anything in the entire world I want to be your wife."

They held each other close, knowing they had just today committed themselves for the rest of their lives. For richer or poorer, they would soon be one.

****

The next morning J was up at first light. He had refused the invite to sleep in the house and had slept in his car. The tool box behind the tractor seat produced a screw driver and sparkplug wrench. He had pulled the plugs and cleaned them with his knife and a wire brush that he found. With the screw driver he popped the distributer cap and set the gap to a guess of eighteen thousandths. Using a piece of old sand paper from the box, he cleaned the points. He went over the old tractor checking the oil, fuel and the battery water. He added battery water. Of course, like most tractors, the key was in it. The engine started within two turns and purred like a kitten. Ford would learn in years to come that this was actually one of the best tractors for its capabilities they would ever build. This was a 1947 8N and it was a work horse. From the driver's seat J moved levers until he found the one that controlled the power take-off. 'Good, it worked, and it sounds great'.

Before Maria called breakfast with the triangle, he had the posthole auger hooked up and working. He was one happy camper. This was working out great. He was smiling from ear to ear as he headed toward the house. He washed up on the porch and as he did he could not help but picture the movies of the cowboys doing the same thing. He was loving this.

After all the good mornings were said he sat down where he was directed. This was his first really western breakfast. J was looking at fried potatoes, gravy, eggs and sour dough biscuits. This feast was accompanied with some of the strongest coffee he had ever had. Chief Hodges spoke, "I heard the old 8N start. I guess you are pretty handy for a city slicker. I will wait to give judgment after a day out there on the prairie. This skirt will work your tail into the ground. We raise 'em tough out here boy."

"I don't doubt a word you're saying Chief, but my daddy, the Engineman, didn't raise a quitter. He wasn't what he called a feather merchant."

"Feather merchant? Is that what you are calling me boy?"

"No sir, I was just saying that is what my daddy would have said if he heard you even hint I was lazy or soft. No insult intended, Chief."

"Well them snipes did work a heap, that is for sure. I always liked being a Bosuns mate myself, when I could, never desired to be a snipe. Well, I better get on guard. You never know about them Pirates," the chief took the last sip from his cup and left with his rifle. Things were quiet in the kitchen.

Maria broke the silence. "By way of explanation, dad is disabled. His heart is bad. He uses the guard duty as a reason to be useful. He knows he cannot do any physical labor or it would kill him. Now that gem of knowledge is not to be repeated. I say again, is not to be repeated. Understand?"

"Sure Maria, I wouldn't do anything to cause him or you any grief." J was looking for any sign that Maria remembered yesterday and last night. He was beginning to think he had dreamed all that, or it was just some passing fancy.

Together they gathered the dishes up and cleaned the table. Maria had started and J just naturally began to help. The kettle of water was boiling on the stove. Maria added some to the sink dish water and started washing. J just naturally fell into the pattern of drying. It was J's turn to break the silence. "Maybe I had better wash and you dry," he suggested, "I don't know where anything goes."

"Good idea, but you may get dish pan hands, which are frowned on by cowboys out here."

"I guess I will just have to worry about that when I become a cowboy," J laughed.

When the task was done Maria said, "I could get used to this."

"What is that?"

"Having a man help with the 'woman's work' as it is called out here."

"Is that all?" J asked hopeful of some indication that Maria remembered last night.

"All I have to say on the subject J-man, is if we are ever to get married, we better fix that fence," she said as she turned into his arms and it was last night all over again. The bells were ringing, his knees were weak and he wanted to scream 'YEAH' to the top of his voice. Instead he experienced the sweetest tender kiss. Time stood still as they savored this kiss and gentle hug.

Tears he could not stop came into his eyes and he said, "I was afraid I had just dreamed what happened last night, and that you were not truly real. Oh, how I love you Maria, my queen." Growing up was not on his mind, but that is what J was doing, growing up.

The embrace was broken and Maria said, "You head on out to the fence. I will saddle Poker and catch up with you." They hurried out the back door and let the screen door slam shut with a bang.

The tractor started without a problem. After he figured the gear pattern, he headed for the fence. He was floating, this was real, and he was in love. He was whistling 'Unchained Melody' when Maria and Poker caught up. The old 8N was so quiet that the whistle was clear above its hum. Maria began to sing along with him. He looked over and smiled. He would have sworn that even Poker smiled.

At the repair site, the first thing Maria had to do was run a string for a few hundred feet to use as a guide to set a straight fence. They had a small bag of flour to mark the post holes. They measured off fifteen holes. The first four or five went pretty slow as they learned how to operate the auger and gauge the right depth. Those holes took about five minutes each. But after that it was three minutes a hole, then a minute to set the pole. They had cut yesterdays time by a big percentage.

"Now, I will use poker to stretch the wire." Maria attached a wire lock and rope onto the barbed wire. She then looped it around the saddle horn and said, "Tight," to Poker. The horse took a few steps and put pressure against the wire. Taking gloves, a bag of staples and a hammer out of the saddle bags, they walked back to the first post. With Maria holding the wire in place and J setting the staples they had the first strand up in no time. Then back to the second, by now they had a system. Back to Poker Maria said, "Ease off." Poker backed off a step and Maria released the wire lock. She walked over to J and said, "Break time." They put Poker in the shade of a Mesquite and found a place to sit. J sat first and she just fell into his arms. They kissed first, and then assessed their work. At this rate they could finish in two days, and still have time to smooch a little. That sounded good to both of them. The rest of the day went great. The job was over half completed, much more than Maria had ever envisioned. Now that she knew the fence would be repaired for Drover, It was time to be thinking about the money. They left the tractor in place, doubled on Poker, and headed home. They were tired but happy. Maria's closeness still put J on cloud nine.

"Well it seems like we will complete the fence repair J-man. You done a heap of work."

"No more than the boss's daughter. You are something else Maria. I would never have thought a lady could or would work so hard on a ranch as you have."

"Well J, I guess I love this piece of land as much as my dad and I do not want to lose it."

"What happens if you lose it?" asked J.

"Oh, it will be the same as most of the folks around here. Drover will offer to rent it to us and we will accept. Then his land will be taken care of like it was our own. We will eventually be beholden to him for everything and he will own us as he does everyone else. That will kill the Chief; he must own his own ship, so to say."

They arrived at the barn. It was not much of a barn, more like a lean-to. After they dismounted, they took care of the expected kiss. Maria showed J how to store the saddle and rub Poker down. They put a quart of oats in the bin and forked some hay over for her. Then they headed for the ranch house. The smell of beans and cornbread hit J, and he realized how hungry he was. They washed-up and Maria gave him a couple onions to peel. The chief had already simmered the potato cubes; Maria drained them and put them in the iron skillet. She diced one of the onions J had peeled, dropped it in the potatoes along with a big spoonful of butter. Supper was on. The ranch house was cozy and warm from the cooking. J leaned against the kitchen door jamb and admired his angel. This was a great life. The dream of riches and route 66 were long forgotten. This was the life.

Supper was ready; Chief came back in from his post. J was helping Maria put the food on the table while the chief took his seat at the head of the table. J and Maria sat across from each other. "Boy, are your intentions honorable toward my daughter?"

"Yes sir they sure are, the most honorable."

"Then I 'spect you can pray. You can ask the Good Lord's blessings on these vittles."

Bowing his head and praying the only prayer he knew, "God is great, God is good, and we thank him for this food. By His hand we all are fed; give us Lord our daily bread. Lord I also thank you for allowing me to meet the Chief and Maria, Amen."

"Be careful trying to bring the Lord in on the brown nosing son," laughed the chief, "pass them potatoes, I am starved."

"Dad, we are half finished. I think we can be completed by tomorrow this time, if the tractor doesn't break down, or something crazy doesn't happen." Maria said as she ate.

"Well count on something crazy happening, it always does. By the way Drover came out today. No honey, I didn't shoot him. We talked, you know he don't mind talking when he knows he is in control. He noticed the Ford out there; I told him a city slicker was helping. He got a good laugh out of that, I laughed with him. He said he would rent to us for two hundred a month after we default. I did tell him we did not plan to default," the chief said as he dipped some more beans. "He said he liked my salt, but he expected eight hundred dollars in two days. I explained it was more like four days, but he laughed and said, what is the difference? You are going to lose it anyway. I told him not to be too sure."

"Dad we have got to come up with the money somehow. Got any ideas?"

J broke into the conversation, "I hate to ask here at the table, but where are your mother's rings you talked about?"

"We are not selling mama's rings, J that is out."

"Okay, but would you mind letting me see them?"

"Right now?"

"Yes mam, right now, if you don't mind."

Maria left the table and went to her room. The chief turned to him and spoke, "You had better not be trying to do something stupid, or hurtful to that girl. Cause if you do, it will be you I shoot before Drover and that is a promise."

"Fine Chief, I will keep that in mind." At about that time Maria came back with a red velvet covered ring box and handed it to J. He looked at the rings, "It looks like you could pay off the ranch and have a lot left over with these," finished J.

"Of course we could, do you think I am a cheap skate boy? I bought them in North Africa while on a cruise. They cost plenty then."

"Maria, are you sure you want to wear these rings?"

"I certainly will when the right guy comes along."

J took the engagement ring in his hand; he got up from his side of the table and walked around. Looking at the chief, he asked, "Chief, I haven't been here but a short time, but be assured I love your daughter. Will you allow me to propose to her?"

The chief was caught off guard. "W-Well go ahead, boy take your best shot, the answer is up to her."

Dropping to the traditional position of one knee, he looked admiringly at Maria, "Maria Hodge, I haven't known you but a little while, but I love you with all my heart and soul. I would be honored if you would consent to be my wife, and I mean my wife forever."

She looked as blank as she could, no expression evident and said, "J-man, what took you so long," she beamed a bright smile and held out her ring finger to accept the ring. "I love you too J, and I would love to be your wife." J slipped the ring on her finger and they kissed.

Chief coughed, "What does this mean? Maria, are you leaving me for North Carolina, or have I got to put up with this city slicker here on the ranch?"

"We haven't talked about it dad. I know that is pretty impulsive, but I was only thinking of how much I love this boy-man."

"Let me put my two cents worth in; I can see Maria loves this place. I don't know about making a living here, but I do know I have enough to pay Mr. Drover. That will take care of the immediate problem."

"You have that much money J?" asked Maria.

"Yeah, you can consider it my cowry," and they all laughed.

"You have this mixed up a bit; it is the girl that must have a dowry."

"Yeah that is right, and do you ever have a dowry!"

The chief got up and went over to the old wood stove, he opened the upper warmer and took out a pie. "I baked this, I didn't know it was for a special occasion, but it is. This is something like my marriage. Her folks just never thought I was good enough for Maria's mama. They thought it was all too fast and I was just a wild sailor looking for a girl in another port. I said I would never say that, if I was faced with it. Now you throw this at me. So kids, I am a US Navy Chief and as good as my word. I wish you the best. This is very fast; I hope your feelings are real enough to take you through some rough places, because you can bet your sea bag mates, they are going to come. Now let's eat this apple pie and celebrate my daughter's engagement."

They were all laughing, Maria stood up and J sat down in her chair. He reached out and gathered Maria into his lap. The pie was delicious, but the feeling was more so. They just looked and looked at each other smiling like it was the happiest night of their lives, and it was. The Chief turned in early. As tired as they were they could not think of sleep for the excitement. Walking outside they held each other close under a beautiful western sky. Here they were, the cowgirl and the city slicker, what future could they have? They talked into the night. They sat on a couple bales of hay looking up at the star-studded sky. As a couple falling stars fell, J said, "Catch a falling star and put it in your pocket. That song is going through my mind but all I want to do is take one and write I Love Maria from one side of the sky to the other. I never knew love before, I thought I did, but I didn't. My Maria, the name sounds so wonderful; I want to be the best husband any girl has ever had. I want to love you forever."

"Sweetheart I have never known love, I have never even dated. I have danced a few times with the cowboys at the fandangos, some even stole a kiss, but you J-man have stolen my heart. I Love you." The kiss that followed was hot, deep and wet.

Stuttering, J tried to talk, "W-W-We had better h-hit the hay. We have a fence to finish; I hope we can do most of it tomorrow."

Reluctantly they both knew they had better call it a night. Maria went in after a last kiss and J headed toward the car. It had become his home. Actually he sorta floated to the Ford. He wasn't really much of a praying person, but he looked up to the sky and said, "Thank you Lord, she is the greatest!" He jumped in the air and spun around, he wanted to yell, but he just whispered real loud, 'YEAH!"

He settled into the pillow Maria had given him off her bed. He smelled her fragrance. Smiling, as a coyote howled in the distance he murmured, 'Find your own girl you old coyote, I have already found mine'. Then he drifted off to sleep.

That chow triangle rang early the next morning, and J did not want to get up.

****

He struggled out of the Ford back seat, knowing there was a lot of work ahead. When his mind cleared and he remembered he was now an engaged dude, he jumped into the air and clicked his heels together, and ran to the back porch. As he washed up he smelled the breakfast and his stomach seemed to growl, yes. Maria was already in the kitchen he kissed her lightly on the cheek and looked down at her ring finger. Then he hugged her and raised her off the floor as he kissed her and they spun around.

"Okay, that is enough lollygagging. Ain't no telling what will happen out on that prairie today. Probably no fence will be strung as you both will be looking at each other like dying calves in a hail storm. Now let's eat these vittles afore they get cold," as he said it the Chief was smiling. Down inside he was happy for the young lovers.

After breakfast J and Maria started clearing the table, "Hey I have plenty of time but you mates don't. So get out of here and get some real work done and I will be the mess-cook for today. It is far beneath my station as a Chief, but for once I will remember what it was like to be a seaman."

Morning ceremonies were taken care of hurriedly and they went out to saddle Poker. The Chief had already fed her and she was ready to hit the trail. The lovers enjoyed every minute of the ride; as a matter of fact to them it was not long enough. At the repair area J started the tractor and immediately punched the first hole. It wasn't long until they were into a routine enough that they could work efficiently and talk also.

"Maria, how long does an engagement have to be?"

"I don't think there is any hard and fast rule. You got something in mind?" She asked smiling.

"You bet I do, I need to find what it takes to get married. I have heard about a marriage license but I have no idea how to get one or anything. Who should I see first?" puzzled J.

"We will ask the Chief this evening, maybe go into town tomorrow and find out something. Anna is going to be surprised. She is my only girlfriend in this area. She said the reason the other girls shied away from me was because they were jealous, and thought I was after their boyfriends."

"Well, were you?"

"Yeah, all of them, I just couldn't decide which one. I thought I might convert to being a Mormon and get them all."

"Now, I know I am wet behind the ears, but the Mormons quit that years ago. Besides it was a man having a lot of wives not a girl having a lot of husbands," he laughed.

"Well, it should have worked both ways, what is good for the goose is good for the gander I always say," Maria smarted.

"Well, I am glad it didn't work that way because now I have your promise, and besides I think Anna sorta liked me."

"Anna could be your mama."

"Well, she sorta liked me like a son so maybe she will give me away at our wedding."

"Boy, I can see I have a lot to teach you in a short time. Nobody gives a man away; only the girl is worth that falderal. You just stand there and wait for me to come to you."

"Well, I am glad you know that stuff because what I am waiting for is the wedding night!"

"Oh yeah, why?" she smiled coyly.

J smiled, "Isn't that when I get to cut the cake?" They both laughed as they set another pole. They weren't working. They were having the time of their lives. They were so much in love that nothing in the world mattered except that magical attraction between a man and a woman. There was that overwhelming feeling that any obstacle was only a small bump in the road, because love would conquer all.

They did not stop for a break or to eat the lunch that Chief had sent. It was three o'clock and they set the last post and tied the fence together. Mr. Drover's fence was now officially mended. The final tie-in was near a creek where they finished, and they were hot. They ran through the water like children. Indeed they had a lot to celebrate. Soaking wet they fed and watered Poker. J pulled the old 8N out of the fence line and shut her down. Maria had spread lunch out. They ate and talked. The pressing work was done. They were relieved and resting and enjoying the sandwiches. It had been a very good day's work. At about three thirty they headed back to the Ranch house.

As they rounded a copse of Aspen there was a clear view of the Ranch house. They could see Drover's Caddy and the Chief holding the shotgun at port arms daring him to come onto the ranch further. Maria kicked Poker into a dead run, leaving J. When he realized he was being too slow, J clutched and ground the 8N into #5 gear and dropped the clutch. He eased the gas lever higher. He traveled at the fastest safe speed the old tractor would make. J knew Maria could handle the situation much better than he, since he was just an outsider.

Poker slide to a four point stop and she asked, "What's going on Chief?"

Drover spoke, "I came out to look over my land and…"

Maria cut him off, "With all due respect Mr. Drover, I asked the Chief. Now, Chief what is the situation?"

"Vice Admiral Drover here thinks he owns this property already. He doesn't read calendars well. Because it ain't his yet, and I don't plan on it being his anytime soon."

"Mr. Drover, Chief is correct, you are welcome on the land, you and your friend who is here as a witness I guess. But remember you are the Chief's guests, you are not the owner."

J had parked the old Ford and he walked on over to the group. As he did Drover spoke, "I heard you had a new hand out here. Got that city slicker I see. Taught him anything yet, can he ride that pretty filly of your daughter's without falling off?" both men in the convertible Cadillac were laughing.

"Good afternoon Mr. Drover, how are you doing? I remember you from in the restaurant in town. Well, things are going pretty good. I can stay on the horse if somebody holds me on but I am improving. I think in a week we can take off the training wheels. My mama would be proud."

"Good, good young feller, I like a man with a sense of humor. We just wanted to see what progress you were making on the fence. You know what is left to repair will be added to the eight hundred you owe, Chief Hodges."

"Drover, there ain't gonna be no extras, 'cause the courts will give us an extension. They always have. I plan to make some money this time around; you can wait on your money a couple months."

"Honestly, Chief, I would surely like to but this time the judge has already told me there will be no extension. Now I am going to do you a favor. I can appreciate a man with sand. You got plenty. After the courts return the land to me I will rent it to you for a hundred fifty a month for the first year, so you can get on your feet. Then I will have to have two hundred twenty five. Ain't that fair?"

"Mr. Drover," it was Maria who spoke this time, "We will be considering your offer. The Chief and me will talk this over. The due date is still four days off. We will be in town in the next couple days to talk it over. Will that suit you?"

"I am glad you have some bargaining sense Miss Maria. We ain't gonna fallout over the fence. I know we can work it out. I am repeating in front of Mr. Johnson here, I require eight hundred dollars cash and a repaired fence or the property reverts back to me. At that time you will become renters at one hundred fifty dollars a month for a year. Is that understood by all?" Everyone was shaking their heads except the Chief who seemed ready to just shoot Drover and get it over with. "Shucks, it seems the old Chief is pretty wrought up, so I won't check the fence today. I will take your word for what is not up. We will just head back to town. Good afternoon to you all."

As the Cadillac backed off the shotgun went to the Chief's shoulder and his finger tightened on the trigger. There was no doubt in J's mind the Chief was going to shoot Drover. As fast as lightening Maria moved ahead and pushed the barrel into the air just as it went off with an ear ringing 'BOOM'.

"It's all right Mr. Drover, the Chief is just celebrating a little early," yelled Maria, "See you in town." The Cadillac had slid around and was spinning wheels stirring up dust and headed for the main road.

"Chief, are you crazy? You were really gonna shoot that varmit weren't you?"

"Yeah honey, I was. I would rather go to jail than lose this place. I dearly love it here."

"Well, that is good, because me and your future son-in-law have some news for your salty old ears. Now, if you can just keep from having a heart attack on us, we will go in the house, put on some coffee and jaw some"

Maria got the grounds and J put the water in the pot. Maria added some wood to the coals in the wood stove. Set the pot on the stove and went in to the kitchen table. The Chief had reloaded his shotgun and leaned it against the wall. He took his place at the head of the table. Maria brought in the rest of the pie while the coffee was heating up.

"Okay Chief, here is the news. The fence repair is complete! Tied in, done!" both Maria and J were smiling ear to ear as the Chief assimilated this new information.

"You telling me that you and this city slicker have poled and strung barb a quarter mile in less than two days?"

"Yep, and my husband-to-be is advancing eight hundred dollars, to keep me from backing out of this marriage deal. How does that sound?" asked Maria.

"Sounds like it is about time for that fandango we have always talked about. What say we have the fandango and the marriage at the same time?" The Chief said breaking into the biggest smile Maria had seen in many a moon. It made her feel so good inside knowing the pressure was off.

"Sir, I need to know some things about this marriage situation. Where and how do I get a marriage license? I am sorta new at this." J said seriously.

"Well son, first of all, it is not I but we. Both of you have to stand before the clerk of court out here and make an application. The beautiful state of Colorado has few requirements for those wanting to get hitched. But you both must travel to Brighton, which is our county seat. That is 'bout fifty miles from here. I think the price has gone up to five dollars now, was three. All you need is five dollars cash and a good driver's license. Maria has one. I assume you do. Are you over eighteen?"

"Yes sir, I am eighteen and have a North Carolina Drivers license. Does that matter out here that it is out of state?"

"No son. The great state of Colorado doesn't care if you are not from here. They just want your five dollars. There ain't any waiting period either. Once you get the license any padre or judge can do the honors." Chief said laughing. "Has my girl said anything about a big marriage, with all the trappings?"

"Well, no sir, we haven't talked about it. I guess we should, huh?"

"You bet, and set up a time. We need at least a couple days to get the word out if you plan a fandango. Folks out here will drop about anything for a fandango."

Maria spoke, "I think it is supposed to be up to me, the bride, as to the kind of wedding. Problem is, we haven't set a date yet. What do you say J-man?"

"I am trying to think with my head instead of my heart. My heart says tomorrow but my head says that the situation with Drover should be settled first. Once that is settled, I want to marry you as soon as possible. Can we make sense from that?" J asked seriously.

The Chief took charge. "Tomorrow we get the Sheriff out here to verify that the fence is repaired. He may be in Drover's pocket but I do not know that. That is the first order of business. Then we go with the Sheriff to Drover's office with a certified check. Drover is a snake but he will not openly break the law. Once he sees our ducks are in a row, there will be no problem. Especially since he thinks I am crazy and will shoot him."

"So that was an act, dad? You had me scared to death."

"Maria girl, I know you like the back of my hand. I knew if I pulled down on him you would jump in and save his life. Now, he is beholden to you and a little afraid of my mental condition," Chief was laughing.

J was shaking his head. What was he getting into? He knew one thing; he wanted Maria Hodges for his wife. He did not mind what was required to make that happen. He wanted it done. "Okay then, right after the land deal is closed, Maria and I will head for Brighton, wherever that is? And whatever a fandango is, we can plan it as soon as possible. Is that a plan?" They all were in agreement.

"Now, if it is all right with you folks, we could all wash up and go into town. I am treating us to a great meal at the Strasburg Hotel Restaurant. We need to tell Anna the trouble she has caused you," he said looking at Maria.

At the Hodge Ranch there was joy. Everyone was happy. The weight was gone and the ranch would be liberated now. All that remained was the legal procedures.

****

J was ready first and took a little while making room for three people to ride. All his 'stuff' went into the trunk. He had wrapped the majority of his money in an oil cloth and stored it in the springs under the front seat. He was smiling as he thought of the past few days, driving in here, hearing the gun fire and thinking he was about to replay his exit from

Las Vegas. Things had taken a drastic turn. He had not even considered how living this far from Mt. Bell would affect his family back home. He hoped his folks would be happy for him, he knew they would once they met Maria. He was pretty young to get married, but it was not unusual in his family. His Dad had married at 17. I will have to call when we get to town. Man, will they be surprised, I sure am.

Maria sat over close to J. and Chief rode shotgun, a fitting description. Thank goodness he was not carrying his rifle. J was feeling goose bumps as he always did when Maria was this close. J parked in front of the Hotel Restaurant, and they entered the nearly empty dining room hand in hand with the Chief close behind.

"Well, what is this I see?" commented Anna. "I sent you out to take a supper and it appears you stayed." J and Maria were grinning ear to ear. "And am I to assume that you are here to collect that free meal that you said you would never collect?"

"Well, I won't lie I did think of it, but the reason we came in was the Chief's cooking is getting pretty rank," laughed J.

"You are getting pretty salty there lad, you had better batten that hatch," spoke the Chief as he walked to the nearest table.

"Hey Maria, did Chief really try to kill Mr. Drover?"

"Nah, is that what he said?"

"Yeah, and it took him a while to calm down. He called the sheriff over and the sheriff calmed him down some." Anna was smiling as she said that. "The Sheriff is right over there now. He will probably come over and discuss the situation. Now, have a seat, what will it be?"

"Why did you ask what it will be," said J, "You know you are going to pawn off the special."

"Okay," then she yelled into the kitchen, "Three more suckers, Thomas, gimme three specials, double the trimmings." In just a minute she had water on the table with a stack of hot steaming homemade biscuits and a jar of honey with the grooved wooden ball on the stick to get it out with. Once a customer got the hang of using the device he could deliver the honey to his plate or biscuit accurately without dripping it on the table. The trick seemed to be keeping the handle twirling in your fingers until you got it above the destination, and then stop twirling until the right amount ran out of the grooves, then twirl again as you returned it to the jar. It was a neat device.

"Now, what do you have to tell me Maria?" asked Anna laughing.

"How do you know I have anything special to say?"

"Well, honey it is like this, I can't ever remember seeing your smile that big, and we have been friends a long time. Soooooo what is it?"

"Okay, you sent J out to the ranch to work, and don't you deny it. Well, it worked; J here is a sucker for a damsel in distress. Then......." Maria paused.

"Well, go ahead, spit it out. Thomas will call in a minute," Anna said motioning for her to finish.

"Okay.. and then this wonderful person proposed to me and I accepted and we are going to have a fandango and dance and get married just as soon as we can," Maria finished out of breath and holding J's hand tight.

"Well, praise be to the Lord and me. I knew he would fall for my beautiful friend but even as brilliant as I am, I never expected it to be this soon. I thought it would take two weeks!" She exclaimed as she jerked Maria up into a big western hug and swung her around. Putting the smaller girl down she said, "Hallelujah, this is great, a marriage and a fandango. That will wake up this dead town."

"Food is getting cold. We ain't making any money with you gabbing and dancing around. You don't want me to make that million so we can get married, do you?" came the voice from the kitchen.

"Excuse me folks, Thomas is just mad because he can't be out here enjoying the good news," and she headed for the kitchen and everything got quiet.

"Whoopee, Whoopee !!! That is great, let's make it a double!" came a man's voice from the kitchen and then they both walked out of the kitchen bringing the meals.

"Don't take him serious, J. Thomas doesn't want to get married. He says that at every happy occasion." Anna said looking at J. Then there was a pause and her face fell. "But does this mean when Drover takes the ranch that you will be leaving? I won't like that and I might just shoot Drover myself."

Maria pulled Anna close and whispered in her ear, "With J's help, we have saved the ranch. But please do not spread that until after we get the papers all signed and legal. I don't want him to be figuring how to circumvent this deal, okay?"

"You got it sugar but I will be waiting to howl, just say the word."

As they talked the sheriff had moved closer and was respectfully waiting for the conversation to die down, then he stepped over to the Chief. "Chief I hear there was a little trouble out at the ranch between you and Drover. What do you have to say?"

"Weren't no problem sheriff but my rifle did go off when Maria jostled me. It was pointed into the air though."

"I figured something like that; I won't interrupt your supper. I'll be seeing you."

As he started to leave Chief said, "There is a little problem I need you to see out at the ranch. Could you drop by tomorrow sometime?"

"Sure Chief, but it will be early; I am headed that way around seven."

"Okay Sheriff, that won't be too late. I was hoping it would be earlier," the Chief laughed.

"See ya then." The chief walked away and they dug into their chuck wagon steaks. Anna and Thomas pulled up chairs and they all talked as the three ate. Whispers and smiles all the way around. This was a happy dinner.

The Sheriff had been contacted easier than they had expected. That was settled. After dinner the crew headed back toward the ranch.

Chapter Three
The Past.. J's story continues, The Marriage.

To everyone's surprise, there was not a hitch. The sheriff looked at the fence repairs, smiled a little and said, "Drover is going to be very surprised with this turn of events. The man is going to be disappointed that he cannot add a few hundred to the land price for fence repair. I am driving over to the Tanner Ranch. I will be back in town and let Mr. Drover know by about noon, if that is all right with you folks."

"That will be excellent Sheriff; we should be ready to face the music by that time. We have a few more ducks to line up, but we will try to see you then," the chief said with a straight face.

Over breakfast, Chief had laid out a plan. After the sheriff was satisfied, they would drive to the County seat. There the kids could get the marriage license and J could get a certified check. There he could have it made out to Drover at a Bank that the man did not 'own'. The chief surprised them both by saying he was going to get everything for the fandango with money he had squirreled back, nearly three hundred dollars. He already had his list made out. He would take care of that at the

Rancher's Dry Goods and Grocery Co-op. There was no reason to worry about Tom over there conversing with anyone in Strasburg because he had no use for old Drover. He was forever complaining how he had to 'push' to collect from the richest man around. He had been a rancher himself, and always said the small ranchers paid on time. Chief, like all the ranches, ran a tab but it was never in arrears.

So after the sheriff was out of sight they piled into J's Ford and headed out. Chief gave directions. They finished their business. The Ford was loaded down and they were back at the restaurant for coffee and pie before noon. They would wait here for the sheriff to show up. He never missed lunch unless it was an emergency.

Maria excused herself and went into the kitchen with Anna. Giggling was heard and plans were being made. At the table, the chief became very serious. "Son, I think you are serious about Maria. But mark my words it ain't always going to be smooth sailing. When the seas get rough, just remember there is a fair haven ahead. I have no doubt that my girl will make you an excellent wife. To be sure, I don't know you, but I do like the cut of your jib. So, like I said, I will not object. I promised myself years ago when my wife's folks gave me such a hard time that I would never do that, and I won't. You can count on it. But pay heed to this, as sure as an anchor must be set, if you hurt her son, I will cut your gizzard out and feed it to the sea gulls. That girl is all I have. Not being mean, just truthful. You do understand that, don't you?"

J looked at the old chief and said, "I think I know exactly how you feel. I understand your concern, but you do not have a thing to worry about. Maria is the love of my life. I will protect her and take care of her to the best of my ability. I love your daughter, Chief."

They sat there looking at each other both lost in their own thoughts. J thinking it was time to call his folks. He would do that after the legal stuff with Drover was done. About that time the sheriff came in. Anna came out to take his order and Maria returned to the table. "What have you men been discussing while I was gone? Wait let me guess. Chief told you if you hurt me he would cut your gizzard out, didn't he?"

"Yes I did, and I mean every word of it."

"Yes he did, and I believe he meant every word of it. So.. pause… since we don't want to lose five dollars, cause they will not give a refund, I guess I will just have to take my chances." J laughed.

Maria hit him playfully on the shoulder, "So if they gave a refund you would reconsider, is that it?"

J laughed, "I refuse to answer on grounds it may incriminate me."

"Maria, looks like you got yourself a jail house lawyer," smiled the chief.

About that time the Sheriff came over, "I was just having coffee today, we can go on over to Johnson's office. Drover said since Johnson is a notary we will just do the formalities there."

"Fine Sheriff, I think that will be just what we need. We are ready." Chief paid their bill and they accompanied the sheriff the short walk to the locomotive shop.

Inside the office everyone was smiles. After all the 'hello's and 'howdy's were said the sheriff started, "Mr. Drover I went out to the Chief's ranch this morning early. The fence is completed. As good a job as I have ever seen. No cow is going to get through that one. The barb is as tight as can be. Also the land looks clear and properly clean. I don't see any reason for penalties toward the closing of your deal."

"Well city slicker, you surprise me. But I am glad the fence is repaired and otherwise all is well. We will just sign the land over to me and then you can sign the rental agreement. If that is agreeable?"

All was quiet for a minute and the chief spoke, "Then Mr. Drover you are agreeing that the sheriff's statements are true, and we owe no penalties."

"Certainly Chief, I trust the Sheriff completely. So, since you do not have the required cash, let's go ahead and sign these few papers. I only need one signature since you are a widower." Drover smiled as he pushed the papers toward the chief.

Looking as solemn as he could the chief picked up the papers. After a minute he said, "Says here the amount I owe is eight hundred dollars, ain't that true?"

"Yep."

Then opening an envelope and extracting the check, "Then this check should cover the total. I only ask that you sign the lien that is stamped on that deed as, 'paid in full'. I will record it at the court house this afternoon and that should conclude our business together. It has sorta been fun at times," laughing out loud Chief Hodges handed the papers back to Mr. Drover who appeared to be in shock. He passed the check to the Sheriff who gave it to Johnson who nodded and passed it finally to Mr. Drover who was getting redder by the minute.

Everyone got dead quiet. Mr. Johnson broke the silence, "Mr. Drover, Chief is correct. You need to clear the lien on that title."

At something between a yell and a scream Drover looked at Johnson, "JOHNSON, I AM NOT BLIND OR DEAF, I KNOW THAT!" Then he was quiet for a minute, his color changed and he started laughing himself. Everyone joined in, not for sure why they were laughing, but Drover's laugh turned genuine and contagious. If you had been outside the office you would have thought they were watching an 'Abbott and Costello' movie.

After a few minutes Mr. Drover held up his hands as if in surrender. "I have got to hand it to you Chief, you got me on this one." He took his pen and wrote 'Paid in Full' across the lien. He handed it to Johnson to witness. Johnson put the deed in the envelope and handed it to Chief Hodges. Chief pulled it from the envelope and kissed it, making sure it was real he returned it to the envelope. "You didn't trust me Chief?"

"Nope, I knew a man on a ship once, who could have put a blank sheet of paper in that envelope with five people looking at him and pocketed the real paper. I was just checking."

"Good thinking Chief, but I have got to tell you this is the first time anyone ever got the best of me. I sure don't like it," and he laughed again, "but I do respect you. You, Maria and the little city slicker beat me taking everything I threw at you. In front of witnesses I give my word the land is yours with no attempt from me to ever recover it. I will even help you if you need it, and on a handshake."

"Thanks Drover, you have been a worthy opponent, and like I said, some of it was fun. Now we are heading for the county seat."

"Wait, before you take off, I have to ask this. If Maria hadn't messed up your aim, would you have shot me?" Drover asked seriously.

Looking just as seriously Chief spoke, "One never knows, does one?" He smiled and they all left the office.

Inside the office Drover said, "What do you think?" No one answered.

****

Everything was light hearted and smiles on the trip to record the deed, free and clear. The Clerk of Court was amazed and they all chatted as westerners will do. Then on the drive back to the Ranch, Maria was close to J. He was driving on the deserted roads with one arm around her and the other on the wheel.

"Now kids, I am planning a big fandango. Before I do any bragging about the marriage and grandkids, or go telling Smokey, Shirl and the band to get ready, I want to know you two are completely serious, are you?" Chief asked.

No one said a word, J glanced down at Maria and she was looking up at him grinning. She said, "Your call J man."

Smiling from ear to ear, J retorted, "Chief, call 'em all. You can call the president. This here cowgirl has said yes to my proposal and I believe her. So, let's have a big fandango and we will start or end it with a wedding. Whichever is proper? To be honest, it is going to be hard for this boy to wait."

"Dad, my answer is the same, I do love this guy and I believe he is real. So like he says let's fandango this coming weekend! J and me will go over to the Reverend's house and talk to him this evening," added Maria.

****

It was a great time on the ranch. Maria and J decorated the place and cleaned the house and yard. They were married at the beginning of the fandango so they could reign over the festivities. J had only one problem. Jealousy. He was so jealous when he learned Maria had to dance with all the cowboys one last time, he had to fight his feelings to keep from spoiling the event. He was able to keep it in and when she was finally in his arms all was forgiven and forgotten. He ended up with the prize, Maria was his and only his now and forever, and he meant it. As Smokey and the boys played, Shirl sang a love song. As he looked at his bride, whom he had known less than two or three weeks, he wondered how a boy from a small cotton mill town in North Carolina could end up in Colorado. Not just here, but married to the most beautiful girl in the world. Life sure takes some strange turns, and our lives are just starting.

The fandango was a huge success. Everyone hugged as they left. When everyone was finally gone Chief said, "Well Son, she is yours now. I have done my best to do right by her and I expect no more or less from you. I don't know about cotton mill daddy's, but us western daddy's don't cotton to no misuse of our daughters, married or not. That is just for clarification. Now I want to welcome you to our family and the ranch. I plan to love you like a son."

"Thanks Chief, no man could want this lady more than me. And no one could love her more, if they had known her all her life. Now we are going to take a couple days off. Our wedding gift from Anna and Thomas is two days at the Inn with meals." His smile was so real he could hardly straighten his face, Maria giggled.

They said good night to the chief and drove off, Maria practically on his lap. Life was wonderful, they were happy. As they drove along J explored where only a husband's hands should be, Maria giggled and held up a room key, "Anna slipped this to me, no checking in." They both laughed.

In the room it was not as easy as J had planned, he was a little self conscious and Maria was too. They sat and kissed for several minutes. "Do you feel a little sweaty and dusty from the dancing?" Maria asked.

"Yeah, as a matter of fact I do, I should take a shower."

"You go ahead, I will bathe last," Maria smiled coyly.

J took some clean shorts, shaving gear and tooth paste and went into the bath, half closing the door. He shaved and brushed his teeth then climbed into the shower and adjusted the water to fairly hot. It was an old claw footed bath tub, which had been rigged with a shower curtain. He had soaped his hair and his eyes were closed tight when he felt cool air and knew his wife had pulled back the curtain and was in the shower behind him. "Need your back scrubbed cowboy?" she asked.

"What took you so long?" He said as he washed the soap from his eyes and turned to his wife. Taking her in his arms he experienced emotions he could have never dreamed were real. That night would be burned into his memory and last for decades. One of his thoughts that night was not original, but it was his, 'God sure knew what he was doing when he made a woman!'

They knew ecstasy that night, and they vowed their love over and over. They left their room only for meals the next day. They ordered breakfast at two in the afternoon. Enduring the jokes and enjoying the congratulations of everyone coming in the restaurant. Most of the community had been to the fandango, so there were comments of how great it was. J was beginning to see that a small western community, even though it was spread out, was just as close as a mill hill back home.

The short honeymoon was over and they headed back to the ranch. J was about to learn what ranch work was all about. Upon their arrival the first thing they noted that standing beside Poker in the corral was a larger white pony. As they got out of the car and was gathering their gear, the chief walked up. "I see you noticed our addition. Tom wanted six cows for him, I gave him four, and one was old Meany. What do you think?"

Maria answered, "I think you talked Tom out of Cotton, because J is from a cotton mill town."

"You know the horse?" asked J.

"Yeah I know Cotton, he can be a little rough around the edges and if you plan to ride him you will work for it. You can bet on that."

"Now my cowgirl wife, just what does that mean?"

"It means Tom thinks he took dad, but I know Chief isn't that easy. Right, Chief?"

Chief smiled, "No horse is as bad as Tom makes out. I knowed old Poker always liked him, he was always calm around Poker. Besides Cotton is an Arabian Stallion. They are supposed to be gentle. I figured something was wrong. So I didn't take Poker over there, he delivered Cotton on the trailer. Then he loaded his cows. He laughed as he drove off and said, 'Good luck, you gonna need it.' I just smiled and waved."

"Okay, I will learn more later. Now we have got to get this stuff inside and I guess I need to learn something about ranching besides stringing a fence, right?"

Chief Hodges was laughing, "Boy you had two days alone with her, didn't she teach you nothing about ranching during that time?"

"No sir, I was just plowing with your heifer, as the Bible would say," J laughed.

"Don't know as I ever read that, and don't know as I like it, Bible or not," he grinned.

****

J took to ranching, he loved the outdoors. He and Maria became quite a team. It was about six months into the marriage when a strange thing happened. J and Maria came in from feeding the stock and clearing a couple water holes, they were tired. Chief had assigned himself to the Mess Cook position four or five days a week. As they came in from washing up Chief was holding a large envelope. "J, the mailman came here with a special delivery letter, hand carried it to me. I had to sign for it. Funny return address huh? Do you know any S'gar (Es-gar) Enterprises? Says MVA Division," pausing then said, "Printed right on it says to be opened only by you."

"Never heard of it, wonder what it is about?" J was holding the envelope and staring at it.

"I have found that if I open a letter addressed to me, I can usually find out what is inside," said Maria innocently with a gotcha smile.

"Right, I would have never thought of that, sure pays to marry a smart cowgirl." J withdrew his pocket knife and slit the envelope. Carefully he took the contents out and laid them on the table. There was a round trip plane ticket from Denver Airport to Pittsburgh International Airport. Then there was a certified check. Finally there was a letter. Staring at the letter he began to read aloud, "Dear J, This letter may change your life forever. If, after reading this letter you do not wish to come to Pittsburgh, we here at MVA will live with that. However, we really do want your input here very much, but if you choose not to come we will understand. If that is the case, you can go to the Denver Air Terminal and cash the ticket in. The money is yours for considering this offer. The check is also yours, and your new bride's as a wedding present. There is no obligation either way. Please continue to read before you decide to throw it away as junk mail.

My name is S'gar. It is pronounced Es-gar. We met a few years ago and I have kept track of you following your life. I felt you would grow to be the type of man we need in the MVA. The MVA is a secret, not for profit organization, presently in its fourth year. This organization is dedicated to doing good and righting some wrongs of our society.

The MVA system is very intricate and involved and cannot be put on paper in a letter such as this. I have a proposal that I want you to consider. It will be to your advantage financially. Hopefully your new wife Maria and Chief Hodges can spare you for three days. During which time you will travel, all expenses paid, to our facility here in Pittsburgh. After the tour you will be free to return and discuss my proposition with your bride, Maria, and her father.

Let me extend my congratulations to you and Maria on your recent marriage. Also for your successful escape from your 'so called friends' in Las Vegas. I will admit I had my doubts about you for a few weeks, but you came through with flying colors.

Please give serious consideration to this offer; I am looking forward to meeting you again and renewing our acquaintance.

Respectfully,

S'gar

PS: This is a hint. If you accept this position you will embark on a journey that will be financially rewarding as well as personally satisfying. Thanks.

Everyone had heard and read the letter. Everyone sat silently.

****

"Well, I never saw or heard of anything to beat this. What do you think J? Do you remember this person S'gar?" asked Maria.

"I am as stumped as you are. I do not remember anyone by that name; you know I would have remembered that strange name. This is very odd, no, this is weird!" Puzzled J.

"Well, what you gonna do boy?" queried the chief.

"You got me Chief. But it looks like I have a week or so before the scheduled flight to think it over. I guess we all will talk about it, it involves everyone, and he even named you guys. That is strange. He sure seems up-to-date on my whereabouts and my business." J said.

Each one at the table took the documents and looked them over again, hoping some secret would be revealed. No new revelations came out. Supper was getting cold.

A decision was made later that week.

Chapter Four
The Past.... Player #2, Buddy ....

Buddy's dad was a successful minister and was called to a pastorate in Mt. Bell, NC. At the time Buddy was eight years old. While at Mt. Bell he made friends, who were to remain so for life: John Morse (Sticky), Tuck (Tucker), and J. Leon (Leon Daniels Jr.). They had many adventures together but the most memorable was during the time they began to shadow a rough homeless man they called Rags. Their goal was to learn all about this man that they just knew was a criminal hiding out in their small town. One night during an overnight camping trip to an island in the Catawba River they found an old sea bag buried in the sand. The sea bag contained two guns that became evidence to convict some bank robbers. This discovery earned them a five thousand dollar reward. Split four ways was twelve hundred fifty dollars each. The boys all were around thirteen at the time. Tragedy and church assignment broke up the group known as the three and a half musketeers. Sticky's dad passed due to cancer and he had to start work to help support his mama. The personal hit was Buddy's dad was assigned a church in Mississippi and Buddy moved with his family too far away. It would be years before all of the Musketeers would ever be reunited.

At the church in Mississippi Buddy made friends quickly. His wit attracted the guys and his looks attracted the girls. School here was no problem. Once it commenced he regained his standing at the top of the class in science and mathematics. He had a love for formulas and treated it like a game to find the unknown.

Quickly, the friends closest were Bill and Belle. They were twins whose interest was martial arts. Buddy had always been into contact sports, mostly ones where his fist contacted some smart mouth guy's nose. He also liked real wrestling not the fake stuff on Saturday night TV. But with the twins, it wasn't long until he was enjoying the slow warm-up exercises, including the required intricate patterns of hand head and foot movements associated with the sport. Isometric exercises were hard for Buddy because he liked fast moving activity. What had hooked him was having Belle throw him about eight feet over her head in a back roll. Bill had suggested he try to put Belle on the grass. She said do it, it seemed simple to Buddy. But to his surprise this little girl sent him flying. As he had approached her she backed away and he increased his speed, she grabbed the front of his shirt and rolled back, placing her foot in his stomach and threw him. This got his attention, he was interested.

The three were fast friends at church, school and after. No romance developed between him and Belle but a deep friendship was there. Buddy continued to do very well in school. Again another separation in his life; Bill and Belle's parents were transferred to Montana. Buddy was now about fifteen and in the ninth grade. He never once used the martial arts in a scuffle; he always reverted back to his fists. They never let him down.

Being a preacher's kid has its disadvantages. If some smart mouth wants to start something, he usually says something about the preacher or his wife. One such incident was in the town park. Buddy was headed home from school when his way was blocked by boys from school who preferred to be called 'The Law'. All three of the boys were seniors. They wore the classic leather jackets and ducktails.

"Well, well, well what do we have here?" mouthed the first guy.

"I am not sure but does his daddy work?" said number two.

"Nah, he don't work, he is a lazy preacher," smarted number three as he smacked a short fat stick in his hand.

"What I see before us is a snotty freshman. No, a creep and a cold-tur-" Number two never finished the word. He was out from a punch that came from the shoulder and aimed at the back of his head through the nose. (That is how Buddy always described his punch, not at the surface but through it.)

Before either of the other two could react Buddy was on them like a mad hornet. They never had a chance. Number one took a solid punch to the breadbasket and went down gasping for air. Buddy knew number 1 was out of commission from the feel of the punch and turned his attention to number three. Three drew back the heavy stick but never saw the upper cut coming that was thrown from the ground. The shot raised his weight off the ground. Buddy knew this would require some dental work. Within less than a minute all three were out of commission and Buddy was standing there, now holding the stick he had been threatened with.

"Now, what was that you were saying cruds?" Buddy was menacing as he stood above them. Slowly he smacked the stick into his palm. "Got nothing to say?"

The three miscreants just lay there rubbing different parts of their anatomy.

"Then I will help you, and repeat after me loud enough that those kids over there can hear you," he pointed to some elementary school kids who had been playing on the swing sets. They were fascinated at the sight. "Repeat this loud and clear boys, 'I will never say anything bad about Preacher Sansbury', now I mean repeat it and do it loud."

The three repeated the sentence, but it was not loud enough for Buddy. They did it again. He flagrantly handed the stick to the one who had it and said, "Next time guys, I will hurt you, and that is a promise." After making the little speech, he turned his back on them and walked off, smug and proud of himself.

Unknown to Buddy, a local boxing promoter happened to be in the park with his granddaughter. His name was Moses McKenzie. He was known state wide as Momac. He took note of the kid and in the next few days found out all he could about him. He liked the fact that the boy was not known to start any altercation, but when forced always came out on top somehow. The other thing that raised his interest was his school record, the boy was smart. This kid had a lot of potential.

It wasn't hard to accidentally run into Buddy so he did just as Buddy was leaving the drugstore where he had had a fountain drink with some friends. Momac approached him. "Buddy my man, I am Moses McKenzie, most folk call me Momac, I think we need to talk."

"Yes sir," answered Buddy, "I have heard of you Mr. McKenzie. You are big in boxing I think."

"Well, not as big as I would like to be. I am always looking for new talent and I happened to catch your show in the park a few days ago, pretty impressive. That was a good sucker punch on the first guy."

"Sorry mister, I don't need a sucker punch, I am fast."

"Be that as it may, I think you have some potential. With my help you might become a good fighter."

"Sorry again mister, I am already good. Did you talk to the guys in the park after I left? Did you get their opinion? I have never lost a fight."

"Son, I have found if a man has never lost a fight, the most folks he has fought have been bums. I'm not here to talk about the past. I want to help make you a future if you want it," smiled Momac showing a gold tooth. "I am pretty good myself."

"Bums? Mr. McKenzie, with all due respect, I have decked some big dudes."

"Ah Buddy, don't get testy. I am not blind I know you can fight that is why we are chatting. I am here to offer you a deal. I just want an opportunity to prove I know what I am talking about. Interested?"

"How you planning to demonstrate this?"

"What you weigh? I figure 'bout 145. Let me put some gloves on you and introduce you to a kid about your age that I call the Missile. I been working with the Missile for about a year. He is pretty good, what do you say?" asked Momac with his serious business face.

"Man I have wrestled in school, but I have never been in a ring or put on gloves, it always seemed pretty sissy to me," Buddy smarted back.

"Okay, I will talk a language you know. I'll give you five dollars to get in my ring and put on some sissy gloves. I'll give you five dollars if you touch him. Okay, Missile isn't any bigger than you, but I will add ten dollars if you deck him or put his knee on the canvas, deal?" Momac finished, still looking serious.

"Yeah? Where do you want to do this?"

"How about six this evening? We will meet you at the Silver Palace Gym."

"Deal," said Buddy, "see you then, but have the bills ready. I always expect a man to be as good as his word."

"Yeah, me too. I'll see you at the gym. I expect punctuality when I am giving out money," laughed Momac good heartedly and he shook Buddy's hand.

Smiling inside Buddy thought about how he had always wanted to get in a ring. Now here was one of the biggest around wanting to pay him to get in the ring. He headed home to see if supper was going to be ready before he headed to the gym. On his way he jogged and shadow boxed as he had seen professionals do on roadwork. This Missile must be good; I know someone like Momac didn't look me up just to give out money. It could be that he wants a cheap sparring partner for this Missile.

One thing was for sure, Buddy was not going to advertise the show. He did not plan to lose or look bad, but it was better to not take chances. It would not do his rep any good if he happened to get knocked on his can and his friends see it. So, he would hold this close to his vest until he checked it out. He had enough training and common sense not to underestimate an opponent. That is how he had stayed on top. But in spite of his caution to himself, he was sure he could deck this guy if he was even close to his size. His attack plan had always been to hit first, second and third. If the guy was still standing to hit again until he went down. It had always worked and it would again today. Then he thought about the money and smiled, maybe $20 bucks for two minutes work. Great!

****

At the Gym: "Buddy my man," Momac called as he entered the gymnasium. "Manny here will show you the locker room, get you some trunks and help you with the gloves," Momac indicated the small guy that was with him, with a nod of his head.

The little kid that was with Mcmac headed toward a door labeled lockers, and indicated that Buddy should follow, which he did. Once in the dressing room, "You can use that open locker there for your stuff," Manny said as he threw him some trunks, "These should fit."

Buddy noticed Manny was getting into some trunks also. He had a pretty good body for a shrimp. It didn't take long to get into the trunks and Manny brought some gloves over and spoke to Buddy, "Momac said tape wasn't necessary this time," he slipped the gloves on Buddy's waiting hands and tied them tight. As they walked out Manny took a pair of gloves from his locker and swung them over his shoulders so they hung on his neck. Manny lead the way to the ring, Buddy noted that the kid walked pretty cocky.

Momac was near the ring and Manny walked over to him as he pulled the gloves on himself. He then held them out for Momac to tie, which he did. During this time Buddy was looking around and could see no one else. Then it dawned on him and he smiled thinking, 'Manny the Missile'. Is this a joke? The silence was broken by Momac.

"Did you boys talk any?" he asked.

"Not much," said Manny, "We just got dressed."

"I see that smile Buddy," laughed Momac, "I want to warn you about judging too soon. Best to wait to see what's in a package, before judging by the size of it. By way of quick intro, this here is my little Missile. And I don't like secrets so I want you to know he hasn't lost a fight since he has been under my tutelage. Okay you two tigers, into the ring. "

They all climbed into the ring and Momac pointed each to his corner. "Listen both of you, don't hold back but be clean. You are going three rounds at two minutes each. I am the bell," and he said, "Bong."

Both fighters made their way to the center of the ring. Fast as lightening Buddy shot a right cross to the jaw, but all he got was air and a little off balance. He received a right left combination to the gut for his trouble. No one ever hurt Buddy in the breadbasket, but it sure surprised him. He was mostly surprised at the power he felt behind the punches. Huh oh, this little guy can hit. While he was digesting this, he caught one on the chin. He back-pedaled and managed to block a couple punches and slide one off his shoulder. He couldn't get set because the Missile kept coming. How did this get reversed? I am supposed to be the aggressor?

He managed to get through the first round. Neither fighter had done any damage. Now Buddy did not have a plan, but he had learned a good lesson. There is more to this than being fast or using surprise.

"Bong," came Momac the bell and both fighters came center ring. This time Buddy is waiting to see what Missile's plans are. Buddy is just not a patient guy. He feigned a left and immediately caught a left to his chin. Fast, this kid is fast, he thought. But even in the speed Buddy noticed when the Missile threw the reflect punch he dropped his right just enough. Let me try that again thought Buddy. He made the same move and the same reaction by Missle, but this time Buddy was ready and let it slide past and it became just a glancing blow. He took advantage of the slightly dropped guard and landed a good solid punch. It felt good. But the Missile countered with a good combination to Buddy's mid-section again. "Bong," Momac ended the second round.

Back in his corner Buddy feels a little better but is thinking, 'this is a little kid and this should have been over long ago. Momac is right, this kid knows some things I don't'.

"Bong," Momac opened the last round. Both fighters moved to the ring center again. Immediately Missile threw a right cross. Buddy blocked it with his forearm and countered with a right and hit nothing, but caught another good combination in the gut.

Back pedaling for time to think he said to himself, 'I am bigger than this guy, why not just charge in swinging and bowl him over. Not wild now, go.' Two more steps back and then he set his feet for a split second and started his charge. Throwing his best available shots, Missile dodged and blocked most of the pepper shots, but two or three connected. Then they were against the ropes. Using this time to get his breath he held the Missile against the ropes. Momac moved over and separated them. They then continued to move around the ring. The rest of the match was uneventful. "Bong," Momac ended the fight.

"All right, both of you done good. To be honest Buddy, I was not sure you could touch him. You got in one good point maker in number two round. Maybe you got in two during round three. But we know who won the fight don't we?"

"Yes sir, Manny is good. He made a believer out of me."

Manny smiled, "You hit me three solid punches, Buddy, one hurt a little."

The gloves came off and Manny offered his hand which Buddy took, "Buddy you have some good moves, I think Momac wants to make a pugilist out of a street fighter. He is good at that. I sure hope to see you around."

"Thanks Manny, I will definitely take that as a compliment coming from you. You got some power behind those fists," commented Buddy.

Momac smiled at both boys, he liked their nature, "Go take a shower, I'll be right here when you get through."

There was a serious talk where Manny talked as well as Momac. Buddy was intelligent enough to listen. Both Manny and Momac used the word pugilist a lot, he was beginning to like the sound of that. A friendship was formed that night between Buddy and Manny the Missile. Buddy had not felt like this since he was thirteen with the Musketeers.

This was the beginning of Buddy's first career. He was going to be a pugilist. Momac took him under his wing and with the reluctant permission of the Rev. & Mrs. Sansbury Buddy began to train in earnest. He was sixteen in his first fight. He won that one by a decision. The preacher Sansbury could not resist, he was in the audience. He never expressed it, but he was very proud of Buddy's fighting ability. A preacher cannot fight, but there were times he would have liked to have taken a punch at a smart aleck or two.

Three weeks later Buddy won the second fight by a knock out. He averaged a fight a month in the tenth grade, not all of them were legal or sanctioned. A couple of them were in the Strong Legion building with a lot of wagering going on. Some were on a big farm pretty far out in the country. But no matter where Momac was by his fighters side to be ready for whatever legal problems they might have. As far as the fighters knew no problems ever arose. Buddy was being billed as the 'Bomb' and Manny was the 'Guided Missile'. Their names were being used among pugilists in Mississippi. Sometimes there was a purse but sometimes quiet money changed hands after the fight.

Only a few folks knew that Buddy's dad had fought a little in his younger years. He gave up the gloves for the Bible. Buddy liked to think of the time in the third grade his dad had taught him the value of the left jab. The Reverend had said, "Son I don't want you to be fighting, but there may come a time you have to defend yourself and at no fault of your own. The fast powerful left jab is like a flash bulb going off. It has a stop action effect." As his fighting and sparring continued he had learned to work any technique off of his powerful left jabs such as hooks, overhand rights, right and left uppercuts. Momac had been impressed with Buddy's natural ability to add the power to the jab.

Of course the Rev. and his wife were always concerned about Buddy's school grades and watched them closely. They remained high as they always had. They breathed easy at the end of the year. But when fall came, Buddy announced he had a job at the local grocery store and was quitting school. He hoped his mom and dad would understand and allow him to live in his room at the parsonage until he could make some better arrangements and get out on his own. Again reluctantly his parents agreed, but the quitting school had broken their hearts. They had hoped he would finish school and go on to college. Since this did not seem to be their son's goal they still hoped, but gave in. Now Buddy would be the pugilist, a son of the preacher man. This won't set well with some of the parishioners but so is the life of a pastor, try to work it out.

Momac was equally disturbed. He had constantly said we do not need any more dumb uneducated boxers. We need wise intelligent pugilists. "You got brains as well as a fighter's mind, the perfect combination, which is why I chose you boy. Can I change your mind?" he asked.

"No sir, I think I will stick to boxing and hone my skills, I am a natural aren't I?"

"Yeah boy, you are. So is Patterson. He is champ now. I like him. But we have this guy Liston coming along, a great guy, uneducated, but a fighter. If Patterson gives him a shot, he will lose the title. Liston will be the world champion, but he will not hold the championship. He isn't smart enough. Son, we need smart educated fighters do you understand me?"

"Momac, I am not losing my brain by quitting school, I will still have it. I am smarter than some of the teachers now," retorted Buddy.

"Buddy, for the first time since our meeting I am going to say something and if you are really smart you had better listen and learn. You just said the first stupid thing I ever heard you say. Think about that. I like you; you are going to be a good fighter. But take my word for it; you are not as smart as any teacher in that school. You might think so, but you are not. Now, if you are not going to school, get your butt over on the big bag and take fifteen minutes on it. Ten minutes on the small bag and then come in and we will talk, okay?"

"No problem boss," and Buddy went to work on the bags. After finishing a fast hard work out, he walked into the office.

"Okay, I have calmed down some. You know I don't like it that you quit school, so I will say no more about that. It is done. Now son, you can make a living fighting. You cannot get insurance, but kids don't think they ever will need insurance so we won't even discuss that. What I want to say is you can earn a decent living for about fifteen years. Now, during those fifteen years you will have to save half of what you take in, because you will not have a retirement plan. That is what smart is. Now listen, you know of Joe Lewis. He was the greatest fighter to ever put on gloves. He was smart, but not educated. Now he is refereeing wrestling matches to pay his taxes. I hope you are getting my drift. You think fifteen years is a long time, but it is not. Following me so far?"

"I think so."

"Okay, for a wakeup call. You have chosen, with my help, a dangerous profession. You can get hurt in that ring, even with those sissy gloves. What happens when that occurs? You have no insurance and hospitals are expensive. To be truthful I will help any fighter who gets hurt in my ring to a certain extent, but I will not support him forever. I can't do that. So, if you get hurt and you did not go on to school and get that law degree, or some BS you have nothing to fall back on. You can get a job bagging groceries, and then you can tell stories of your glory days." They both sat there looking at each other.

"Now, I have painted a bleak picture. I just want you to think of what may happen. The only thing I ask is for you to please think about it. There is still time to go back to school. Now, get out of here." They were up and Momac gave him a fatherly shove out the door.

Buddy did not go back to school. He worked several jobs and he did save his money; from the jobs and his fights. The jobs were secondary, his focus was his workouts.

He fought during the year his classmates were juniors. He won every fight. The name Buddy the Bomb was well known. The night his class was graduating he fought one of the top rated fighters in the state called 'Freddy the Fighter'. It was not an easy fight, but in the last round the left jab he had perfected, set up his right haymaker, as he called it. Freddy went down for the count. Freddy was slow getting up and staggered leaving the ring after congratulating Buddy. Manny had won decisively that night also and Momac took his Missile and Bomb out to celebrate. They had the biggest and best steaks money could buy. Everything was right with the world. The two pugilists were on their way to the top, Mississippi first, the South second then the World. Nothing could stop them.

Buddy did not have to work the next day which was Saturday, but he went in to work out as usual. As he walked through the door he heard Momac calling his name. He headed for the office. Momac was not smiling. "I just got off the phone with Matthews, Freddy's manager. Freddy is in a coma. He had a seizure after the fight last night and went into a coma. The Doctors do not know if or when he will pull out of it.

Just thought you should know. There is nothing you can do, and it is not your fault. It is one of the tragedies of this game. I have tried my best to convey that to you and Manny. This is one of the things that cannot be explained. A guy takes a thousand punches the exact same place, but one does him in. It is a mystery but it is boxing."

"What do I do, go see him or his family? Do I send something?" Buddy was still in sort of a shock.

"Nah, nothing you can or should do. I will send our regrets; you just go on as usual. You cannot let this stop you. You don't quit driving if you have an auto accident and someone gets hurt. You have to keep on driving. Do you understand that Buddy?"

"I think so Mo."

"Well, go home and cut the grass or something, skip the work out. Run some if you want, but stay away until Monday, Okay?"

"Sure Mo, see you Monday." Buddy walked out of the gym. He could not get that last punch off his mind, it felt so good. But it might have killed someone. Momac tried to tell you stupid, folks get hurt in this game. He went home and worked around the house doing things he had promised his mom, but he had put off. He kept thinking of Freddy. He could take it no longer so he went in the house and called Momac.

"Not much change so far, Buddy. I spoke to his manager about an hour ago. He blinked his eyes a couple times, but nothing else. The doctors say that is a hopeful sign."

"Hey Mo, do you mind if I call back in a little while to check."

"Nah, I don't mind, you know that. Don't let it weigh on you too much son, hopefully things will be all right," Momac spoke in his best fatherly voice. "Better wait about three hours and call, I may know more by then."

"Sure Momac, thanks. Bye," and Buddy hung up feeling a little better just hearing Momac's voice.

As Buddy turned he came face to face with his dad who spoke to him, "Trouble, Buddy?"

"Yeah dad, a friend got hurt, probably could use a prayer or two."

"Has this friend got a name?" asked his dad. "You know I like to use names when I talk to the Lord about someone."

"Oh yeah Dad, the name is Freddy."

"Like in Freddy the Fighter? Like in the fight you won last night by a knockout?"

"Sure is dad, how did you know?"

"A dad who has a great son like you, must keep up with his life you know. And besides I just got back from the Hospital where I had prayer with a Fred Johnson who happens to be as you call it, a pugilist. He is still a little groggy but the doctors say he should have no lasting affects from the fight." As they talked the phone rang. Buddy answered it.

"Hello, the Rev. Sansbury residence."

"Oh, it's you Momac, Yeah thanks. Dad just told me…….. Yeah Mo my dad knows everything. He has better contacts than you and me………. Hey thanks for calling that is great news. Take care. Bye." As Buddy hung up he looked at his dad who was looking concerned.

"That was Momac calling to say Freddy was better."

"I figured that from your side of the conversation. My question is, are you all right?" His dad asked, showing his concern.

"I think so dad, but I never realized I could hurt someone that bad. I might have to think this through a little more." The Rev. Sansbury was no slouch physically. He grabbed his son and put a bear hug on him that nearly took Buddy's breath away. "I love you son, I know you will do what is right."

"Thanks dad, I love you too. But it is you who always does what is right."

"Son, I wish from the bottom of my heart that was a hundred percent true. And by the way, this Freddy said you have a lot of potential. Says you have some confusing moves and that is good in the fight business. He also wanted you to know this was part of the game; we all take our chances he said."

"Thanks again dad. Knowing he is all right eases my mind a lot. I still have a lot to think about." Outside Buddy felt so much better. He had cleaned the basement and had everything out side. Moving everything back inside was not half the chore knowing Freddy was going to live. I wonder if that will affect me if we fight again. What do I mean if we fight again, sure we will. I'll just have to handle it.

****

Over the next four months, the training and fights continued. Buddy still won, but not as decisively. His punches were never as deep. It was a Saturday morning, his road work was done and his gym workout went well. He was in top shape. He ran home as usual, it was about four miles. He felt good at the end of the run and lay in the back yard just enjoying the fresh air and passing the time making things out of clouds. That had always been his past time. He saw animals, cars, people on a nice day with some wind the clouds changed by the minute. His day dreaming was interrupted by his Mother's call.

"Buddy, you have a registered letter."

Inside he held the large brown envelope. The Return address was S'gar Enterprises and in parenthesis just say Es-gar. MVA Division. The letter came from Pittsburgh.

He took out his pocket knife and slit the envelope and placed the contents on the kitchen table. A round trip ticket from Jackson Municipal to Atlanta to Pittsburgh and back, a cashier's check for $350.00 and a letter. He sat for a minute staring. His Mother was curiously looking over his shoulder also. Buddy picked up the letter.

Dear Buddy,

I am sure you are curious. This letter is being sent after a lot of thought. The MVA Division of S'gar (Es-gar) Enterprises is about five years old now. I have watched you for years as you grew into a man. I have to admit I was disappointed when you became a high school dropout. Then we discussed it and figured that was a small problem we could overcome. So you remain in the running for a very special job and assignment. The work is completely legal, but secretive. It cannot be divulged in open correspondence such as this letter.

As you have found in this envelope there is a check and a ticket. If you are not curious enough, or do not want to investigate the job, feel free to get a refund on the ticket and cash the check with my blessings. However, in my judgment, I am quite sure you will board the plane. I know you have never flown and cannot pass up a chance to do it at no cost to you.

I would like to assure you this is not a trick of any kind. It will be a bonafide offer. To clear up one thing, it is not in connection with pugilism (I know you like that word).

It has been a few years since we met; I look forward to renewing our acquaintance. The date is on the plane ticket. You will be met at the Pittsburgh Airport. Look for my name or your name on a placard in the baggage claim area. I hope you choose to come; the trip will be well worth your while. I am sure you will seek counsel from the Rev. Sansbury and Moses McKensie, the man you call Momac.

I am looking forward to seeing you in Pittsburgh on the date specified on the ticket.

Regards,

S'gar

PS: You cannot locate us in any telephone directory. We are legitimately buried inside our parent corporation. We are not foolish. We understand you could, at a lot to expense, locate who and how the plane ticket was purchased, but it would be a waste of resources and time. Come on up, Pittsburgh is cold, but nice this time of the year.

******

"Wow Mom, what do you make of it? I am flabbergasted; I think that is a word."

"I don't know son, it sounds so crazy, but the letter was registered. Let's think about it. Your dad will be home in a little while. I'll continue getting ready for supper tonight. I am fixing chicken and dumplings, everybody's favorite." His mother said.

Man, this is something, thought Buddy. The man is right I will talk this over with dad and Momac, but I am boarding that plane. Buddy smiled at the thought of flying, wow.

Chapter Five

The Past..Player #3, Tuck

Tuck was nearly as restless as 'J'. He could not stay around Mt. Bell either. In High School it was J and Tuck in one high school and Sticky in another. They were no longer the tight group they were since the death of Sticky's dad and Buddy moving to Mississippi with his family. Buddy's dad was a preacher, and preacher's families move. The moves are not normally this far, this was hundreds of miles.

Sticky was very occupied from thirteen years old on throughout high school. He had to put enough jobs together to support his mother and himself after his dad's untimely death. Sticky was the unique one of the group. He had inherited his dad's desire to operate heavy equipment, and actually did operate the old Cat that they all called the 'Sucker'. The Three an a half Musketeers never were together as a team again. It had been a wonderful childhood. There was a song out now by Peter, Paul & Mary, called 'Puff the Magic Dragon', it sorta signified their lives now, they were growing up. There was no longer the 'magical musketeers' to sustain the boys.

During high school the inevitable happened, girls came into the lives of the musketeers. J and Tuck had migrated to two cute girls, Marta and Maggie. The M & M's they called them. They were sweet on the girls and they finally paired off. There wasn't much in the way of romance, just some holding hands and stealing a kiss or two. At first it seemed It was J and Marta who were going to be the item. But over the high school years, for one reason or the other Tuck and Marta ended up more serious. With Maggie and J double dating in the back seat of the 1948 Chevrolet Fleetline. There was never a problem between J and Tuck, they were too close. They had too much history to get really upset at each other. Their friendship was nearly kin, it was just too close for anything to break up.

Never the less, Tuck always felt that Marta never got over J. Also, down inside Tuck knew J was too wild for his conservative nature. So it was that right after High School Tuck joined the Air Force instead of heading for Vegas with J. He passed all the tests with flying colors. He expressed his desire to investigate, so he was promised a job with the Air Police.

Before either boy left dear old Mt. Bell, they all went to Tony's in Gastonia for a school's out and a going away celebration. They had their favorites; hamburgers and livermush sandwiches with mayo, lettuce and tomato. That was followed by one of Tony's famous giant thick milkshakes.

They sat inside the ice cream parlor for an hour talking about the future. J was his restless self and was looking for a car. Both he and Tuck had received their reward money on their eighteenth birthdays. The reward was paid for the childhood discovery of some evidence that convicted two bank robbers. Since they were underage, the government had held it in trust with interest, until they turned eighteen. Tuck had opened a savings account and deposited his money, but J had the cash in hand and was headed for Las Vegas and riches just as soon as he bought his car.

The girls were acting heartbroken, but they were glad to be loose to either go to college or find a college boy. The M & M's knew that neither J nor Tuck could ever settle down like a college man. But the night was fun. They reminisced about their high school years and joked about how they had switched partners. They all knew down inside this was a good bye to high school relationships. They would all be friends forever, pretty much like the musketeers. No romantic notions of marrying and living happily ever after. They had had a lot of fun; the times would never be forgotten.

All of that had been light hearted and fun, but now at Lackland Air Force Base, near San Antonio, Tuck was lying in his rack. It was close to two in the morning and he was one homesick puppy. 'Man this is stupid, I wish I could go to sleep and wakeup and this whole situation just be a bad dream. I would give a month's pay to hold Marta right now'. He had gone over this same thing every night of basic training. Of course it never happened, because most mornings he was jarred awake by the yell of Sergeant Hawes, his Company Sergeant. Now Sgt. Harris was a different story. He was what military folks called a short timer. He did not have long left on active duty and would soon be discharged. You never knew about Sgt. Harris, he may come in singing to the top of his voice, "When the big ship left manila sailing proudly over the foam, get up 'cause you boys cannot go home!" One morning he came in ringing a small Liberty Bell. He was the bright light in an otherwise bleak world of basic training. He was a short-timer and everyone knew it however, being short did not falter his drive to get everyone in shape. It was his passion. He was fun on the parade field also. He would challenge the most physically fit to a push up race, one arm or two, he always won. And after he had run the company two miles, he could lecture calmly. He wasn't even breathing hard. And there was the morning he gave a ten minute lecture, as he performed one arm pushups. He had a way of inspiring the troops to want to get into shape.

Tuck had signed on the dotted line, he was in for at least four years and that was it. He knew it was a commitment and could accept that, but he recognized he was 'home-sick'. For the first few weeks he had called Marta every chance he could. He kept change handy to feed the pay phone. Many times, as he fed the pay phone, he wished he was with J out there in Las Vegas feeding the slot machines. He just knew J was winning and had beautiful girls hanging on his arm.

One afternoon, after the troops were dismissed to get ready for chow, Sgt. Harris called him aside. "Tuck, you are no different than the rest of the troops. It is normal to get homesick."

"Hey Sarg, you got me wrong, I ain't homesick."

"Oh, yes, you are Tuck. You are so homesick you are nearly green. I just wanted to tell you it will get better. It ain't a bad outfit. Just keep your nose clean and you will do okay. Go into town and relax some. Texas is a good place, enjoy your stay. Now get your butt in there and get ready to march to chow. I might even give you all a break and not double time you this evening."

After that little talk the calls to Marta became less frequent. He somehow knew she had never gotten over going with J in the first place. He could tell by her voice she was becoming distant, probably had another guy on the string. But mainly his homesickness was going away and he was discovering he did like Texas.

On the fourth weekend he had a pass. Since he had no car he took the military shuttle bus to down town San Antonio. This was the largest city he had ever visited. Charlotte was near Mt. Bell, and he had been there many times, but this was San Anton and he was alone. He was the first of his friends to see the Alamo. This was really more like a dream, this place was world famous. It was in history books. Now he could actually walk inside where those brave men had fought and died. He couldn't remember when he did not know the battle cry, 'Remember the Alamo'. After entering by way of the decorative entrance he began to read the plaques honoring the ones who died here defending the Alamo. He was engrossed reading the names he had studied in history. Now he was in the actual place where Bowie, Travis, Davy Crockett and about two hundred other brave souls actually stood, fought and died. It was a humbling thought. As he turned from the plaque detailing the actions of Jim Bowie he bumped into a young lady who was reading over his shoulder. Of course he was wearing his uniform, and knew he was supposed to be especially careful not to give a bad impression. He immediately apologized and stepped aside, to ensure he had not hurt the girl.

"Please excuse me, I did not realize you were standing there, are you hurt?"

"Of course not. I am not that fragile. I see you are in basic at Lackland, first off-base pass, huh?"

"Yes mam, it is. But how do you know so much about the routine of the Air Force, are you from San Antonio?"

"No, actually I am from Tennessee. I just wanted to see where so many of our volunteers fought and died. There were more men here from Tennessee than Texas, actually," she smiled at him as she finished.

"Well, how long will you be in the area?" J asked.

"Well, like you, that is subject to the Air Force, you see I am an airman stationed at Kelly AFB. I finished Basic Training a few months ago."

"Please forgive me for saying so, but you are the prettiest airman I have ever seen," Tuck said, loosening up a little to flirt.

"Don't get the idea I am easy Airman, just because we are talking."

"I would never think that," smiled Tuck. "So you are doing the local sites too?"

"Yeah I usually come with friends, but I decided to drive down myself and take in the River Walk." She was smiling a little more herself.

"By the way, I am Tuck, short for Tucker and I know your first name is Airman, but I don't know the rest," commented Tuck.

"Well Tuck, I am Airman Second class Vickie Conrad. Nice to meet you," they walked on through the main building at the Alamo. They were enjoying each other's company. As they finished up the outside tour through the old barracks and stable area, Vickie asked, "Have you been on the River walk yet?"

"No and I have no idea where or what it is. I have heard back on base it is a great place, but a little expensive if you are looking for food and drinks."

"It is also called the Paseo del Rio and it is lovely and not all that expensive, come on I will buy a new Airman a taco."

"I will follow you all right, but as far as the buying, I just got my first Air Force payday, I'm buying," said Tuck proudly. Tuck was surprised how close the river walk was. Just across the Alamo Plaza and down some steps by a beautiful fountain. It looked like they went through a hotel lobby or something and there was the river. It looked more festive than anything he had ever seen. It appeared that there were tourist laden 'tour boats' in the river. The river looked like one of the canals he had seen in history books of Venice in Italy. It was all so spectacular to a guy from a little cotton mill town in North Carolina. Both Airmen were just standing looking at the sites. All so Hispanic in the décor, there was even a wandering troupe of musicians in their gala Spanish costumes. "Nothing like this in Mt. Bell, we do have Stone Park with a dance area and a miniature locomotive to ride on though."

"Of course there is nothing like this in the world, Tuck. This is San Antonio the home of the Alamo, there can be only one. Come on let's go over to that outdoor café and get that taco." She was pulling Tuck along toward a table that was just emptying. They sat had a taco and watched the boats go by. There was also a continuous string of tourists passing them at water's edge, 'doing' the river walk.

This was definitely the best day Tuck had had in the Air Force. He could get to like this. It was getting a little dark and he remembered Sgt. Hawes last words, "This ain't no leave you are going on boys, your pass expires tonight at taps. I expect to see every one of you here and sleeping like babies. No hang over in ranks tomorrow morning. Now get out of here, I am tired of looking at you!"

Well he was not worried about the hangover. He had never learned to drink and his family frowned on it anyway. They were very fundamental in their religious beliefs. The brief thought brought back memories of Buddy's daddy who had been a great pastor, and had understood boys. Wonder how old Buddy is doing?

"Hey, Airman Tucker, are you still with me here?" laughed Vickie.

"Yeah Vickie, I was having a flash back. I have to be back in the barracks before taps, you know this is the first time they turned us loose."

"Sure I remember, but that is three hours off. I can drive you back to the base in less than twenty minutes. Let's take a boat ride. I have never done that since being in San Antonio."

"If you are sure? I really don't want to have Sgt. Hawes peeved at me; he can be nasty when he wants to be."

"You have got to be kidding me. You have Sergeant Ralph Hawes as company Sgt? I did too. He just couldn't get used to having a girl in his company. Shoot, it frustrated him no end. Most all the recruits loved seeing him upset; of course it cost everybody at times. We did a lot of pushups and double time."

"I can imagine it did, just seeing him get mad because someone is late for formation is bad enough. He still loves pushups. I think he just uses any breach of what he considers discipline, for an excuse to double time our company to the chow hall or class. We are not lucky enough to have any females in our company."

They continued their conversation as they made their way to the ticket stand to get tickets and board the waiting boat. It was a pleasant evening. San Antonio was very nice in the evening and the sights were great. Tuck found he really enjoyed Vickie's company. As they were walking back to Vickie's Pontiac she suddenly stopped, "Is Hawes's cousin, Sgt. Harris, still with him. I know he should be getting out about now."

"Cousin? You are kidding me! Yeah, Sgt. Harris is still there. Harris is a nice guy and Hawes is a pain in the rear. How could there be that much difference?"

"Aw, they are really buddies. The way I understand it Harris just asked to be assigned here for his last four months. He came in towards the end of my basic training. Yeah, you are right though, everyone liked Sgt. Harris because he is fundamentally just crazy! But I have found out something in this flying club. Short timers just get crazier the closer they get to their time to get out. We have two where I am assigned; both have big short-timers calendars."

True to her word she got him back to base in plenty of time. There was no good night kiss; he just couldn't build up the nerve. Since they were both off the next Saturday, they agreed to meet at the Lackland Library about fourteen hundred. They both had really enjoyed the accidental date. Of course they joked about who picked who up, a military joke. Vickie did ask Tuck not to mention the fact that the two sergeants were kin. She figured they did not want everyone to know until after basic for some reason.

At this period of Tuck's training there was a National Crisis. The United States, under President Kennedy was preparing to go to war with Cuba. President Kennedy had asked and received permission to use military force to remove Russian Missiles from the Island Nation. All Military personnel were on alert. Anyone due to be discharged was extended by order of the President. This did not affect Tuck of course, but it did his seniors. Sgt. Hawes's cousin, Sgt. Vernon Harris. He was due to be discharged in thirty days, now he was extended. Harris made no secret about it, he was not happy. He already had a good civilian position lined up and they would not hold the job. Hawes was real serious about this development. An attack on Cuba would mean a huge role by 'His' Air Force. Tuck thought, 'you would think Hawes owned this outfit'.

During the next week Tuck actually found some of the training interesting and some of it was fun. The time with Vickie had sorta stunted his desire to make the calls back to Mt. Bell. Texas and the Air Force weren't bad at all. The week's classes were mostly about General Orders, Security and the USMJ (Uniform Code of Military Justice.) Sergeant Hawes seemed to love the threats in the UCMJ. He seemed to prefer talks about Court-martials and the firing squad. But then every once in a while he would smile; Tuck figured it was just to confuse recruits.

Saturday morning was titivate and spit-shine time. Sergeant Hawes was to inspect. Anyone failing did not get a weekend pass and had latrine duty. Tuck worked hard at his bunk and uniform. He pressed the uniform one more time and did the final touch up on his shoes. Inspection time, he stood tall. When Hawes stepped in front of him he reached up and brushed an imaginary piece of lint off the shoulder of his uniform and frowned, "Those collar devices could be straighter Airman Basic Tucker."

"Yes sir, Sergeant Hawes."

"Tucker, I'm not an officer. Haven't you been listening in your military orientation classes? Who do you address as sir, Airman Basic Tucker?"

"Officers, Sergeant!"

"That was not an attempt at brown nosing to make sure you get that pass, was it?"

"No s-si...I mean, Sergeant it was not!"

"Good, you just passed by the skin of your teeth, work on that uniform." Sgt. Hawes did a sharp left face and stepped in front of the next airman. As the heels of his spit shined shoes clicked loudly he barked, "Airman Basic Shoemaker, you look as bad as Tucker there. I should have you both cleaning latrines for the rest of basic training, neither of you will be worth a flip when we fight Castro. You will........"

'You are a pain in the backside Sgt. Hawes,' Tuck was saying to himself. But later, as Hawes dismissed the troops, Tuck could have sworn he saw a slight smile of satisfaction, on the stern face of Sgt. Hawes. 'Maybe miracles do happen, he might be able to smile after all,' thought Tuck.

Following the inspection the barracks was a roar. Two men had failed and were headed for the latrine duty. The rest were getting on their best for a day and maybe a night on the town. The inspection was forgotten and a date with Vickie back to the forefront. He still did not have any civilian clothes so he would change into another uniform and save this one for inspections.

True to her word Vickie was at the library. They talked for awhile then opted to just drive around and look at the sights in nearby towns, only if Vickie would let him fill the tank. So they agreed and were off. He always felt a little uneasy until after he cleared the Air Policemen at the gates. Once outside he breathed an audible sigh.

"I know exactly how you feel Tuck, I am just getting used to driving thru without wondering if they are going to stop the car to check it out. I was not worried about it, just always thought they may find something or even plant something. Paranoid I think the word is. But I am okay with it now; they have a job to do "

"Yeah, that is what I figure. I hope to get into the Air Police as an investigator. At least that is my thinking now," said Tuck.

"This alert has everyone at Kelly excited about the possibility of kicking Castro's butt. However, if those missiles are nuclear, they could do an awful lot of damage if they got through."

"We covered some of that this week. We have what is called the SAGE system, which will help identify any incoming stuff. Our defenses in the Keys are supposed to cover that, and be able to shoot them down."

"Sounds good, I hope it works," answered Vick seriously. "What direction do you wish to go my Airman?"

"Let's drive out highway 90 to Hondo, that way we can go through Castroville. I can report back to Hawes that Castro is home and asleep and no threat. Harris will be glad to know that, and they will call President Kennedy and call this whole thing off."

"What if he is not asleep and waiting for you when you get there?"

"Then Airman Third Class Vickie, you rush back and tell them to attack ASAP." They both laughed as the Beatles hit record, 'Love Me Do' came on the radio, which stayed tuned to KISS radio. KISS rocked the San Antonio area.

"This is sorta fun Tuck, what do you think of this new group from England, the Beatles?"

"I hear they need a haircut, and Sgt. Hawes would gladly give them one if they came to Lackland."

"I don't doubt that," commented Vickie.

They rolled through Castroville, a wide spot in the road, then on to Hondo. Tuck had read 'Hondo' by Louis L'Amour, and really liked it. The book had nothing to do with the town of Hondo, but he liked the name. They both liked the Texas country side and just sat back and let the fall air circulate through the car. All the windows were down and it was a comfortable ride. There was nothing to speak of at Hondo, but they stopped at a service station and bought two Pepsi's, paid the deposit so they could keep the bottles, and continued on their way.

It was nearing mid afternoon. They could tell they were approaching a community. It looked like a golf course on their right or a small air port. They crossed a small steam and started up a small rise in the road. They saw the city limits sign. It read "Welcome to Bandera, Cowboy Capitol of the World."

****

The First National Bank of Bandera had been in business since

1920. No expansion was needed or tried. Now the new bank president had put things into motion to add a small branch south of town, in a small shopping center. The building had been given final approval and the transfer of funds was to be today. This had been kept secret. Wells Fargo was going to handle that part. The senior man, Thomas Turner, with twenty-five years experience now sat at the wheel. In the back compartment was Jose Perez, a younger guy but with fifteen years experience. Their records were unblemished and they had never lost a penny entrusted to them. For the past twelve years they were a team. Jose was due to get his own vehicle in two years.

The route chosen was not a direct route, but one with the least hazards and areas for possible hidden dangers. Both men lived by the code, you can never be too careful and never assume. Remembering an instructors warning, 'Assume, break it down. Never assume because you make an Ass of u and me'.

The transfer had gone by the book. The times were secret. Only a very few trusted personnel knew of the times so no one with mischief in mind should know of this money move. They had just turned South on Texas 173. Thomas was cautious, he had signed for over a million dollars in currency and six thousand in change. That is enough money to make a man nervous on a Saturday. Thank goodness today paid double time he could sure use the extra coin. Up ahead he saw an old pickup truck facing him on the shoulder on his side of the road. Two cowboys had the hood up. Thomas noted that a few yards further on down was a tire leaned up against a box. The standard orange triangular signs were out for a warning of a traffic hazard. 'They are under the hood, why the tire?' the thought went through his mind as he swung into the left lane to give plenty of clearance. He spoke into the communications mike to Jose that he was swinging wide of a stalled vehicle. As he passed he looked into the right side mirror the Cowboys had slammed the hood and dove into the ditch. He yelled, "Red alert" into the mike as he saw the red/orange explosion and heard the loudest explosion he had heard since Korea. The shaped charge was set off even with his back tires. His eyes then went forward to catch a form rise from the left side ditch with a tube on his shoulder. His Marine training said bazooka as he witnessed the back blast of the tube and the projectile hit his right windshield and on through the passengers window and exploded harmlessly in the road bank. Hearing the projectile hit the windshield is all he remembered. For Thomas, everything went black.

In the back compartment Jose was knocked unconscious as the shaped explosion hit the side and undercarriage. He was unaffected by the explosion from the front. The vehicle came to a dead stop. Its rear wheels, axles, tires and protective undercarriage blown completely out from under the Wells Fargo Truck. The rear compartment door swung on its hinges, these men knew explosives. Everything went perfect.

Before the vehicle came to a complete rest, the pickup was started and backed at an angle to the disabled truck. One man went in and pushed Jose's limp body to the side ad started passing money bags out the back. They took all the currency and two bags of change. Everything was thrown on the back of the pickup. One guy grabbed what was left of the spare and threw it on top of the money bags, and jumped into the open bed. The other two crooks were in the cab, the man in the rear yelled, "GO!"

The Driver did a spinning turn and headed South away from Bandera, "What the….." was all the driver got out.

Vickie and Tuck were having a great time away from the base and military authority. It was Saturday and they were free as birds. The music on the radio was more rock and roll from KISS of San Antonio.

Together they saw the smoke rising from an armored truck as a Pickup spun out from the back of it and headed straight for them. Vickie yelled, "Brace yourself!" Tuck just had time to place both hands palms first against the dashboard. The heavy 1952 Pontiac didn't budge much as it went head on with the Old Chevy pickup. Both vehicles came to a complete stop. Tuck was out. He knew these were crooks. One had gone air borne from the truck bed and was unconscious on Vickie's crumpled hood. The driver was shaking his head as Tuck drug him out the open door and hit him as hard as he could right square on the nose. Blood flew everywhere, but the driver collapsed. It took only a couple seconds and Tuck had his belt off and around the crooks wrists. He then took time to look over at the passenger who was coming around after hitting the windshield. Tuck saw blood running down into the bad guy's eyes, but the crook raised an old 44 revolver without blinking and pointed it directly at Tuck. 'This can't be the end,' thought Tuck.

"Don't even think about it son," came the quiet steady voice of Thomas, who had approached the vehicle behind the crook. He had spoken as he placed his forty five against the crook's skull through the open window. "I would surely like to take your head off after what you just done to my truck."

Slowly the crook lowered his pistol and immediately Vickie reached over and took charge of it. Then she turned toward the front of her car. Two steps put her beside the crook that was just regaining consciousness as he lay on the crumpled hood of her car.

"W…what happened? Did we git the money?"

"I don't think so buddy, but you sure have made me mad. You have messed up my car and my weekend pass, I should shoot you, stupid," Vickie was fit to be tied.

"Can you guys watch these idiots; I need to check on Jose?"

"Sure go ahead, they had better not move, Vickie is an expert with a pistol, and pretty mad about what these fools did to her car. They would be smart not to move." before Tuck was finished, Vickie had thrown the pistol she had to him and Thomas handed her his pistol. Immediately he was running toward the rear of the Wells Fargo truck as fast as he could under the circumstances.

A cowboy drove by in a pickup. As he slowly worked his way past the accident Tuck yelled, "Get the Sheriff as soon as you can. There has been a robbery."

When Thomas heard Tuck yelling about the sheriff he turned to see the cowboy, "Tell him we need an ambulance too, my partner is hurt. Thanks man!" The driver gave the thumbs up to Thomas and hit the accelerator on the pickup and burned some rubber, as he headed into Bandera.

Thomas had found Jose trying to climb out of the wreckage and helped him through the jagged torn steel. Then he had him lie down on the road, he quickly removed his own jacket to use as a pillow for his buddy. Jose could not hear because the blast had broken both ear drums. He was also incoherent, but otherwise seemed all in one piece. That was a miracle in itself since the shaped explosive charge had hit just under him full force. This was the first time Thomas had taken time to look at his truck. It was a total wreck, but they were alive and the money was still here. His head was still not clear, but it seems like the couple of airmen had the crooks under control. He finally got it through to Jose to lie still, trying to explain he had to get back to the pickup and secure their money. He ran back to the wreck.

Glancing to make sure the two airmen had the crooks under control; he started locating the bags of money. From experience he had remembered the exact number of money pouches. All the currency appeared to be there, but not all the change. Automatically he figured some of the change was still in his vehicle, he wasn't completely at ease yet, but he definitely felt better. He now had Jose's weapon, so all the good guys were armed.

He noticed the male airman had found some rope and had hog tied every crook. They were trussed up like Christmas turkeys. "Is everything okay with you guys? Thomas called out from the truck bed.

"Yeah, everything is peachy. That is my Pontiac that steam is coming out of the broken radiator," called back Vickie.

"Mam, I sure hate that, but I think Wells Fargo or the bank will surely take care of that problem. You just foiled a million dollar robbery. And I for one want to be the first to thank you for the help."

"No problem I guess," Said Vickie, "but we were having such a great afternoon."

"Yeah, I was too!" said Thomas then he broke into a big smile as he heard the radio in the Pontiac.

They all started laughing, because about that time the Disk Jockey on KISS put on 'Bill Haley and His Comets' with their old hit, "Rock Around the Clock". The old Pontiac seemed to be singing at the top of its voice and steam just a piling out!

'We're gonna rock around the clock tonight,
We are gonna rock rock rock 'til broad daylight,
We're gonna rock we're gonna rock around the clock tonight'.

They laughed as the tension went out of all of them. They all heard the sound of the siren in the distance and in just a minute or two the Sheriff pulled up. The identifying whip antennae just whipping as he stopped.

The sheriff came out of his car with his pistol in his hand. He was looking at Thomas; the Wells Fargo Uniform was obvious, "What is going on here?"

"Sheriff, I'm Thomas of Wells Fargo that is my truck blown to pieces over there. The turkeys you see trussed up there are the robbers that created this junk yard. As you can see the two airmen foiled this robbery and now have the crooks tied and packaged. If it hadn't been for them Wells Fargo would have lost over a million dollars. Oh by the way, could you call for a back up truck for me. I can't leave this money to do it."

"Sure Thomas, I have a couple deputies coming, I hear the cars now. Just as soon as we get these crooks in a lockup position, we will do that." The Sheriff made a walk around, first to see that the robbers were secure. He was satisfied with that. Then he went back to Jose, who was starting to regain his senses. "Just lay where you are son, we will have an ambulance here in a few minutes." Jose was shaking his head, like he did not understand.

"Sheriff, I think his ears are gone, he was in the back when the charge hit. I sure hope it isn't permanent."

Understanding, the Sheriff motioned for Jose to lie back, the message got through to him and he seemed to relax. But it was obvious he was moving his arms, hands and fingers to see if they were all working. Satisfied, the Sheriff moved back to Thomas. "What in Hades were you doing in Bandera with a million dollars on Saturday?"

"No one was supposed to know. This is the seed money for the new branch bank for the First National Bank. Today was the 'secret' transportation day. That seems to have been a loud secret," he paused a minute, "It would be good to call the bank president, he won't be too happy, but the crooks didn't give us much choice. They sure know explosives."

"I have a wrecker coming."

"I can't let him move the Wells Fargo truck until my boss and the bank representative are on the scene."

"He will have plenty to do with the pickup and the Pontiac. Did the airman drive directly into them on purpose to stop them?" asked the sheriff.

"You know sheriff; I haven't even taken time to think that far. I really don't know." At that the sheriff walked over to Tuck and Vickie who were in deep conversation. He spoke to Tuck first assuming it was his car. Tuck directed him to Vickie.

I would appreciate it if you would fill me in on the last while, from the time you entered Bandera. You can give me the Reader's Digest version, because I will need a full report at the station. I am sorry to ruin your Saturday, but as you can guess this is pretty important in Bandera. Vickie quickly gave her version with Tuck nodding his head in agreement. As she was finishing, the deputies arrived, followed by the ambulance. It wasn't long until the wrecker drove up, then the bank president. It wasn't long until they had a crowd and Thomas was getting more nervous with a million dollars in an open pickup truck, and no way to count it, etc. To help, the deputies cordoned off the Wells Fargo truck with yellow tape to prevent the casual observer from taking a chance on entering the truck.

The Sheriff and his deputies took custody of the crooks. Since Miranda was still a few years down the pike, the Sheriff simply said, "Come on boys you are being arrested for the crime of robbery. Ain't attempted Robbery, 'cause you boys robbed Wells Fargo and was getting' away clean. 'Pears you'd a made it, if it hadn't been for the Air Force there, indicating Tuck and Vickie with a nod. "Kinda changes this ex-jarhead's opinion of that US Flying club. Makes you tough guys look bad, yeah, real bad."

The three only grunted as they were forced into the back seat of a squad car. Once the three crooks were inside the car, the Sheriff took control and started sorting out the situation. Instructing one deputy to relieve Tuck who had started directing traffic and the other to get the Polaroid and take some pictures before the vehicles could be moved.

While all this was happening, the medics examined Jose and determined his ear drums were both destroyed. Otherwise he appeared ready to transport so a doctor could determine his complete physical state. From the stretcher he waved to Thomas. They saluted each other with a 'thumbs up', meaning to both, we did not lose the money and we are alive, partner. The ambulance sped away towards San Antonio.   Jose was in good hands.

Tuck went over to Vickie and put his arm around her. She was standing looking at her treasured Pontiac. There was a tear in her eye. "I think the car can be saved, but you will be without it for a week or so. I guess it is a good thing they require insurance on cars tagged for the base, huh?"

"Yeah Tuck, but we are in a little town called Bandera. In case it hasn't hit your brain yet, hero, we do not have any wheels!" Vickie answered.

"Oh I have thought about that. Sgt. Hawes could march me that far, if he was here," Tuck responded smiling.

They walked over to the Pontiac; Vickie reached through the door and shut the radio down. They just leaned against the vehicle and watched the commotion. "Hey Tuck, you are fast on your feet. You were on that crook like stink on manure. Thank goodness the driver Thomas was able to get it together and halt the passenger. Of course I was right beside him, I would have done something. I would not have let him pull the trigger."

"You know what Vickie, I firmly believe that. To be honest I about said my prayers looking at his bloody face and staring at that big revolver. It all worked out great. It was sorta fun, except for the Pontiac of course."

While they had talked a black Caddy drove up and in a few minutes a Wells Fargo truck arrived. Everyone got in a huddle and was having a conference. When they broke up the replacement truck pulled up blocking the road and the new driver and Thomas began to transfer the money. The Wrecker also arrived and was waiting on the other side of the Wells Fargo truck. The driver got out and walked by speaking to everyone as he passed and came over to them. "Who is the lucky owner of the pretty Pontiac?"

Vickie held up her hand like she was in school, "I am, wanna buy it?"

"Nah, got plenty just like it," he smiled holding out his hand. "Tom, with Tom's Wrecker Co. Me and the red thing down there are the company. Anyplace particular you want 'er towed?"

"I honestly have no idea, you have any suggestions Tom?"

"Well Jason's here in town does a good job on repairs and is a lot cheaper than taking it to San Anton, but I will take it anywhere. I'll wait for my pay if you have insurance. I see the base sticker and the uniforms, so you probably got insurance, right?"

"Now, if you take it to a dealer in San Antonio he will probably have a loaner car, old Jason might, but it'd be a junker and you wouldn't get it on base. It is something to think about. I can tow the pickup first and give you time to mull it over if you'd like."

"Please do that, I might make a phone call or something." Jason walked back to his truck. It was apparent the Wells Fargo truck was preparing to pull out.

"Pardon me," spoke a man in a suit as he approached. He had been in the huddle, the one out of the Cadillac, "I'm J. Lieck, president of the First National Bank of Bandera. I understand I have much to thank you guys for."

"I'm Vickie," as she held out her hand to meet the bank president's hand. "And this fast thinking soul is Tuck. He did most of the work."

"Well I don't have much time right now, but the Sheriff says you will be at his office for a little while. If you can wait there for me we need to talk more in detail. I have to run over to the branch bank and take care of the money situation. I have called in the vice president to handle that end. As soon as he comes I will be right down, but to ease your mind, the bank and Wells Fargo will furnish you transportation and rooms for the night. That is if you will be our guests. I have to run. See you at the Sheriff's office." He was turning as he finished and jogged to his car.

"Man that does make things simpler, I sure am glad he came over."

The rest of the time there was just watching the wrecker move the vehicles. Vickie sent her car to Jason, whoever he is. Then they rode to the Sheriff's office. The three crooks were already booked into the Bandera Jail when they go there. Both Tuck and Vickie sat for about thirty minutes and wrote out their statements. The crook's photos were shown and they identified them as the perpetrators. There was a good chance they would not have to appear in court. Vickie was expecting orders to school soon and she did not want to be delayed. She had chosen to enter the engine mechanics area of the Air Force. She had passed the test with very high scores, passed the stringent physical and was accepted. All she was doing now was waiting for an opening in the next starting class. Of course Tuck had about five weeks left of Basic Training and only the Air Force and God knew what would happen to him. They enjoyed the chat with the Sheriff and his deputies while waiting on Mr. Lieck. The men had only good to say about Mr. Lieck. He had been a local rancher for many years before getting into the banking end. So he wasn't your average stuff shirt and the ranchers of Bandera County and surrounding areas trusted him. The bank had expanded. It was too bad that something had to happen as he was expanding. But they were all quick to point out he would have been in much worse shape if it had not been for the Air Force.

Tuck was smiling to himself when he and Vickie were referred to as the Air Force. He wanted to say, no that is Sgt Hawes not us! But everyone was treating them as heroes. They had been interviewed already by a reporter from the Bandera Courier. This was big news in this small town. As the reporter was leaving he met Mr. Lieck coming in. He got a quick statement from the bank president to add to his story.

"Well, I see our local reporter had a chance to talk to you."

"Yes and he was very nice, but we are wondering when this hero stuff is going to end. Both of us did what any citizen would have done in the same situation," Vickie said.

"Well guys, I talked to the supervisor of Wells Fargo on the phone. Tentatively we want to reward you two for your acts of bravery." Tuck started to interrupt, but he held up his hand, "Please hear me out. Both the bank and Wells Fargo have a contingency fund. I know something about insurance Airman Conrad. If they payout to fix your car, they will raise the rates. We have decided to do one of two things, if you agree. We will let you pick a car of equal value or we will pay to fix yours. In the mean time the bank has rented you a car for three weeks. It should be here by early evening. When do you have to be back aboard the base?"

"We both have the entire weekend off, so I am clear until 0800 Monday, but Tuck here is still in Basic Training. He must be in by 2200 hours Sunday night."

"Good, if you will accept we have reserved two rooms at the Bandera Tourist Lodge. Here is a hundred dollars for meals & entertainment, not much of that here, but the food is good."

"We appreciate it, but don't exactly know what to say," stammered Vickie, "But I am sure we both will accept, this is very good of you."

"By the way, I ran into Tom outside. Here are the keys to the Pontiac. He parked it outside the fence at Jason's Garage. He figured you might want to get in and get some stuff. If you are through here, I can drop you at the Tourist Lodge. The car will be delivered there." The sheriff said he was through with them and thanked them; they got to ride in the Cadillac. Mr. Lieck continued to praise their actions.

The evening went well, still no romance. They had dinner and took the rental out for a drive. It was the end of an exciting day. Both of the airmen were beat. At the Tourist Lodge Tuck stopped at Vickie's door. She turned and he kissed her. She smiled and said, "Thanks for an exciting date Airman Tucker you ain't half bad."

"Yeah, we only lost one car," They both laughed.

"But we saved a million dollars, and they wouldn't even let us see it." Vickie said.

"Good night, what do you say we have a late breakfast in the morning, say nine or ten?"

"Okay with me, but since we don't have a change of clothes, we will just have to use what toiletries we bought and act like we are on maneuvers." She said.

They had a good Sunday, no church today, and they headed back toward the base. Vickie wanted to get to the Provost Marshall's office and get a temporary pass for the rental. Mr. Lieck and the Sheriff had given her a letter explaining what had happened. She dropped Tuck off outside the gate since she did not have the vehicle pass yet. The AP's light heartedly gave him a hard time because they had seen him get out of the car. They made a couple comments about his real late date. He did not try to explain anything, just smiled and walked aboard the base and back to the barracks. He was still tired and turned in early.

Monday started off as usual, marching to chow with Harris threatening the ones with hangovers with double time. Tuck was beginning to like the mess hall food. It was very good. He took his time. They no longer had to march back from chow, and they were allowed to straggle. You just had to be aware of officers you passed. Remembering to salute was still a problem to an independent thinking Tucker.

Sgt. Harris had everyone in ranks. They marched off to the first class of the day. The morning classes were about fire arms. Everyone needed to know how to fire the Carbine and the .45 pistol. There was always guard duty around the aircraft. These classes were some Tuck liked. Then Sgt. Harris had some calisthenics for them before lunch. He straggled back from lunch and lay on his bunk for a few minutes before the call to 'fall-out'.

With everyone in ranks, Sgt. Harris called out loudly, "Airman Tucker, front and center!"

Tuck had never been called front and center. But he did his best. When he stood in front of Sgt. Harris he reported, "Here Sgt. Harris!"

"Heck, Tucker, you think I'm blind? I can see you are here. My question is why are you messing up my schedule? I have a note here that says you are to report to Sgt. Hawes and you two are to report to the Base Commander. Is there something the rest of us should know? Have you been playing around with the Base Commander's daughter or worse, his wife?"

"I-I don't know Sgt. Harris honest?"

"YOU don't know whether it was his daughter or his wife?" there was some snickering in ranks. "Any of the rest of you want to go with Tucker?" Things got quiet.

"No, I mean I have no idea why, but do I have to go?"

"Son, when the old man says report, and you are on the can, you had better cut it and go, got me?" said Harris with a half smile.

"I don't think you are in trouble Tucker," he said quietly. Then he raised his voice, "Now get out of here and report to Sgt. Hawes, he will take it from there! Move it!"

Tucker reported to Hawes and they took a jeep over to the Base Commander's Office. When they stepped in flash bulbs flashed and when his eyes cleared Tucker saw cameramen, Mr. Lieck, the Sheriff and some more folk. Behind the desk was Colonel Wilmot. The Colonel stood and walked in front of his desk.

"Airman Tucker, it seems that you had an exciting weekend. According to these men You and Airman Second Class Conrad from Kelly captured three bank robbers and saved the First National Bank over a million dollars. The Air Force takes pride in men with initiative. I cannot promote you while you are in Basic Training, but upon graduation you will be promoted to Airman Second Class and given the duty of your choice, that you qualify for. On behalf of the United States Air Force I want to commend you for your bravery and courage."

There were several photos shaking hands with everyone. All Tucker could say was "Thank you Sir." The whole process took less than fifteen minutes, including the presentation of two checks from the First National Bank and Wells Fargo. Each check was for five hundred dollars. After he was dismissed and in the Jeep Sgt. Hawes said, "That was some piece of work Tucker."

"Thank you Sgt. Hawes but it was not a big deal, I was lucky."

"You are right of course, so don't expect any special treatment from your Company Sergeants. You have a lot to learn. You study and maybe I will let you kick Castro's behind one day," Tuck could see Hawes was about to break a smile.

He was dropped off at the firing range where everyone was firing for familiarization with the weapons. He joined them. Sgt. Harris turned and gave him a big smile and a 'thumbs up'. He had known all the time, the rascal.

"Well did you ask the Old Man when he was going to give me my discharge?"

"I was so busy posing for the cameras I plumb forgot," said Tuck with a smile.

"Well, I hear you did the Air Force proud, good for you! Now get over here and I will show you this forty five, next time you can shoot the suckers, Okay?"

****

The next few weeks finally passed. He and Vickie saw each other as much as possible. She decided to get her Pontiac repaired. Jason put a whole front end on it and gave it a complete paint job. He added a two tone job at no extra cost. It looked like new. Vickie's orders came in she was headed for the West coast and some special engine training. She was excited about it. They went out for one last time. They were able to talk about everything. Tonight they were nostalgic over the past few weeks. "Tuck, you are something. Never once did you get fresh with me. We have had a good time. I wish the spark had been there but it just wasn't. It was great just having a friend and not having to fight all the pawing and stuff."

"Well you know it wasn't that I didn't want to, Vickie. You are a great looking lady. You are also a lot of fun. I wish you the best. I do want to know how you are doing, and what is going on in your life. So keep in contact."

"You bet, and I want to know about you. Send me a picture of that special lady when you find her." They sat and talked the night away. Neither one had a curfew now. Tuck was graduating in a couple days. He still did not know where he was going. They finally kissed good night. It was a warm, sweet but not sexual kiss. Tuck got out and headed for the barracks. After a few steps he turned and watched the Pontiac go through the gate. 'Bye Vickie, it has been a blast. Well that relationship is one for the books. I never knew you could like a girl just like a buddy. A fellow learns something all the time'.

"Whoa there, Airman Tucker," it was Sgt. Harris. He had the duty today and had awakened everyone with his rendition of the Air Force hymn this morning. Tucker was heading back to his bunk after shaving. "After graduation, and after you are promoted to Airman Second class, you are to head to the Orderly Room and see your favorite Sergeant, Sgt. Hawes. It is about some strange orders you have. I have been around this flying club long enough to know your orders are weird."

"What do you mean, Sgt. Harris?"

"Okay Tuck, you can dispense with the Sgt. Title, call me Vernon. You graduate today and you will be real Air Force. We use a lot of first names, a little opposite of the Army, Navy and the Marines. Anyway about your orders, let's just say you are getting what you asked for."

"What do you mean, Sgt, I mean Vernon?"

"I can't get into that, that is Sgt. Hawe's bailiwick, he loves that kind of stuff. He is all Air Force, as you already know. I'll tell you something you do not know though, we come from the same home town you do, Mt. Bell, North Carolina."

"You are kidding?"

"Nah, who would kid about something like that? Hawes comes from the National Mill and my folks worked the Imperial? Small world, huh, Tucker? Now get dressed and ready for graduation. We will do old hometown stuff after you graduate."

Now Tuck's head was spinning. Strange orders and both the Company Sergeants are from Mt. Bell. What a turn of events.

The graduation ended without a catch. He went front and center for his new stripes. He made every facing movement sharply and the smile on Hawes and Harris's faces let him know he had done well. The Sergeants were on either side of the Company Commander as he made the announcement of his meritorious promotion. He was proud himself, but he kept his mind on the military ceremony. After the presentation he saluted, did an about face and returned to ranks. His buddies whispered, 'good job' as he returned to ranks. The Company Commander turned the Company over to Sgt Hawes and departed.

Sgt. Hawes did not dismiss the troops; instead he gave the command, 'At Ease'. With everyone attentive, he began, "This will be short and sweet. Every man and woman here is now a full-fledged Airman in the world's greatest Air Force. You are no longer a boot or basic. I am proud of each of you, even though Tucker did show off some; we are all in the same outfit. I would be proud to serve beside any one of you. You all have your orders except Tucker. You will be on leave for ten days, it is up to you to be at your assigned duty station on the day specified. I want to see Tucker in my office immediately after I dismiss this company. TEN HUT! DISMISSED!"

Yells, congratulations, goodbyes and everything else was going on. Families that had come to see the graduation filtered in looking for their airman. It was a festive occasion. Tucker said good bye to his closest friends, waved to some and headed for the Orderly Room to find out his fate.

"It's like this Tucker; you wanted to go into the Air Police. That is not possible at this time," Tucks face fell, "But don't look down, my Air Force knows what is best for you, remember that. You are being groomed for Special Investigations. That is a highly sought after slot, son. Seems the Air Force has chosen not to tell me what your orders are. They are classified. You can go into the Old Man's office. He is not in, but it will give you privacy. Go in, close the door and break the seal. Look inside and you may get an idea what the Air Force has in mind. Now move Airman Second Class Tucker, by the way why aren't those stripes on yet?" Hawes was laughing as he said it.

Upon opening the manila envelope he found it contained only one page. It read:

A/2C L.V. Tucker will proceed to Mt. Bell, NC, your home of record, where you are to spend your ten days leave enroute to a private contractor. This company, 'S'gar Inc' located in Pittsburgh, Pennsylvania, has been chosen to instruct you the basics of investigation and interrogation. The address and details are listed below. Your accounting and flight data along with an airline ticket will be mailed to your home of record. At the end of your ten days leave, you will report to Mr. R.D. Fletcher at the address and times below. The length of time of your TAD (Temporary Additional Duty) is undetermined and classified. You are to protect these orders and are not to discuss your destination with anyone.

Given under my hand this day,

D.D. Wilmot, Col USAF, COMMANDING.

Wow, thought Tuck, what have I gotten into? Well at least I know I am going to Mt. Bell. Outside in the Orderly Room he had a long talk with Sgt. Hawes and Sgt. Harris. Since they were no longer his official bosses they had a good time talking about Mt. Bell. They did know a lot of the same folk, but since these were old guys, they did not know the same crowd. Goodbyes were said and Tuck was homeward bound. He had names of folks to say hello to from the Sergeants. Little did Tuck know that in just a few years Sgt. Harris of the USAF, would become Top Sergeant Harris of the 82nd Air Borne. He would become a hero as a Green Beret. And the biggest surprise of all would be becoming Brother's in law. That was to be later in life. Today Tuck was one happy guy; he was headed home on leave.

After grabbing his blue duffel bag he boarded the bus headed for the airport. Many of his company were aboard, and they had a lot to talk about. The airport was no problem and his plane was on time. In no time he was aboard and flirting with the pretty stewardesses. He had a window seat, headed for Atlanta then Charlotte, NC. He had a lot of thoughts, but most of all was these strange orders to S'gar Inc.

Chapter 6

(Out of the Past)

The Fourth Player, Sticky

The gang had spread from here to there. After graduation they seldom saw each other. J had left for Las Vegas to get rich quick. Buddy had moved with his family to some ungodly place in Mississippi. Tuck had joined the Air Force. Now he, the Stick, was the only one to stay here in Mt. Bell.

Life had not been easy on Sticky. His desire to operate heavy equipment like his dad was always overshadowed by his mama's plans for him to be a doctor. His life had been both tough and exciting. After losing his father to the dreaded disease cancer, he had set goals for himself. Before his fifteenth birthday he had already successfully loaded his favorite piece of equipment, the Sucker, onto the old flat bed and driven it to jobs that were procured by his uncle. Sticky became known in his own right. He could do the quick small jobs that the big guys did not want to bother with. Unlike his dad, however, Sticky learned he needed to charge more than operating expense, and with the help of his uncle, he learned to price low, but still make some money.

Never did Sticky forget the things his dad had taught him about the Sucker. But mostly he held foremost in his heart the teachings of life and business. It was no secret around Mt. Bell that his dad, Willie Morse, had left Mt. Bell as a kid. He was a rough piece of coal. He had driven back into town a few years later with his own flat bed and a Caterpillar Dozer, he called the Sucker. Willie had driven the Sucker the entire length of the Alaskan/Canadian Highway as it was built. When he returned to Mt. Bell he knew heavy equipment better than most men who had been in the business for many years. He was no longer just a lump of coal, he was a diamond. Willie was doing well and his reputation was gaining strength when he was struck down by cancer. By default, Sticky had inherited the truck and the dozer. Even though he was still just a lad his mother needed him. What he could earn working part time for Uncle Harold and running errands went to help around the household, except for the little he could shave off the top to buy diesel fuel. Unknown to his mother he was also practicing privately on the Sucker until he could operate it like a man. From there his Uncle Harold had helped him in the business.

Near graduation, his mother had reluctantly agreed that his ability to move dirt, and his love for that profession, was probably to be his apple in life. His ability to picture a job's completion and work to that end was amazing. His feel for 'level' astounded folks who hired him. He could finish a slab level, fifty by a hundred feet within an inch and a half of level without the assistance of a transit shot. This astounding ability got him contract after contract. Sticky was on his way and ready to own his Grading Company soon after graduation. He proudly lettered, 'John Morse Grading' on the door panels of the old truck.

Sticky knew if he was going to advance he would need to trade up, or buy a loader with a 'three in one' bucket. The Sucker had a blade on the front. The three in one bucket allowed the operator to pick up dirt, where the Sucker could only push it. It had worked on small jobs but now to move to larger jobs he needed a loader. By now the Sucker was an antique. He had been contacted by a man from the Pittsburgh, Pennsylvania area. This man wanted to buy the Sucker and the low boy. Sticky wanted to keep both but he was a logical person and knew that was impossible.

One of the deals of which he was very proud was with J's brother Mark. Mark was older than Sticky. He had a past history with some secret Government agency. His building career had been mostly overseas. He had returned to work locally. He was now a local contractor. Mark needed some land cleared, so Sticky did the dirt work and in exchange Mark had worked wonders with the low boy. The bed looked like furniture. He kept the sucker clean and it looked good on the truck. He hated to part with it.

The date would soon arrive that it had to be delivered to the Pittsburgh address on that date and at a precise time. The whole thing seemed strange to Sticky, but the retainer he had been given was more than the actual value of the rig. He was naturally happy and sad. In a way he felt like he was letting his dad down, but in reality he knew that Willie Morse would do what he had to do to make his dreams come true. There was a stipulation in the sale deal. He was to tell no one where he was taking the Sucker. That had to remain a secret. So he was going to sell the Sucker, and eventually have the money to build his mama the house that his dad had promised her. Not many people knew of the agreement between Sticky and his dad, but Sticky never forgot. When the promise came to his mind he could hear his dad's words, "Sticky, the Lord is taking me early, I promised your mama I would build her a house. I ain't been able to do that yet. Your Grandpa thinks I ain't worth a hill of beans. Now, you are a kid but I have taught you a lot. Use that knowledge and the Sucker and build your mama that house." Sticky's answer had been, 'Yes sir'.

Sticky had stopped by the service station. He was pumping diesel fuel into the old truck at Groner's Station when he ran into Perry. "Hey Sticky my man, how is it going?"

"I am working hard and getting rich. How about you?" Sticky laughed.

"Well, you are looking at a reformed man. I have enlisted in the United States Navy and I leave for Great Lakes in a week. You believe that?"

"Hey, that is great. I will go if I am drafted, but until then I need to support mama."

"Yeah, Stick, we all know that. It doesn't have a thing to do with Hattie does it?" laughed Perry.

Sticky had topped off the tank and was putting the cap on, "Can't keep a secret in good old Mt. Bell can you?"

"Nope and that is a fact. Oh yeah, Sticky, all the recruiters are tight over in Gastonia. The Air Force guy was in to see the Chief I was talking to and asked if I was from Mt. Bell. He said Tuck would be coming home in a week from Lackland on leave. He said he was some kind of hero. Busted up a bank robbery and captured three crooks."

Sticky was startled, "For real?" he asked.

"That is what he said. I got to get going Sticky, keep it cool old man. The next time you see me I will be wearing bell bottoms."

"Yeah, congratulations Perry, now you be cool your own self, and I can't wait to see you in bell bottom trousers with all them buttons on the front. I always wondered what a sailor done when he was in a hurry," laughed Sticky.

Tuck captured some bank robbers, wow, that is great. I guess the next time I see him he will be in uniform also. Sticky had secretly always wanted to be a marine, but life wasn't headed that direction for him. He definitely had other fish to fry. Perry was right; Hattie had a lot to do with his decisions. He had a logical mind. And he used it. This deal with the Sucker would put him on the road to success and competition with some of the big operators. This collector was paying enough for him to buy a dump truck, a Cat Loader, and a flat bed trailer to haul it.

He finished checking his load, signed the ticket and climbed in the cab. This was done all by routine; his mind was on his trip to Pittsburgh. Jim, at the station, had given him the maps to mark his way to Pittsburgh. He would sit down with Hattie and map out his way. They would have to figure the time it would take him to get there because he was going to deliver on time, he had given his word and took the man's money. His daddy said your word is your bond; you give it you keep it, no exceptions.

He had three jobs scheduled before he was to leave headed North. As he drove he thought of Tuck. It would be great to see him again and find out how the Air Force was. Of course he was most curious about the bank robbery affair.

The next week was busy. Sticky worked fourteen hours a day but completed every job in record time. He had started a routine scheduling calendar. He had jobs tentatively scheduled two months down the road. He was using a big desk calendar, and Hattie was helping when she could.

His meeting with Tuck was the highlight of his time. Tuck looked good in the Air Force Blue. He passed off the robbery deal as something unavoidable due to the head on collision. If he hadn't acted, the crooks would have. So he was first with the most. Tuck was secretive about where he was going after his leave was over. Sticky was equally vague about where he was delivering the Sucker. Tuck stopped by to see Mrs. Morse and enjoyed some sticky buns and coffee. It was a pleasant evening, but Tuck had to get home, his dad was due in from the second shift. He was temporarily filling in for a super who was sick.

Three days before Tuck's leave was up, Sticky climbed into the cab of the old truck. He had an ice box with a lot of sandwiches and some quart jars of sweet tea. There were some pint jars of pintos. He had commented to his mom, "I am just driving six hundred fifty miles. I should do that in a couple days, but I am allowing four." Mama had retorted that she knew how he ate; he would run out in a day and a half. Sticky smiled remembering her laugh. He also knew she was right. His plans were to sleep in the truck. If the truck stops were anything like they were around Charlotte that would be no problem.

Sticky hit the road. The truck was full of fuel and if he got into a bind the Sucker had nearly a full tank if he needed to siphon some. He was not at ease leaving his comfort zone. The area he was leaving was very familiar to him; but nearing the Virginia line he was feeling a little better. It was all just roads, and he kept referring to the notes he and Hattie had made to keep him straight. The problem was, on a map you could not see elevations and now he was starting to see mountains.

In school he had read about the Shenandoah Valley, now he found himself driving through it. It would be hard to describe this to Hattie. He would have to bring her up here one day. The mountains on either side of him were hazy blue. And even though fall was near, things were still green and beautiful. He planned to fill up when he reached the half mark on his fuel gauge. It was time so he started his routine. Everyone was friendly and all the drivers were passing the time. Several drivers mentioned his low-boy; they had never seen a bed like that. One wanted to know if he was transporting the antique to a show. It was all just trucker chatter. Soon he was back on the road again.

He took VA 250 over to US 220 North. These mountains were not what he expected. He really began to wonder about his brakes. He did not want to wear them out, or worse set them on fire. He had an extinguisher of course, but he did not want the delay or damage to the man's truck. As he slowed for a small town called Franklin, he was thirsty for a Pepsi and maybe a bologna sandwich. He passed a place called Thompson's Tourists Cabins and spotted a small Café that had outside service. With plenty of parking room he eased off the road and set the brakes.

Two men were sitting at the picnic table on the porch. He nodded in recognition as he stepped past the drink machine and up to the window. He ordered a bologna sandwich and turned to the drink machine.

"Bubba, I thank I'll go out and carve my initials in that truck door, this beer can cutter oughta do a good job. What do you thank?"

"Go ahead Billy Bob, that boy will prob'ly 'preciate it."

The man on the inside spoke up, "I ain't wanting no ruckus here Bubba, so jest calm down, the man is my customer."

"Ain't gonna be no ruckus Tom, I'm just gonna decorate the boy's purty truck."

Sticky was thinking to himself. 'Oh man, why did I stop here?' He looked toward the two guys and smiled. He was holding one Pepsi and he took another dime out of his pocket, put it in the machine and got another. He shook both of them a little as he walked toward the picnic table. "Boys I am just passing through. All I want to do is get a Pepsi and sandwich and leave. I am buying you boys a Pepsi to show I am a friendly guy." Both of the men were still sitting at the table. As Sticky approached he slammed both cans down on the table and put pressure on his grip; he had strategically pointed the pull tabs towards each person. The result was Pepsi hitting both men in the eyes at about a hundred and fifty pounds per square inch; temporarily blinding them. Sticky released the cans and immediately grabbed a wrist of each of his antagonizers as the cans spun off the table releasing the rest of the pressure and soda build up inside.

"Now you two rednecks listen to me. I know you are not smart enough to understand physics, so let me try to explain in layman's terms. The average man has a grip of about a hundred pounds. What you are feeling now on your wrists is about a hundred and fifty pounds per square inch. You can feel that can't you?"

Both guys nodded vigorously. They were wildly rubbing their eyes with the free hands and trying to figure what has happened.

"If anyone touches that truck this grip will be on his neck, is that clear?"

Nothing.

"Okay, just for your information, at last check I was close to the world's record in grip. I can go over two hundred pounds. Now note, this is about one hundred and forty pounds per square inch," he increased the pressure and he heard a definite whine. "Now, is this clear yet?"

"Yeah, yes sir, please turn my wrist loose," Bubba said, "My eyes are burning like hell."

"Nah, boy they ain't half as hot as the preacher says hell is. Now what I am gonna do is hold your arms a few more seconds and turn them loose. Then they are gonna hurt, they will burn for about a minute. And boy," he shook Billy Bob's arm. "If that is a knife you are reaching for in your pocket, don't take it out. Because if you do, I'll make you eat it. What you don't know is that unless it is a switch blade you will not be able to use this other hand to open it when I release your arm. You will have a closed knife in your hand and you will be dead meat. Do you understand, boy?"

"Y-yes sir, I got it," stammered Billy Bob.

"Now, I ain't no preacher but I suggest you boys find a church to attend and pray some. I don't know what good it will do you but it sure can't hurt. Give up this fake life, cause boys, you ain't too good at being bad. Somebody will come along who won't be as nice as I am and you will get yourself killed, I guarantee it. You boys are amateurs at being bad so you had better give it up for your own health."

Sticky released a little pressure, but then tightened back up. "would you guys like to replace the twenty cents I spent on the Pepsi's?" Both men nodded. Sticky released the wrists and in a couple seconds, both men screamed as the blood started circulation causing extreme pain in their hands. As Sticky turned the first thing he saw was a Smokey Bear hat and a set of khaki with a star on the vest. He was very relieved when a smile appeared on the sheriff's face. "Well, that was a show worth seeing. Our town tough guys saying yes sir to the better man. I'm Sheriff Dillon. Are you okay?"

"Yeah, Sheriff I'm okay. I'm John Morse from Mt. Bell, North Carolina. Those two just threatened to damage the truck out there and it doesn't belong to me anymore, and I just could not allow it."

"No problem Mr. Morse. I just hate the little town of Franklin gave this impression. I just wanted to fill you in on a situation around here. We have had several truckers that stopped to help a lady who appeared in trouble. For their generosity, they were robbed by a man who appeared like out of nowhere with a double barrel shotgun."

"Thanks Sheriff, I just want to be on my way, if that is okay."

"Certainly, John, just watch these mountains. I know Mt. Bell and you don't have hills like this down there," grinned the sheriff.

"You are right about that," Sticky said as he took the brown bag from the cook. "I was worried about my brakes." Then to the cook, "What do I owe you?"

"Mister, you don't owe me a thing. I replaced the two Pepsis. I'll collect for them in a minute when the boys over there stop crying. Shucks, when I tell the folks around here what you've gone 'n done, these boys will be cut down to size for a long time, thanks."

As Sticky climbed into his truck with a fresh cold Pepsi, Bubba and Billy Bob were still rubbing their wrists and hands trying to get the circulation going. He smiled to himself, but declared not to stop anywhere except at truck stops from here on out. The truck started on less than two turns of the engine as always, and he slid her into gear, released the brake, checked his mirrors and eased out into the road. 'Whew,' he blew, 'I'll be glad to make this delivery and get back to Mt. Bell.'

The mountains were very tough, much tougher than he ever expected. But the scenery was great. After a couple mountains he entered a beautiful valley. A clear mountain stream raced beside him. It was clear and crisp looking. Entertainingly splashing and dashing against and upon the rocks and logs that were anchored in its run. The stream was cool, relaxing and inviting. The traffic was so light that he seldom saw a car. When he did they threw up their hands in salute. He had all but forgotten the incident back at Franklin. Hattie was on his mind now. He missed her already. Lost in thought he was caught off guard by the woman on the side of the road waving at him. She was beside a car with the trunk and hood open. It was apparent she was crying. He eased the truck to the side of the road and it hit him. This could be exactly what the Sheriff was talking about and I bit hook line and sinker. Damsel in distress, right!

Sticky reached across to the passenger's door and opened it. Then he opened the driver's door so the woman could see it swing open. He quickly slid to the other side and down to the ground. Quietly he retrieved a four foot piece of half inch rebar he kept behind the seat and moved to the rear of the truck where he heard voices.

"Dang it woman where is he?"

"I don't know. He ain't got ow' chet."

"Well git to cryin' and go on up there, or I might jest shoot you."

"OH-AWEEEE!" the man screamed as he dropped the shotgun he had been holding. Sticky had rapped him hard on the fore arm with the four foot iron. Then with a mighty right to the side of the man's head, Sticky put the skinny guy out.

The woman came running around the rear of the lo-boy. She froze when she saw Sticky standing there with the shot gun. "D-don't kill me mister, he makes me do this. Says he'll kill me hisself if'n I don't."

"Just hold up your hands and turn all the way around so I can see if you have a weapon." The woman did as he said.

"Mister, if 'n I'd had a gun, I'd a shot him long ago."

"Well mam, you just stand aside." Sticky reached down and picked up the man like he was nothing. Jamming the rod in the ground he slammed the hood then recovered the rod. He opened the driver's door and put the man inside. The keys were still in the ignition switch; he removed them and threw them in the river. He then took both ends of the rebar and bent it into a 'U'. He broke both the front and rear windows and put the 'U' around the man's neck with an end out each broken window. He then proceeded to tie it together around the door posts. All the time checking to make sure the crook could breathe, but ensuring that he could not get away. Once he was sure the man would not get out on his own he went to his cab and retrieved a can of spray marking paint. He then painted 'Call the Sheriff, this is a crook!' in large orange letters on the car's side. By now the crook was coming around. He was trying to figure out what had happened.

"Now mam," Sticky addressed the woman, "If you are innocent and forced to do this, you tell the Sheriff. Someone is sure to call him soon. Come on up to the cab with me." Sticky had a pint jar of pintos, he handed them to the woman. Stay here until someone comes. Ignore whatever that fool says. I can't stay; I have a schedule that can't be changed. I am John Morse, you tell the Sheriff that I am the one who done this and describe my truck, he will know who I am. I also have your partner's driver's license that I will mail to the Sheriff."

"I'll do it, but I ain't his partner. He took me from my mama when she would not pay him for something. I was the payment," the woman said crying.

"Well, I can't stay. Ask anyone passing to call the Sheriff. Here comes a car now. I have to go. I wish you the best." Sticky climbed back into the cab and drove on down the road. Looking in his mirror he saw the car stop. After a little while the woman got in the car. 'Good' he thought to himself. I was worried about her, but I am out of that and on my way to Pittsburgh.

The rest of the trip was uneventful. He actually arrived a day early and found the address. Once he located the delivery point he then drove back to the nearest truck stop to have supper and rest until in the morning. He had made it. Soon he would be on a bus back to Mt. Bell.

Chapter 7
MVA Headquarters

S'gar stood staring vacantly out his office windows. A smile creeps across the solemn face. 'Finally, bringing these boys together again has been a dream. I know some will accept the challenge of the MVA. I sure hope they all will. I never took time for children; I think I have adopted these boys at least in my mind. Man oh man, I feel sorta like a kid at Christmas. This is real excitement, a plan coming together right before my eyes.' His 'eyes' have reported that all systems are on go. All four boys are headed this way, and what a pleasant shock they are in for. Looking at his watch and noting that it would all come together in two hours.

Smelling the steaming coffee and absent mindedly taking a sip, his mind returned to a time when the boys were about thirteen. He was then the well known Dr. Jerry Wiley, recently AWOL from the CIA. Hiding in a small town called Mt. Bell. Very confused and depressed staying in the woods and living in a cave. His only friend was a dog named Satan. The boys tagged him Rags and in a few months the town knew him as Rags. He had observed their lives from a distance. After pulling himself back together he returned to the present world, but not to the field of medicine where he had gained his fame. He now was the CEO of his brain child, the MVA. Right now there was some of the everyday paperwork to be done lying on his desk, but today he could not get his mind on it. That work would just have to wait while he took pleasure where he could.

****

Buddy was aboard his first airplane. It was a relatively short flight, three hours, but he was going to enjoy every minute of it. The first thing that caught his attention was all the electronic gadgets aboard. He was fascinated by the orientation speech of the stewardess. If the oxygen masks fell they must be dropped by a relay controlled by some sensor. Could it be altitude, pressure or oxygen sensor? His passion since he could remember was, 'how does this work?' At the early age of four it got him into a little trouble when he took his dad's flash light completely apart.

Aroused by the winding up to the engines he became aware of his surroundings. He loved feeling the power of the engines as they lifted this big piece of aluminum off the ground He had a window seat and began straining to see everything he could on the ground. 'This is great,' he thought, 'I wonder what mountains those are down there. Do folks live out in those wild areas away from towns?" Those and hundreds of more thoughts wandered through his mind. He had had two cokes and two packs of the airline peanuts. Of course this guy S'gar was on his mind. Where could I have met him? Maybe he saw me fight.

"Your Attention please, the pilot has turned on the fasten seat belts sign, we will be landing in Pittsburgh, Pennsylvania in a few minutes. Take this time to look around you and gather your belongings. For the passengers who will be leaving us here, thanks for flying the friendly skies with us. For those continuing to Detroit and points beyond, please remain seated. We will be on the ground for only a short time. Again, on behalf of the pilot and crew, thanks for flying with us today."

Buddy wondered it all stewardesses were this pretty, these girls were knockouts. A guy might even take a 'dive' for one of these .... maybe, he laughed to himself.

****

Tucks orders had been specific. He was not to wear his uniform when reporting to this civilian corporation. Boarding in Charlotte and transferring in Atlanta he was now nearing his destination, Pittsburgh. The flights had been good the sky clear and no bumps to speak of. He had spent his time just mulling over what had took place in the last few days. Marta had been distant but friendly. She did not say it, but there was another boy, he sensed it. They had gone out once, sorta. He had borrowed his dad's car and with Maggie, they all had gone to Tony's for old time's sake. It was good to see everyone. He was amazed how nice it was to see mom and dad, and eat mom's cooking. Well, I guess that is life as you grow up.

Old Sticky seemed to be distant also. They had enjoyed a good visit. But for some reason this was a busy time and he had been working from sun up until after dark the whole time he was home on leave. I wish we could have had more time. About that time he heard the ding and saw the 'Fasten Seatbelts' light come on. He looked down and saw a city coming up to meet them. The flight was over. Soon this mystery of my training will be explained, I hope.

****

"Your attention please, the pilot has….."

The announcement startled J awake. He shook his head trying to figure where he was and what he was doing. Then he remembered he was supposed to be landing in Pittsburgh. He had said goodbye to his young bride and her dad in Denver. Yeah, the mystery would soon be cleared up. The mystery of this S'gar fellow would soon be over. Where could he have possibly met someone by the name of S'gar, and not know it? The stewardess came by tapped him on the shoulder and pointed to the seat belt and smiled. He returned the smile, turning redder than he was, and fastened the belt. Looking down he saw several other planes as they circled awaiting clearance to land. He loved the looks of things from up here. One day he would have to try sky diving. Maybe Maria would like to do that. Just the thought of her name, and he missed her.

****

Sticky awoke early of course, sleeping cramped up on the seat of the cab. He had used some old blankets that would stay with the truck. He could endure anything for a night. Down deep he also wanted to spend the last night with the Sucker and his truck. He washed up in the truck stop and after breakfast he climbed up on the Sucker, just for old time's sake. Tears came to his eyes as he remembered the night of his daddy's wake. At twelve years of age he had climbed up in the seat where his dad had sat for years. Where he had sat while building the ALCAN Highway. He had sat on his dad's lap many times. That night of the wake he had tried to smell the seat and handles, just to feel close to the man who had just left. The man who said God was taking him early. "I still miss you daddy," Sticky whispered.

"Hey, son," he barely heard the words. He looked down and saw an elderly black guy that he recognized as a truck driver from breakfast. The man continued, "You okay up there?"

120

"Oh, Oh yes sir. I was just saying goodbye to a part of the family here. I sure hate to part with this old Cat and the truck, yes sir, I surely do." Sticky climbed down for the last time.

"I know how you feel, I got that old Mack over there, folks say I should get rid of her. She has over six hundred thousand miles on her, but like you say, she is part of the family. And as long as I can hold on to her I will. But come a time, I'll do what I have to do, just like you."

"Thanks for stopping by old timer, I appreciate the words, I needed them. Now you keep it between the ditches, you hear?" his eyes glistened but Sticky smiled his biggest smile.

"I hear you son, best of luck, I'm gone," the old gent waved and turned toward the old Mack truck at the end of the lot.

Sticky arrived at the delivery address and pulled into the parking lot. He was fifteen minutes early. He had done it. For a guy who had never left the Mt. Bell area he had done well. He was proud of himself. In just a few minutes a long black stretch Limo pulled into the lot. Sticky watched it and wondered who needed a vehicle that size. Then he realized the Limo was headed toward him and figured this must be the buyer. He climbed out of the truck holding the brown paper bag. Inside the bag was his coat and dirty clothes.

The driver jumped out and opened the side door, but no one got out. The driver turned to him, "Please sir, get your belongings and have a seat inside the vehicle."

"Bud, this is my belongings," he held the bag up, "And I drove all the way up here from North Carolina to deliver this rig. I need to see the buyer, get my money and find the bus station."

"Please sir, you will see him in due time, I have several more riders to pick up before I return everyone at the same time to the MVA and S'gar. My orders are to furnish you a ride. I know nothing about money but if S'gar owes you money, you can rest assured it will be paid. Now, we must hurry." The driver nodded to the door and Sticky got in. the driver shut the door quietly, got under the driver's seat and drove out of the parking lot. "You will find snacks and cold drinks in the compartment at your side. Feel free to enjoy some refreshments as we drive to the airport." The voice came over the speakers.

"Excuse me, can you hear me?" Sticky asked a glass wall.

"Certainly sir, what can I help you with?" asked the chauffeur.

"You said Esgar, I don't know an Esgar. I am just delivering a dozer and truck."

"The name is pronounced as you said it, Esgar, but it is spelled S'g a r. The boss has only one name and that is it. It is sorta like Elvis and forgetting the Pressley. Or more like Liberace I guess. One never knows what S'gar will collect or what he will do with it. This surprises me though; I did not know he collected things like that."

"I guess I will have to wait for my money, but I will have to find the bus station. Can you help me there?"

"I can tell you where it is. I cannot speak for S'gar, but I am sure he will have someone drive you there; he would be inconsistent if he did not."

The guy sure thinks highly of his boss. Sticky took out a Pepsi and opened the bottle with the opener provided. It was ice cold. He also opened one of the Milky Ways. Now this is living. One day I'll have to take Mama and Hattie for a ride in one of these. It wasn't long until he realized they were nearing an airport. This one was bigger than the one in Charlotte. He watched as the driver passed up a long line of traffic and pulled up to a gate that said 'Absolutely No Admittance'. The driver lowered his window the Policeman acknowledged him with a nod and opened the gate. The Limo glided through. "This S'gar must be someone important, huh?"

"You could say that. I would say, one of the most important." The driver said as he parked in a no parking zone. "Please wait here, if the airlines are on time I will return within twenty minutes." With that the driver got out and entered a door that said 'Authorized Personnel Only'.

What ever it is he is mixed up in it must be big. There was a radio playing low. He tuned it to a Rock and Roll station and sat back to finish his Pepsi.

****

Tuck held his small grip bag; in military slang it is an AWOL bag. It carried his orders and a change of clothes. He started walking up the concourse to the terminal something caught his eye. Thinking to himself, 'I would swear that looks like old Buddy from the rear. But it has been a long time. What in the name of common sense would he be doing here?' Curiosity got the best of him and he increased his pace. As he came along

122

side he realized he was right, it was Buddy. He moved close and spoke quietly, "Okay fella, your money or your wife!"

True to form, buddy said as cool as ever, "Man, take my wife, don't shoot!" He looked over at Tuck and a smile broke across his face, "Tuck, Tucker you sucker, what in blazes are you doing here? I heard you joined the Air Force." Both guys moved to the side of the concourse, dropped their bags and bear hugged each other. The crowds smiled knowing this was a happy reunion, and then continued in their own worlds.

"Well, I honestly can't say too much. I have some crazy orders. It appears I may be stationed here in Pittsburgh. What are you doing here?"

"Man, it is a weird story. I got a letter saying I had a chance at a great job here. The letter had a check and a plane ticket in it. To be honest I came out of curiosity and to get an airplane ride. I don't think anything will come of it."

They had both picked up their bags and started up the concourse to find the baggage claim area. They talked as they walked, took the escalator down to the baggage claim area. They went to different carrousels to get their bags. Once the bags were retrieved, both of them were looking around. They both spotted the S'gar sign at the same time. They also noticed someone who looked very familiar talking to the man holding the sign. They both realized it was J. Both of them yelled together, 'All for one and one for all!' J turned and a smile lit up his face like they had never seen. This was old times week.

"What are you guys doing here?" asked J after they had all bear hugged.

"Hurumph," said the sign holder to reclaim their attention, "Look gentlemen, I am here to pick up three passengers for S'gar. I am assuming it is you men, am I correct?" Everyone nodded, "Then you can talk as we go, this way please." And he stepped off toward a door that said Authorized Personnel Only. Beside it was an armed security guard. They all noticed as they approached that the guard smiled, greeted the driver by the name of Corey and proceeded to open the door. He wished them all a good day as they padded past.

"Did you guys get a crazy letter about a job?" asked J.

"I did," said Buddy.

"Man you won't believe this, but the Air Force sent me here under orders. How much pull can this guy have?" said J as they approached a stretch limo. The Chauffeur quickly opened the trunk for their bags, and closed it quietly after all bags were deposited. He then went to the passenger side rear door and opened it."

Inside the Limo Sticky had seen his old childhood friends coming toward the limo and a plan emerged for some fun. He moved as far as he could toward the front of the long stretch. Flipped off the lights around him and sat quietly in the shadows. The three getting in were coming in from the bright sunlight. They would be momentarily blind and hopefully would not see him. They were all inside and talking furiously. The driver quietly closed the door and went to the driver's seat. As soon as he was seated, Sticky said in a normal voice, "You can drive us to the office now."

Taken aback the driver answered, "Yes sir."

"Now I don't want any crap out of you guys, my name is S'gar, it is said as Esgar but spelled S' g a r. Is that understood?"

"Yes Sir," everyone answered.

"Now, all I want to know is why are you musketeers up here in Pittsburgh?" And he moved to the rear to bear hug as many as he could reach.

"I ought to whup your butt Sticky. You noticed I called you sir, what are you doing here?" laughed Buddy.

Now everyone was talking at once. No one could remember anyone remotely called S'gar. Now, Sticky was more confused than ever. He had a reason to come up here. He was selling some equipment. This cannot be a coincidence.

The limo pulled into a busy parking lot and right up to the portico. The chauffer opened and let them disembark. Informing them that their baggage would be taken care of and be available when they needed it. He also took Sticky's paper bag and deposited it in the trunk. "Just step inside the door and give the receptionist your names and tell her you have an appointment with S'gar. Nice meeting you guys, I think." The driver headed back to the driver's seat to depart.

They were given ID tags and sent to the elevator labeled private. As they approached it, the door opened. Inside they pressed nothing and the elevator door closed and took them to the top floor. The ride was so smooth they could hardly tell it had ended. The doors slid silently open. They got their first glimpse of what money can design. The walls were a great combination of teak and cherry woods. All the cabinet doors matched the paneling. There was a beautifully hand carved desk from solid cherry wood. Sitting at the desk and looking at them like they had just arrived from outer space was a middle aged lady whose desk plate, also carved from cherry, read **'V. Jane McGarity, Executive Assistant'**. There was a half smile and she said, "Mr. Daniels?"

J held his hand up.

"Mr. Morse?" Sticky did the same.

"Mr. Tucker?"

Tuck said, "Yes mam."

"So you can speak," she said without humor.

"Mr. Sansbury?"

Buddy said, "Yo."

"S'gar has decided to interview the four of you together at exactly 11:30, which will be four minutes and thirty seconds from now. Please be seated," she indicated the leather chairs by the window. Unspoken were the words, 'sit down, shut up and don't bother me'.

Each of the former musketeers sat there uncomfortable without talking with each other, even though they wanted to very much. J sat there in a cheap brown suit he and Maria had found in a bargain basement in Denver. He had never been one to spend money on clothes. He had grown up with a mother who made his shirts from feed sacks. When a collar was warn she broke the seams and turned it over. Cuffs were done the same. He pulled at his collar and thought, 'why in common sense am I sitting here awaiting an interview with God only knows who. He says I know him, I know I do not. This is so weird'.

Buddy was thinking, 'Who is this dude? What is wrong with me? I am scared stiff; look at these pictures and awards on the walls. If I wasn't in this frozen state, I'd get up and walk around and look at them. But then Ms Storm Trooper over there might have me shot. What have you gotten into? Funny isn't it, all my friends are here and I can't even talk to them'.

Breaking the silence as he stood up, Sticky spoke. "Lady, all I want is the money that is due for a delivery I made on time and in accordance with all the instructions I was given. I didn't expect nor want an <u>interview</u>; I just want to get back down the road."

"Mr. Morse, isn't it?"

"Mr. Morse was my daddy's name; I'm Sticky, now about the m...."

He was cut off by a professional voice, "Mr. Morse, or Sticky if you prefer, I understand you have business with S'gar. His instructions to me included nothing about money. I am sure he will explain everything starting in the next 45 seconds. I am sure you can wait that long for an answer."

Sticky shook his head at the other guys and sat back down. Ms. V. Jane returned to her work. 'Mama and Hattie sure look good about now. The first thing I am going to say to this dude is exactly that, give me the money, I'll sign the title to the truck and I am out of here'.

Lastly, Tuck was deep in thought. 'I wonder what the rest of the guys have to do with this assignment. Somehow I have been assigned to a corporation that is also interested in the rest of the guys. This is very curious. But at least we've all been able to renew acquaintances. Surely the government can't draft these guys into the Air Force. And what about old J, he didn't get rich like I thought he would. But he was the first of us to get married. I can't believe it, old care free, give-a-crap J settled down on a ranch with a cowgirl. Amazing he says he is happy and will live in Colorado'.....

Everyone's thoughts were interrupted by a very soft bell. Then the announcement by the commandant, "S'gar will see you now, step lively he is a very busy man," she indicated the wall at the rear of her desk. There were no visible doors. As they approached the walls two large teak pocket doors slid silently open on non slip quick drive Teflon tracks. They were opened by two 'Quiet-Run DC motors'. Evidently these doors were controlled by a switch at Ms McGarity's desk.

The four entered into an office of unbelievable beauty. These walls were of solid mahogany. Hand tooled to match the door panels. There was an intricate roping carved into all the recesses. The Carpet was a deep green color and felt like it was three inches thick. A man stood looking out the large solid glass window behind an ornate mahogany desk. He was dressed in a white suit. You could tell beneath the suit he was a well built, probably muscular man. Everything was quiet for a few seconds then the man, without turning, said, "Please have a seat and make yourselves comfortable gentleman. I am still trying to put into words what I want to say to the four of you."

Everyone moved to the seats in front of the desks. "Excuse me Mr. but I just came to get my money for a truck and dozer. I delivered them this morning. They were delivered on time and to the place specified. I need to get paid, find a bus station and head back to Mt. Bell," said Sticky a little uncomfortably.

Indicating the view out his windows, "I love these mountains; the view never ceases to amaze me. I have always been impressed by you; you are always the logical one of the musketeers, right Mr. Morse?"

"Well, yes sir, but I can't see any reason to be here other than to get payment on a deal I made in good faith," Sticky said his voice softening.

Still looking out the window, "Let me say this, I want you to stay and have lunch with me. We can talk a little before lunch. If you still feel an urge to leave I will give you a check for the amount we agreed on, and you can get back in the truck and drive it back to Mt. Bell. You will still have your Sucker, and the check. Is that fair enough?"

"Like you said mister, I am logical, I'll stay, but this is a little confusing."

As S'gar turned, there seemed to be dampness in his eyes. He looked each one of the old musketeers in the eye. Taking his time he smiled and said, "Each of you have done well. If I were a parent I would be very proud. You have grown since we last met," as he spoke he fingered a scar on his forhead.

Tuck spoke, "Mr. S'gar, we..." he was interrupted.

"The name is S'gar, no mister."

"Fair enough. S'gar none of us remember ever meeting you, we are baffled." Stammered Tuck.

"Ah, maybe I can clear that up. We, you and I Tuck, have scars from our meetings. Just below your rib cage you have a three and a half inch scar, and I? I have this crease across my forehead from a rock fired from a well aimed slingshot."

"RAGS?" all four men said at once, "RAGS!"

"Yes gentlemen, you knew me as Rags. As a matter of fact you gave me the name, if I am not mistaken. But we are not here to discuss our past. We are here to discuss our future together." He walked around the table and shook hands with each of the guys. "Now men, I have watched your lives from the time I first saw you wandering through the woods. Let me explain."

S'gar went through a Reader's Digest version of his life. Down to where he lost a kid labeled 'B' in a CIA operation. It was a rescue in South America which included the President's nephew, and is still classified.

He explained to the boys that something in him was afraid for them. That he had kept having this overriding feeling that one of them would do something dangerous, and be terribly hurt. True to his fears, Tuck had nearly drowned. Thanks to his watching, and his ability as a surgeon, Tuck was saved. S'gar was sure that his own salvation had come about from that tragedy. Following that incident, and with the CIA following him. He had returned to his Corporation here in Pittsburgh and formed a secret, nonprofit corporation called the MVA.

"The MVA has been in operation for nearly four years now. We are expanding all the time. What I would like is to hire all of you to work for the MVA."

Tuck spoke, "How can you hire me, I belong to the Air Force. I am curious and so were my instructors at Lackland. How and why am I here?"

Everyone was paying close attention; their interest was piqued of course. "Yes Tuck, there is that. But to explain, in this building and in the sub basements, I have developed the best investigative and counter intelligence schools in the world. We are selective, but we accept only students from countries and groups that are sympathetic to the USA. The school is not non-profit; it is a money cow that finances part of our main endeavor. That endeavor is what I want to hire you guys to join me in. But back to you Tuck, when you finish this course you will be Second Lieutenant Tucker. So you will be receiving a commission from this school."

"Now, before lunch let me quickly go over what the MVA is. Please let me finish the introduction before you start with the questions. The initials MVA stands for 'Modern Vigilante Association'. Yes gentlemen, it is exactly what it sounds like, a Vigilante group. It is not government sanctioned. I know that the CIA and FBI are aware of our existence, but so far have turned their collective heads. Vigilantes have always been necessary. As our court system gets bogged down and some slick lawyers twist the intent of the law, crooks sometime walk free and thumb their noses at the law. Likewise some citizens, because of their position in life such as wealth, political or professional status, judges and lawyers get away with breaking the law where Joe six-pack may be locked up. I determined to do something about some of these cases. Are there any questions?" S'gar walked behind his desk and sat down.

"If we work for you, will we be breaking the law?"

"Seldom, but we do use strong arm tactics and intimidation. I do not apologize for it. Let me give you a couple examples so you can see the spread in the scope of our reach. We have helped a teenager, who was being shook down for her lunch money daily. There was every indication that the gang was going to start requiring her body. She now goes to school unafraid and is on the honor roll. She doesn't know that the MVA stepped in. No, we did not use violence against the gang members, but now they do not shake students down. Then there was a district attorney in a major city that was milking the poorest of the citizenry. This was done with threats of sending them to jail for misdemeanors if they did not come across with a sizeable cash deposit to his favorite charity, himself. Oh, he is alive and practicing law, but he no longer is a DA. Those are examples of what we do."

"That sounds like a noble cause, but why us?" asked Sticky, "And besides to be honest, from what I have seen of this area, I don't want to live in Pittsburgh."

"Yeah, that has been going through my mind also. I just got married and I love that ranch out in Colorado. If I were to ask Maria to move here, she may balk pretty badly," said J.

"Gentlemen, I think all that can be worked out. No one, except Mr. Tucker, is being asked to relocate, unless you want to. I have some ideas I would like to put forward later," The doors slid open and two servers pushed serving carts into the office and headed to the conference table. Small name plates were placed and the food was distributed quickly and efficiently. Drinks were poured and a silver coffee pot was left plugged in on a serving tray. Without a word the servers departed. As they reached the door S'gar said, "Thank you Tommy and Janine."

In unison they said, "You are welcome sir," and the doors closed as if on command.

"Shall we, gentlemen?" S'gar indicated they should go to the table.

Choosing the seat at their name they all found that their favorite meal was being served. No one said anything for a few minutes. "You are wondering about the food. As I told you, I have followed you all very closely. Each of you has a unique potential and I want to cultivate it. Yes, I know a lot about you. As a matter of fact a certain Sheriff Dillon is interested in talking to Sticky. Seems someone bent a length of half inch re-bar around a thief's neck and left him attached to his car yesterday. Do you know anything about that Mr. Morse?"

Sticky laughed, "The fool tried to rob me, something in me just don't like that."

"These things that happened to you are what I want to correct in this world. I have no illusions that we can solve the country's problems, but we can solve some. We can solve enough that someone will live a better life and may reach the American dream."

As they ate one of the best meals of their lives S'gar continued to explain the MVA. "I have some cases on video that I want you to watch. These should drive my point home. You knew me as Rags. But that was not me. I was born, here in Pittsburgh, with a silver spoon in my mouth as the saying goes. I have had everything a person could ask for. I am not ignorant; I know the world is not like that. Of you four, Sticky here has faced and overcome the largest obstacles so far, but none of us can see the future, who knows which one of you will be next."

After lunch they all sat around and listened to S'gar talk about his love for the MVA. Following the videos, they were all becoming very intrigued with this 'project' put before them. "Now gentlemen, have I peaked your interest enough to give me another day?"

Everyone nodded their accord, so S'gar continued, "I have arranged rooms at the oldest Hotel in town, the Omni William Penn. You will have the evening meal and breakfast included. You have unlimited long distance calls, so I want you to call your respective homes and explain that there will be a delay in your returning home. I would appreciate it if nothing was said of work being discussed. If you must, use the term, 'investigations', that should suffice. I know it has been awhile since you 'three and a half Musketeers' got together, so you need an evening to catch up. The driver will drop you off this afternoon and pick you up at nine in the morning. Enjoy old home week and everyone catch up on what has been happening in your lives. I am sure J will tell you of his narrow escape from assassins in Vegas. Anyway, relax and I look forward to seeing you all, or Y'all as you guys say, tomorrow. Have a good evening."

Wonders would never cease, as they walked through the outer office, The Storm Trooper woman had turned into a smiling bubbling lady. "Well, I can tell S'gar thinks things went very well. I do hope you boys will decide to attach yourselves to the MVA. I would enjoy working with you all. Enjoy this evening, Pittsburgh is a great place once you get used to it. See you guys in the morning, have a good time," She was even laughing as she spoke. "Over the past few years we here at the MVA all kinda think of you boys as S'gar's sons. Don't disappoint him, you hear?"

All of the boys were caught aback, except Buddy of course. He whipped a quick smile at her and asked, "Which of these performances was an Act? Before or after?" and they all laughed. Vickie Jane just smiled and winked at Buddy. The elevator opened for them and they headed down.

They were met in the lobby by Corey who was now smiling like they were old friends. Corey was close to six feet tall and in good physical shape. He had bright red hair and wore it in a flat top. "Before we leave I want you to meet Ben, we are like brothers except he is an old man! He has been with S'gar longer than I have and he is fast becoming 'The Man's' next in command."

After all the glad handing Ben said, "We have followed you guys so much I feel like I know you. I hope you like what you see around here and want to join us; we do a lot of good things. He handed each a card, if you need anything you can call me direct. Now as the boss said, have a good evening."

"Come this way guys," Corey said as he lead the way to the front door. "Also for your information, the boss said the limo was yours for the evening. He figured you might just want to cruise some." Corey put his hat on, stepped in front of them and opened the door. He shut the door quietly after everyone was aboard.

In the limo everyone was talking when Corey came over the speaker, "I'll cruise around some. Just yell when you want to head for the hotel, okay?"

"Yeah Corey, I like the idea of riding in this stretch, could you run us down to Mt. Bell, drive around and let us show off, This is my first experience with the red carpet treatment, mama would like this," said Sticky.

"Can't do that Sticky, I couldn't get you back to the hotel in time. By the way, I am enrolled in school here. S'gar is allowing me to pay my tuition by driving. One of my courses is driving. I have a race car driver called 'Slick'; his real name is Wayne Carter, out of Florida. He has the most even nature, I don't think he has ever been caught napping, he takes everything in stride. S'gar is sure he will need expert drivers, so one of the things I am learning is how to 'really' drive. Slick learned from the best. He worked with Fireball. You would not believe what this guy can do with a combination of steering wheel, pedals and momentum. Now, I will shut up and drive. Just let me know when to head for the hotel.

"Thanks Corey, anyplace special? You pick."

The reports continued as the Limo maneuvered around the city and across the Monogahela River. "Hey guys, I am going up on Coal Hill. You will get a complete view of the city."

"Drive on," said Buddy with everybody yelling. 'Yeah, drive on'.

They all got out on top of the Hill and Corey explained that the locals called the Monogahela River simply the Mon. "This is the best and the most famous view. I know you probably saw the city coming in on the plane, but this is up close and personal."

"Hey Corey, you are not from here, how did you get tied up with S'gar?" asked J.

Corey thought for a minute, "One of the 'assignments' was out in Utah where I was learning the basics of building. S'gar was on the job personally and I met him. I was not the object of interest, but I worked for the guy who was. After the 'assignment' was completed I got the same strange letter some of you got. S'gar likes that approach. The rest is history; I will be a full time employee once school is out. I am looking forward to it. This is an exciting and worthwhile life. I didn't get to drive a car with 650 horses under the hood as a carpenter. You guys are lucky. If you stay on you may get to work with me. I have worked with Ben on several occasions. Man he is good, cool as a cucumber, you will like working with him.

After about fifteen minutes they agreed it was time to get to the Hotel and clean up for supper. As the limo headed to the hotel, they were all just basking in this reunion. What a day of surprises.

Chapter 8
The Hotel

Excitement was not the word, ecstatic would be more like it. Corey went to the Hotel restaurant to have coffee and watch the recently developed color TV set. The boys checked into the hotel and headed to their rooms. All the rooms were adjacent, of course. They decided to take forty five minutes to make some calls, then shower and get dressed. To each person's surprise there was a new change of clothes, including shoes. As they had come to expect, they fit perfectly when they tried them on. They were finding their summons by old Rags to be incredible. From what they thought was a homeless bum to an ultra wealthy man, was a little more than mind boggling.

In Tuck's room his mind was a whirl. Rags! This was the illusive man that disappeared after performing a miracle. Tuck's mind went back to that day years ago when he was going to be Mr. Cool and hang the tire swing at the swimming hole. Everything had gone well until he decided to try the swing. He had done a flip from the tire and hit his head on a rock ledge. Before he completely blacked out, he remembered being under water and thinking how stupid the other guys were going to think he was to be there without them.

That was when Rag's fears came true; one of the boys needed him. Unknown to the boys or anyone in Mt. Bell, Rags was a renowned medical doctor and surgeon. He had quit a job as head of Duke University to work with the CIA. During one CIA operation a child designated only as 'B' had died. The death had thrown him into a depression. He left the CIA and went AWOL. As a result of his hiding, he ended up living in a cave just outside Mt. Bell. The boys had given him the name of Rags. Rags had rescued Tuck from the creek, and eventually, before reaching the hospital, he had performed open chest heart massage. He had made the incision with a borrowed pocket knife he had sterilized with a pint of vodka. Tuck was in the shower and his hand went instinctively to the scar just below his rib cage. I owe my life to this guy Rags, I mean S'gar. It is astonishing how unpredictable life is. Now, we are back together. Tomorrow I will have to thank him for what he did.

****

After everyone had showered and put on their new duds, phone calls were made. Everyone here and back at home was excited to know the Musketeers were back together for a reunion. They tried to keep the noise down in the hallway but it was impossible. When they arrived the table had been prepared and Corey was waiting. All of the guys had decided they would not go anywhere after dinner, they just wanted to sit and talk. After they all were seated Buddy looked over at Corey, "Hey Corey, after we eat if you got things to do take off. We are not going anywhere. I just want to find out what all these guys have been up to, and I know they are going to want a blow by blow description of my latest fight!"

"Yeah, I do have a little studying I need to do," Corey said, "But I am here for you guys, if you want a Limo ride I am the man. I can certainly understand you have a lot of catching up to do. Naturally I know a lot about you guys because S'gar considers you boys family. At one time or the other everyone in MVA has had a shot at observing your lives. I hope I am not speaking out of turn, but he has kept close tabs on you. Here is just one hint of how close. Ask J about his last ride out of Vegas when he jumped in the bad guy's car and left them standing. We, that is S'gar, had a team close by in case you really needed help."

Completely stunned J stammered, "You mean you could have stopped those guys? You let them take shots at me? Man, I coulda been killed!"

"Nah, Ben was the leader of that team. He said you appeared to handle yourself well enough to get out of that little scrape."

"Little scrape? My telling the story will not show it as a little scrape!"

"Better roll up your new pants legs," chimed Sticky. "This will be another of J's wild ones and it will get deep!" They were all slapping each other on the shoulder and laughing as the waiter came to take their order. They tried to settle down enough to order dinner, even though they all insisted it was supper.   Then the chaos continued. Corey had called attention to J's exit from Vegas so J ran through his experiences while trying to get rich quick in Vegas. It was not the story Tuck and the boys had expected.

They were amazed that J was married, settled and learning to run a ranch. They had all wanted to be cowboys, now one of the Musketeers was becoming one. He told them of his solid white horse. So white he looked like raw cotton and his name was Cotton. His father in law, Chief, had got him that horse. He had said it would remind him of the cotton mill towns back east. J had told him he did not want to work in a cotton mill. Chief did not want him to leave so he wanted him reminded daily of raw cotton and the work required by it.

"What are your thoughts on school?" asked Tuck.

"I never liked school," said J, "but then what boy does? I thought Buddy did, but now I hear he quit. But Tuck, it did sound like S'gar expected anyone working for the MVA to have a degree. I don't really understand, the more I know the more confused I am."

Tuck continued, "I guess I have no choice, I was ordered here. And.."

"Yeah, what is this about you and the Air Force, I know you hated authority, now you have every Tom, Dick and Harry ordering you around," cut in Buddy.

"Oh Buddy, it is not as bad as it sounds, we all follow orders to a point all our lives. Except maybe if you are president, then his wife probably tells him what to do," Tuck laughed, "Don't boxers, excuse me, pugilists have trainers who tell them what to do?"

"Touché Tuck. I guess you have a point," conceded Buddy.

"Okay, let's go around the table. I started so Tuck?" J indicated.

"Well, you know I am now in the Air Force. That is obvious. I haven't been out of basic long; as a matter of fact I just finished my basic leave before coming here. Boy, was it a shock to see you guys. I think I am more confused than any of you. I spoke with old workaholic Sticky while in Mt. Bell. Oh yeah, I am also a certified hero," he stood making a mock bow and showing a muscle builder stance.

"Cut the crap, you ain't been to war yet to save us from the communists!" said Buddy.

"Oh, he is a hero all right," said Sticky, "He made the papers back home, went to Texas, some town called Bandana…"

"Bandera, if you're gonna tell it tell it right," joked Tuck.

"Okay, a big town in Texas called Bandera. Anyway while he was AWOL, he nearly single handedly helped his girlfriend capture the entire Jessie James Gang," mocked Sticky, "That is the true story, but he will probably tell it differently."

"I wasn't AWOL, it is not a big town and there were only three of them that Vickie captured, under my guidance of course."

"Now, tell us Tuck. What really happened?" asked J.

Tuck went through the time he was in San Antonio, including how beautiful the city was and how good it felt to actually be at the Alamo where Davy, Bowie and the rest had fought and died. He was a little embarrassed about the awards, but he told about them anyway. "By the way, do you guys know any Hawes or Harris's in the Air Force?"

"I think Shirley and Ernie down on the National had an older brother that was Air Force."

"A long time ago when we had the run in with Chief Harris, I think I remember him saying his older brother, Vernon, was in the military somewhere, what do you want to know that for?" asked Sticky.

"Well, believe it or not, Hawes is a sergeant on Lackland and he was my Company Commander. Chief Harris's brother Vernon came aboard as his assistant while he was awaiting discharge. Hawes is a stickler for rules and regulations. Sgt. Harris knew how to cut some of the stress of basic. He can be a comedian at times. It was hard for me to believe but they are also cousins. Looking back on it, they did a good job playing the good cop bad cop routine on us, but it worked. I figure it was Hawes' idea. This thing with Castro and the Russians has Harris involuntarily extended and he is not a happy camper. They didn't explain any of this to me until after basic. Sgt Harris wants out of the United States Air Force."

"Anyway, when I got these orders they were baffled, as baffled as I was. But you know what? I think this is the greatest thing that has ever happened to me. I mean all of us. This is sort of like a dream. Even though I am bound by the Air Force, here we are being offered a chance to be together again."

"Well, I don't understand some of the things Rags, I mean S'gar has said. I came here to deliver the Sucker. Now he tells me he will give me the price we agreed on and I can take the price and the Sucker back to Mt. Bell. Talk about confusing."

"While you are talking, continue. What have you been doing except goofing off?" smiled Buddy.

"This guy hasn't been goofing off, Buddy. The talk around Mt. Bell is that he is the next Vanderbilt. The dude has a rep as a miracle worker in dirt," chided Tuck.

"I've been doing all right. I hated to sell the Sucker but to compete with the others around the area I needed a loader and big dump truck. This sale was my way to do that. Now I am a little confused. I plan to move North Carolina red dirt. I don't see how I fit into S'gars's plans. I sit here about to enjoy a good meal and cannot figure how this can work."

The meal arrived as Sticky was finishing. They were all excited, but not too excited to eat. The Omni William Penn serves some of the best food in the world. These boys from the small southern town of Mt. Bell were significantly impressed. "I never ate like this in Mt. Bell, Vegas nor on the ranch, but if you ever meet the Chief, don't tell him I said that," said J with food in his mouth.

"Don't talk with food in your mouth," laughed Sticky.

"Cowboys can do that, Sticky, I have learned a lot in Colorado. Why I remember once on a cattle drive up in Montana …."

"Like I said, roll up your britches legs!" that was Sticky. They were all laughing and having the time of their lives. As the meal progressed they were mostly silent as they ate. The eating gave them time to think of the situation. This was honestly, to each of them, the most confusing time in their lives. None of them could wrap their thoughts around the situation they were in. They were happy; there was not doubt on any of their minds. And if nothing else came out of this weird meeting, they were together in a way they could have never dreamed.

Everyone had blackberry pie a la mode for dessert. That is except J, who said, "I don't care if this chef is the best pie baker in the world, you can't beat butter pecan ice cream." So he had a large helping of the local butter pecan ice cream.

"Okay Buddy, you were the brains of this outfit. I, or we, know you threw a mean punch, but you were Mr. Electronics. I figured you for some kind of engineer, so you are a pugilist now, how did that come about?" asked Sticky.

"I knew more than most of my teachers," Buddy said as he laughed, "I couldn't waste this brain on the simple stuff they were teaching. I really have developed a couple things that I think are very interesting in electronics. I haven't dropped the subject. But yeah, I was always pretty fast with my fists." Buddy went on with the story about how he was discovered. He also was honest about how he felt after really hurting an opponent." Everyone knew that Buddy was joking about knowing more than his teachers; he, more than the rest had respected learning. They also knew their friend had a soft heart, to go along with his hard fists.

It was late, the tables were cleared, and they headed for their rooms, everyone saying good night. They all had more phone calls to make. Every one of them was bursting to tell what the other musketeers had been up to. Tonight had been the cat's meow; as they used to say, back when they were all Cool Cats.

Back in their rooms all the phone calls were made, no one was ready for sleep after all today's excitement. Each room was equipped with the newest development in TV, the color set. Each one of the musketeers went to sleep watching Johnny Carson in living color.

Chapter 9
Some Major Answers

Everyone was up early. Breakfast was great and they all were anxious to get the morning started. There were some comments to be spread around from family members to make sure everyone knew that the rest missed them. The atmosphere was charged with excitement. There were so many questions they wanted answered. Today should be that day.

It was no surprise that Corey's timing was perfect. The limo rolled to a stop as the doorman opened the door. Corey was all smiles as he opened the rear passenger's side door. "Corey, you don't have to do that stuff for us. We aren't used to it," said Sticky.

"Speak for yourself, Stick man, I am enjoying this high cotton treatment," spoke out Buddy. "To the S'gar farm my good man," he said to Corey as they started to roll. "And where is my morning Wall Street Journal kind sir?" he finished smiling.

"You, kind sir, will find it in its normal place, just to your left, on the light stand, along with today's Charlotte Observer. WE from S'gar Enterprises strive to please and anticipate men of higher caliber's needs," Corey said with a smile in his voice!

"Gotcha," laughed Sticky, "Seldom see you speechless old Buddy."

"Now, if he could just read," slipped in J.

"Aw, he can read," said Tuck, "He copied all my papers in school," Tuck ducked as Buddy made a fake lunge, "Hold that pugilist Sticky, he's gone crazy!"

It was just like they were kids again. Not many boys get this chance that fate was dealing them. They were all wondering just how a man like S'gar could bring this about. None of them in their wildest imaginations could figure how they could possibly work together. At the present their goals were in all different directions. They would like nothing better than to be together as a team. The limo pulled into S'gar Enterprises and Corey discharged his passengers professionally.

Inside they picked up their picture ID's and were again directed to the elevator. On the top floor they were greeted by a smiling V. Jane, "Well I see you guys survived the night, go on in. Ben and S'gar are waiting."

All the greetings were accomplished and they were seated around the conference table. Each position had a stack of papers with their name on the cover. "Gentlemen, this is Dallas, you might remember him. He is lead counsel here at MVA and a great legal mind. He was the one who gave you the unguided tour of my cave when you all were kids. As you know, I had to depart Mt. Bell in a pretty big hurry with the CIA reps too close for comfort." Everyone nodded. They were all thinking about the time when the man named Rags had sent this lawyer to Mt. Bell. He took them on a helicopter ride that ended at Rags home cave. That is when they saw inside the cave that Rags had called home. They remembered seeing the dog Satan. The dog that was so faithful to defend Rags. Mark, the friend of Chief Harris, had the dog eating out of his hand, they even got to pet him. He was just as docile and loving as their pets. They remembered seeing the goat for the first time. A Monk had given Rags the goat so he would have milk. The whole set up was out of some fantasy world. Of course, the boys recognized Mr. Fletcher, even with his graying hair. They smiled as they thought of the fun day Fletcher had led them on.

"Dallas is going to cover some of the questions you may have about the MVA. He will cover the points of law in which you will probably be interested." S'gar was seated and indicated Dallas with a nod, "They are all yours Dallas."

"You guys sure look good, and have grown to be fine young men. Yes, I remember going on that mission to Mt. Bell for S'gar. I remember it as the strangest thing he had asked me to do up to that point. Who could forget the three and a half musketeers? I will not discuss the other more bazaar missions he has sent me on since that time," he smiled in S'gar's direction. Dallas went on to tell about the first discussion on the MVA, its problems and some of the successes. He went over the requirements of each employee (considered a partner). One of the requirements is to have at least a four year degree. When he saw there was going to be questions at that he held up his hand to indicate wait, "I am only giving an overview.

We will get into details later. He continued with a lot of details, all of which were interesting. Then he asked if there were any questions, as he broke into a big smile, like: is that a stupid question?

"Aside from the education requirements, will we be asked to break the law?" Tuck.

"Yes," next?

"Is there a lot of personal danger?" Sticky.

"Yes," next?

"Okay, how am I going to get an education to qualify for the MVA, and learn to run a ranch?"

"I don't know," next?

"You know, I have the same question. I want to move dirt and as much as I like the sound of the MVA, how would I ever qualify?"

"I don't know," next? With this Dallas was starting to smile, as the troops were starting to all mutter and talk at once.

"Hold on Dallas, for a lawyer you sometimes run a meeting into the ground. These men want more than: you are going to become a crook, you are going to be in danger and I don't know anything. You are the one with all the answers, aren't you?"

"No," a pause then followed with a big laugh, "That is your department. Guys I have been pulling your leg. S'gar can answer your questions; I just do what he tells me to do. He has never told me wrong nor asked me to commit a felony, (pause) not many times," and he laughed again and indicated the meeting was S'gars'.

"Before I try to restore some decorum and sanity to what my friend has created, I want you to hear from Ben. He is a senior partner, a trusted friend and has many times over the years watched each of your backs. I do not apologize for keeping an eye on you. I knew you guys had something special; I want to take advantage of that. Not just for the MVA, this is for you also. It is something I never had in my youth, the deep trust, faith and love for each other. I want to promote the camaraderie I saw in you guys. I want that in the MVA, Ben."

"Gentlemen, I am a professional. Handpicked, like you, and taught by a compassionate man. Never in my wildest dreams did I think I could find a job that gave so much satisfaction. Listen to S'gar, trust his word. If he makes a promise you can count on it. Dallas and I have discussed this many times. He relayed to me his many doubts when S'gar came up with this idea. But since it has been in existence, we both know beyond a shadow of a doubt, we have saved lives and we have changed lives. Yes, I have skirted the law. I have broken the law, but life is not always black and white. There are many gray areas and that is where we deal a lot. I wanted to speak to you today, I asked S'gar if it would be all right, and he agreed to give me this slot. I know you have heard it from some folk here at MVA that you guys have been a focus from here for awhile. Nothing in your private lives was compromised, but everyone here came to love you. We began to cheer for Buddy in every fight; we couldn't wait to hear the results. We held our breath for J in Vegas. We were caught with our pants down when Tuck ran into a bank robbery. We had just dropped back to give him some privacy, because we thought he had romantic notions toward Airman Vickie. However, Tuck exceeded our expectations, we all cheered. And you, Sticky my man? What can I say? You have turned into one of the most responsible men I have known at such a young age. You are a prince among men, a good honest business man. I know you wanted that contract with Williams; we threw the monkey wrench in. It hurt to see you upset when you did not get the job. But we could tell you were glad you did not have that contract when he went to jail." The guys were shaking their heads learning just how involved S'gar had been in their lives. This was amazing. "Well, I said what I wanted to say. You have my card. If you need anything call me. That goes either way, if you stay or not, still call. It's back to you S'gar." Ben smiled, excused himself and left the room.

"I knew you would have many questions. Dallas or Ben could have answered your questions. They indulge me in my little games. Now as I said yesterday the only person being asked to relocate is Tuck. Of course he isn't being asked, he has been ordered here by his superiors in the Air Force. We have a great relationship with all branches of the service. We have men here from every branch right now, except the Coast Guard. Their crew just graduated. Also, Tuck does not have to come aboard the MVA until his military obligations are filled, but he will be trained here whether he joins us or not. You are clear on that Airman Tucker?"

"Yes sir, I understand. I am sure I don't fully comprehend but I have learned to follow orders because they are orders," Tuck sounded confident, his voice strong.

143

"My next fairly simple concern is you, Buddy. We learned from several sources that you continued to tinker with electronics after you quit school. Your teachers, without exception, say you are brilliant. I would prefer you attend school here at MVA; however I have a friend at MIT. He informs me after looking at the data we furnished; with certain requirements bent a little, you can attend MIT. He suggest six years, I said do it in two. He said thirty months with you taking double loads he could get you to a master's level, and then you could return here for the fun time with Tuck. It is something to think about. You would have very little time for boxing. Forgive me, Momac says you prefer pugilism. And for your information, that man is brilliant in his own right; 'he says tell the kid to use his brain. He don't have to prove nothing to me or nobody else'. I tend to agree with him. If I am not mistaken, MIT is where you dreamed of going, wasn't it?"

Overwhelmed, Buddy forced himself to speak, "Mister that dream has been voiced only three or four times, I didn't think anyone remembered or knew. Yes it is a dream; they have a course covering space technology and satellites. I am very interested in that. But aren't you forgetting something, I quit school dadgummit, how smart can I be. That was stupid."

"No Mr. Sansbury, we haven't forgotten. I did not say it was going to be easy. I have a crew standing by; they are going to teach you the test. Yes, we are going to cheat to get you in. You will pass the entrance exam, because in a period of three weeks our experts are going to teach you the test. We are not going to participate in complete fraud and allow you to walk across the stage and receive a real Master's Degree. You will only get the knowledge; there will be no sheepskin from MIT. Is that fair?" S'gar asked.

"You bet, and I will bust my butt to learn everything I can. Are you sure this is not a dream?" Buddy asked.

"No dream, and if you think Momac was tough you wait until you encounter these teachers. You will probably think along the lines of hell on earth. But sometimes we must pay for stupidity. That can be a lesson learned."

"While Tuck and Buddy are doing some soul searching, here is something for each of you to think about. MVA is not necessarily a full time job. So I expect you to do one of two things. Start your own business or have a flexible job. We at MVA can arrange flexible jobs but I would prefer that you each have your own business. Of course, Sticky has that one covered. To prove how much we want you to have that business, MVA will provide you with an interest free loan up to five hundred thousand dollars. No payments due for the first two years. We will discuss salary once you digest what has been said. Now, how about some good coffee, and try the sticky buns from a new recipe? The recipe for the sticky buns comes from a wonderful lady in North Carolina; you are all familiar with her." As if on cue, the doors swung open and serving carts entered, the smell was from their youth, the Morse home, sticky buns!

Once every one had a bun or two and coffee, S'gar began again, "Sticky, in our look-see, we learned your grades were exceptional. Also some folks, including your mom, wanted you to go to medical school. How about a degree from UNCC in Business Administration? Before you answer think about something. Do you know Billy Moody?"

"Certainly I know Bill, he just retired awhile back."

"Could he operate your gear and run your company in you absence?"

"Sure, but he isn't working for me or anyone else. I know he retired and is doing a lot of fishing."

"Think about this. Bill fills in for you while you are in school. That will be only three days a week. Right now you work six days a week. You would be cutting your week's work in half."

"Somehow, we are not communicating. Billy is fishing!"

"We have been looking into this for a good while. Hear me out. Bill has done what a lot of men do; they retire and in a month regret it. In Bill's case he cannot replace his equipment, but he will work for you." Sticky started to say something, "Wait, I am not finished yet. The MVA will pay Bill to work for you while you go to school. Bill is chomping at the bits to work part time. We don't take anyone's word for things. We researched Bill, and the man is solid and trustworthy. Now, can we work from there?"

"What is that line? Here is a deal you cannot refuse? Sounds like I am leaning to your understanding S'gar," putting one last bit of a bun in his mouth and smiling at Tuck.

"J, I have some bad news for you. That ranch of the Chief's is not a great investment. He has been losing money constantly every year he has had it. I know he has told his daughter and you differently, but he is a proud man. He has used his military retirement and a few personal loans to keep it going. Maria does not know this, but we have a feeling she suspects it. Our number crunchers tell us he needs about two hundred acres more and about a thousand head of cattle for a paying ranch. You will also need a couple hands to handle the extra load. You heard my proposal to Sticky. Our folks have located a couple of retired ranch hands. These two are tired of hanging around the local watering hole telling stories; they are ready and willing to work some. Our guys have also looked your personal situation over and talked to experts in ranching. They have suggested that you build a nice home for you and Maria. Attach an apartment in the rear for the hired help, grab two hundred acres and go to school. You can let Chief add the cattle, he would love that. Am I talking something we can discuss seriously?"

"S'gar, like Sticky says, you are presenting deals that cannot be refused," said J.

"Well, to be honest that was my plan. Boys I have no family, the people here know I look at you guys as part of my family. I hope you can see it my way. What I have laid out is not equal among you. I know you boys share and share alike, you always have. So, since Dallas is so smart, I will assign him the task of leveling the playing field." S'gar rose out of his chair and faced his mountains. All was quiet for a moment, and then he continued.

"I did consider making you my heirs, but I will not saddle you with that. However, I will provide the means for you to make all our dreams come to fruition. Mine, the MVA and yours, whatever your dreams are," as he turned tears were streaming down his face. "I do not want this to appear that I have bought a family, but to have you guys as part of me, as my family, I would do it."

There wasn't a dry eye in that ornate office. This was a touching moment. But as Sticky's dad had been heard to say, 'The Northern Lights have seen strange sights, but this is the strangest I ever did see."

Tuck, 'old give a crap' Tuck, stood walked around the table and grabbed S'gar in a big hug. Through tears he said, "Last night I made up my mind to thank you for saving my life, this is as good a time as any. Thank you for taking a chance and saving the life of a stupid kid. Thanks, I love you for it."

The next few minutes was filled with hugs and thanks. It was a scene none would ever forget. "Since I am only half a musketeer, but I am the smartest and wisest of the group. I want to say on behalf of my brothers here, we would love to be your family. I think everyone is ready to look at things the way you see them. Last night none of us could see how this could be possible. All I can say is thanks and, we as a group, will work to see the MVA whatever you envision. Your vision will be our vision. Right guys?"

"Hear, hear! All for one and one for all, we share and share alike!" they all spoke as one. Everyone began to settle down, eyes were wiped and more coffee poured. No one spoke, all eyes were on S'gar.

A moment later he spoke, "Now we must discuss salary. You will be on the books at $300 a week until school is finished. All expenses for your education will be paid. Several times during your schooling you will be called here to participate in an active case as an observer to learn how we operate first hand. Like this trip your transportation will be paid or furnished," he laughed. "Sticky won't have to come up in his truck next time. You will be given ample time to make arrangements. In most cases you will not be here together. Is that agreeable?"

S'gar went on to tell the salary after school and financial arrangements for loans and so on. He explained that the MVA was not like most entities. It was not self propelling. When he died, the MVA died. The school would continue as long as it was feasible and profitable. All was arranged in writing to take care of each of them should he predecease their graduation. They went thru the agreements that were before them on the table. Most blanks were filled in on the application. They were now employees at large of 'S'gar Enterprises', Pittsburgh, Pennsylvania.

The day was full with a working lunch. All the wrinkles were ironed out, and they were beat from all the excitement. Sticky was told he could fly back to Charlotte, and a qualified driver would deliver the Sucker back to North Carolina. He first refused, but thinking about what all he had to tell Hattie and mama, he changed his mind. Sticky found a certified check for the amount they had agreed on for the truck and the Sucker in his stack. He attempted to return the check but it was firmly refused.

S'gar stood to address the group, "Well, I guess this is the end of a very profitable day for everyone, including the MVA. As I walked around

Mt. Bell, I heard the name Rags. I actually started accepting it as my name. Once in Mt. Bell, when Chief Harris stopped me he addressed me by saying, 'Excuse me Rags.. I mean sir.' At that moment I had the realization that I did not take offense at being called Rags. I told the Chief that, and I began to like having one name. No one has ever questioned the name I chose, in my presence. That is except Dallas. He even laughed and suggested some names FDR, Elvis, Tulip or Squirrel. Now I want to ask you, what do you think of the name?"

"I think it is strange, but I think I like it," said Sticky

"Well," said Buddy, "Logically it is good, it is short, like Rags, It has four letters like Rags." Pausing making a quick note, slid it over to Tuck who was sitting beside him. Tuck smiled, "As a matter of fact the same four letters as Rags, just backwards! Well, I'll be hog tied, why didn't we see that before?"

"What took you so long, Buddy?" asked S'gar laughing at the looks on their faces. "You are the first person that has put that little fact together. I was surprised Dallas didn't see it at first, but with so much on his mind at the time, it slid right past him. When I returned from Mt. Bell I sat in my office thinking. It had been my Dad's old office. He always said that bums and fools should turn their lives around. Just after that incident with Tuck in Mt Bell, I came alive again. So, before leaving Mt. Bell, I had decided to turn my life around. As I sat there pondering, I decided that I would turn my new name around also, hence, S'gar, I like it and the mystery it holds for those who do not know."

The meeting was dismissed. Everyone left with detailed instructions for the next thirty or forty months. There would be no summer breaks. They would all be driven by their new found fortunes and goals. Ahead was a future life of good deeds. There was also the knowledge of being backed in business by a financially strong Enterprise, S'gar. There were times when each of the four boys wanted to throw in the towel and say it is not worth it. But a phone call from a fellow Musketeer always brought their thinking back to the real goals, working together. It was always, all for one.

The absolute highlights were the times that Ben called OJT (On the job training). That was when they were called to observe an 'event'. Later they actually got 'feet wet' as Ben called it, they took part. The feeling was so exhilarating it was hard to explain.

Other things happened, unrelated to school. Sticky and Hattie were married. On one job that sent Buddy to England for a few months at Oxford, he met a lady he could not live without. He and Dianne were married. He called her Princess Di. Later there would actually be a real Princess Di. Of Course Buddy said, "Dianne was always real."

Tuck went home to Mt. Bell when he could. He was courting one of the Adcock girls, Rose. He called her his Rosie Mae, until she clipped his horns a couple times, now it is just Rose. Because she says 'just one Rose will do'. There was a twist in the tale. Sgt. Harris, Tuck's Assistant Company Commander from Lackland had finally got his release from the Air Force. He had returned to Mt. Bell and courted one of the Adcock girls also. He had married the older sister, Janet. So Tuck and Harris were brothers in law. Would wonders never cease?

So by the end of their tough and in-depth schooling they were all happily married. In confidence all the wives knew what their husbands did in their secret lives. When the call came, it was understood everything was dropped, MVA came first. Everyone had met and adored S'gar, and Dallas.

They were also trained and all held the highest awards in three of the leading martial arts. They were experts in weapons and explosives. They understood psychology and some psychiatry as dealing with the twisted or criminal mind.

With some more OJT as a team, they were ready for use. They were also well paid; a part time job was paying more than the average attorney earned per year. No one complained about salary or the times that calls came in.

Chapter 10
The early years with MVA

As the years passed S'gar 's dream of the MVA had progressed as he had planned. The boys, now grown men, had their own businesses. Sticky was now in a position financially to bid on small state road projects. This brought him in contact with North Carolina state officials. They could not ignore what they saw. This man was honest and produced a good product on every project. He was encouraged to bid on larger projects.

Sticky had reached this point in the business world by using his head. He never stretched himself so thin that he had to ignore quality to meet a deadline. Sticky had been used on many short term 'incidents' for the MVA. Bill had handled the construction well in each absence, so he and Sticky had become like hand in glove. As an employee Bill was earning more part time than he had been when working for himself full time. There was the added bonus that he did not have the responsibility of meeting a payroll or buying new equipment. Like most heavy equipment men it was in his nature to protect the equipment. He did not have to be told not to overwork heavy gear and to keep it maintained. Sticky could see and appreciate Bill's efforts. Above everything except Hattie he loved his equipment most.

The main reason Bill loved the part time work was that he had the money and time to pursue his second hobby. Fishing was his first, but restoring an old Studebaker was his second passion. Having two or three days a week in his garage was his idea of retirement. His present project was a 1956 Hawk; even his wife loved this one.

The MVA 'events' many times required acting. Sticky was a natural. He could be a preacher or a high rolling gambler. He was unique in that his personality could change on a moment's notice to match his clothes. Put the man in a clerical collar and he became pious and could quote scripture. He could even deliver a message if needed. No one made a better gambler. Add a gold tooth and a $1000 suit and he could take Vegas. He was the perfect shill. Nothing thrilled him more than when Ben asked him to be a hobo. He was the perfect bum, with the old stove pipe hat and an unlit short stogie. He enjoyed his private life as a partner in the MVA. Like everyone in the MVA he knew the risks, and several times he was in danger. Of course, these times were never mentioned to Hattie.

Lately, there have been rumors that the North Carolina Highway Department has an interest in Mr. Morse from Mt Bell. Some think tank had brought his name up. Their rationale was that with his ability in business he would be able to bring costs under control and raise the quality on North Carolina roads. His record in such a short time was impressive. Nothing firm and no offers had been made.

****

Tuck and Buddy had developed their own companies. Both companies were involved in investigative services, serving personal and commercial businesses. Buddy leaned more to the electronic end and Tuck was more involved in the covert area. Tuck's path had been a strange one. It was one that amazed all the Musketeers. Near the end of school in Pittsburgh Tuck was visited by a couple FBI agents. In their hands was a discharge from the United States Air Force and a contract with the FBI. Once he finished the school in Pittsburgh, he was completely away from MVA for a year and a half. During that time he went through SEAL and counter intelligence training. He became an Agent-at-Large. As an Agent-at-Large he was surreptitiously assigned back to the school at Pittsburgh as an instructor under S'gar.

After a year at S'gar Enterprises, the same two FBI agents returned. This time there was a release from the FBI, which he was directed to read. After reading for a few minutes he looked up puzzled. The FBI was releasing him. They would disavow any knowledge of his association with the FBI. There was to be no record of his ever being attached to The FBI. "This is all your records; pay, physical and performance," said agent number one, indicating the one inch stack of papers and folders he held. He then started feeding them into the shredder.

While the records were being fed into the shredder, number two spoke, "We don't know who you know and we don't want to. I don't know if you have a great contact, or you have made someone so angry that you are about to disappear. As you know we can't be concerned about that. Please sign that release you are holding," and he handed Tuck a pen. "I will also need your ID, shield and piece."

Still confused, Tuck signed the paper and handed the pen back to the agent. He also handed him his FBI credentials and weapon. Then he asked, "There is only one copy here, so where is my copy?"

The agent took the copy from Tuck, "There is no copy," and he fed that copy into the shredder. "Because there was no original, it is pretty hard to have a copy."

The agents stood to leave. They shook his hand and one said, "I have been with this agency for twelve years. He," indicating the other agent, "has nine years. We have never seen or heard of anything like this. I don't know whether to be glad or sad for you. You have our best wishes. We just shredded some of the best records I have ever read. I was envious. Good luck to you." They turned and left.

Tuck sat in his office, dumb founded. His life had been a whirlwind for the last few years but this, wow, this takes the cake. 'Rose ain't gonna believe this one' he said to the walls.

There was a knock on his office door. "Come," said Tuck, only half meaning it. Ben stepped through the door.

"Well are you sufficiently confused?" asked Ben.

"You could say that. I assume you are here to clarify what just happened," mumbled Tuck.

"Brighten up Tuck; you have just been released from your obligations to the United States Government. You are officially a civilian again. Now, your contract with the MVA and S'gar Enterprises takes effect. You are welcome to remain on the job here. If you decide that, the only thing that would change is that your salary will be paid by S'gar Enterprises instead of the U.S. Government. However, S'gar says if you want to pursue your idea for an investigative service of your own, as two of your friends have done, you need to see Dallas. He has the necessary paperwork to establish you in the PI business. He has the applications for national and international licenses you will need. As you know we try to cover all bases."

"Ben, this is unbelievable. Does this happen often around here, I mean something this bazaar?"

"Nah, this is normal, sometimes things really bazaar happen. Like four kids show up and are offered a wonderful future," Ben laughed.

"Touché," said Tuck, "How soon we forget. After I collect myself, I'll see Dallas."

From that time on Tuck set his mind and efforts toward establishing a unique private investigative service. His business would be the old fashioned strong arm tactic PI. He rapidly learned that strong arm tactics worked great for the lower level that he had first aimed at. But, he was quick to realize if he was to 'Aim High', as the Air Force had taught him, he would need other sources as well. J and Buddy were already underway with their own unique services, they got together to help Tuck put his organization on a footing to compete with other PI's. Brain storming produced the ideas for a third successful service. He called it 'Line Investigative Service', specializing in covert activities. This would be making the best of his FBI training. He targeted industrial espionage. His operatives would be inside corporations to get the information then out before any action was taken sanitizing them for future work at that corporation. His aim was to keep any agent from becoming 'snake bit'. That was his term for being discovered. Because once an agent was snake bit his usefulness was greatly impaired in other corporations.

Thanks to contacts of S'gar and his friends Tuck quickly gained a couple clients. Both those cases were ongoing and seemed headed in the right direction. He needed success so it would spread among CEO's. His vision was to work no lower than one level below the CEO. From that level his investigation could cover the whole corporate ladder. It was not unheard of for a person high up the ladder to get greedy. One who was privy to some very valuable development's worth would save a lot in future R&D for another corporation. Money and ambition have turned many a good man's head especially if all he has to do is spill something to make himself eligible for a step up to CEO in another company.

One case broke. Matt was embedded into the Moderntronics Corporation as a temp hire with expertise in expediting. His job was to speed up the newly developed growing process for modern chips. By doing this he was involved in the company secrets in the process. Early on he spotted an official who took more than a passing interest in the process. He reported this to Tuck, who immediately put Luke on the suspect as a daily tail. Photos taken by Luke of the official passing data to a competitor put a quick cap on the investigation. Matt was replaced by someone else from the temp hire company. On Tuck's advice, bad data was fed to the crooked official. When added to the process he had stolen, it would completely ruin the mole's credibility. Millions were at stake on this particular process. It gave Tuck the inside track he needed. When you save a corporation millions they tend to be appreciative. Tuck was enjoying this success. Matt and Luke were also elated. This was their first assignment with Tuck. He was very pleased.

****

J had continued to operate the ranch, mostly at a distance. Maria, of course, backed her J one hundred percent. She was thrilled with the information he had brought back from his first visit with S'gar. "I had a feeling dad was covering up the finances of the ranch. I let it go hoping I was wrong. I couldn't burst his bubble because he wanted to be a rancher so badly. I just tried to put it out of my mind."

After J explained what the expert's opinions were, he and Maria set up a plan to take advantage of information S'gar had supplied. With land prices down, Drover needed some cash on another investment to keep it from becoming a disaster. If it failed Drover would be up the creek without a paddle. There was two hundred fifty acres adjoining their land with fifty head of prime white face on it. S'gar's experts were sure if Maria offered thirty five thousand cash he would, after negotiations, settle for forty thousand cash.

In town at Drover's office, "Are you crazy Maria, I buy land. I don't sell. It is a fact I don't give it away, and that is what you are asking me to do. I tell you what I will do; I'll drive the cattle off and let you have it for twenty thousand down and a note for forty thousand."

"No, Mr. Drover, J has a better idea. He has found a thousand acres in Wyoming for forty thousand. It has a nice little home on it and the Chief is about ready to sign on. He said he would like to stay here if he could get more land, so to humor him we came in. Since forty thousand is what J has inherited, I think we will do just that, buy and move. By the way I think Chief will let our place go for twenty thousand if you want it."

J spoke up, "Mr. Drover I have really enjoyed living around here, I like it. But that place in Wyoming is big. I think we will really benefit from it. I hate to think of the winters, but the house is warm."

"Now, don't be too hasty, Forty thousand you say? I like the chief; he has sand. Tell you what. I will give the land to you without the cows for forty down and a note for ten thousand."

"Nah, Drover I told dad I would offer you thirty thousand for the whole shebang, which would leave us ten thousand to work with to improve that shaggy herd you have on it."

"Shaggy herd? Those are prime white face, girl.   You can't improve that herd. But everyone knows I am a fair man. Forty thousand cash and I drive the cattle off."

"I know you have probably gone as low as you can, and I appreciate it. To be honest I hoped you wouldn't take my offer. Now, I can tell the Chief I made the offer. It'll probably be a week or so before we list the ranch for sale. So, if you are interested, of course you have the first refusal. Come on J, let's get some lunch."

They said their goodbyes and headed to the Hotel Restaurant. "Do you think this is wise Maria? It looked like he would have taken the forty thousand for it all."

"Well, as your concerned wife, and a great judge of Drover, I think he will walk through that door in a few minutes and take my offer," she said grinning.

They had a lunch and talked, both became pretty nervous when nothing happened. They paid the tab and J said, "Let's go over and finish the negotiations, Maria, we don't have a thousand acres in Wyoming to fall back on."

"I wanted to commend you for catching that little fabrication and following through on it. I thought that about the weather was a good touch."

"But you aren't going back to Drover's are you?"

"Nope, Drover will come to us." Maria said.   But she had lost a little cockiness.

They had made the trip back to the ranch in silence. J and Maria were lost in their own worlds of thought. They brought a sandwich for the Chief and gave it to him. He drew himself a big glass of butter milk and sat at the table with them.   "Well, what is the verdict? Will Drover sell the land?"

"Chief we…" J started but was interrupted.

"Drover will be out after awhile to finalize the agreement. What do you think about thirty five thousand for the two hundred fifty acres and the cattle?" asked Maria.

"Dang it girl if you done that I will hug your neck. I can't believe anyone took old Drover. That is all worth near eighty thousand if it is worth a dime."

"I think you are right dad, but remember the papers are not signed yet."

Maria messed around the kitchen cleaning up some stuff. Chief and J were listening to the radio. It was getting dark and Maria was losing her confidence, what little she had left. "What time is that sucker coming out Maria, it is getting mighty late?" called the Chief.

"Well, dad it is like this," Maria started to speak when they all saw headlights come across the curtains. "That should be him now."

There was knock on the door. Chief answered and invited Drover in. They all sat around the table looking at Drover. He took a folder out. "Chief, this is my final offer, I don't want you people moving off to Wyoming, so I have decided to let good business be forgotten and use my heart. Thirty five thousand, five hundred for the whole shebang as Maria said. Here are the papers. We will all sign them. I expect a check by tomorrow afternoon for Thirty five thousand five hundred dollars."

"No, Mr. Drover I s...." she was interrupted by J as he gripped her arm.

"That is okay, Mr. Drover. Maria was about to say we appreciate your offer and we will accept. You will have the check by close of business tomorrow." J was holding Maria as tight as he could without hurting her.

"I wasn't too keen on moving to Wyoming anyway. I am glad we were able to come to an agreement. You know I really do love this land," spoke the Chief.

"Well, sorry to show up so late, but I have been pretty busy. I am surely glad to have you folks stay on here. You know I am taking a loss for old time's sake."

"We appreciate it, don't we Maria?"

Maria nodded her head to keep from screaming. Mr. Drover left a copy of the papers and departed. J relaxed his grip on Maria. "Well, I never... I could have got that five hundred back," she nearly yelled.

"Honey, when I tell S'gar you got the whole thing for thirty five they aren't going to believe it. Take a victory and calm down."

"What is this about Wyoming?" asked the chief.

Both J and Maria broke out laughing and told the whole story about the whole day. The Chief agreed to buy cattle monthly at the auction to increase the herd. Life was good on the ranch in Colorado. J started college and the cowboys were hired to help on the ranch. Before the end of college J started his Investigative Company. The ranch became mostly supervisory and Chief Hodges loved every minute of his dry land ship. He was the skipper. Maria was happy. She had J and assisted in the organization. She hired Reece and Steve both black belts in two martial arts. They were actors and for a bonus they both understood and used some electronics. They made the ideal agents. Maria, with the help of S'gar enterprises, helped the young folk get Private Investigator Licenses. Reece and Steve were quick study actors and could fit about any situation.

****

From the beginning Buddy felt he could investigate most corporation and government problems electronically. He soon learned he needed help from humans who knew electronics. He decided on applicants who would act as well as understand electronics. Once he had the qualified agents he   could then get whatever bugs he needed planted or find passwords, etc he would need to invade the company's computer systems. He searched for and hired the best. His core was both young and old, but everyone either had a degree in electronics or had grown with the industry. With his wit and winning personality he was already working for several 'Fortune 500 Companies' and he had been contracted to several overseas companies.

They very seldom had a chance to get together, but when S'gar called them all in at one time, they were in their element. It seemed that success fed off success. Today they all arrived in Pittsburgh and were taken directly to the office. Being called all at once they knew it was very important to S'gar. After all the funning that they all enjoyed, they settled down with Ben, S'gar and Dallas standing at the head of the table. S'gar spoke, "Men, we have what seems o be a very serious problem. One I should involve state police and more than likely the FBI. You know me; I won't send anything to the FBI without iron clad proof. It may not be proof that can be used in court but enough to let them know what I present is worth their time. This is extremely big."

Chapter 11
Problems in the Judicial System

With everyone seated, S'gar took his time, "In the beginning of MVA my first idea was to put out phone help lines. I blanketed the net works with ads saying if you needed someone to talk to, call xxx number. I put professional psychologists on the lines. Most of the problems were solved by advice. But ever so often it was the wife who was being abused and could talk to no one, but needed to vent. Several times it was children who were abused. When we could we took action. Now, we are more sophisticated. We still have hot lines, but along with that we have many electronic gathering gadgets. Now, with the advent of the internet, our information is coming from FBI, SBI, and police reports. It is very technical but you guys have put together a filtering system that is almost automatic.

Something has come up that sends up red flags from almost all of our sources. We now have a pattern. Some are complaints, some are cries for help and some are copies of reports from law enforcement. What they seem to show is a pattern by a judge of sending innocent people to prison or work houses for profit. I have ascertained to my satisfaction that when mentally handicapped or under privileged children and some vagrants appear before a certain judge there seems to be a pattern that his decisions put these people in a private institution no matter how small the infraction is. Sometimes there is no infraction just being in the wrong place. That institution is then paid by the state to house these people until they are judged fit to return to society, or a family member yells loud enough that they are released." S'gar then nodded to Dallas.

"Guys, S'gar is on target. I want to play some calls from the help line. Listen and give us your impressions." He hit the remote play button that brought up the Phone banks. "When an operator gets a call he feels is very important he gives the high sign, and the other operators who are not busy all listen to the caller."

Caller, "I can't tell nobody else so I want to talk to you. Okay?"
Operator, "Certainly, that is what we are here for."

Caller, " Wu-well it is about my frien, my frien Phillip. He went up in front of Judge Black and I ain't seen him since. Phil ain't right in the head, but he is a good guy. He don't hurt nobody and his mama don't pay much attention to him. I don't think she cares at all that he's gone. I miss him cause nobody else won't talk to me, least he listened. I asked that policeman West who took him and he said to mind my own business. Is that right? Ain't my friens my business?"

Operator, "Certainly, what is your name so I will know what to call you?"

"Doan wan' to give a name, okay?"

"Sure, can I just call you David?"

"Yeah, that will be good, I like David."

"Okay David, I like it too, I have a son named David, and he is twelve. How old are you David?

"Thirteen, but why you ask that? "Can't we just talk?"

"Sure David, what else is on your mind?"

The rest of the call was innocuous. There were three other calls approximately the same. Then there were the reports. "All these people went before Judge Black. None returned to the street. The Police reports show that only one had been picked up before so most were not repeat offenders. As we all know, these usually are back home or on the street in a day. All totaled, there were twenty three people that had been traced just from MVA reports. We hired Buddy's outfit to come up last week and with computer experts they were able to find over three hundred in the last thirty-six months. Now, gentleman that is over ten million dollars a year cost to the state and federal government. Under the present laws both pay some of the freight. A cursory study by Buddy shows Judge Black is living a little above his means. You know to the MVA that is enough to say 'do something'. Now I know that you have questions. We need a lot of answers and some good suggestions."

"Does anyone see a way to get any solid proof without getting on the inside?" asked J.

"I think it is impossible without stretching this investigation out over a year," said Buddy.

S'gar spoke, "You gentlemen know me. I hate dragging my feet when I know someone may be suffering. We have tried electronically but that doesn't give us much. We can find out more about Judge Black but that does not say what is happening, and who all is involved. I honestly don't want to approve anyone going inside unless we have at least two ways to monitor them and an emergency escape hatch. So, if you are seriously thinking of sending someone inside, I want some pretty good proof we can protect them. I want Ben to remain here with you guys. Dallas and I have some folks in the legal business to talk to. This is important to me, I repeat, very important to me. Come up with something that we can seriously bat around."

Everyone gave him the high sign and turned to the coffee that was just arriving. Sticky was the first to speak, "I don't have much to say in a case like this, except if you need me for anything just say so, I will listen and if I see a place where I can input I will."

"Well, what I have up front to go inside is two good agents, Reece and Steve, who are young enough to fit the bill. I am sure they will tackle it. But let's see if we can protect them," put in J.

Buddy, "From what I see it may be very complicated. First, we have to look at the facilities where the Judge is sending them."

The Belt Electronics Labs had developed what was being called the cell phone. All the Musketeers carried their four pound bag phones. The reception was good in cities, but shaky in the field. Tuck had just taken a call. It was Josh. "Okay, I told you guys I have this young fellow, Josh. I just got off the phone. He is sure he is on to something concerning the cop West. He did a match of dates the ones we know were sent up, and this man West's bank account increased three to four hundred dollars within three days of each collar. When it fell on a pay day, the deposit was increased accordingly. So, at least on the surface, we have increased the culpable level one under the judge."

"Where are the kids being sent?" asked Sticky.

"There are three facilities owned by the corporation. The subjects in question all are sent to one in particular. The others seem legit," input Ben. "With some foot work and Buddy's troop's electronics magic we have located them in the county. All three are built on land formerly owned by our friendly judge's family. Now, it is part of the Lighthouse Eight Corporation. The Corporation purchased the land from the Black family about ten years ago. It is a strange contract. The selling price was ten million. The land at the time was worth about a million. But it is an interest free loan, with an eight year delay in the first payment. We are still trying to unravel the paper trail to ID who Lighthouse really is; but to get back to the facilities. From their policy statement they are built as minimum security facilities. However, Buddy suggests that J & Tuck both take a close look to see if that is actually the case. He suspects it is more medium to high security."

Buddy held up his hand, "I took the liberty to lease the closest building to the facilities. It is an old TV repair shop with living quarters in the rear. It is a two story building with some clear view of the first facility and partial views of the last two. As of now we are licensed and have permits to remodel it for a computer repair shop. The sign is now up, 'Computers for U' opening soon. We are keeping a little activity going, construction trucks etc. So far we haven't learned very much. We are hoping with Tuck and J's folks we can develop a good strategy."

Sticky spoke, "Now from a common sense position, we don't know about the inside. So why don't we see how we could get someone inside, without sentencing them to a hard life, without a possibility of parole."

"Good starting place Sticky," kicked in J. "My first impression is to use Steve and Reececup as brother and sister, bumming into town. One of them could appear to be a sandwich short of a picnic."

"Yeah, they could be runaways, but how do you get them and West together?" queried Sticky.

"If I am not mistaken a friend of mine from my short FBI stint retired awhile back and is on retainer by law enforcement here in Pittsburgh. I think it would be possible for the two kids to come to his attention, and maybe he could call West, since he doesn't get involved in delinquents. Now old Woody is a by the book agent, he doesn't mind denting a skull when necessary, but mostly he handles problems with his brain," put in Tuck.

Buddy pointed out, "That sounds plausible. Maybe you could fill him in just a little; he could honestly say the kids looked healthy to him. I would hope it never happened but if it ever came to needing a respected voice to swear to that, he would be good."

"Politically speaking, the more in the dark the FBI is the better witness he would be. We don't want it to look like he is IN on an investigation of a department who hired him, and I would not expect him to lie under oath."

"Good point Sticky," said Ben, "This must be as tight in security as possible. As it looks now, we are dealing with tens of millions of dollars. At that level lives could depend on this. No reflection on the friend Woody."

"What if West actually takes them someplace else?" asked Sticky.

"We will have them with some ID. If they go to another agency that is straight, you can show up in clerical garb as their pastor and take charge of them to return them to their parents who are worried sick about them."

"All right, but this time I want to be a Priest, never been one of them before Brother J." Sticky said in a deep pious voice. That got a needed laugh. It was Sticky this time, but they all knew how to break out with humor at the right time. It was just part or their deep partnership.

They all refilled cups and sat silent for some time. "I would sure like to figure a way to keep Reececup and Steve together, but that is probably a pipe dream," mused J.

"Yeah, that is impossible around the clock, because of the sleeping arrangements, but there is a co-ed working area. They have contracts for state uniforms and are using these guys for free labor and calling it rehab and therapy, we think. There is also a small farm that they run to supplement the cost of food," said Buddy.

"We will need to find out what charges or reasons subjects are sent to the production facility. I want some interaction if possible between the two," said J.

"Okay, the biggie as I see it is communications and an ability to monitor them. S'gar wants double coverage if possible. I am in the dark, what is on your minds on this part?" asked Sticky.

"Good question, Stick. I have a couple ideas, but they are theories. One is a negative response system. In other words, IF I can produce a small transmitter that sends a signal for, let's say ten days, and if they are ever in serious to mortal danger they could switch it off. We would monitor that twenty four hours a day. If that happened we could take the place apart, to get them. The signal would show exactly where they are in the facility. That would give us the advantage of knowing where to point our efforts and we would not be looking in the dark," answered Buddy.

"I have a heat seeking system that can cover the buildings to show body heat in the buildings. It works on the twelve second sweep. Every twelve seconds it scans the building. So, we have five times a minute reports. At night we can tell whether there is a roving patrol in the buildings. That is in case we want to penetrate and converse with the kids at night. I know that is a touchy thing but we have done it before," said J.

"I am working on a miniature transmitter, but it is still not small enough to conceal during a body search. I envision one small enough that it could be a hearing aid or a watch like Dick Tracy uses. However now, we are not that small," said Buddy. "But we are not through yet. We could still come up with something."

"Hey J," snapped Tuck, "We need that heat seeker set up as soon as possible so our guys at the HQ out there can be getting an idea of routines. Guard changes and routes and so on."

"Sure, I can have the guys bring it in with them when they fly in tomorrow, that is a good idea," answered J, as he picked up the phone to call.

"The continuous signal you talked about, Buddy. Where are you going to install it?" asked Sticky.

"I don't know yet. First I have to build it and see how much battery I need. The battery is the big thing," said Buddy.

"What about in their shoes? That is if they do not use uniform shoes there," Sticky suggested.

"Good point, we need to list what we need to know and why," said Tuck.

"Got it so far," said J, holding up his notes.

"How can we get information from inside without sending someone in as an inmate," asked Buddy, " What about some phone taps?"

"Bugs?" was one of Sticky's questions. "You PI types do use bugs don't you or is that just in the movies?"

"We gotta consider the taps and bugs," said Buddy. "Problem with the Bugs is getting them in place. We have used fake salesmen, phone men, plumbers you name it. We just have to find the right vehicle."

Tuck, hanging up the phone again says, "Okay, here's some firm information. The outfit that handles the security is 'Call It Secure'. They furnish the swings, mid shifts and weekends. The corporation handles things during the week days. They are now looking into a couple guys who work there, maybe get some personal views."

"I wonder if the same troops are there most of the time." J was thinking out loud. "We might bribe or replace one for a shift or two to place some bugs."

"It would be better if OUR man was hired by the Call It Secure company," Buddy said excitedly, "I bet between us we have a couple of guys who would fit the bill. Shoot, we could have their rich uncle go by employment and 'buy' them a job, because they want to be policemen so bad. And they need some experience to put on the resume. And besides, they are becoming a little more expensive than I like."

"By Jove, I think he has hit on something, lets flesh this idea out," said J, with an exaggerated British accent. Smiling, he continued, "And I was thinking you were about washed up."

There were chuckles all around. But now they had something to really get their teeth into, adrenaline was kicking in. Ideas began to fly. Good, wild and some crazy sounding ones, but they were ideas. After about thirty minutes of knocking the idea around they had settled on what they figured was the best route to take. They all agreed that the Security Guard(s) was the best way to go. But before they could make any final decisions, they needed more information. First, they had to decide on the volunteers willing to become guards. A plan had to be made to ensure they would be assigned to the Lighthouse Eight Corporation. Who owned it, and who did the hiring? Was the Lighthouse assignment a plum for guards or did they hate to be used there? They needed answers to the questions and all the information possible on 'Call it Secure'. They decided to make this a priority for Buddy and J. Tuck would continue to look at the Lighthouse Eight Corp. for as much detail as he could glean.

They agreed if they could get the information this way there would be no need to send anyone on the inside. Tuck has said even if they had to get several agents on the Call it Secure payroll it would be safer than sending our folks to jail.

This was their element. All together, working to fix something that was broke. This was something that caused pain and suffering while others made money from it. This group, the musketeers and the MVA were for free enterprise, but not slavery; slavery, whether to others, alcohol or drugs was still slavery.

Chapter 12
Time to Get Inside

Enough information on the security company 'Call It Secure' was gathered that the MVA felt they had enough to attempt to 'bribe' or motivate the personnel man to hire a couple agents into the security company. They had agreed that, more than likely, any new employees would be assigned to the Lighthouse Eight Corporation. It was considered the dregs. The shift was a monotonous night of walking and clocking. Most men, who hire out to security, want to become law enforcement officers. So, they do not want to be unarmed night watchmen. Well, most of the guys carried a knife along with the night stick and clock keys. But what they really wanted was a high profile job, like a bank, where they could at least carry a side arm. S'gar had chosen Ben to go in and play the rich uncle to two agents. His job was to 'grease the skids' for the two agents listed as his nephews. The homework on the personnel manager had been simple. He was in debt up to his eye balls. The group figured any extra money would be appreciated. He would also know that he could fire these bums, if that is what they turned out to be, and still have the incentive money paid by Ben.

The S'gar stretch limo pulled up outside the office of 'Call it Secure'. Corey got out and opened the door for the nattily dressed gentleman. Ben nodded to Corey as a thank you and turned to the business front entrance. Upon entering he spoke, "I am Julius Timmons, I have an appointment with the personnel manager in a few minutes, I believe."

Typical 'cute' young secretary chewing gum says, "Please go right in, Mr. Timmons, John is expecting you."

Upon entering Ben looked around as if inspecting. The young man behind the desk seemed very nervous. He stood and walked around the desk, "Mr. Timmons," he spoke, as he looked out the window at Corey standing at attention by the limo. "Your secretary said this was important so I hurriedly made time. What is so important, may I ask?"

"Certainly you may ask suh," drawled Ben with a fake Southern accent, "Because that is why I am here. I flew up from West Virginia.

165

Fortunately, your governor was nice enough to get me some transportation. You see suh, I've got two nephews who are worrying my little sistah to death. They want to be policemen but do not have squat to put on a resume. I promised mah little Sistah that I would try to find them employment where they could get some experience. That is why I am here."

"Mr. Timmons, you could have had your secretary ask that over the phone. We are not hiring at the present, but I will be glad to take the names of the nephews and give them consideration on the next opening. However, I cannot promise anything, our standards are pretty high."

"I see suh, I have not made myself clear, and I seem to ramble at times. These two youngsters are the picture of health and both have associate's degrees in law enforcement. They are not bums as you may be picturing them. Now, with all due respect, I am pretty smart in judging folks. I see into your eyes that you could use $1200 cash in the next few days. Just a guess mind you. Now, I promise these boys are pretty sharp. Even without me you would hire 'em, but I believe in greasing the skids as my old pappy used to say. I want to make mah sistah happy. Now, look deep into your inner self and think hard. Could you find two night watchmen jobs with a six hundred dollar advance, and six more after mah sistah calls, jubilant, saying her boys have jobs? I mean it can be minimum wage with no benefits, I do not care. Think young man, can we work something out?"

With his eyes on the fat envelope Ben had just removed from his inside coat pocket the young personnel man cleared his throat and spoke. "Well, Mr. Timmons since you put it that way I just might be able to use two sharp night watchmen." He accepted the envelope from Ben. "Just send the boys around and tell them to identify themselves as your nephews. I am sure when I see them I will not be disappointed. You have described them very well. "Call it Secure' will be happy to put them to work, at least as night watchmen."

"I think you are in for a surprise suh. You are probably looking for bumpkins; these boys are much more than that. But I will wait to hear they have a job. Thank you for your time, and God Bless." Ben shook the personnel man's hand then turned and left.

Looking out the window, he could see the professional chauffer take on his passenger with grace, close the door and drive off. The tag was covered with a dark vinyl and unreadable. The personnel manager quickly opened the envelope and counted six crisp one hundred dollar bills. He kissed them and slid them into his pocket. 'I don't care if they are bumpkins Suh, just bring on the other six hundred and I'll fire them if I want, SUH!' he said quietly. He then told the secretary to expect two applicants in the next couple days.

Inside the limo, "Corey Suh, take me home, Suh!" said Ben.

"Yes Suh, Mr. Timmons Suh, am I taking you all the way to West by gravy Virginia, Suh?"

"Nah, Mc Donald's and we will get a coffee. I have a good time with these acting assignments," replied Ben.

"You got it. Coffee coming up."

****

During the time Ben was enjoying himself at 'Call it Secure', back at the MVA the two prospective agents were being briefed. There was a tentative layout of the buildings and the schedule of the guards. The watcher/interpreters assumed by the schedule that there were clocking stations; the schedules were pretty tight so the guards did not have a lot of time to dilly-dally to get to the next clocking station. They were shown recent photos of Reece and Steve if inserting them into the equation was required. The locations of the several offices were needed and what was actually in the buildings. They were given instructions on the latest low light spy cameras they would be using. They were briefed on the main players in this 'Event'. Just what their roles were and the reasons they were there. Keep a lookout for abuse or abused. Are there any places you cannot go? The briefing was as in detail as it could be. At the interview they were not to appear incompetent, but not to appear as the sharpest knives in the drawer either.

****

Hourly, more information was being discovered and cataloged. The team was going over everything and what they found was being reviewed by S'gar and company. Electronics were becoming a wonder for data. Josh was heading the E-Team that consisted of the electronics guys from all three investigative arms. They were able to break the simple codes and hack into the system main frame. They had payrolls and employees records. They were accumulating the amounts of government finances pouring into the Lighthouse system. Then, into contracts and communications, they had learned what was expected of security. They were able to copy the shift procedure and clock in times that were expected of the guards. There was one solid warning in the procedures:

"LPO stands for Lighthouse Personnel Only. All doors, cabinets and closets labeled as 'LPO' should be secured at all times. If one of these doors is found unsecure, the head of Lighthouse Personnel is to be notified immediately, at any time of night or day. At no time is the guard to enter the unsecured door, but should remain by the door to prevent any unauthorized entrance. The guard is to remain there until given a directive to continue his rounds by senior Lighthouse Personnel."

Upon learning of this little jewel of information, Buddy wanted to know who was the manufacturer of the time keeping and clocking devices used. Josh assured him they could find out but it would take a little longer, as the building construction plans were not in the local database. He would have to find the architect and hack into their files. He hoped it would take less than a day. With this new thing called the internet there was a wealth of knowledge. They were all just learning how to manipulate it.

****

Tuck had asked Matt and Luke to take the jobs of security guards. At their final briefing Ben was there. "Now boys, I laid it on pretty thick. I am sure they are expecting two complete incompetents. We want you to surprise them, but not too much. I want you to be aggressive, ready to shoot anyone who goes against the rules of 'Call it Secure'. You are supposed to have an associate's degree, so you are no dummies. Tuck says you guys know how to play it by ear, so give it your best shot. But remember, we want you at what they call the 'Crazy House'. That is our main objective."

"You have your applications that Ben brought back. The information is pretty accurate so you have nothing to remember except that your last name is now Davis. And your SS #'s are fifty counts off from your real SS number." They had ID and SS cards to match their new names. "We have noticed they do not record SS# or employees for six weeks. We hope to be out of there by then. Tell them you are ready to go to work now," said Tuck.

"It just happens that two of the guards who are scheduled for tomorrow night will no doubt call in sick. They share an apartment together. Tomorrow, as always, we expect them to order their Pizza from Papa Giorgio's Greatest Pizza. If our plans do not fail us, it will have an extra added ingredient; we hope they will be in the bathroom most of the afternoon."

Matt and Luke received their final briefing and headed out to their interview at 'Call It Secure'. They had a big four wheel drive Hummer. Luke was in camo and Matt in black. They both had 'obvious concealed weapons'. The Hummer was loud and when they drove in the personnel man went to the window to see the pair carrying what must be the applications and slapping good naturedly at each other as they approached the door. The secretary had been instructed to look over the applications, and direct them into his office.

"Good morning gentleman, what can I do for you?" he asked innocently.

"Our Uncle said this would be a good place to apply for a job. He even brought us the applications. I'm Matt and this is my brother Luke, but don't tell anybody." Both boys cracked up laughing.

"Yes, he is correct. We do have openings for some hard charging men who want to become law enforcement officers."

Luke trying to appear serious said, "Well buddy, you have two of the hardest chargers. We are ready to shoot anybody that 'Call it Secure' says to," and he patted his obvious shoulder holster.

"I am assuming you have a permit for those pieces you are carrying, so I will go ahead and tell you. Your first assignment will require you to leave them at home. That is, if you are hired. Some of our customers will not allow fire arms on the property. It would be too easy for an inmate to take possession."

"Huh, you don't know me 'n Matt here. Ain't nobody gonna take our guns."

"Oh, I have no doubt of that, sir. But it still remains our policy that we give a man a thirty day trial period before he is sent on an assignment with a side arm. I'm sure that with your back ground in LEO training that you can appreciate that."

"Well sir, let me tell….." Luke was interrupted.

"What my brother is trying to say is that we do understand completely, and to land a job with this good organization, we will gladly follow the rules of 'Call it Secure'," broke in Matt, giving Luke a fake stare.

The personnel man took his time moving some papers around then looked up, "Okay, we can hire you both. The pay will be minimum wage during the trial period. It may be a few days before I can brief you, but I will call the number you left with the secretary on the applications. I hope you will be happy here and the secretary will give you a copy of company policy and your benefits for the first thirty days. If you have any more questions, call the secretary, she will be glad to answer any questions you may have. Good day gentlemen." He stood and shook Luke's and Matt's hands before they left his office. They flirted with and winked at the secretary and walked out the door. Outside, they gave a big yell and ran to the jeep like they had won the lottery. They put on a good show for the personnel manager as he stood by the window shaking his head.

On the road in the Hummer and headed back to headquarters, Luke looked over at Matt, "I think we convinced him we are half nuts broooo!"

"Yeah, I think Ben will like that. I can't wait to get inside and do some snooping. Have you done anything interesting lately?" asked Matt.

"Nah, oh well, yeah I did. I had a chance to infiltrate a gang in Dallas. Tuck was looking into one of the oil companies that they were trying to shake down. I got my tail in a crack once. I made a mistake with my accent; Texans are different than the rest of the south. I had to whip a big Hispanic dude who was supposed to be king of the hill. I am sure glad we had to learn four of the Martial Arts, I had to use all of them, plus a little old-fashioned brawling, to save my neck"

"Well, were they convinced?"

"Yeah, most of them were. They have this macho code, if you can whip one of the big guys, you must be all right. They firmly believe they can lay any law and order guy out. What have you been up to? We haven't had time to just talk."

"Tuck has been farming me out to Buddy a good bit. I am picking up more of the electronics stuff. He has developed some great little bugs, and he is working on something he calls a 'You are It' transmitter. Buddy says they used to play a game of tag. When tagged they said 'You are it'. He hopes to power it with body heat. He thinks it is even possible to have a doctor implant these in people. He is talking about those rich dudes that are worried about being kidnapped. With this type of homing device they could be located and a rescue would be made less complicated. None of them are easy. Of course, we both know that. He is using the same idea of his magnet transmitter. So basically the 'You are It' is like that magnetic transmitter we have put on cars to keep track of them, instead of trying to keep the tail too close. I hope he can get them to work." They finished their conversation as they pulled into the S'gar Enterprise's parking lot.

After checking in they went to Ben's office. "Okay, we are in," Matt said, after the formalities.

"Good, I hate to waste grease, if it doesn't help."

"Whadaya mean?" snapped Luke smiling, "Man, we were shoo-in's without the grease. All I had to do was tell him how bad I am. They would have taken Matt just to get me."

"Yeah Ben, he is right." Laughed Matt, "I only had to smack him three times."

"We have that phone line forwarded to your bag phone, Matt. I think tomorrow you should get a call, probably about an hour before the shift. You will probably be pushing it close to get there. It is according to how long the 'sick' guys wait to call in. Their usual policy for trainees is two trips around the security route of the building with an experienced man, and then you are on your own. Be especially on the lookout for computer and personnel areas. Also, look for a door that you can slip Josh in. We want him to have a few minutes with their computers. Okay, I know you guys will do a great job, now get out of here." They all shook hands and the guys headed up to find Tuck.

When they reached Tuck's working space, Steve was there. Tuck was briefing him on the pizza delivery intercept. Steve was going to play a part as a friend of the two guards. Everyone knew each other, and there were handshakes and high fives all around. "If you are going to jail, as I heard thru the MVA grapevine, won't you be exposing yourself needlessly? asked Matt.

"Hey Matt my man, I am an actor, a man of many faces," he got laughs with his facial expressions as he spoke, "Nah, this will be easy, a wig, some glasses and a small limp, the delivery boy won't know me an hour later, especially when I show him this fifty Tuck just gave me."

"That should do it."

"But, don't be spreading rumors about me and my partner Reececup going to jail. I hope we get to, but Tuck says if you guys can get enough evidence and photo proof, we won't push it. I agree, even though this would be a challenge."

Luke spoke, looking over at Tuck, "By the way Tuck, we are hired, we are now awaiting indoctrination as agents of 'Call it Secure'. We already told Ben."

"That is good news, come on over to the table and let's all talk a little," invited Tuck.

Chapter 13
Matt and Luke, on the Job

"Papa Giorgio's, may I help you?" Listening, "sure same as yesterday?" "The large Georgio Special, 2215 N. 23rd Apt 2, right?" Listening, "Sure, and today you get a free 2 liter Coke with that. It will be there in about a half hour, Thanks!"

"Hey Louie, gimme a special. That guy from Apartment two on North 23rd could say, 'gimme the same'. He has ordered the same thing for two months. Heck, even I would get tired of my pizzas every day. But, why am I complaining? They pay, God bless 'em!"

Steve was parked in front of the apartment building. He had picked a spot just a little distance from the entrance on the street. He was waiting for the pizza delivery to arrive. He had the small container of powder in his pocket that he had picked up at the lab. When he saw the car swing in and park in the no parking zone he jumped out in time to intercept the delivery. He was wearing torn jeans and a Pirate's T shirt, dark rimmed clear glasses with curly blonde hair sticking out of a Pirate's baseball cap. A front tooth was also blacked out.

"Hey, that wouldn't happen to be for apartment 2 would it?" Steve asked as he blocked the driver's path.

"Yeah, every day, excuse me, I gotta hurry. He don't tip great, but he does tip if I beat thirty minutes," said the kid.

Steve flashed the fifty dollar bill, "Will this take care of the cost and the tip? I want to deliver it, we are old friends. I want to surprise them, it's been years. Don't ever mention this to them, you might lose your tip next time. Cause I am gonna make them beg!" laughed Steve.

"You got it brother. Thanks, this is the best tip I ever got, come back tomorrow!"

"I might just do that, but I had better get this to Apartment 2 or I will lose my tip!" They both laughed as they turned in different directions.

In the stairwell Steve sat the two liter down and raised the lid on the hot pizza. He sprinkled the powder over the hot cheese. It melted and

173

blended in as promised by the lab boys. He looked at the ticket taped to the box and mentally noted the price of the pizza as he walked to the door. At apartment 2 he rang the bell and yelled, "Pizza".

The door opened, "Well, it's about time, hey what happened to the regular guy?"

"I gotta be honest, I am taking his place cause he needed to see his girl for a couple minutes to patch something up. Natch, he didn't want the boss to know, that will be twelve fifty."

"Well, it is not your lucky day, Jake; it has been thirty three minutes. But here keep the change." The guard handed Steve thirteen dollars.

"Thanks, I gotta run, enjoy the pizza!" Steve said over his shoulder as he headed for the stairs. He was smiling.

****

"It went smooth; here is the thirteen dollars of company funds. When he came to the door the dude was thinking of 'no tip', he wasn't even looking at me. I hope he enjoys the pizza. It did look great. I may try Papa Giorgio's pizza, but without the additional ingredient," said Steve.

Tuck answered, "Well, he will probably enjoy the pizza because the added ingredient is a tasteless concentrate of magnesium citrate. Those guys will be clean enough for a colonoscopy by tomorrow. They could be out two days."

Matt, Luke, Reececup and Steve were in Tuck's working space. They were getting reacquainted. They were also throwing out ideas of how to exchange data in the event Reece and Steve did go inside also. Matt said, "Luke and I will get as much info from the briefing guy as possible during the orientation rounds. I would like to nail these guys good, and fast."

Their conversations were interrupted when Buddy knocked and entered. He was excited about an idea of magnets. "Hey guys, I have been doing some simple tests with magnets. I got the idea from reading about a breakthrough in medical diagnosis. Some medical research guys have been using what they call nuclear magnetic resonance imaging or NMRI. I discovered, with a little trial and error testing, that a small magnet puts off just enough heat that it affects Tuck's heat scan. The magnet shows up red. If we can get a magnet on you guys, we can keep track of you on the heat sensor. Got any ideas?"

"Hey, I have a grandma who swears by her magnetic bracelet. Reckon they would allow us to wear one if we insisted we would 'die' without it?" asked Reececup.

"That would be a possibility if you could convince them that you are so mentally attached to the magnets that you would go into a depression without them. I think their goal is not only to keep these victims incarcerated, but to get good production out of them. Even the crooked mind knows which side of the bread the butter is on. If I was in their place I would let you keep them just to keep the peace. I would bend if I thought that was all you needed to keep you happy."

"I first thought of a magnetic belt buckle for me," Steve added, "but they will probably take my belt, even in minimum security."

"Yeah, we will have to work on that," commented Buddy, "It's something to be thinking about. But, about Matt and Luke, you guys are the priority. I have been updating a little 'cheater' device I used once on a clocking station. It also uses a magnet to attach to the clocking device. It can clock you in at predetermined times, and uses a random number generator to vary the times by up to five minutes so every 'clock in' is different, it produces a realistic record. We can use them on the second time you go in to give you more time to check the doors of interest. I know I don't need repeat this, but never guess or assume a door is not alarmed."

"Any progress on the small transmitter?" asked Steve. "I know you were thinking about trying to install it into a shoe, like Maxwell Smart's shoe phone." Everyone laughed at a reminder of the TV series 'Get Smart' and it's bungling hero, Max.

"We can probably forget that. We will have to wait to find out the daily procedures regarding inmate searches and so forth. Having someone on security, they can plant a transmitter where you can get it. If there are no searches after the check-in strip search, we will be home free. A lot depends on what Matt and Luke uncover. I think they will be able to break the case without having to go through all the gyrations of guaranteeing contact with inmates. That can be iffy and S'gar knows it. So we plan for the worst scenario and hope for the best and easiest."

"Naturally, Steve and I want to go inside, but if the bad guys are caught, that is the goal of the MVA," commented Reece.

"If there is nothing else here I think Luke and I had better head to our little apartment to await the news that we can go to work. We can be at 'Call it Secure' in ten minutes from that address. Wish us luck, I hope this is a full night. I am anxious to see the inside of that place. I might just like my new job."

Everybody wished the guys luck and they headed out the door to the new adventure. The adrenaline was flowing because the event was about to begin. They were the lead-off hitters. Both Matt and Luke had been excellent baseball players. Matt had always been the lead-off hitter on his teams. He was very familiar with watching and waiting to see what the new pitcher had. Now, this was a new game. He had done his hitch in the National Guard with two years active. He loved the excitement of the Army, but this was different. Here he was on the line, again in his life all eyes were on him and, of course, Luke. Luke had picked the USMC. He had done his straight three years, mostly as an MP investigator. Luke's adrenaline was also max. Waiting was the hard part. They were quiet as they headed across town to their new apartment which was compliments of S'gar. It was a nice place. They had the minimum gear here, a couple changes of clothes and their weapons. Snacks were in the refrigerator but now they weren't in the mood to eat. Inside the apartment Luke took some time to do some **Choi Kwang Do exercises.** This was the latest in the martial arts. It was not for competition but for those who expected they would need a defense and offense to save their lives.

Matt was also proficient in martial arts but was doing some pushups to relieve the tension. The room only had two folding chairs and a couple sleeping bags so they had plenty of room.

When the phone rang neither jumped, they took it in stride and let it ring five times. Matt answered, "Yeah?"

"This is Paula at 'Call it Secure,' I am trying to reach either Matt or Luke."

"This is Matt, what can I do for you, good-looking?"

Giggling, "The boss said he knew you guys were anxious to get started so he has moved some folks around and you can start tonight if you are ready?"

"Hey baby, we were born ready! Are you going to be there? What time and where do you want us?" Matt was flirting.

"I'll be right here, but not on the job. You should be here, where you interviewed for the job, at sixteen hundred. Oh, I'm sorry, that is four o'clock. We use military time around here."

"Honey, we know sixteen hundred. We both wore a uniform. I am really looking forward to seeing you again. Look for us fifteen minutes early, all military men know to be early," Matt finished.

"Okay Matt, see you at Sixteen hundred, I mean fifteen forty five. Good b…. wait, wait, I almost forgot. The boss said for you to please leave your weapons at home this time, okay?"

"Sure sweetheart, we wouldn't want to shoot anybody on the first night anyway. See you in a little while. bye!" finished Matt.

"I guess Steve did his job, the boys must be spending some time in the ceramic room. Too bad, but I am glad we are on. I guess we will be in different buildings. I always sort of like the unknown. I think it keeps you sharp," as Matt talked Luke did not vary his exercises but answered with one word grunts. Luke was completing his final routine; both were proficient in **Choi Kwang Do.** Matt knew the routine was coming to an end so he waited to finish.

Matt and Luke were dressed casual, since they had not been issued uniforms yet. They figured the uniforms would come when they got to the office.

Chapter 14
First Night

Matt was making his rounds as ordered. It was the norm in his occupation to be very cautious. As he walked he looked for the possibilities of camera monitors. He did a close check on all doors and mentally logged the type of alarm, if he could decipher it. There were some he made notes to ask the team leaders about back at MVA. Half the shift passed a little too fast.

In the Dormitories Luke was doing the exact same thing. He made it through the female dorm with no incidents. His key gave a 'thirty second free time' with the alarm system, at each entry and departure. On the second floor of the male dorms he ran into his first problem.

Out of the corner of his eye he caught a movement, and saw a figure move back into the shadows. He was about twenty feet out, slowed his pace to prepare for a confrontation.

"Y-you ain't supposed to be here, it is supposed to be someone else," the voice said from the shadows.

"I'm sorry, but the other dude is sick and I am his replacement. Why don't you step out so we can talk man to man," Luke spoke softly and as nonthreatening as he could.

"I-I...g-got a gun you know."

That brought a new view to the game. Now, Luke was wary and moved to the shadows himself and slowly bent and palmed his ankle gun. "We don't want to go there do we? You don't even know me. You might like me if we could talk," Luke said, trying to use a non threatening tone. "What is your plan?"

"Th-the dude was supposed to let me out tonight, I got twenty-five dollars. I was going to get him a hundred more when I got home."

Luke decided to try a guess. "Are you Phil?" asked Luke.

"H-how you know that?"

"Your friend called and asked me to check on you."

"Huh uh, cause I ain't got no friend. G-got you t-there."

"Oh yeah you do, young kid about thirteen. He likes to talk to you. He says you are the only one who listens and he is sure worried about you."

"H-Harold that must be Harold cause we used to talk a lot. No joke he called you?"

"Yes, he did. He wanted me to find out how you are and when are you coming back to talk to him. He really misses you. So why don't you just bend down and put the gun on the floor. We don't want any big trouble, do we?" Luke said as a friend.

"W-what you gonna do if I do? Gonna r-r-report me?"

"No, Phil, this is between you and me, and honestly I hope I can help you. But you cannot mention that we talked, because I have things I must do myself. Can you put the gun down now that we are friends?"

Phil stepped out of the shadows and he had a weapon or something in his hand, it was not threatening but he had not put it down. "Stop, Phil, please. Put the gun down, do it now!"

"A-at's what I am trying to show you," as he raised the weapon up but not pointing it at Luke.

Instantly, Luke raised his gun, leveled it and took the slack out of the trigger, and at the last split second saw that what Phil held was not a gun. Luke lowered his weapon, bent and slowly slipped it back in the snap holster at his ankle. "Hey Phil, my man, you sacred me pretty bad. You should never do that. What you got there?"

"I been playing with the soap bars we have here. Thought I could make a gun. I did, but it won't shoot." He handed Luke the formed soap.

Luke put his arm around Phil and gives him a little squeeze. "Where do you bunk, Phil?"

"I am in 206; I am by myself now, m-my r-room mate left two days back. C-can I go now?"

"I'll make a deal with you. You cannot go outside now, but maybe later next week. Let's go to your room and talk a little, okay?"

"I-I'd like that."

Luke was able to learn a lot from Phil. He was treated okay, but they expected a lot of work from him in the fields. There was always something to do to get crops in or plant or prepare the ground for planting. They were not allowed to eat anything as they picked, it all had to go to the cooks. He had seen a couple boys who were whipped for not obeying the rules. Phil said the reason he thought he needed a gun was that the guard had cheated Tommy and Billy. The guard had promised to let them out for money, but when he got the money he didn't let the boys out. He just kept the money. He told them they would go to a real jail if they told anyone. The guard was the one with the scar on his face. Phil couldn't remember his name.

Judge Black had told Phil if he followed the rules he would get out soon. But he was beginning to think the judge had forgotten because it had been too long. They talked about fifteen minutes. Luke was going to be late clocking in, but he would think of something. He tucked Phil in, and eased back out into the passageway.

The rest of the half shift went too fast for him also. It was time to take a break and find out what Matt had been doing. As he entered the break room Matt spoke, "Hey Bro, I like this, I think it is going to be a great job," as he spoke he rolled his eyes up, Luke glanced over Matt's shoulder to see the video monitor with the red indicator on indicating it was active. So, taking the hint, he answered.

"Yeah Matt, I think it is going to be great. I want to get to a more exciting place though. Something, like a bank or savings and loan. But, to get something on a resume, this is good work."

They got snacks and a drink from the vending machines and continued to talk and put on a show for the monitor. Close to the end of the break Matt said, "I think I will head down the hall to the latrine before time to start back to work," he got up to put his wrappers and napkin in the garbage.

"Good idea, I better leak my lizard before going back too."

Down the hall they both filled each other in. Matt was shocked at the story of Phil. "Wow, what luck to run into someone who's name you knew. And I am glad the sucker did not have a real gun. Wow, my man, you would have started this job with a bang."

They talked a few minutes passing what information they could remember on the spot about the different doors and alarms. Then, they separated to finish the shift for their new employer.

When the van arrived to pick them up, they were in no way tired, but they gave the impression to Bobby of a long shift. Back at the office they grabbed their civilian clothes, said good night and headed for the jeep.   Their destination was of course, MVA headquarters and a debriefing.

Tuck, Buddy, J, Sticky, Ben and S'gar himself were there waiting. Their arrival coincided with that of Steve and Reececup, so the four of them entered the building together and made it to the conference room.

Coffee was brewing and some light cookies. After the informal howdys and handshakes S'gar asked Matt to cover his area.

"My post was the Admin/Production building, number one on our briefing. The place is fair on internal security. I am 99% sure that the security alarms on the LPO doors are the Standard Lock Company's 'Gold Standard'. I have a 75% entry rating on that one, so I am not the one to open it in this case," stated Matt.

"How many doors have the 'Gold Standard', Matt?" That was Tuck. Just as Tuck spoke Buddy flashed the floor plans for the three levels labeled building one.

"I counted four positive here, here, here and here," Matt used the pointer to indicate each one. "There are two possibilities, here and here. I may know more after my next shift which Bobby said is tomorrow. The office in room 106 looks like the admin, payroll and records area. Probably the best bet for information."

"Anything unusual or unexpected, Matt?" asked J.

"Yes, this area here," pointing to the third deck floor plan, "Has a solid wall across the end of the passageway. I have an idea it is an in-house modification. The work is not professionally done and I am sure it violates the present fire code. I could not find a way into the enclosed area from my post. I would have to enter one of the two doors I mentioned that were 'possibly rigged with alarms'. It may be nothing more than a storage room; however, it is a point of interest."

There were a couple more questions and Matt was through. Luke took a position in front of the now displayed floor plans of the dormitories.

"I could see only two doors that I am sure are alarmed. I am assuming a computer terminal hooked to the Admin system next door. That is taking what Bobby said when I asked him. He said the terminal and the black box below it were important." Luke covered the buildings as well as he could and saved his encounter with Phil to the last.

"Now, I will digress," said Luke.   "On my first circuit I encountered what I thought was a big problem. I saw one of the inmates moving in the shadows. He was expecting the regular guard. I knew that because he said, 'you are not supposed to be here'. He then said the words none of us like to hear, 'I got a gun'. Immediately I retrieved my ankle gun and moved into the shadows myself. This will surprise you; it was Phil. Yeah, the kid one of the calls was about in our briefing. He was expecting to be released for twenty five dollars by the guard. He had the gun, or what he said was a gun which was made out of soap, to ensure the guard would let him out. Evidently promising to release an inmate was a pattern, and the guard had a history of reneging on his promises after taking the money."

Luke finished his brief after going into detail of the things Phil had told him.

"Thanks fellows," said S'gar. "That was a successful first shift. And, since Bobby said you guys would be working again tonight, the pizza must have done its job. The floor is open for discussion, what do you think?"

J began the discussion, "First off, I think the guards shaking the inmates down should be dealt with, after we settle the real problem. I do not see them as related. I think one more shift should give us some solid data to go on. Then, as soon as possible, we should put the computer people inside to dump what they have stored in their system's memory."

"I agree and I have a guy who can handle the "Gold Standard". He has a one hundred percent success record. His equipment is the best, because we developed it," said Buddy, "Oh yeah, and knowing the time clock model I can set up my cheaters to clock you in automatically, giving you a little more freedom."

"Well, hopefully we will not need for anyone to go inside, but if we do, communications should be no problem with two guards of our own making the rounds every once in awhile. That will make life much easier," suggested Tuck.

Sticky had been silent. "I know we have looked at this from a lot of angles, but could this just seem a little too simple. I hope we are assuming correctly that this security group has accepted our guards at face value. Our records show they have made no back ground checks, that don't seem normal. Even for a truck driver I do some investigating into his past. I suggest we tread lightly for another night or two."

"But, what if 'Call it Secure' sends these guys someplace else, when Roscoe or whoever gets over this stomach problem. If that is in the cards we need to get inside and out just as soon as possible. Maybe even tomorrow night," said Buddy.

"Both Sticky and Buddy have valid questions. So let's kick around tomorrow night. What do you think? Pros and cons of you guys going in tomorrow night and dumping the computers. Give me some good reasons for and against," S'gar spoke, using the voice of authority.

"It would be great to go in and get the data and exit," said Tuck, "And, what if the job is blown? We have a back up. We might could even fake a break in and leave the guards in the clear, by bumping one on the head after we disable the one who does the 'bust' from wherever. I say, let these guys do half shift investigating full time while Buddy's remotes do the clock work. Then the last half of the shift they let us in so our guys can erase the alarms and let the geeks at the computers."

"Maybe I was too cautious, and even if not, in my opinion, anyone suspecting anything wrong would not expect us to hit this soon. I know I want to be there and ready on standby it there are any problems. But, what is the problem with getting our guys in as soon after the shift starts as possible, this could take longer then we expect. I believe we should have as much back-up as possible to protect our guards and the job. If it is blown, Matt and Luke can disappear and leave this caper completely, I'm in," said Sticky.

"Okay, this will be tight. My Gold Standard man is in New Mexico right now, but I can get him here, I think, let me check," Buddy immediately picked up his phone. Every one waited silently. "Hey, Joey the one, I need you in Pittsburgh later today, check it out and give me a call......(pause).. Yeah, use my mobile number and I need to know ASAP okay? Yeah, ..., Okay, I am waiting, adios."

"It won't be a problem if the airlines have a vacancy and a flight," said Buddy.

"Let's assume for planning purposes that Joey can make it. Who else do we need? I know we need the geek crew. Josh and Raymond are already here, they arrived today. They are setting up in our 'TV Shop' already," Tuck.

"I think Tuck, Buddy and I should be inside also, for support if there are any problems. In this case I don't think we will be in anyone's way. Joey will be there inside also until the job is over because he will have to reset the Gold Standard alarms. That will be added muscle, if needed," said J.

"Uh.. J, I may have given the wrong impression, my man Joey is a beautiful little lady. She is cool and can provide some support in the defense area, she knows karate and two more Japanese words, but she's brains not muscle," laughed Buddy.

"My bad then Buddy, we can always use brains," laughed J.

"Hey Matt, yeah you and Luke, about what time did it appear you were alone. When did the staff go home?" asked Tuck.

"It looked like they made an exit from the admin building just as soon as I was posted," said Matt.

"No one was in the dormitories when I took the post, the man left with a wave just as soon as we walked in," replied Luke.

"Then, using Sticky's idea, which I like, we could have six or seven hours to roam at will and do some full scale investigating. I think there will be room for Corey and Ben inside, their experience would prove invaluable." S'gar smiled and continued, "If the probe is blown, I want all defense squashed immediately. I want this clear. I expect all the MVA troops to march out, not run. Think about this, get some sleep and let's hit it hard about 0800, is that all right?"

There were nods of agreement throughout, as they stretched and headed for the door. Everyone was ready for rest including Matt and Luke. This should give them about five hours sleep. That would be enough sleep during an operation.

Chapter 15
Just another event with the MVA

The smell in the conference room was the standard that had been set from the beginning of the organization, coffee and sticky buns. Excitement was in the air. These guys enjoyed the intrigue and danger; they loved it out on the edge for justice's sake. Everyone was completely sold on the MVA cause. This time it was not just an individual, but it was an organized attempt to make money off the melancholy of the underprivileged. This was their cup of tea, and they would right this wrong.

"Okay folks, let's settle down and find a seat, we have a lot of work to do. First, Buddy, can Joey make it with her equipment?"

"Yes sir, she will board in about thirty minutes. She will be here by thirteen hundred."

"Okay then, we can proceed with ideas you have come up with, let's hear them, starting with J here on my right," concluded S'gar.

"I like the KISS procedure here, 'Keep it Simple'. Matt and Luke take their posts as scheduled. They give a prearranged signal after all the workers have departed and they have placed the clock cheaters. We drive up, go in, the vehicle returns to the TV Repair Shop to await our call. The good guys disarm the alarms and we suck the computers dry. Do some physical file schmoozing, reset the alarms and leave. That is how I see it," said J.

Next was Tuck, "My thoughts too, J. But the signal must be something that cannot be traced. No phone calls, etc. so maybe we give Matt a radio. After Luke secures his area he comes to Matt. When Matt is secure he contacts us on a 'shorty' radio. They open the front door for us and we march in. Hopefully, there will be no after hours visitors. But we will have to cover that possibility."

"We cannot ignore the actual security of the plant. So the guard assigned to the dormitories will have to check his area often to make sure the inmates do not take charge of the asylum. What we do know is that 'Call it Secure' actually has a Corporal of the Guard. They make surprise inspections but they are so infrequent they are hard to predict. Since we know it can happen, we have to plan for that possibility. Everyone will need to have a rabbit hole to climb in if we have a 'red alert'. I would suggest that the place be behind the LPO doors. I don't think anyone will look there during a spot inspection. If a random inspection by the Corporal of the Guard would happen, one thing required is to remove the 'Clock Cheater' from the clocking station on the first level, because it is visible. Left in place, it would be disastrous," injected Sticky.

"I am making some notes. Buddy, are the cheaters hard to install and remove?" asked S'gar.

"Negative, they are held in place by 'solid suck' magnets, and even do the work via magnets, so they are simple to use," answered Buddy.

"Okay, let me make a couple assignments. Ben will be the 'eyes' looking forward, or watching for any incoming vehicle. I estimate about three minutes lead time from the time Ben would see an arrival, until we would have to disappear. Does anyone see anything different?"

"I agree with the time estimate, I believe it is conservative. It will probably be four, but I believe you are on the money with three minutes for practical purposes here," said J. "But Buddy, what is a 'solid suck'?"

"Ha, I thought I would slip that by you. It is a suction cup I designed that will hold like a weld, until its little ear is pulled, then it releases like a little lamb. It is a real sucker!" laughed Buddy, "but I also agree on the time involved."

Everyone else seemed to agree, "Okay, Corey will grab the cheater and disappear. I agree with the idea of everyone having a hidey hole. So that is the first order of business once we get inside, an alternate place to be during the surprise."

"Is that stair well near the offices clear, Matt?"

"Yeah Tuck, it is clear, and would be a great place for someone to duck into. Luke and I have already made ten duplicate keys for the doors just in case there is an emergency and the team gets separated. The keys disarm the alarms at the doors, for thirty seconds; I have only one squeaking door. Luke says he has none. I am carrying some spray lubricant tonight to solve that problem in the admin area."

"I know everyone involved has been notified, but as usual, double check that everyone concerned be either here or at the TV Repair Shop. The techies will be at the shop and the troops who are going to do the grunt work will meet here," said S'gar. "Now get your heads together and put the teams in place on the board so we can see where everyone is going to be as well as you can. We use the buddy system on this event, instead of the number system or roll call. Okay, let's do it," S'gar ended his speech and headed for the coffee pot.

By nine thirty all was in place and Tuck went over the event. Using a laser light he briefed everyone by going through the plan as much in detail as he could. Everyone was listening intently to see if they could find a glitch they had missed.

"What do we do if someone in management decides to drop in for a little catch up work, or some lady forgot her purse?" asked J.

"I have thought of that also," said Ben. "And if the hidey holes don't pass muster and we are discovered, I think we should immobilize the intruder and finish our work, and when we leave take the person back with us. After we have the person we have several options. We can leave him absent with a farewell letter or get his speech pattern down and have one of our 'actors' call in and report him sick. I am sure one of you brilliant types can think of more. Corey could just scare the dude speechless; I have seen him do that."

"Everyone work on that, can anyone see any more possible holes?" pause…. "Okay work on the intruder idea. I want this to be surreptitious but as was mentioned earlier, I don't care if they know there was a break-in; I just do not want them to know who. We also don't want to leave Matt or Luke hung out to dry. I want them to appear to be victims also. I don't care if we have to taser the intruder, cover his eyes, and put on a fake beating of our guys for the intruders benefit. There are a lot of ways; we just want the most convincing."

****

By two in the afternoon all decisions had been made, plans firmed up and Joey had been retrieved from the airport. All was ready to implement 'The Plan'.

Matt and Luke reported for work and were posted as normal. This time there was no accompanied rounds thru the watch area. The best way to deliver the cheaters was using a fake 'DASH' courier. A courier delivery would not raise an eye brow. The service was growing in popularity and being used even by smaller companies. Since DASH uses subcontractors and they use their own vehicles any vehicle could be used with magnetic DASH signs on the doors. Once Matt called in the all secure the fake driver would deliver to the front door a box containing all the cheaters needs for the clocking devices. Each one was labeled and pre programmed. The day seemed to end normally and all the workers had left for home. Luke secured his area and made his rendezvous reporting all secure to Matt. Matt pulled out the radio and made the call. Within a minute there was a yellow Volkswagen with a DASH sign on the door driving up in front of the building.

With no fan fare, Matt signed for and accepted the box and the driver left. Inside they divided the cheaters and proceeded to install them. Meeting again after the installation, Matt made another call. Within minutes a dark limo pulled up and several people got out and entered the building as a door opened. The limo sped off. The 'event' was under way.

Joey, without fan fare, headed to the door which Matt indicated and with Buddy standing by she worked her magic. "Voila," she said as she opened the door, "Now stand back and let me scan the room." In just a few minutes she indicated all was well and said, "Next?"

As Matt led Joey and Buddy and two more tech's away Josh took a man with him and started looking at the computer system. He smiled as he saw one he was very familiar with. He sat the brief case down. The assistant brought over a small black box and they went to work.

Joey opened two more doors with no incidents and the systems were being invaded as planned. For an hour the plan went flawlessly. Luke had made a couple trips to make sure the dormitory side was quiet. So far all was going as planned. Ben was watching the front drive but also monitoring what was being accomplished. The CEO's safe and office computer was also being drained. They had taken a chance to include Steve and Reececup in this trip counting on no one breaking up their party. Those two were versatile. Both are actors, musicians, singers and computer nerds. They had been assigned the CEO's office.

Josh and his assistant were winding down their dump of the financial and physical data. Buddy, J and Sticky had been quietly and proficiently going through the files and photographing any suspicious papers.

"Alert!" spoke Ben loudly. The word was repeated by everyone who heard it, 'ALERT!'

Everyone headed for their assigned hidey hole; Joey immediately reset the lock on the CEO's office yelling secure, and headed for the other doors. She was able to secure them and reset the alarms. She settled in the stair well with Tuck and Buddy. As the front door opened Matt yelled, "Halt, this is security, who goes there?"

"Good job guard, I am Tim Kelly, Lighthouse CEO. I am sure you are familiar with my photo," Kelly said very authoritatively.

"Yes sir, but I would still like to see some ID, if you don't mind. As you know, I am new," said Matt, all business.

The CEO complimented Matt on his alertness and headed for his office. "Shucks, be ready," whispered Tuck. "Steve and Reececup are locked in the CEO's office I am sure. They were supposed to be here and they are not."

Matt had followed the CEO to his door, speaking loudly, "Excuse me sir, but are you going to be here long? I ask because I need to make another round before break time."

The CEO shifted his bag phone to use his right hand to free up the alarm and unlock the door, "Go ahead, Matt, isn't it?"

"Yes sir, I'm Matt, and if I can be of assistance, just call. I'll be back this way in about thirty minutes."

"Well Matt, as CEO, I may very well have a very private meeting in my office. If I do I would appreciate not being interrupted for anything other than a fire, am I clear?"

"Oh, very clear sir. I can guarantee you complete privacy. That is part of my job."

Inside the office, Steve had closed the lap top when he heard the alert. But he had to wait to be sure its monitor lights were out. He then grabbed the external drive he had dumped the laptop data onto and positioned himself behind a heavy drape. They both knew it was too late to leave the room, Joey had signaled the door alarm was reset. Reece was closing the safe and putting the picture back in front of it when the door opened. She barely had time to drop to the floor and squeeze under a credenza. Everyone except Matt and Luke had pulled ski masks over their faces just as soon as they heard the word Alert. The door opened and the CEO flipped on the lights and walked to his desk. Spinning in his high back executive chair he reached for his phone and dialed. Outside the door and to the side, Matt stood, alert. He too assumed Steve and Reececup had been caught inside, but was not positive. He breathed much easier when he heard the phone conversation begin.

"Hey honey, it's me. ......Yeah I know but I had some free time, my wife is shopping and I wanted to hear your voice. I just stopped by the office for a few minutes. Would you like to come over? Got a nice place here as you know."

The conversation went on for a few minutes as the rendezvous was planned. Steve was bracing to attack and secure this dude He knew that Reece was ready. They had worked together so many times they could anticipate what the other was going to do. Just as the conversation was ending, the bag phone rung, "Hold on sweetheart, let me get rid of this caller and I will be right back with you."

"Hello, Tim Kelly here." He spoke and was silent..... "Oh Honey, through already? I expected you to take hours. You know I don't care how long you shop or what you spend." ..silence.

"Oh, sure I understand, I'll pick you up shortly, love you, bye bye." Then to the other phone.... "Hey Baby, I am sorry, that was my battle ax, got to go. I will get back with you......I know, I promised I would tell her and I am going to, it just has to be the right time. Got to get out of here. See you in two days. Bye now, sleep tight." Hanging up the phone he spoke out loud, "Darn it, the best laid plans of mice and men. Any other time she would want to shop all night." He retreated out the door. He closed and locked the door then reset the alarm. He headed toward the door whistling.

"That didn't take long," said Tuck. "Thank goodness."

When Ben signaled that all was clear, Joey rushed down to the CEO's door, cleared the alarm and let Steve and Reececup out. The team assembled in the lobby. "Are we all clear? Did we accomplish the mission?"

Buddy, J and Tuck had already interrogated the team members, Tuck answered, "This part of the mission is accomplished."

The radio in his hand came to life and Ben said, "We are ready." Across the road lights came to life and the limo jumped at the accelerators command. No one talked about the close call. There would be plenty of time at the debriefing. Right now it was time to close this session of the 'event'. As quietly as they came, they departed. Luke looked at Matt and winked, "We just about had some excitement, huh?"

"Yeah, but I am glad we didn't; now we go back to work and finish our shift."

"Spoil sport," laughed Luke, as he headed back to the dormitory area.

****

Inside the limo the cameras were all passed to the techies. The limo pulled into the TV repair shop parking lot and dropped off the technical personnel and equipment.   It then continued on to MTV headquarters. At headquarters coffee and sticky buns were available. It was just approaching ten in the evening and it had already been a good night's work. Everyone grabbed some coffee and a bun and took a seat.

"I know we are going to have to wait a long time for the computer data to be analyzed, but did you learn anything pertinent to our cause by eyeball?" asked S'gar.

"We had one interruption. The CEO came in for a few minutes. Steve or Reececup can tell the rest of us what happened. They were in the CEO's office when he came in, Reece?" said Ben, indicating for Reece to explain what had happened inside the office.

"Well, gentlemen we have a philandering CEO. He came to the office to set up a little tet-a-tet with his lady friend but thank goodness his wife interrupted and called him home. Thank heavens for those bag phones. They can keep a husband on an electronic leash." Everyone laughed, "It was heading to a situation in which we would have had Ben's earlier scenario concerning an intruder. I know Steve was about to nail him for sure. Anyway we were not compromised and our end went well. Oh yes, and the time in the building gave Matt and Luke a chance to show us where they would hide keys and radios for us to use if we must go in."

"It will probably be good to know the number of the lady friend, in case we need some pressure over time," said S'gar, "Can you get that J?"

"I have it," piped in Reece.

"How do you have it, Reececup?" asked J.

"You know I memorize things; he has one of the new digital phones that use tones for numbers. I have memorized them all, here it is." She smiled as she passed the sheet of paper over. "I was within two feet of the phone, right under his feet, I heard it clearly."

"Will miracles never cease, that makes tracing it much simpler, good work, Reece," complimented J.

"The team of Steve and Reece aim to please," she said with a wave of her hand.

191

"Okay, what else do we have?" S'gar brought them back to the business mode.

"We found several pages of numbers in the CEO's safe. I am sure a couple of them are off shore bank account numbers and codes. There are a variety of banks and account numbers. They will show up on the film we used," said Steve.

"There was probably five hundred thousand dollars in one hundred dollar bills in the safe also. I gave Ben one of them off the top and bottom of two stacks as he requested," broke in Reece.

"We will run them for prints to see if we can identify anyone other than the CEO who handled the money," Ben explained.

"By the way," said Steve, passing a small plastic bag over to Ben, "here is the pen he was playing with while he talked. I placed another black pen on the desk when I took that one. It should make it easier to get his prints."

"Great work guys, this should get the ball rolling," stated Ben.

Nothing else of significance was brought up. They knew the heavy stuff would come in after the analysts looked at the computer data and the developed film. They had folks working now, and it would be around the clock until they got some answers. Toward the end of the meeting Matt and Luke came in to report all was well and they were relieved with no hint of question. They were scheduled to work tomorrow night also. Maybe the data would lead them into something they could check out then. The meeting broke up with everyone feeling good about the evenings work.

****

Back at the TV repair shop Josh was reviewing some files. "Hey troops, look at this." Everyone gathered around the monitor. "Give me your first impressions."

"It is a scanned document, with several signatures."

"It looks like an official document. You can make out the embossed notary seal," said another.

"Exactly, it is the original document setting up the Lighthouse Corporation, but friends it is not the one filed with the state and federal government," Josh scrolled down to another document, "This is the one filed for a 'Not For Profit' corporation called 'Lighthouse'. Notice whose signatures are missing from the one submitted to the state?"

"Judge Black and West the cop," they said in unison.

"Yep, that surprises me. I didn't realize West was that big in the players. Now get back to work and find me some good stuff, we want to make a big splash. MVA wants to make these crooks pay and pay dearly," Josh was making notes and also spinning these forms off to a copier tape. The tape would be printed once he had filled it.

Back in the dark room film was being developed and prepared for printing. Before morning, hundreds of prints would be made and labeled. These groups of techies from three investigative organizations were working together for one cause. They were all dedicated to get the bad guys.

These workers were the pride of S'gar. His confidence in four boys many years ago had paid off. J, Tuck, and Buddy had put together some of the best. They were well paid investigators, but to them the pay was secondary, this group wanted justice. The forth boy, Sticky had turned into a man to be reckoned with. From a child he had been a dedicated heavy equipment operator. Childhood circumstances had forced him to grow up faster than the other three. He now owned and operated one of the larger road construction companies in North Carolina. He knew injustice and hated it. Sticky had been named correctly; he was the glue that held things together in the early years.

In all of MVA's years of operation this was the most complex case it had tackled. This was going to reach into many areas, some of them governmental. It was going to entail more people than they had dealt with before. As Josh perused records and documents he was seeing tentacles weaving to other areas of the country. One of his favorite TV programs growing up had a deputy in it whose favorite saying was, 'This is going to be big!' Josh was realizing that this indeed was going to be big.

****

As morning approached, the technical investigators had plenty of paper evidence that could incriminate Judge Black, the CEO, one policeman and a couple other folks. But nothing substantial that would shut down the working system. They had no proof that innocent people had been incarcerated. They had several solid, crooked money trails; everything so far was strictly white collar money crimes. The FBI could use leads and disbar a judge, maybe give him a few years in a nice 'hotel type' prison. They could do the same for several people, but that would not solve the Rehab center problem. It was possible that someone else would take over and operate it as usual. They all sensed something was wrong. Innocent people were being locked up but they found no proof.

Josh called the whole group together, "I am going to have to report to J, Tuck and Buddy this morning. What can I tell them?"

"We need physical evidence," someone said.

"We have names of several inmates we know should not be there, can we approach them?" asked another.

David in the back spoke up, "The ones I checked that I feel were innocent of a crime of any kind have juvy records, and it would hurt their testimony. We need a clean guy. Yeah, what we need is to find 'Mr. Clean' who is locked up."

"I know we have a back up. My friends, Steve and Reececup, are standing by to go inside. Personally, I do not see any other way. We have good stuff here, but we all know it ain't worth a nickel in court," Shorty said.

"I just wanted to hear someone else say it, I feel the same way. The place is as crooked as a barrel of fish hooks, but not a good thread that will unsnarl it. How do the rest of you feel?"

After about fifteen minutes of going back and forth everyone agreed, it looks like someone will have to go inside to get the physical evidence. It must be documented. By documenting it, it could possibly give exposure to MVA. "Well troops, you have done good, get to the motel and get a bath and some sleep. I am going to headquarters and give what we have. We have nothing to be ashamed of; no one could have done better than you have done. Thanks again."

All the evidence had been neatly packaged and a couple guys carried it out for Josh, as they headed for some well deserved rest. Josh drove a cherry nineteen fifty nine Ford Fairlane 500. With the data safely in the trunk, he fired up the 332 cubic inch engine and headed to headquarters to make his report. He loved driving his Fairlane. It was Turquoise and white with stainless steel fender skirts. The 332 Cube engine developed 235 horses, all the power he ever wanted. He was reporting as a techie, but he knew what he reported would eventually bring some degree of danger to the two who would undoubtedly go undercover inside a crooked prison that fronted as a rehab center..

194

Chapter 16
Plan B

Josh made his presentation to the MVA leaders. He put it to them straight, the only way he knew. With the main data being passed around everyone had questions. Josh fielded the questions like a battle commander, clear, precise and to the point. For an hour Josh made his presentation and fielded questions. The coverage was very thorough. Josh informed them that the team would be back on the job around fifteen hundred today. They would tweak what they have and follow all the paths of money with a flow chart. Using their legal expert, along with Dallas, MVA's top legal mind, they would try to determine what laws were broken and the possible penalties.

"By tonight we should know the amounts in each off-shore account and what names are attached. I am not saying it is straight forward, but with programs we have, and some we are developing, we can be pretty precise. Some of the stuff we won't have to decipher, thanks to the contents of the safe. I have already recognized several account numbers and code words required, within the data Steve and Reece retrieved from the safe," he paused and smiled. "About last night, you guys know I am not a second story man. I am comfortable in an office environment. Last night was exciting to me but I have to tell you, when I heard Ben call 'alert', I was shook. I have been thinking a lot since then. If I had been locked in the office like Steve and Reece were, I'm not sure how I would have handled it," he finished his statement, laughing along with everyone else as he warmed his coffee and took a seat.

"So, it is plain that you guys from the technical side think we need to have more physical data; what about the rest of you? Let's go around the table." S'gar indicated Ben should begin.

"Well Boss, it is pretty clear we can give the FBI enough to start with, and they can get some real convictions. But the major charges would concern financial misappropriations. I am in agreement with Josh and his technical team; with what we have, we cannot prove anyone was intentionally incarcerated for money. What I believe you and MVA want is a modern day charge of slavery. That is what I see it as. So, it seems to me we had better revise our plan to record and document our guys who are going in. We want it plain that they are not indigent and that they have broken no laws. It must be plain if they are sentenced or 'held to await some decision', like that order by the judge, is inappropriate. It must be obvious to the most casual observer that they do not deserve it by any stretch of the imagination." Ben nodded to Buddy who was beside him.

"I have to agree with Ben's view of the situation. In the beginning we discussed having a friendly face inform the good Officer West of two youngsters who needed some guidance. At that time we wanted help without the friendly face getting involved or knowing what is actually going down. Now, it seems we need him on our team, and willing to testify for the FBI when the time comes. I think we want him to know he is being filmed and recorded. That may take some doing," warned Buddy.

"Woody was my idea," said Tuck. "Let me contact him later today and set up a time to talk. I do think the complexion of the situation has changed. We will need Woody to ensure the kids meet with West. I don't know how he will like it, but if it comes down to it, would you like to take on a temporary hire?"

S'gar responded to the question, "Tuck, I will accept your opinion on that. Of course, if he is not coming on board full time, I wouldn't want him to know the entire MVA inner workings, but use your discretion. This is very important. I don't want to close down the MVA, but I would sacrifice it to stop slavery."

Unusual for Reece, she stood and getting everyone's attention she spoke, "Steve and I have discussed this at length. We want to go inside. We know that there were strict requirements in the beginning for our protection. I want to go in, Steve shares that desire. We want to get the goods on this group; the risk is secondary, in our opinion." Steve was nodding his agreement.

"I think we can handle the cover now that we have two guys inside. Of course, we do not know if their assignments will stay as is," said J.

"Maybe I have an in there, Paula slipped me her phone number," said Luke, Matt's head snapped around and their eyes locked, "Don't look at me like that, Bro, I know you thought you had the inside track, but she apparently likes me, after all I am the coolest."

"Nah she must like her men flaky bro," laughed Matt, "But you may have an idea, call her and take her out, then whisper some sweet nothings in her ear. Hey, y'all, he did that to a girl in Denver once, talked sugar in her ear until her nose ran Karo Syrup."

"Jealousy doesn't look good on you, brother!" smiled Luke, "But I will suffer thru an evening with sweet Paula, maybe I can do some good with our schedule. I'll tell her you are scared to do the big jobs like a bank, ha!"

"Okay kids, back to business. Follow up on that Luke; see if you can insure a fairly permanent setup. In the mean time we can see about getting the other guys hired by another security outfit, if Luke's plan doesn't work," said Ben.

"I know you all need to get some sleep, but there is one more thing, Josh. Then you can go get some rest. If you can set it up I want you to be ready, on a moment's notice, to drain every off-shore account and transfer them to these numbers. The codes are attached. Now get some rest," S'gar handed Josh the list and he said his goodbyes and headed out the door.

The conversations continued, some assignments were made and the meeting broke up. "Hey Buddy, do you have your super wheels up here?"

"No Luke, I flew up, why?"

"Oh, I thought if I had the super Mustang I could really impress Paula!" said Luke. "Josh won't let anyone borrow his Fairlane." Buddy's purple mustang was well known within this group. It had more than once gotten one of the troops out of jeopardy, either by a flash get away or a split second arrival. It truly was a piece of work; it had everything in the book, plus some, done to the engine and the chassis. To the average observer, it looked like a cherry antique except for the oversize tires.

"Well, for the cause of young love and the MVA I would loan it out, but since it is not here, your uncle's limo probably would impress her," suggested Buddy as they all headed in different directions. Luke gave Buddy the thumbs-up sign.

Tuck went immediately to a phone to call Woody.

197

****

"Is this Anna?" asked Tuck on the phone.

"Yes it is. Who is calling please?"

"Anna, this is Tuck, I worked with Woody for a short time. I was in your home once a few years ago. We had a jam session and I entertained your son Jonathan who was sick that night. I found out he did not want to be called Johnny."

"Oh sure, Tuck now I remember, that was a long time ago. Jonathan still feels that way about his name. So, you left the agency, I heard. You do know Woody retired don't you? So what can I do for you?" asked Anna.

"I need to see Woody as soon as I can about a possible job, could you get me in contact with him?"

"Not today, he is on the street and is not carrying his phone. How about tonight, he is having our pastor and a couple guys from our church come over for a Jam session. It would be like old times and I know he would love to see you. Would that work?" she asked.

"Yes, it sure would. I'll bring my axe over and see if he is as good as he used to be," laughed Tuck.

"I don't know how long it has been since you saw Woody, but don't be shocked. He has lost a little hair and is gaining that spare tire you guys used to joke about. What about seven, he is cooking on the patio as usual, so bring your appetite. Do you have our address? Forget I asked. You are from the group of people who know everything just like Woody," she laughed, "See you tonight, Woody will be thrilled."

'I hope so' Tuck thought, then said, "Looking forward to it. Bye now."

****

Tuck approached the door of a nice ranch style house and rang the doorbell; it was about ten 'til seven. The door opened and there stood Woody, older, balder and a little heaver, but no mistaking it was Woody. Tuck spoke, "I heard there were some pretty good pickers here tonight, I just wanted to see how good," he said, smiling.

Woody stepped onto the porch and smothered Tuck in a bear hug, "Man, you are a sight for sore eyes. So, the mystery is here, now, maybe I will learn the truth of your quick departure from the agency. Come on in and meet the guys," Woody carefully took the guitar Tuck held and ushered him into the living room where everyone was already set up. "Let me have your attention, this is Tuck, he can't pick worth a nickel but he is here to learn. Tuck, there is Stan, next is Will, and our pastor, Mixon." Everyone greeted each other and made a seat for Tuck to crash and pick.

"I don't mean to intrude, but I am not in Pittsburgh often and this is a chance I did not want to miss. I have been hearing rumors that Woody needed a few picking pointers, so here I am. Thanks for allowing me in the group on short notice."

Anna came out of the kitchen to hug Tuck and welcome him, "I will be departing in a few, and leaving the house to you monsters. Don't tear it up!" she laughed. "I am headed out with Ora, Mixon's wife, and some ladies from the church. We are going to do something nice, while you guys sit here and contaminate our pastor. Have a good time. If you are still here I will see you later this evening. If not, I hope it won't be as long before the next visit. It is great to see you, Tuck."

Mixon started the session off with a Chet Atkins number, 'Guitar Blues'. Seconds later everyone was with him. To Tucks surprise, he lost himself in the picking and singing. They did gospel, hillbilly, rockabilly and blue grass. The group was good and Woody was as good as he ever was, maybe better. It is always a challenge to notice good moves by a new picker and try to use it in your own repertoire. Most pickers and musicians will share their talents. This group was all good. They took a break and Woody invited them into the kitchen, where he and Anna had set up a buffet. The food was delicious. Tuck hadn't had home cooking in a couple weeks; Rose was a great cook, having learned from the best, her mother.

Over to the side, Woody asked, "Okay Tuck, I know you didn't come here to pick and grin. What is up?"

"You are right of course Woody, it is a job. Do you mind if I stick around after everyone leaves and we will discuss it, okay?"

"Sure I'm open-minded, but it better be more than following some drunk to a rendezvous. Sure we can talk later, as a matter of fact I will be glad to," Woodrow was smiling.

Things were a good bit slower after the meal; they even went back to the old 'Shipboard' songs Woody loved so much. They generated sea stories by Woody and Stan who was also an old swabbie. It didn't take long for Woody to lead out with, 'When the big ship left Manila sailing proudly o're the sea, the deep blue sea....'.

The pastor was a military man himself. Mixon had been an Army Chaplain and had done a good bit of his time in 'Nam'. Some good, some bad, but he considered all the time 'for the good'. The music was really fun and the fellowship great. Tuck found himself dreading for it to end. Around nine-thirty everyone was packing up, saying good night and complimenting each other on the good music. Mixon was the last to leave. "Woody, if there is anything you need, please do not hesitate to call." Turning to Tuck, "Nice meeting you Tuck, I really enjoyed the evening. Try to get with us again. Come by our church if you stay in the area. Good night to you both. I sense you have business to discuss. Take care and God Bless."

"Come on in the kitchen while I straighten up some." In the kitchen, they both started clearing up the mess and filling the dishwasher. As they did, Tuck hit the high spots with Woody. He could not read Woody's feelings and felt like he was sort of shooting in the dark. After about twenty minutes the kitchen looked livable. Woody smiled, "Okay Tuck, grab a cup and let's get down to business out back, I am ready to get serious."

"Woody, the group I work for is on the edge of legal, but very patriotic and pro law enforcement. You have been a straight arrow, by the book, but can you remember a time when you wanted to bend the rules? When you were up against a case where you knew without a shadow of a doubt you were right, but because the rules were skewed toward the crook, he was going to walk?"

"Sure Tuck, many times, but I was FBI and I had a list of parameters, hard and fast, and I followed them, so?"

"You ain't gonna make this easy, are you?"

"Nope, I am sure you did not expect me to."

"You are right, before we go any further, what are you doing now? Are you full time?" asked Tuck.

"They want it full time, and are pushing me. Tuck, I am a free agent for the Pittsburgh area. I draw about half pay, work about 4-6 hours a day. I am looking for signs of federal crimes. I follow up on leads given to the area command. Most is strictly 'hunt and peck' or 'Easter Egg'. I have done some good but I am beginning to feel sorta useless. As a matter of fact, I am at the point where I really want to fish. Know what I mean?"

"Good, how much trouble is it for you to resign this free agent deal?"

"Well, since a week ago they brought another man in who retired. The boss indicated all he needed was a phone call from me to terminate. Is that simple enough?"

"Okay, let me put it this way. If you are seriously ready to retire and fish, I think I have a way you can leave with a big bonus and a feeling of accomplishment." For the next hour Tuck laid out what was happening and what was needed. He also asked Woody's advice on what approach could be used to steer West to the kids. Woody seemed excited to be included. He was for crushing a crooked judge. Of course, he knew West casually and had heard of Black. He had heard no information or had there been any hints on the streets of anything untoward about the two. They agreed to meet at noon the next day to work out an agreement if, after a night of hashing it over, Woody still wanted in.

Then the conversation went on to the lighter side. Joking, Woody wanted to know about Tuck's fast disappearance from the FBI. Tuck told him exactly what happened. Telling Woody he was as shocked an anyone else, he had enjoyed his schools and was very satisfied with assignments. Then slam, the door closed. All part of showing how much leverage MVA or really S'gar had with the government. Tuck even told about Rags and their first encounter with him. Woody loved the story, "It is almost like a fairy tale, I love it," laughed Woody. "I like what I hear Tuck, but you know me, I need to sleep on it. But, I will be there for the meeting. Glad you came over and, right now, I think I am glad you brought this offer."

They finished their third cup and said good night. As Tuck was leaving he met Anna Mae coming in. They spent a few more minutes passing news and Tuck left.

After Tuck was gone Anna Mae eased up to Woody, imitating the famous movie actress, Marlene D, "Okay, this strange man coming for a visit was no accident, big boy, tell me everything. You know I am very curious, I will find out, I have my ways" she purred.

"No more, I can take no more. I will tell everything, he reached for her, swung her around and kissed her." He stopped, held her at arm's length and smiled, "How would you like to spend a lot of time fishing at our little cabin up on the Lake?"

"You mean it Woody, you think you could actually settle down and be a real retiree?" she asked, hopefully.

"Well, let me tell you a story," and Woody laid it out as much as his feelings and knowledge of security would allow him to. They had sat on the couch during the telling. They discussed the possibilities and the time frames Tuck had laid out.

Anna spoke, "I have lived with you as a policeman and as an FBI agent. There have been times when you were gone and the phone rang I was afraid to answer it. I knew that at any given time some idiot, drunk or bad guy could take your life. I was a little more relaxed here in the Pit, but I know it can happen here. I think it is time to quit. Be honest with me, will there be any danger? I mean truthfully Woody, I deserve it. I have friends, wives of policemen, who have buried their men and never got to fish. I want us to fish, Woody."

"I will know more tomorrow, honey. Right now, I don't see any life threatening circumstances. The situation is dirty but honestly I don't see any blood, mine or anyone else's. I will honor your thoughts when I make my decision tomorrow. Honey, you know I want to fish with you in upstate New York and I want to go south and fish Lake Okeechobee with you. I want us to enjoy getting old together and have the money to do it with. Trust me, Okay?"

"Purrrrrrr, I always do, big man. Let's go up and continue this interrogation. I will get out the hand cuffs and rubber hose!"

"Anything but that!" Woody laughed, as he pulled her off the couch for a big bed time kiss.

Chapter 17
A new player

Tuck returned to MVA headquarters to discuss his meeting with Woody. He informed everyone of the coming meeting and shared his opinion, he was optimistic but 'guarded' in his hopes Woody would come on board. "There is a lot of pressure on a man to give up a secure job with the FBI, even if it is part time," said Tuck. "It would be too much of a conflict of interest for him to be working for the MVA and the FBI," he laughed, "too much alphabet soup is dangerous to a person."

"Why don't we go with the idea he is coming aboard," said Steve. "How do you want us dressed and give us an idea of how you see our characters. We have our own ideas. Let me throw this out. We will have about a hundred fifty dollars between us. Reece will carry most of the money; say a hundred-ten dollars. I have the rest in small bills. She will be pretty bright and I will be a little slow, and we need names."

J took over, "You have the right idea. We have decided on a couple of names. We feel you should be simply Jill and James Jackson. You are from a large family in Jackson County, West Virginia. You lived in the back country on Sandy creek. With thirteen kids at home, you wanted to move to a city, work and save money for the family. The name Jackson is used because there are a lot of Jacksons in Jackson County. Here are your ID's; they are worn library cards from the 'Public Library in Ripley. Ripley is the county seat. Both of you will have some old receipts in your pockets from towns on the way to Pittsburgh. You will arrive on the bus, so hold onto your stubs. Your tickets will originate in West Virginia, but you will get aboard over in Green Tree. Here are the dossiers we have put together. Look them over in the next couple days and memorize the basics. You will wing-it a lot after you get into character, we all know that," concluded J.

"Hopefully, Woody will say yes and we can get Plan B into action," said S'gar. "I would like to have you guys 'arrive by bus' in a couple days. I think everything has been laid out and ready. Buddy has the small radio transmitters ready for the guards to plant on their next shift. There will also be strong magnets to replace any you have lost by searches. As you will recall the magnets are to keep us abreast of where you are in the buildings. We hope to have good communications between the members of MVA. I have decided on one 'last resort' effort, which I think I can live with. I want at least six of our 'aggressive' men at all times at the TV Repair shop. Steve and Reece should familiarize themselves with the fire alarms. In an emergency, one or both should set off the alarms. When we get that warning our troops are to go immediately and secure the building. One well dressed man or woman will meet the first responders to apologize and explain profusely that an inmate has triggered the alarm. A call should be made to 911 immediately to say the same thing. By the time any emergency vehicle arrives, I want MVA to own that building and our people. Using stun grenades, flash bangs, electronic screams anything to preserve our troops. I think you get the idea. Using the SEAL philosophy, we leave no one behind."

"I like that idea, boss. I have one more idea to add. I think it would be an advantage for our intel analysis at the TV Repair shop to know where our guards are at all times. I think our guards should carry magnets to let us know where they are. The problem in my mind is, how can we separate the signals, guard and inmate? Let's put that in effect on their next shift to give the watchers something to get familiar with," added Sticky. "Does that make sense?"

"Makes perfect sense and for a neophyte, that is getting pretty good," said Buddy. "I think we can differentiate between the four by magnetic strength. We give the stronger magnets to the inmates, since they are the most vulnerable; we must know where they are at all times."

"I ain't been around you guys all this time without picking up something. I knew about the stronger magnetic strength, just didn't want to steal your thunder. One of these days I will let you guys learn some real work and put you on a loader, when I think it is safe," laughed Sticky.

Reece and Steve left to find another space to read and plan their own important part of this plan. The others discussed the different possibilities then took off before one AM.

****

Woody picked today's meeting place. They were going to meet at the 'Dirty O', the local slang name for the 'Original Hot Dog Shop'. Woody had said it is great food, delicious fries but the place lives up to its name, it is dirty. So, use the head before you get there, their head is in the basement and it is filthy. It's safer to use the alley if you have to. Woody could never escape the old navy term head for the toilet. The reason he gave for meeting there was that West was known to hate the place and there was no way they would accidentally run into him. Lots of Pitt students gathered at the Dirty O. It was a big hang out during the day.

Woody was there and had already ordered chili dogs and fries. Woody read Tuck's mind, laughed and said, "Hey, at least I ordered diet drinks!"

"Hey, Woody my man, I never eat a large order of fries," said Tuck, as they shook hands.

"Son, you ain't from here I can tell. This IS the small size fries, you can't carry the large."

Tuck sat and they began to devour a great looking chili dog and it was good too. "These fries are great, what do they do to them?"

"They cut them fresh, and fry them twice, I don't know what that does to them but they are the best in Pittsburgh and we are the French fry capitol of the world, I think," answered Woody.

Tuck finished his dog, leaned back to look at the crowd. There were suits, jeans, overalls, dresses and baggy pants all sitting side by side devouring tons of French fries and dogs. He took a sip of his soda, "So, what do you think, Woody?"

"I think they out done themselves on the fries again," he paused to see if Tuck would rise to the bait, which did not happen. "Oh, you mean about this little job you mentioned?"

"Yeah, but I do appreciate you introducing me to one of Pitt's more famous places. You really do sorta forget the dirt, when eating the good food."

"I thought you could appreciate it. But yes, Tuck I called the office this morning, they are processing my papers as we speak. I am unemployed. So I guess you can figure Anna Mae is going to allow me to work with you, but for a short while, good pay, right?"

"Great to hear it Woody and about the pay, to be honest we were hoping for pro bono," Tuck could not do it. He wanted to pull Woody's leg but just couldn't. "Nah, friend Woody, I have never heard anyone complain about S'gar's pay. You will be very well rewarded. If you want to give me a figure, I will be glad to present it."

"I won't do that, Tuck. But a guy has to be curious how your association earns its' living just doing good?" Woody finished off his chili dog and took a swig of his cola. "I just want to know something about how you operate, financially."

"To start with, our founder, who is called S'gar, is a billionaire. The home offices of his holdings are here in Pittsburgh. He operates a school for special needs of governments around the world. Many FBI agents, including myself, have attended. The fees are high, because he produces winners. Also, we from law enforcement have always laughed at the statement 'that crime does not pay', because we knew for some it does. Well, he has determined if he finds a criminal that has earned money from crime, and we can, we borrow that money permanently. It is taken as a gift that is then used to fight crime somewhere else."

"I think I would like to meet this guy," said Woody, as he finished the last of his fries.

"Follow me, my good man, and you will do just that. How did you get here by the way?"

"I took the Port Authority bus like every good Pittsburgh citizen should."

"Good, lets walk a block," and Tuck lead the way out to the sidewalk and headed on up Forbes toward Bigelow Boulevard. The limo was parked in a no parking zone with Corey, in full uniform, standing beside it. As they approached, he opened the door and Tuck ushered Woody inside as Corey closed the door quietly and moved efficiently to the driver's seat. Inside, Ben was waiting.

Tuck introduced the two and Ben said to Corey, "Hey bro, head toward headquarters," then turning to Woody, "Good to meet you, I haven't had a chance to get anyone to the Dirty O. Glad you introduced Tuck to it."

"My pleasure, I see you guys go first class. I feel honored."

"It is we that are honored, Woodrow. We need you and are looking forward to working together. I am assuming we are, since you are here."

"That is correct, Ben. As I told Tuck I tendered my resignation this morning, I am unemployed."

"Good, our people will solve the unemployment bit pretty soon and you should not miss a payday, that is eleven hundred fifty nine fifty a week, isn't it?"

"Pretty well informed, I see. Yeah, you are right. But, as you know, part of that is my agency retainer."

"We are aware of that, and that will continue. We intend to pay you two thousand a week above your retainer. The organization power has told me to ask you if thirty weeks pay in advance would be sufficient. We are hoping it will be only a few weeks, but he likes to be on the safe side. From our research and Tuck's opinion, you trust your wife completely, so on that knowledge we have made the following arrangements. The money will be placed in an account in Anna Mae's name in upstate New York, same county of your cabin. She will inherit sixty thousand dollars; it will be tax free, from a long lost relative who loved her. You, Woody, in addition to that, will be legally salaried at three hundred dollars a week, taxable, for consultant work, if that is all agreeable with you?"

"Ben, you seem like a nice guy, I know Tuck ain't. But, of course, this is a sweetheart deal; I promised Anna Mae that there would be little danger. I was going by what Tuck told me last night. This sounds like a lot more than that. Am I right?"

"Woody, S'gar places a high premium on justice. The cost is immaterial to him. Last night he made the statement he would sacrifice the entire organization, if it took it, to sink this injustice. We will be at the office in a minute and you will get the whole story. We know you, maybe not as well as you know yourself, but we know you will walk if we have lied to you, money or no money. We have considered that."

The meeting with S'gar was a success. Woody was comfortable within minutes. He also fell victim to sticky buns and coffee. He had what sounded like the perfect way to drop the info about the two kids. MVA has already followed West and knew his habits. Woody also knew his normal haunts.

The time schedule for the arrival of Reececup and Steve was now tomorrow, that was earlier than had been planned. Being here tomorrow would give them time to spend one night on the street, and a chance to make some inquires for employment before Woody would 'accidently' meet them the following morning. Woody could bump into West later in the day.

S'gar called a meeting of all the players, including the technical troops. By sixteen hundred everyone was apprised of the locations and approximate times of the meetings. Josh assured the group they had the long range mikes to pick up the voices and two positions for the cameras. The first meeting would be covered by a cleaning truck, the second would be by a utility van and the same cleaning truck.

By way of information, Luke informed everyone that his date had gone well. After the cat calls and rude comments, he explained that they were semi permanent at the 'crazy house'. However, he added, "Now I have a few follow-up dates to endure." That generated more comments and laughing. Luke took it on the chin, "Okay, that is enough, so it is a tough job, but someone has to do it." He laughed with everyone else. Woody was last to laugh. Tuck had just explained the situation.

Things were coming fast now; this happened fairly often with the MVA 'events'. S'gar did not like dragging his feet and everyone who worked for the MVA liked it that way. They were all prepared and getting tighter by the minute. They all knew their jobs and departed to get ready for the main event. They were going to put their people on the line to rectify an injustice.

Corey came over to Tuck, "You guys want a ride? I have plenty of time to take Woody home. You can ride and I will drop you at your place."

"That would be cool, let me impress Anna Mae with my new found employment," they all laughed and headed for the door. Time was moving on.

Chapter 18
Time to Rock and Roll

Reece and Steve boarded the bus in Green Tree. Half the seats were empty and no one paid any attention to them. They found sets with no one in front or behind them so they could talk more freely. They were wired (mentally speaking) and ready for the Event to unfold. Both of them knew there would be times they would have to improvise, they lived for that part. "The idea of having you a little thick in the head will cover some mistakes," commented Reece.

"Okay, but don't make me too empty," laughed Steve.

"I don't know exactly how Woody plans to do it, but he said there was always a plain clothes guy just outside the bus station. He wants to make contact with us near him thinking that guy may contact West also. He figured if this scam was paying off West would have feelers out. It would be good to have more than one input to West. This whole thing depends on West turning us over to the judge," said Reece.

"I would sure be disappointed if I am acting dumb for nothing," laughed Steve.

They got off the bus. Steve was carrying one battered small suitcase. They played the parts, looking around the big terminal and then walked out on the street. They started looking around at the buildings and traffic like it was the first time they had seen the inside of a city before. Then, on cue, they headed west on Main Street, at a snail's pace. They were being jostled by others in a hurry. Steve felt the attempt of the light touch of a pick-pocket. He appeared ignorant and easily foiled the attempt. Within minutes Woody made his appearance.

"Hey kids," he called from a few feet away, getting the attention of some of the folks on the sidewalk. "Do you need any help? I see you are new to Pittsburgh."

"How you know that?" asked Steve.

"Ah, well, it was just a wild guess. I might be able to help. I'm Woody," and he stuck out his hand to Steve.

"Good to meet you sir, I am James Jackson, this is my sister Jill Jackson. We came up here to get a job and get rich."

"You will have to excuse James, Mr. Woody. He is a little impulsive. We have come to get jobs and earn enough to send some back home to help our family. If you are a policeman, we are not bums, we have money and are looking for work," said Reece.

"Well, I am not a local policeman but I am recently retired from law enforcement. If you are looking for a place to stay for the night try the Catholic Home on Ninth St. Continue on Main and make a right on Ninth. They will help you get a job or point you in the right direction. And about the money, I wouldn't tell anyone too much about it, they may want it more than you."

"I doubt that," said Reece, "We have about a hundred fifty between us and we are keeping it. Steve here is slow with figures, but not with his fists."

"A hundred fifty dollars?" repeating the figure, Woody continued, "That is a lot of money over in Sharpsburg, so be real careful." Woody was relieved to see a vagrant moving closer looking uninterested, but Woody recognized the guy, they were now connected.

"Sharpsburg? I thought we were in Pittsburgh?"

"That you are missy, but Sharpsburg is the area you will be in. So, take it easy. You might ask about work in the hotels as you walk that way. You guys take care. Remember, right on Ninth!" Woody called to them.

"Thank you Mr. Woody, we will," Reece and Steve headed west on Main.

Walking the opposite direction Woody noticed the vagrant heading to the bank of pay phones outside the bus station, 'homerun, I hope' thought Woody. He got in and headed his car to West's normal haunt on East Main. He parked in a NO Park Zone, slipped his FBI card on the dash and headed for Aspinwall's 'Five Guys'. Just as he arrived West actually about ran into him.

"Whoa Mr. West," laughed Woody, "Remember me? Woody, recently of the FBI, we have talked a few times."

"Sure Woody, what are you doing in these parts?"

"Looking for a good burger, but since I ran into you I thought you might want to keep an eye on two young kids that just arrived from West Virginia. They seem too innocent for this part of town. I suggested they head for The Catholic Bed & Breakfast on Ninth. They are looking for work and they say they have money, so they shouldn't be a problem. Probably good for you to know since it is your turf. Look young, one not too bright."

"We get that all the time, Woody. They will be here until their money runs out then go back home. They usually just want to see the big city lights. But Thanks. I gotta run, enjoy your burger." West took off like a man on a mission.

Woody stepped inside, found the pay phone and dialed Ben's mobile phone.

"Yes?" was all Woody heard.

"Heads up, I would bet fifty bucks West is headed toward the kids right now. He already knew about them I am sure."

Ben said, "Got it, head to your spot on Ninth St. Just stay in your car and watch as planned. Use the Pub if it gives you a clearer view."

****

Ben quickly notified every one of the head's up, letting the recording crew know they might have to reposition. Then, he sent one crew in a van to Main Street to look for Steve and Reece. This wrinkle may be rough to smooth out. The plans were for Steve and Reece to be at the sidewalk pizza place before West caught up with them.

On impulse, he told Corey to head east on Main looking for the two. Immediately, Corey did an expert U-turn in traffic. They spotted the two walking just west of the Blue Beltway. Corey did another slick U-turn and Ben popped the door open to the surprise of the street crowd who watched as Steve and Reece wasted no time jumping in. Immediately Corey hit the gas and was back in traffic. The pickup was done in less than ten seconds.

Steve and Reece were trained in this situation not to waste time asking questions, they knew the explanation was coming. Quickly, Ben laid it out. They were just getting a ride to the 'set' area for the show to begin. Corey told Ben that the van crew he dispatched had read what was happening and returned. Corey drove the back streets to Church and Clay. At the corner he stopped and looking into the back of the limo he said, "You are right behind the pizza place. Walk one short block west and you are there. They have great pizza by the way, get the special. Good luck, we better split with this limo. It wouldn't look good for two homeless kids to be seen in a limo." He laughed.

As they drove off Ben thought to himself, one wrinkle ironed out. This is early in the game to have a problem. I just hope that is no indication of how this whole 'event' is going to go.

****

Woody was stationed as an observer. He was to be a witness to the fact that West did pick up the two, if it did happen. From his window seat in the local pub, across the street, he sipped a diet drink. He was surprised to see Steve and Reece walk out of the side street and walk up and order at the window. He thought, 'how in heck did they get here this soon? Did they run? Slick outfit the MVA. They have made sure West talks to the kids live and on the air. Someone did some quick improvising'.

West had driven up Main Street looking for the two. Thinking he had missed them he turned up Ninth to circle back, 'wh-what the heck? That must be them, right clothes and one beat up bag. Come to papa my new fish.' He turned the corner and parked in a NO Parking Zone. Got out and walked back to the pizzeria. He took his time looking them over trying to guess their ages. Girl is around seventeen to nineteen, boy could be thirteen to nineteen can't tell by his looks and his clothes. He got a drink and walked to their table on the sidewalk. "You are new in town, mind if I join you?"

"We weren't expecting company, could you take another table please?" said Reece, sounding a little nervous.

"No, I will sit here; you see I am Officer West of the Pittsburgh Police. You are on my turf and I like to know who is here and why, just a rule of mine, you understand," as he sat down and took a piece of their pizza.

"We ain't broke no laws and we come to get some work," said Steve.

"Yeah, and what would you be called, and what work can you do?"

"I'm James Jackson that is my big sister Jill. We can do about anything. I can dig, plow, weed and cut wood; just anything."

"And you, young lady, do you plow too?"

"No need for sarcasm Officer West. I can cook, wash clothes, clean and prepare hotel rooms. And yes, I can also garden. As my brother said, we are not breaking any laws. We are not vagrants; we paid for the food and will pay for tonight's lodgings. Now is there any reason we cannot stay in this big city?"

"No, Miss Jill Jackson, there is no reason you cannot stay. Please forgive an old man for being suspicious. We have some bad folks come into our town, and I can see that the Jackson's are not any of those. But, just to satisfy my professional curiosity how much money do you carry into town and where did you come from? You don't have to answer, and I cannot force you to. I just want to keep you and my area safe. The more information I have the better job I can do."

"Of course, we understand sir. We are from Jackson County, West Virginia. We have ID on us and close to a hundred and fifty dollars. We plan to go next door to get a place for the night, if that is all right with you," said Reece, softening.

"I have to ask this, how old are you two?"

"I am twenty two and Steve is twenty," said Reece, defiantly.

"More like seventeen and fifteen would be my guess, but whatever you say is fine."

"It is certainly all right with me. And I will take the call in the morning when you call in to report someone molested you, hurt your brother and took your money." West got up as if to leave.

"Wh-what do you mean by that?"

"You have landed in the worst section of Pittsburgh. I get calls every day to that exact place. Oh, you would be safe if you were sixty years old, drunk and broke. But, you are young and beautiful and have some money. You won't last three hours in there."

"Th-then just what can we do?" asked Steve who had been staring intently at West, convincingly taking everything in.

"I can take you to a place down town; we will have to go by the station first to set it up. But I think I can get you in before it is filled since this is early. And it won't cost you a thing for the night. How does that sound?"

"Not that I doubt you Mr. West, but do you have a badge or something to show you are with the police?" Reece asked.

"Good thinking Jill, yes I have a badge, we call it a shield." He took it out to show both of them.

"Okay, we will go," said Reece.

"I ain't finished yet, let me eat this last piece, Jill!" begged Steve.

"Sure son, take your time, I think we have time to make it without too much rush."

Steve finished, wiped his hands on his pants, looked at Reece who was shaking her head no. "I forgot again Jill, I'm sorry." Reece put her arm around his shoulder as they followed West to his car. He put them in the back seat and headed down town. Discreetly, a van followed about a half block back.

"Okay folks, that is a wrap, I think we are in. That is all we can do for awhile. Let's go back to HQ and see what we have." Ben ended the conference call and they headed to HQ.

Back in West's car, "Jill this is scary, I ain't never been in a real police car before. Looks like a little jail. Did you notice there ain't no door knobs, how do we get out?" asked Steve, loudly.

"No problem, James. We haul a lot of bad guys and they would try to jump out and run. This is the only car I have so it will have to do, but I will let you out, don't worry about that," West spoke up from the front seat. In just a few minutes they were pulling into the parking lot at the downtown precinct.

Inside at a desk, West talked to them both for a few minutes. He made a couple calls. Then he took a manila envelope out. "Now to be on the safe side, I need for you to empty your pockets in here; I will seal it up and give you a receipt. It will be returned when you are released."

"Released, are you arresting us?" asked Reece.

"Heavens no, it is a precaution, you will be protected where you are going to make sure no one bothers you. I am used to dealing with criminals, sorry for using that word. Come, on empty them, and we will find you a place to stay."

Reluctantly, they both emptied their pockets. West put the envelope in his desk drawer and locked it. He stood up and said, " you guys come on with me."

"Aren't you forgetting something?" asked Reece.

"Oh, I almost forgot." He sat down wrote, something on a sheet of paper, folded it and stuck it in his shirt pocket, then headed out the door. The two followed through lots of halls and several stairways before they came to a locked door. West pressed the buzzer.

"Yes?"

"Got a couple nice folks who need a place to rest for the night, this is West. I will be back in the morning to pick them up." The door opened and a matronly woman let them inside.

"What are the charges?"

"No charges," West winked, "They were over in a bad section of town and they need a place to stay before Black comes in, in the morning. He will probably have a better place for them to stay." West turned to leave.

"Officer West, I will need that receipt," said Reece.

"So you will, I'm sorry, here it is," West handed her the paper and was out the door in a flash. When Reece opened it, it was something like she expected, 'Received personal property,' not signed.

"Who is Black? West mentioned that a Black would have a better place for us," asked Reece.

The matron replied, "It is not Black, it is Judge Black, and I would remember that if I was you two."

"But we are just here for the night because it was too dangerous at the Catholic House, West told us."

"Never heard of the Catholic House being dangerous, but West is on the streets, he knows more than we do. Anyway, let's get you a place to sleep."

They were assigned rooms across from each other. There were noises coming from behind a door that was heavily barred. "What's in there?" asked Steve.

"Nothing to concern you, son. You are on this side as long as you are nice and obey the rules. They are posted on the wall inside. It is getting late, get ready for bed, lights out in thirty minutes." The matron returned to her desk and Steve gave Reece the thumbs up and turned to his room.

****

They were awakened at six AM by a whistle. "Wash up. You will get breakfast in thirty minutes, then exercise. You are to be ready at oh eight hundred to see Judge Black. Officer West will pick up at seven thirty." The meal was an egg sandwich and a carton of milk. It really wasn't bad. They had a chance to clean up some and brush their teeth.

At seven thirty Officer West buzzed the door and took the two of them down the stairs. "Officer West, we appreciate your getting us a place to stay, but there is no need any more, if you will just return our stuff, we won't be any more bother."

"Oh, it is no bother, just normal procedure. When you get free nights' lodgings the Judge likes to have a talk with you about the responsibilities of being in our city. As I said, it is just normal procedure, nothing fancy or complicated about it. You will go right into his private chambers, not everyone gets that chance. If you follow his advice and instructions everything will go all right. Do you understand?"

"I don't." said Steve.

"I don't either, but if we must, before we can leave, we will."

"Atta girl, you are getting the idea."

Upon entering the Judge's Chambers, he smiled at them, looked at Officer West and asked, **"Is this our two vagrants from West Virginia?"**

Chapter 19
Reececup and Steve Inside

It was obvious to Reece and Steve that they were going to be railroaded; their aim was to make it appear they did not like the idea.

"Vagrants? How can he say that Officer West? You know….." Reece was interrupted by the Judge.

"Young lady, we are in chambers and this is still considered my court room. I can cite you for contempt for interrupting me. So hold your tongue until I finish. You will get a chance to explain yourself, but until then I am in charge and I was talking, am I clear?"

"Yes, sir, but…"

"No buts, you listen. Officer West helps to keep this city clean. That means when someone comes to sleep on the streets of Pittsgurgh, steal or pan handle he brings it to my attention. It is my understanding you spent the night in Juvenile lock up, so what do you have to say for yourself?"

"Judge, my brother and I arrived in town yesterday. We have about a hundred fifty dollars. We bought a pizza and were eating it when Officer West offered us a place to spend the night where it was safe. He said I would be molested if we stayed at the Catholic place. He took our belongings, so he knows who we are and that we have money."

"And what about you young man, it says here you are James, the younger brother."

"Y-yes Mr. Black, my name is James. I am a good worker, Jill had most of the money and we are gonna get jobs and send some money back home to help daddy and mamma. We had a nice place to sleep last night."

"Officer West, now let me hear your reasons for bringing these two in on vagrancy charges?"

"He didn't…." Reece was cut off again by the judge.

"Young lady, I can do this with or without you present, you can sit still while I hear Officer West or I can have security come in here, hand cuff you and tape your mouth shut, is that clear?"

Feeling she had pushed far enough Reece said, "Yes, sir." The judge nodded to West to continue.

"I ran into these two at the pizzeria on Ninth. They had ordered a pizza, and could not pay for it. I paid for it, they ate it and I brought them in. As for all that money," West handed the judge a sealed manila envelope which he tore open and dumped the contents for all to see. Out fell three dollars and nothing else. "They saw me seal the envelope last night your honor, that is it."

Reece was holding up her hand to speak, "Yes Jill, what is it?"

"Judge, your honor, there was close to a hundred and fifty dollars there, James' 'Old Timer' pocket knife and our identification in that envelope last night. Something is terribly wrong here. We are honest people, raised poor but honest. Something is bad wrong."

"Okay Jill, give me your phone number and I will call your folks and verify you had the money."

"Judge, we ain't got a phone, never had one up on Sandy Creek. We don't have any electric wires even. But we are Jacksons from Jackson County. We are distant kin to the seventh president of the United States, Old Hickory, Andrew Jackson. Daddy said he was the best president this country ever had and we had to be honest and live up to his name. We are poor, but we are not vagrants."

"That is a good speech Jill, but are you saying Officer West here is lying?"

"I wouldn't say that, but he must have the wrong envelope or something."

"Kids, I am not a mean man. I am a judge. So what I am going to do is take your address and names. I will have this all researched and find a way to contact your family. When I do and verify what you have said, the best I can do is buy you a ticket back home, and apologize for your bad experience in our fair city. But let me point out, forgetting this misunderstanding for a moment, Officer West has done you a favor. You could have easily been molested and hurt if he had not intervened. You are too innocent to be walking these streets without proper supervision."

The judge took down the pertinent data they gave him and then said, "Okay this is what I am going to do. Jill, you and James will be taken to our county facility and housed there for awhile until this is cleared up.

You will be given a clean place to sleep, entertainment, and good food. It will be like a vacation until this is cleared up. Are we clear on this?"

"I don't see as we have much choice, but if you call Deputy Bright in Ripley, he'll go up on Sandy Creek and tell daddy and daddy will call you when he gets to town."

"Okay kids, I promise I will call that Deputy Bright, we will straighten this out in no time. In the mean time, I think you can enjoy our services here, and I am sorry you have had such a bad first encounter here in Pittsburgh."

Outside the Judge's Chambers West stopped them, "Okay, just so we don't get lost from each other I am going to fasten you together with these nylon tie-wraps," said West. I will hold onto Jill and you follow, James. In a few minutes they headed to West's car and on their way out of town. As they left the building filming was started again with a minute by minute narration and times noted as the trio made it to the car. The van again followed a safe distance filming all the time. The filming continued to the security buildings and did not stop until they disappeared inside. Later, West was filmed leaving and the times noted.

****

Steve and Reece aka James and Jill Jackson were logged in, paperwork filled out and rooms assigned. Steve had a roommate; Reece was in a room alone. There was the other bunk, but no occupant at present. The matron said it could be filled in a day or a week, she did not know. They were told to stay in their rooms until the lunch bell was sounded. Then they were to stand outside their rooms until given instructions. Both of them settled down to study their surroundings, escape routes and good hiding holes if needed.

Steve's roommate was not in the room. He he was assigned to the garden force and was working outside. When lunch was sounded they were directed to the cafeteria. It was like a school cafeteria line and everyone ate at one time. They worked around, Steve moving back until he was with Reece. They did not say much except described their rooms as you would expect new arrivals to do. The food was pretty good. Looking around there were a few bruises and a couple casts covering broken bones, apparently. No way to know if the injuries were from here or brought in with the lock up.

After lunch, Reece was assigned to Peggy, an inmate. Peggy was to show her what she would be doing while here. They headed for the production building and the sewing machines. Reece told Peggy there was no need to learn much, she would be leaving soon. Peggy smiled, "That is what we all said. I've been here over a year. Judge Black said a week at most he would contact my family and I would probably be released. Same story with most everyone here. Does your mama care where you are Jill?" asked Peggy as they approached the machines.

"I think so, why?"

"Cause it seems that when a person is from a family like mine, who couldn't care less if I am around or not, we never get out," said Peggy and Reece saw the starting of a tear.

"None of that lolly-gagging girls, let's get to work," that came from the bossy looking woman at the center table. It appeared to be a sort of combination inspection station and desk.

"Better do as the boss says, if you want supper," said Peggy. "Sit down here and I will show you what you will be doing. Maybe we can talk a little without any trouble, as long as I can keep up production. By the way, truthfully, can you sew?"

"Yes, I am pretty good at it."

"Well, don't let it show. That way I can spend more time teaching you and we can talk some. I don't get to talk to folks much." Peggy said, while she kept an eye on the boss.

In the next four hours they got two ten minute breaks and since Jill fit in pretty well, they were able to talk a good bit. Things that Reece needed to know. The afternoon really did go fast.

During the same period Steve was assigned to the grounds crew. One of his co-workers had the broken arm, the other a black eye. Neither was very talkative. At first they appeared not to trust Steve, and were not completely sure of how much he could understand, since Steve, aka James, was supposed to be a brick short of a load. Steve used the same ploy as Reece, "Fellows, I won't need to learn much 'cause I won't be here long, my sister is pretty smart, she will have us out in no time."

"Yeah right bright boy, I have been here almost two years waiting for my quick release. All you are going to do is keep this place pretty so the government folks will think we are real happy. They come around every two or three months, and for sure you will learn to smile and bow real good," said broke arm.

"Hey, they might let him in the garden so he can grow us some vegetables. You never know, he might just grow one of them bean stalks like old jack, and climb right out of here," commented black eye.

They were digging around some bushes. "Look guys, I am a little slow, but I ain't stupid. I don't plan on climbing out, and I don't plan on being here no two years, that is for sure."

"You think I planned it? My folks kicked me out of the house 'cause I smoked some weed, it was my first time. I was hungry; I didn't have a thing, so I stole a sandwich from the deli. Old Officer West collared me. Then he took me to good old Judge Black. Says the Judge, 'son I got just the place for you. You can stay there a week or so while I talk some sense into your mom and dad. I'll get you back home in no time'. I really believed the old guy," said black eye, mimicking the deep voice of the judge."

"All right you crap heads," came the booming voice from a big man in a brown uniform, "I see and hear more yapping than work, you are supposed to be teaching dummy here not giving Sunday School lessons, now get to work. We got two more beauty gardens before supper. If you get supper," the guard said as he slapped the stick against his leg making a popping sound.

"Yes sir," the two boys said together.

"That's dummy's first mistake, I will let him slide on that one. You tell him how to answer his superiors, if I don't get a sir from him next time, you all will suffer," he said as he walked off.

"James, always answer with a 'yes sir'. He will brain you if you don't and believe me that stupid, flat stick hurts," said broke arm.

"You mean he will really hit me? He will be in trouble if he does. I will be onto him like stink on a skunk!"

"How the heck do you think I got this black eye? I will say I fell if the government man asks. I don't want another one. And besides, they ain't no way you gonna tackle him. He would kill you and nobody would know the difference. That happens around here too, but you didn't hear that from me."

Steve learned a lot his first afternoon, also. The work was done on time and they headed for the shower room at the sound of the whistle. All the boys showered together. Steve saw a lot of bruises as he looked around. Steve found out that the same shower room was used by the girls and boys at different times. The girls bathed in the mornings and boys bathed before dinner.

In the cafeteria they were all allowed to visit and talk. The workers milled in and around all the tables, so no one talked 'out of school'. Steve and Reece ate together again. They were able to talk enough to learn they had something to report. The plans were to make contact with either Luke or Matt that evening. They both had been able to retrieve the magnets that had been planted in the main restrooms in the dormitory. They had a secure feeling that now someone was monitoring them.

Everyone was allowed to exercise for thirty minutes while the cooks and helpers cleaned up the kitchen and washed the remaining dishes. Exercise was a small walking track; it was crowded and at times shoulder to shoulder. Then they were directed to their rooms. Once in the rooms no one was allowed to leave. Each room had a toilet and sink for personal needs. The doors were closed, but not locked. The punishment was severe for breaking that rule, so it was seldom disobeyed.

Steve liked his roommate. At first, he was stand offish, but in just a few minutes opened up. He blurted out a lot of illegal things that had happened. He had been here almost two years. He had had no contact with his family in all that time and was not allowed to try to contact anyone. He also mentioned that a couple boys had disappeared, and it was rumored that they had been killed and buried in the garden area. He did not know where. Steve made sure he got the name correct. His roommate had worked in the fields all day and was tired. He crashed and was dead asleep at ten o'clock.

The plans were to keep an eye out to make sure the guard was either Matt or Luke, if so, they were home free. There was always a possibility that a last minute change would be made and the MVA guys might have the mid shift. The first meeting was to be at ten. At their first break Matt retrieved one radio and checked in with the TV Repair Shop. The goal was to find out if they could tell which rooms Steve and Reece were in. As hoped, the magnetic fields pin pointed the exact location of the two. Luke would meet with Steve first and he would be free to head for the planted radio to call in his report. If that failed, he would check on Reece to do the same. Fortunately it worked like clockwork, just as planned. Both troops made their reports and returned to their rooms before time for Luke to leave his shift.

At the end of the shift, Luke had a date. He called and begged off saying he had to do something with Matt concerning family. The two then headed for MVA to find out the status and results of the inside reports. No info was passed at the worksite to save time. Everyone knew there would be a debriefing and Matt and Luke would learn what they needed to know then. This looked like a real, by the book, operation. The event was going smoothly.

Chapter 20
From the Inside

Matt and Luke arrived in time for the late night briefing. This time they drove directly from the shift change. Most of the players were assembled. They had had the data for about two hours. The techies had run missing persons checks on the four names given. Of the four, two were listed as missing, nothing on the others. People, on foot, would start trying to track down the four first thing in the morning. It was obvious that these kids were being held on bogus charges and not being allowed to contact their family, and families were not being contacted as required by law.

By far the greatest interest was concerning the fact that deaths may have occurred and not been reported. The charges, if this were true, would range from manslaughter, accidental death or murder. This was on the level with slavery and, with a body and DNA, this could be the death knell of the Lighthouse Corporation and its select few.

Many things were discussed, but it seemed to come back to the possibilities of someone dying inside those walls and the fact not being reported. It was infuriating to people who respected justice. To think a human meant no more than an animal. Bury and forget.

"Josh," S'gar spoke over the small roar, "Josh, can you take the data we have and do some manipulating? Check the souls taken in, the souls remaining, and the ones who have been actually, physically released?" Everyone became silent listening to what the boss was saying.

"Yes sir, I have been thinking the same thing. I think in a day or so we could write a program that would bounce and juggle the names around, using names in and names out. That would leave the remainder inside. Then check the remainder against the present population. We should come up with a list of names to start with. There will be a percentage of error of course, but we will have something solid, some names, to work with," Josh answered firmly.

"Good, make that your priority, I am extremely interested to know if we are dealing with people who do not actually value life. Do we have not only folks dealing in slavery but also a killer mentality?" S'gar said firmly. "Okay, we know what needs to be done. For starters, do the families, of the names we have, know where their children are? And also, do they care? After that, we determine the names not accounted for at this fine institution? So, we continue, as we are, keeping track of our guys inside. Luke and Matt will remain on the job as long as we can keep them there. Oh, by the way, Ben has contacted the competitor of 'Call it Secure' and they will be contacting the two guards with an offer of more money. If they accept we are probably set for a couple weeks. I don't want the kids in there any longer than that. If there have been deaths that is a whole new light on the subject. We just might be endangering them much more than our original assessment. I want them informed at tonight's phone report. Unless someone has more, we are through."

No one said anything and the meeting dismissed. Some hung around, others took off as if on a mission. Things continued following the same routine. With each nightly report, new data and new names were added.

****

Three nights later at the mid-night session S'gar made an announcement to those who had not heard. "Folks we have a list of twenty names. These twenty people are logged into Lighthouse Incorporated but are not on their records as being released. Neither are they on the present list of inmates. I believe that some of these names either never made it inside or somehow the record of their release is missing or destroyed. There is no way to place a percentage of error on this list so we will have to trace down every name. We are doing as much as possible by electronics means, but a lot of work is going to be basic shoe leather and asking questions. We have created a fake Government agency. It is called, Youth Off. It was created by the state to find and help youthful offenders. You who hit the streets will have calling cards, ID and an official badge to show as you make inquiries. The number on the cards will take the caller to the Youth Off desk here at MVA. WE have had a lot of success with this type of thing in the past. Most of the success comes from a call later. Many people in the areas you will be going will not openly cooperate with law enforcement, some with good reason. Results are usually gained later via phone."

"Are we going to wait for some digital input or start right away?" asked J.

S'gar gave a nod to Sticky, "I think we will begin tomorrow, mid morning," said Sticky. "I was in on an earlier discussion, I am not the investigator type, but I can surely direct," he laughed, "I have some addresses and areas. I have already notified the four people here who will go with me, so if you haven't been talking to me, just continue to do what you are doing."

"For everyone's information, we have located ten of the families or custodians of the names we have been given by Steve and Reececup. So far it splits down the middle. Half are just glad to be rid of the child and don't care where they are. Those who do not appear to care have too many other problems and no time to be concerned about the lost children. It is truly a shame. The other half is worried to death, having no idea of the whereabouts of the child. It is sort of strange that with all that concern, only two are listed as missing persons so far. We know how tough many families have it. Some of the mothers are druggies and the grandmother is the responsible one. In some of the families there are so many children it is hard to think one would be missed. The stories are heart breaking," reported Tuck.

"How did you approach it? And did you tell the folks where the kids are?" someone asked.

"We used the Youth Off line, along with the badges. We did not tell them that we know where the kids are. I didn't think it was time yet, and S'gar agreed. As we proceed the job becomes easier. We are getting a pattern of knowing somewhat how the contacts will act. We are developing several anticipated responses," finished Tuck.

"I know you all will have recognized right away that some sticky legal problems exist here for the police and the Lighthouse. One is having a child locked up and not runing the missing persons report by all the lock ups. That is a violation of policy. Second, which is worse, if the list was run by Lighthouse and they did not report, 'hey the kid is here', then the plot thickens. By omission, proving they do not want to lose a producing worker," injected Ben. "Of course, Josh and the technical guys are keeping an electronic record of all this."

"That covers what is coming up, what about you guys," S'gar indicated Matt and Luke. "Is the job still going without a hitch?"

"Luke and I were just talking, it has been too easy. No problems with the nightly reports and no problems with the inmates. It just seems too easy. We agree, we are going to have to tighten up, we don't want any surprises," answered Matt.

"All monitors and indicators we have show nothing that would indicate we have anything other than an ideal event, let's hope it remains that way. See you all tomorrow night." S'gar dismissed the meeting.

****

The next afternoon about an hour before work the phone rang in Matt and Luke's apartment. "Yeah, your dime," Luke answered.

"Oh Luke, I am soooo glad you answered, the boss is outside and doesn't know I am calling. He told me awhile ago that I can't see you no more, and I ain't supposed to tell you, just make some excuse, but I can't do that. I just wanted you to know that I can't keep our date tonight. But this may blow over soon, I sure hope so." It was Paula.

"What is the problem?" asked Luke, trying to sound nonplussed.

"I don't know. He took a call a little while ago from his boss and... I gotta go here he comes," Paula hung up fast.

"Matt, we may have a problem. The Boss told Paula she could not see me anymore. What difference would that make to him? What do you think?"

"It is probably nothing more than a streak of jealousy. He may think she is getting too serious with you. He may have had his eye on her all the time. Just to be safe, you had better inform Tuck, they may have some ideas at HQ," said Matt.

Luke made the call, and later they reported for work as usual. Paula informed them the boss wanted to talk before they were posted. So they went in. "Oh, there you are. Well, you guys have been here a week and doing great. How do you like it so far?"

"Good," said Matt.

"I'd like it better if there was more excitement," said Luke, "It is pretty boring over there."

"Well Luke, that is law enforcement, it will bore you to death, then all of a sudden, you have more than you can handle."

"I doubt that," said Luke flexing his muscle.

"Well, I just wanted to touch base with you, no problems? No one leaving their rooms, no sex and violence I should know about?"

"Negative," said Luke.

227

"Okay, hit the road and let's protect the Lighthouse." Just as they got to the door the boss spoke again, "Do you guys go home after your shifts or go hit some bars to unwind?"

Luke answered, "Sometimes I have a date, but she cancelled tonight, so we will probably just hit the sack, why?"

"No reason, just that we don't want any of our guys picked up for drunkenness."

"Don't worry about that, we got better things to do," Luke said as they walked out.

****

Upon being posted, Luke left his post and went over to Matt's post, "Do you feel sorta funny about anything?" asked Luke.

"Yeah, to be honest I do," said Matt, "There is nothing I can put my finger on, but keep your eyes peeled."

They talked a few more minutes and Luke headed back, taking a short cut, and made it on time to his next clocking station. The rest of the night went without a hitch. Reece and Steve made their reports. Each one talked to Luke a few minutes and went back to their rooms. Steve and Luke's reliefs came on time and their shift was over. They had time to run by and change clothes before the nightly de-briefing. So, they drove by the apartment.

As they approached the door, Matt motioned for Luke to hold back. He quietly eased up to the door, checked the small piece of transparent tape they always placed at the top of the door. The seal was broken. Luke gave the thumbs up, showing he understood. As Matt placed himself to the side he said, "Dang, Luke I can't find my key," at that moment he unlocked the door with one quiet move, "you will have to use yours." He motioned he was going to turn the handle and Luke was to kick the door in with his full body force. They both would roll into the room, Matt first. Both had their ankle weapons in their hands.

"Okay," said Luke, "Let me put this stuff down." As the last word was out of his mouth he kicked the door with a solid follow through motion and with liquid smoothness Matt rolled in and was on his feet. He was immediately followed by Luke. Both came to their feet. Matt had the two, they now knew about, under his weapon. One had a very broken nose from the door. They had trained on this maneuver so many times it was almost second nature. They knew the sound of the door hitting a body to tell the secret of where at least one perp was and both of them had observed the other guard stunned by the surprise entrance. Matt said, "I got two," Luke knew the second guy thru the door would scan the room for anyone other than the guy behind the door. He had already eye-balled the room and ran to the bathroom.

"Nothing here, I guess it is just these two clowns," said Luke as he walked to the closet and returned with some nylon tie-wraps to use as hand cuffs. "Okay, you naughty boys, you know the drill, up against the wall. He patted them down and emptied their pockets. He removed their weapons, knives and wallets and then handcuffed them very tight.

"Okay, have a seat gentlemen. To what do we owe this visit? We are going to have a serious talk. Why the little surprise? Why not just take us at work? But, my biggest question, why bother two of your mates at all?"

Silence… The only noise or movement was broken nose trying to stop the bleeding with his shoulder. "Hey Luke, go ahead and call the boss and make him aware of the situation. Ask him if he wants us to cut fingers off until we get info or just go ahead and shoot them and give them the prepared acid treatment."

"Come on Matt, let's not ask him anything. I would love to do the finger trick on old broke nose, he hasn't seen any blood yet. I like to see the mean ones faint," said Luke. "I'm gonna tape their eyes first anyway. I like this new flesh colored duct tape. After I draw eyes on them we can walk them to the car with no problems."

As the partner watched, Luke taped the eyes shut and expertly drew two eyes on the tape. He then did the other. One of the men started to speak and Luke said, "Too late, Matt asked nicely, he just didn't mention that this is a one strike and you are out deal. This will shut you up," and he taped their mouths.

"I'll call," said Matt, "they aren't going anywhere," and he dialed the phone. It was answered immediately by Ben. "This is Matt, we have a problem."

"We know, we are on our way to the Lighthouse site. We just received a call, the fire alarm is going, there is a chopper there and strange activity by our inside people. Are you on site?"

"No, we are in our apartment, holding two of our brother guards who were waiting here to welcome us. We are in control. We are headed for the site as soon as we get rid of these guys," and he hung up.

"Okay Luke, kill 'em, something went wrong at the Lighthouse!" Both prisoners began shaking their heads frantically.

"Let me screw this silencer on,"

"What is wrong with you guys, evidently you know who we are, you know we don't take prisoners and that we play for keeps; I thought that was understood. What? Are you trying to tell me something?"

Both guys were frantically nodding their heads yes, "listen and listen well. Luke loves to shoot folks, it is just his nature. Now guys, please try hard and understand this, you get one chance. If you yank our chain we are out of here, we will find someone who truly wants to talk to us, we always do. So pay attention, only one is going to talk so which of you is in charge, in other words, who knows the most?" Broke nose was the indication by nods. "This is how it is, I am going to remove the tape, you yell you are dead, okay?" a nod yes. "Now what is going on back at the 'Crazy House'?" Matt ripped the tape off his mouth.

Sputtering, "Ah-all we know is we were supposed to get you guys, someone is picking up the two undercover guys over there, and they are flying them out in a helicopter. We were just supposed to take you back to the office. That is all we know?"

"How did they know about the undercover guys? And how do you know who we are working for?"

"They added some cameras during the other shift that you guys did not know about. They saw Luke talking to the guys and saw them on the radios. They got the frequencies from the radios and monitored last night's calls. All hell broke loose at the office because they cannot find out who you are, but they don't think it is the FBI. Honest, that is all we know. Please don't kill us man, we liked you guys really." Matt put the tape back over his mouth.

"Are you in the blue company car?" heads shake yes. "Is it out front?" heads shake no. "Out back?" Yes signal.

"Grab the keys off the bed Luke and move it to the service entrance." All the time Matt was talking he was preparing two needles. He handed one to Luke and nodded. Immediately after the injections the bodies went limp.

"You get the car; I will get a laundry cart, and meet you at the service entrance. Before I leave I will take time to call Ben and tell him what we know." Luke took off like a shot. Matt grabbed the phone.

Luke positioned the company car and ran to the room. Matt was leaving the room pushing the laundry cart with the men loaded inside. Matt had placed all the stuff taken off the guys in a pillowcase along with some wide nylon tape and more nylon tie-wraps to further secure the men. They, unceremoniously, dumped the men in the trunk. Luke took the car and Matt ran for their Jeep. They were both still in uniform. They had decided to drop the car off at the TV Repair shop, leave the men in the trunk, and go to the Lighthouse Barracks.

****

Earlier that night on shift they had gone about their rounds as usual after Steve and Reececup had made their reports. Nothing was unusual. Even the reliefs were a few minutes early. As they drove out the driveway and turned onto the main road, they did not see the forms moving from the shadows toward the dormitory while on top of the main building a flare was lit and a distant light in the sky headed toward the flare.

In Reece's dorm she was resting peacefully. She did not hear the door open. But her sense of survival stirred her; she had not seen the dark figure move beside her bed. That is when she felt the most awful pain. Even in the waking mode her mind said: stun gun or taser. She was hit with 950,000 volts for five seconds. She had experienced this in training; once a body is hit with this voltage it doesn't forget it. As her mind said taser she lost all control of her body. When she did regain control of her senses she was being carried toward a thump, thump sound, 'a helicopter'. What th.. who, and how? Was going through her mind as her survival instincts were coming around. She had been taught and believed there is always something you can do.

At approximately the same time Reece was being stunned, in Steve's room things were different. He was awakened by a yell. His roommate had let out a blood curdling yell. Through the dim light in the room he saw forms over the bed. Fortunate for Steve, his roommate had wanted to change beds to be further from the window. Steve's sense of survival came alive, in his underwear he sprinted through the door and down to the hall. The night guard was coming up the stairs as he reached them. He silenced him with a quick chop to the carotid artery area, but he heard some men coming behind the guard. He turned and remembered a canvas awning below the windows opposite the stairs. Out of the corner of his eye he saw the group leaving his room carrying his roommate. One of the men seeing Steve said, "We can forget him. The others will get him if he is needed, we have our cargo."

At that very moment Steve remembered the fail safe plan. He ran the few steps back and hit the fire alarm at the top of the stairs. Immediately, the emergency lights came on and the bells started ringing. Turning, he ran toward the windows and dove through the glass with his arms in front of his face. Just as he had hoped he landed on the taunt canvas and slid to an easy rolling fall. There was panic all around. Above the noise and confusion he heard the thump, thump, thump of a helicopter, it was getting airborne. He ran toward the sound and was able to get four numbers off the fuselage before it turned.

Then he realized he would be pretty obvious in his skivvies. Just then, he saw one of the ninja dressed intruders approaching him with a hand gun. He wilted, giving the impression he was giving up. When the man got close enough he saw a maniac. Steve seemed to fly straight up in the air, do a 360 degree turn and caught the guard with his right heel. Steve landed lightly. Hastily, he loosed the guys belt and quickly grabbed the trouser legs and removed them, then he easily slid the stretch sweater off his victim. He then headed for the shadows to dress. No one had paid any attention. Steve glanced in the back doors, looking through to the entrance, and saw the good guys from MVA arriving. He ran to meet them. He quickly identified himself and told them what had happened. The black dressed invaders headed for the surrounding woods. The alarm was now silenced and the inmates were being herded back inside.

Then, they heard the sirens of the local fire department and what was beginning to be called 'First Responders'. Everyone knew their jobs. Fortunately, Buddy was already in a suit and ready to meet the emergency vehicles. With his calm voice of authority he would explain the situation. At least that was still the plan. The results had been predicted pretty well. Buddy was able to talk to the duty chief and they walked inside to see that order was restored. No smell of smoke and no fire. Through the door walked Matt and Luke in uniform to make sure all was well. Buddy signed the required papers. Yes, He agreed Lighthouse would pay the minimum for the false alarm, no problem. It was late, everyone was glad to head back to the station. One of the units was going to stop for Krispy Kreme on the way in. The fire fighters were in a good mood, no work at this site, no hoses to clear and restore, just a ride to wake them up. Now coffee and donuts sounded good to them.

Once the emergency crew was out of earshot, Steve told Buddy what had happened from his standpoint. Someone had already searched for Reececup and she was reported missing in action. Everyone assumed she was on that helicopter with Steve's roommate. Steve gave the four numbers he had been able to read along with the type and style of the chopper.

All MVA personnel departed taking the guards and the one stranger that had been a party to the kidnapping. Each one was blinded with tape and secured. Steve and Luke informed them of the blue company car with the keys under the mat and of the cargo in the trunk. They remained as the 'Call it Secure' guards. After Ben and the crew sorted some things out, they would be relieved. Both of them were looking forward to visiting the 'Call it Secure' office. If at all possible, they wanted to be there when the boss came in, if he wasn't already there.

Chapter 21
Untangling the Web

To S'gar this was a tragedy of epic proportions. His right hand man, Corey, was at his door within minutes of the MVA alert. Thanking Corey, he dashed past holding his phone and headed for the limo. Refusing to allow Corey to do his usual 'open the door for you' ritual, he got the door first, telling Corey, "Get in and drive son, like you never have." Once they were both in place, S'gar called out, "Get to the TV repair Shop."

Corey had been trained well by 'Slick' Wayne Carter, the stock car driver out of Central Florida. He handled the limo using all its power with an aggressive skill. Hoping he would not get the attention of a late night policeman he let it all out. He did not have time to explain to the locals why he was driving this erratic and fast, but at the time he concentrated on the road. In the back, buckled in, S'gar was on the phone. His first call was to Josh. Josh seeing on his computer screen who was calling, answered immediately, "Yes sir?"

"Did you get the arrangements set up to transfer and drain all the off shore accounts?"

"Yes sir, all I have to do is activate a pre-programmed macro and the entire process will all be done in less than five minutes," answered Josh.

"Do it and make me a hard copy of the amounts transferred. And Josh, thanks. YOU have been the bright star in this event. I will see you in about ten minutes," S'gar then dialed the chief of police.

"Tom, this is S'gar. I need a favor." That was all that was needed, a few words and every cop would know to escort or ignore the limo. S'gar had helped many of the local policemen and their families, along with footing the bills for some of the Policeman's balls in the last twenty years. The chief knew he could count on donations to any worthy legal cause involving the police.

"Okay Corey, you are clear, hit it!"

"Excuse me S'gar," said Corey, thru clenched teeth as he darted around traffic, "I thought I was!" Corey and S'gar smiled at the retort.

"Of course Corey, I am just so frustrated." They talked a little more. Corey, of course, understood his boss's concern. S'gar was not used to being the one over a barrel. Now, he was.

The TV Repair shop was a two story building. All the electronics were on the second floor, along with a make shift office. The five prisoners were on the first floor. The two Matt and Luke had brought were in one room on the floor and the remaining three in the other room on the floor. These were sleeping quarters. There was another small room that appeared to have been a large laundry room. There was some plumbing here and a couple tables with power outlets. The prisoners were guarded by one man in each room with a sawed off shotgun and a side arm. The prisoners were all alert but trussed up like Christmas turkeys. Their mouths and eyes taped securely closed.

S'gar went directly to the second floor where J, Buddy, Tuck and Sticky were gathered in the small office. S'gar nodded, took the proffered coffee and sat down, "Give it to me. Everything you have."

Buddy was the spokesman, "To cut to the chase, we have lost Reececup! The whole plan was blown because we underestimated the resources of our opponent. Not an excuse, just a fact. They evidently got suspicious and planted a few new cameras that we, Luke or Matt did not spot. They saw the radios, found them, got the frequencies, and monitored at least one session. We are not sure how many. Steve was very lucky, he was not in the bed he was supposed to be in. He and his roommate had switched beds at the roommate's request. The roommate was taken. If they don't know by now, they will soon know that they have the wrong guy. We worry about his safety. They used a stun gun or a taser, so the victim could not resist. Our only lead is four digits of the helo's fuselage number. The techies are trying to ID that as we speak. Steve was able to set off the alarm and dive through a second floor window. He used a canvas awning to break his fall and he is unhurt. He also disabled one of the attackers. We have him, along with the two guards tied up below. The plan we had worked perfect with the First Responders. They took my explanation and will bill Lighthouse for a false alarm." Buddy sipped some coffee and continued, "When Luke and Matt stopped at their apartment to change clothes on the way to our nightly de-briefing they were met by the two guards they have been replacing. Of course, they subdued the amateur guards and learned about the cameras and the radios. We are 99% sure they have no idea who we are or why we were there. The guards say that 'Call It Secure' has come to the conclusion we are not FBI. Matt and Luke brought the two guards here. They are also below, secure and under guard. Matt and Luke are at Lighthouse to cover for the guards we removed. They want reliefs as soon as we can get them. They want to be the ones to meet 'Call it Secure' in the morning. I tend to agree it is a good idea, with a couple of us near in case we again get surprised. That is it as far as my notes go," looking at the assembled crew he asked, "Have I covered it all?" Everyone nodded.

"Well, of course as of now, our top priority is to find and rescue Reececup unhurt. EVERYTHING else goes to the back burner. I don't care if the techies continue during a lull, to ID the missing folk. But Reececup, we must find her. Second, of course, is the innocent kid taken by mistake, which should go without saying. Now give me ideas?"

"My first impression is they will try to contact us. They only have a couple points that I can see where they can do that. That would have to be the fake guards and the radio frequencies. Luke and Matt have their phones and will be expecting something. We here are monitoring the radio frequencies because the radios are gone. They are fairly short range, ten miles max. They will know that," said J, "Buddy, I just thought of something. We need Luke and Matt here. Do you have someone who can relieve them, ASAP? If they get a call we need to try to trace it. There is no way we can do that with them at the Lighthouse site."

"You bet." Buddy hurried from the room.

"Ben and Dallas are here working the phones to try to locate anyone, anywhere who saw a helicopter during the times we know it was flying. They have a contact at the airport who is asking around," said Tuck.

"I want all the pictures of every person in management in Lighthouse and Call it Secure, put on slides or some type of video. I want them shown to the whole crew separately or at once. We need some eyeball data so everyone will be on the lookout. We need to recognize these guys on sight," inserted S'gar.

"I'm on it," said J, as he too left the room. It was only a couple minutes until Buddy and J were back.

"How are we going to treat the dudes that we have trussed up below us?" asked J. "I think the one with the most info would be the dude with the kidnapping crew. Next, would be the guys who had the duty on the mid watch, they must have been in on it."

"I want to know something now. You two go on down and have a talk with the latest three," S'gar said to Tuck and J.

"First of all, he ain't gonna be easy to scare, but let's try that first," said Tuck, "I will be the one who wants to erase them this time."

"Okay let's do it," said J as they left the office. S'gar wished them luck.

****

Entering the room, Tuck spoke to the guard, "Get a cup of coffee." Tuck was great with improvising; He spotted an old cotton type scale in the corner. He went over and drug it out, stood on it and weighed himself. Amazingly, it worked. "Okay, let's get to it. I don't see why we can't do like we did in North Carolina a couple weeks ago. Just use a back hoe and bury them fifteen feet deep. Ain't nobody gonna find them. Why does the boss want to be so technical, weigh 'em? I think this is silly and a waste of time. But we may as well do it, drag one over here."

As J started to drag one, he was wiggling. J dropped him. "I know you can hear me dude, this can be easy or hard. I am just moving you to the scale." He grabbed the back of his belt and with Tuck's help hung him there by his belt. The guy was swinging.

"Hey dude we can't weigh you and you moving. Let me explain something. Feel this?" he touched the guard's cheek with his very sharp knife. "This is an ice pick. I am not a patient man. If I push this thru your ear into your little brain I bet you will be still. Nobody told me to keep you alive, just weigh you." The guard became as still as a mouse.

"That is better, remember this, you weighed 179 pounds the very last time you weighed. Now I will subtract five pounds for clothes," not bad. Tuck took a black marker and wrote 174 on his cheek and on his fore arm. "That's 174, next."

The other guard was next; they went thru the same procedure, J is wondering, where Tuck is going with this. "This hog is only 167." He wrote it on cheek and forearm.

While the last guy was hung, Tuck wrote as he spoke, "Only 163 here. The boss ordered ten barrels of acid. I wanted to just dump half and stuff them in, but no, it must be done right so the barrels will weigh right when they go aboard the ship. He knows how long it takes to dissolve a body so we have to remove the exact amount of acid, as the body weight. Now, I have to figure how much to take out. The acid weighs five pounds a quart," pausing while he calculated, " Gotta take out 35 quarts for the fat guy. He walked over and wrote '35 qts' on the guy." He went thru the procedure with each guy.

"Are you sure the boss don't want to talk to them first?" asked J.

"Nah he said they were too far down the food chain. He was sure that they wouldn't know enough to take the time. What I am looking forward to is the big guys; we get to water board Judge Black and the CEO. Man, I love it. The boss does want to watch that," Tuck said. The whole time they are talking the three are making all kinds of motions with their heads and grunting to try to say something.

"My silencer is in the truck, you got yours?" Tuck was quietly screwing a silencer on his weapon as he spoke.

"Yeah, here just use my colt, it is already rigged," J paused, "Are you sure you don't want to hear what they got to say? They are fidgety about something."

"They just want to cry or ask you to tell their mama something, makes me sick. Everyone is supposed to know when we get in this business that we can make a million and live in high cotton or lose everything, and they just lost it all." Tuck pulled the trigger on a silenced pistol 'pffft'.

The round hit the concrete right next to one guys arm, throwing little shavings of concrete against him. The slug went harmlessly into the wall. "Come on, no playing around man, we are professionals," the words were spoken low and as serious as J could make them.

"I'm not playing, I needed to check your piece out. This colt handles good. Now, I'm ready," said Tuck. "Okay guys say your prayers. Nah, you don't have to say 'em out loud. Mama told me God knows what you are thinking, so just think your prayers and get ready to meet Him."

"Come on T, the guy in the middle really wants to say something, don't you?" They all nodded their heads frantically.

"Okay, but make it snappy, I want to get some coffee," retorted Tuck.

Quickly, J moved over beside the guy. "I'm taking the tape off. You had better have something important to say because I have seen T take a long time, using a lot of shells to waste a man. So don't make a mistake and end up leaving this life slowly. Okay, knowing that, do you think you still have something important to say?" The guy nodded frantically. J ripped the tape off his mouth.

"Man, don't shot me….." J interrupted him.

"I said important, say something important, understand?" The guy nodded yes, "Go ahead then."

"I know who was flying the chopper, I know where he was going when he left. Do you want to know?" he gasped.

"It is according to what the boss says. If I like what you say you will at least get ten minutes while I find out."

"You still gonna shot me?"

"Probably, but we know one thing for sure don't we, I am going to shoot you if you don't tell me. Because I ain't gonna climb those steps without a name, I might end up in a barrel. I would rather he never know you knew anything. That way we are still at square one. So, do I hear the names and places?" asked Tuck, with as much 'I don't care' as possible in his voice.

"Yes sir, the chopper belongs to Dan Gibson and he was flying it. He is headed to a little place called Robinson. That is out close to the Airport. Dan owns some land there and it is real private. I can take you there and guide you through all the security stations. I helped set them up. This is all the truth, man; please talk to your boss. Man, you need me," he pleaded.

"You are wrong. We don't NEED anyone. We have the fuselage numbers already, but stay right here I will be back in a few," said Tuck. With that, J put more tape over his mouth.

Speaking low, as if only to the prisoner, "That might do it, but something else would help. I'd advise you to think hard while we are gone," whispered J, "I don't think these other guys know doodle." The other guys were nodding and grunting frantically again. J left the room as the guard reentered.

****

Up topside, Tuck and J informed S'gar and the others there of the pilot's name. Josh immediately entered the name. All the information came back, including his helicopter fuselage number that matched what numbers they had. His small flying company was a contract outfit. He owned thirty acres in the small community of Robinson. If what the prisoner was saying about security is true, it may be much more than just a flying club.

"I am betting he knows more," said S'gar. "In my CIA experience a smart guy holds out a little with which to negotiate. I want you two to give it one more shot. Then, as the final decision maker, I will go down if we feel it is necessary. Sticky, take Corey and one other guy and head out to this address as soon as Corey can get you there. It is still dark. I'll call the Chief and have him clear it with the Sherriff also. Observe and make contact only if absolutely necessary. You know where the weapons are stored in the limo. What am I saying? Use your own judgment son, we all know the objective on this one is to get Reececup back without losing anyone else."

****

Down below again, Tuck and J walked back in. "Take another break guy, but get three of the barrels ready, okay?" said J. The watcher grunted as he left as if disgusted.

"Sorry son, no cigar, they already had that info from the fuselage number of the chopper. The boss did tell me to ask you if you know something that public records doesn't. Something he can use. To be honest, I told him it didn't look like you knew anything else."

"Wait T," said J, "Son do you know anything else worth a hoot?" He frantically nodded his head yes. "Okay, same rules, do you want me to remove the tape again?" Same indication, J ripped the tape.

"We had two vans out there fully gassed for a long drive. Now, I don't know exactly where they were going but I know the general direction and the approximate driving time. Also, Gib's place is going to be a Militia Battalion. That is why we put in the security. Okay, I know more but without some proof you ain't still gonna shoot me, it dies with me. I really ain't stupid."

"Okay, hold that thought," said J. as he replaced the tape. "Tuck, can I see what these guys are in an uproar about?"

"Negative, I came in here planning to shoot somebody, not listen to some blabbering. If I keep putting this off Matt and Luke will be back from the Crazy House. Luke will want to do it. Luke is an up and comer that thinks he is better at this than I am. I plan to prove him wrong."

There was noise from outside and the doors opened. "What is going on in here?"

"Go on up stairs Luke, I'm taking care of this," said Tuck.

"You gonna do it ain't you, Tuck? Not gonna give me a shot, huh?" asked Luke.

"You two homicidal maniacs shut up. Luke, you and Matt go on up topside, the boss wants to see you. Something important has come up, we'll be up in a minute," said J. Then under his breath he said, "If it wasn't for me and Matt you two would kill everybody you meet."

"Look J, it is just a job. One you don't like but it is part of the job. You know as well as I do, that these guys have been here long enough to make up some stuff to try to save their rear ends. And, from experience, you know it will be lies and we'll just have to go thru this again. Am I right?"

"Yeah, you are right. Let's take this little bit up to the boss; I am getting a little tired of climbing the stairs. You guys don't leave, we will be right back," the two guards were becoming almost violent trying to get their attention. "Calm down, you guys are gonna give yourselves a heart attack," J said as they left.

****

After hearing the latest, S'gar said he would go down and talk with the prisoner. They needed to know more. A helo had been spotted near the air port. The controller's report confirmed that it appeared to be Gibson's helicopter because it disappeared near where his place is. But they were busy and knew it was out of the flight patterns so not much attention was paid to it. Not much else had been learned. This latest info was the best they had so far.

Down in the room with the prisoners S'gar said, "Remove the tape, J."

"Yes, sir," J ripped the tape again.

"And, what is your name?" asked S'gar.

"Billy, Sir, and I will help you to the best of my ability, if you will spare my life. I have had a lot of time to think, nothing is worth this."

"Billy, I run this outfit. I have lost one of my best people. You have no idea to what extent I will go to get her back, or the extent of retaliation and retribution if I don't. So, starting from there if everything you say proves out to be correct, you will live. I will allow you to board a plane once this episode is complete, and you can start a new, less exciting, life somewhere. Do we completely understand each other?"

"Yes sir, I swear to God, I will be loyal to you and tell you all I know in exchange for my life."

"Okay, I agree, what else can you tell me?"

"The vans were prepared to travel for approximately eight hours. They were going south. Now, that is an educated guess because the only part of the directions I saw and heard was South Interstate 79."

"Okay, what about Gibson's place?"

"Once you are in Robinson you take Washington Rd to Church Lane. Take a right turn and Gib's place is at the dead end. There are three red lights on his little tower. If all three are lit all security is off. If two are lit Perimeter is on. If one is lit, everything is set to monitor, that is laser and motion detectors."

There were a few more innocuous points, but S'gar was convinced Billy was telling the truth. "It seems that we have enough information. You can continue Tuck, skip Billy for now."

The other two appeared to be nearly hysterical, "What is the story on those two, did they know anything?" asked S'gar.

"Nah, I figured they were just scared. Some folks don't like to pay the piper," said Tuck.

"I'll pull the tape and we can see," said J, "Can't hurt. Tuck really wants to waste them. I don't blame him much, but it won't take but a minute to check."

"Go ahead, I will trust you guys to judge the info, I am not coming back down, I have a lot to do," said S'gar, dismissing any negotiations.

"I really hate to look like an idiot, but you heard what I said about important information, I have a recorder, when I take the tape off don't be stupid and start asking us not to shoot you, we have enough sense to know you really don't want to be shot. So, don't waste our time telling us what we know, we are interested in what we do not know, understood?" heads nod yes. "Now, Billy will also be listening, I expect him to tell me you are lying or telling the truth, if he knows, so let's get this part of the show on the road," and he ripped the tape off the first guys mouth.

There was no interrogation, just ten minutes of the two telling everything they knew about this morning, Lighthouse and Call it Secure. Much of the info was useful. The same process was used with the two guards that Matt and Luke had brought in. They too told everything they knew painting a pretty clear picture of the workings of the company and their ties to the organized militia groups. Every member of Call it Secure was also a member of a militia group. The only exceptions were Matt and Luke. None of the guards could understand why they were hired. They did not know about the bribe Ben had paid.

The one question was answered that had puzzled them all. 'What had made someone suspicious of Matt and Luke or Reececup and Steve?' It seems that Matt and Luke had been doing too good a job for people who had to be bribed into such a low paying job. Without exception, no guard had ever made a complete round on a regular basis. Clocking stations were used on a hit and miss basis. Matt and Luke had been so consistent that they were never over three to four minutes off schedule. In other words, they had been too good.

All the new data was being assembled. Vans were being put together and stocked with a computer and a generator. Tuck, Buddy and J were busy picking equipment, arms, ammo and explosives. It was decided that two crews would head south and await instructions. Before anyone departed, S'gar met with them all. "We will leave a skeleton crew here. Josh, I would like for you to stay so we can keep in touch, you have all the data bases here. We know Reececup is somewhere south of here. Until they make contact and we can try to trace, it is like looking for a needle in a hay stack. Josh has put together a digital slide show of all the parties we are aware of who are involved in this event. Look and study the faces. There will also be hard copies in each van and with all team leaders. Run it Josh; we need to get the vans on the road as soon as possible."

Josh, started the show. He read the notes on the pictures as they came up. The crew silently read along and stared intently at the photos to retain a mental image. About six pictures into the show Sticky asked loudly, "Josh can you go back one?" Josh did. It was a picture of the Lighthouse Inc treasurer.

"I flew home and back yesterday. Come to think of it, it was day before yesterday, to sign some papers for my corporation. That guy was on the plane, he got off in Charlotte with me. I wouldn't have remembered but he was across from me and when the stewardess reached for his briefcase offering to stow it over head, he got nasty for no reason, calling attention to himself. I forgot about the incident during the flight. I got in late signed the papers and took the red eye back. But, at Charlotte, Hattie picked me up and I am almost positive he climbed into a cab in front of us. If it was him getting in the cab he headed West on Wilkinson Boulevard in front of us. I remember the Crown Cab because one tail light was broken and Hattie complained about it. The bright bare bulb was kinda blinding her but I didn't have reason to pay any more attention."

This definitely got everyone's attention. S'gar stopped the slide presentation to bounce the subject around. Then they finished the show.

"Sticky, this is a shot in the dark but at present it is all we have. Charlotte is within the half circle we have drawn for an eight hundred mile van trip. Take one of the PI types with you and catch a plane and head for Charlotte as soon as possible. Ask around, do some gumshoe work. Use all the pictures and the names of everything we have here, any questions?"

"No questions, I'm on it. I will take whoever the guys say would be best." Sticky immediately discussed this with the rest of the guys and they decided J should go, rather than send one of the more junior troops. Sticky called for a flight to Charlotte.

Chapter 22
Back to Mt. Bell, Where it all started

Everyone connected with MVA knew when an event was in progress and an alert was out, everyone worked. S'gar called Vickie Jane who was at her desk. Within fifteen minutes she had a flight booked for two thru Atlanta to Charlotte. Delta Flight 1935 departing at 0730. The timing would be close but this team was used to that. Things were a little rushed, but a few things were packed. Sticky and J headed for the airport, stored the MVA auto and caught the flight with a few minutes to spare.

On the flight to Atlanta they discussed some ideas of what direction to take. Sticky was sure the broken tail light would help ID the taxi. J was sure he could find out which one. Most cabs left the terminal and headed toward downtown Charlotte. A fare going to Gastonia was probably rare. They discussed what the guards had said, and the possibilities of why the Lighthouse treasurer was in this area. Several ideas, maybe they were going to try the scam here in North Carolina. Since they were finding that militia's were involved on the outside, maybe it had something to do with security forces. Josh had found that 'Call It Secure' was a subsidiary of Lighthouse Inc. So, since they were joined at the hip, the militia idea could have merit. Also, the man could have family around here.

"We are both from here, so we know something about this area. I don't think he would be going much farther than Shelby or he would have flown into Asheville. What do you think?" asked J.

"You are probably right. I have been thinking since this came up, I wish we could have gotten here ahead of the eight hour driving time, but we have missed that by hours. I was over at Gibson's place by two this morning and nothing was moving. So, I figure they were gone around one or one thirty. That would make the eight hour driving time ending around nine. We will get in around 1:30. Even though this plane makes a stop in Atlanta, it goes on to Charlotte. So, let's grab a couple hours sleep if we can. I have a feeling the hours are going to be long. I hope Reece is doing all right."

"Sticky, that girl has worked for me for awhile now. She is as savvy as they come. Man that girl is one hundred pounds of pure dynamite and as sweet as your mother's sticky buns. I would be hard pressed to keep from killing anyone who really hurt her. She has been trained well, she will handle it as well as any man I have, but in this business it is hard to predict. My opinion is she will be fine for a couple days. If we don't know anything after that I will really worry. Yeah, let's try to get some shut eye before I cry all over you, dadgummit," J was wiping his eyes, he loved everyone who worked for him, they were like family, but there was a special place in his heart for that girl.

****

While Sticky was renting a non-descript car, J was making his rounds with the cabbies in the queue outside the terminal. Sticky would drive to the taxi area once he had the car. J was armed with the number one incentive, twenty dollar bills. The money got their attention and then he asked if they had a fare to Gaston County or further west in the past two days. If they had, the picture and another twenty came out. Every driver was asked if they had noticed a Crown Cab with a broken tail light. He hit pay dirt at the sixth cab driver with a calypso ring to his voice, "Broken tail light, mon? Shure, mon. Dot dere is Jose, he have one showing white. Got heem a ticket too! Say he 'aven't de time to 'ave it repaired," he finished as he accepted the first twenty.

Easing another twenty into view he asked, "Is Jose around, or can I find him? It is very important," J added another twenty.

"You in luck, mon, he just pull in de back of d'queue," J gave him the money with a big thank you and headed to the last cab.

He walked past the cab, to ensure the lens was broken, reversed and opened the front passenger door and got in. "Jose?"

"Yez,' the driver answered with caution, "Sorry, sir, I cannot take a passenger until I am at the front of the line." There was a slight Hispanic accent.

J lay two twenties on the seat between them, "I might want a ride later, but right now I am only paying for conversation," he flashed an old FBI shield, and Jose's eyes showed question and apprehension. "Jose, this has nothing to do with you personally. It does concern a passenger of yours that we are very interested in. This is just a preliminary investigation. Have you had a fare in the past couple days toward Gaston County?"

"Si, yes. Two trips, one was an older gentleman; the other was a lady and two keeds."

"Is this the older gentleman?" Jose looked at the picture then back up at J. J knew at that instant, he was onto something.

"Will this get me into trouble? Is the law gonna look at me after this?" questioned Jose with his eyes as well as the words he spoke.

"Cooperate with me, and I will add three more twenties with those and you will be completely forgotten," J said sincerely.

"Yez, that ees the man I drove to North Mt. Bell two nights ago, he ees a very unhappy man. He also does no tipping," said Jose. The taxi was nearing the front of the queue.

J had kept his eye out for Sticky to come around with the rental car as he made his rounds talking to the cabbies. "Could you take me to the address where you dropped him?" Just then the rental car was driving slowly by the taxi line. As it came abreast, J signaled with crossed wrists and pointed ahead; crossed wrists is the standard combat signal meaning meet me, the point meant ahead. Sticky headed out of the terminal area.

"Si, mister you have paid for more than the trip, but I must wait until I am number uno before leaving," Jose replied, apologetically.

"No problem man, and believe me, you will get a tip for this trip. Once we turn on Wilkinson Boulevard and head west, pull off to the side of the road at the Bear Cat Lake Grocery. I need to explain to my partner what we are doing. He was in that rental car that just passed, okay?"

"Sure, we will be leaving in a couple minutes." When Jose's time came he pulled out and headed toward Wilkinson Boulevard. On the way they passed Sticky who had pulled over to the side of the road. As they passed, J motioned for him to follow. The rental pulled out and followed as they passed.

The rendezvous with Sticky was made, and Jose headed toward the Catawba River Bridge which separates Mecklenburg and Gaston counties. J was very curious as to where this particular cab ride would end. This was his old stomping grounds. He, Sticky, Tuck and Buddy had grown up here in Mt. Bell. Many memories passed through his mind. It was here where it all began; it would be so strange if this event ended here. In their childhood, he and the boys were known as the Three and a Half

Musketeers. J smiled to himself, he had been the half. This is where we first came into contact with the guy we named Rags. The guy whom we had thought was a bum, because he was a recluse and lived in a cave. That man has forever changed our lives, because he was really a famous surgeon. Rags had performed an open chest heart massage on Tuck in the back of an old pickup truck. Using a borrowed bottle of vodka to sterilize and a pocket knife for a scalpel, he had saved Tuck's life.

Rags was, at that time, a member of the CIA, but not in good standing. He later inherited a huge corporation and changed his name to S'gar. Over the years S'gar had been their hero and mentor. Now, J is thinking, 'this event means a lot to S'gar but more to me. God, let this be the place they have transported Reececup. What a break if this is it'.

He was aroused from his thoughts by Jose. He realized they were passing the Abbey. "Do you want me to take you to the building or just drive past?"

"Thanks Jose, yeah, just drive past unless it is a dead end," answered J.

Jose passed the volunteer fire department and pointed ahead to the ACME Mill on the right. "I dropped him off in front of that building," Jose said, pointing to the offices of the ACME. The cab passed the mill and they went up the small grade as the road curved back to the right.

As they were out of sight of the mill, J told Jose, "Turn right just past the top of this little hill, and go a couple blocks. There will be room to pull off the road on the left. Let's wait there until my friend gets here." J got out and walked around to the driver's side and Jose let his window down. Sticky parked behind and came on up beside the cab.

"Well, was the rear of this cab familiar?"

"You bet!" said Sticky.

"This is Jose, he said the passenger he brought here was not a nice guy and did not tip. He dropped him off at the front of the old ACME Mill. I think they are out of business. Can you think of anything Jose might know that would help us?" asked J.

"Hello, Jose my man, I am glad you didn't get the tail light fixed. That is the only way I had to remember you. Did your passenger say anything about why he was here, where he came from, anything?"

"No, senior sir, he said nothing much. What he said was 'this is a hick looking place'."

J offered his hand to Jose who took it to shake hands, he found a loaded handshake and ended up with another twenty dollar bill, "Thank you very much Jose Mendez. Yes, I read your name and I will remember it, but it is for me, not my government. I remember friends. If this works out it will be the best thing you have ever done in your life, and I mean it."

"Thank you sen.. sir, I have been in the United States ten years, I became a citizen two years ago. I want to cooperate with my government; am I free to go?"

"Certainly Jose, we know you didn't have to tell us anything, but you did and we thank you, go with God, amigo." Jose waved and drove back toward the airport. Much happier and with a little more in his pocket than he would have had if he had stayed with the queue.

Sitting in the rental, Sticky and J discussed their options. Agreeing that the one thing they needed to do was find out if Reececup was in that building. It was a stretch, but if this was the destination ninety percent of the battle was won.

"Didn't Reececup have a magnet when she was picked up?" Sticky said, raising his voice, "Man, we need that what-ever machine of yours right now."

"Stick you are brilliant, let's get to a phone!" said J.

"Here, try my bag phone. Sometimes it will work around here." Sticky said handing J the bag phone.

The phone had a signal and worked. All the gears were put in motion. The scanner was in one of the vans near the Southern end of I-79. The vans were at Coon Skin Park near Charleston, West Virginia. That was about four and a half hours out. Everyone would remain on hold until a good survey was done. Dallas was using the info on the ACME to see what the public documents could reveal. Calls were in to the Chief of Police of Mt. Bell, but Harris had retired. Jessie James was now the Chief. He took a lot of good natured kidding about his name, but he was used to that. He had a good record of fairness but he did not know S'gar. Sticky knew him and would drop by to see him and try to read his mind. At the same time someone was locating John Harris and the one called Mark David to see if they had influence on the new Chief. Wheels were rolling but not fast enough for J. Reececup was on his mind. "We promised her she would be covered."

"Yeah, I know," said Sticky, "But the best laid plans of mice... I am driving back by the ACME but first let's drive down Suggs Street and see if we can see behind the mill." Off Suggs, they drove Julia. They could see the top of a light colored van. "Call S'gar and see what color Billy said the vans were. I am going past the front and then turn down Cason and see if I can see more from there."

J was still on the phone when Sticky stopped on Cason Street and took out a pair of binoculars from the end compartment of the bag phone........ "Bingo," he yelled, "the van has Pennsylvania plates. I think we are in." said Sticky.

"S'gar is no slouch, he has already asked that question, the vans were both cream colored Fords."

"Well, we have a cream colored van with PA plates, I have never believed too much in coincidence!" said Sticky, I believe we have hit pay dirt.

****

Early that morning Reececup had been in her room alone, she remembered the pain. As she lay on the helicopter floor listening to the thump thump of the blades, she was trying to put together what had happened, where she was and where she was going. Without moving, she could see three people. Apparently, it was the pilot, then a man beside him and the legs of one beside and above her in the bench seat. The other form on the floor must be Steve. He didn't get away, and that is terrible. The deck was uncomfortable but she knew how to disengage her brain from the pain to focus on her present position. There was conversation, but the noise level was so high she could not make out but a few words, none at the time made any sense, but she filed them away for future reference. Acme, van, weather and food were the only words she was sure of. Some half words but, so far, she could not file them. She figured it had been about fifteen minutes. She could tell they were on the descent. She closed her eyes. The chopper landed gently. The noise ceased rapidly down to a whup whup whup of the coasting blades.

"Put them into separate vans," were the verbal orders, "Thanks Gib, you will get a check soon," said one voice.

"No problem, glad to help, you sure you don't want to tell me what is going on?" asked Gib.

"You don't want to know. Your brother Battalion is going to house us for a few days until we straighten a debacle out. These pigs are just going to be fake bargaining tools. Oh, forget what I just said, we got to hit the road. Thanks again." They saluted and the vans departed after everyone was aboard.

'Well, good luck guys, I hope you know what you are doing'. He thought. Before the vans departed he had lowered the security. Turning everything off and showing three red lights on his tower. "Time to get some shut eye, got that early job in a few hours," he said aloud to no one as he went inside, removing his flight jacket.

Inside the van, Reececup was on the floor, at least it had carpet. A voice interrupted her thinking, "You don't have to fake it, and we know you are awake. You guys must think we are stupid. We were onto you within hours of you being admitted to the Crazy House. You don't have to talk yet; I will leave that to the experts. You will be glad to talk to them after a few minutes alone. They are very convincing."

Using her time wisely as she had been trained, she was constantly listening and mentally filing. Trying to get directions proved useless and a waste of time, it was impossible from her position. She was wracking her brain to see if she could figure where they went wrong. What gave them away. Maybe I need to sleep. It was hard but she did drift off as she was thinking.

She was awakening when she felt the van come to a stop. It was light outside. They were at a service station. "If you need to use the bathroom this is your only chance and I will try to make it as private as possible, there is a bucket in back for you to use." Reececup nodded. "I have the taser and if you even act funny you get it."

She was released to relieve herself then retied, and back to the same position. "A few more hours then you will be home," the voice said. She had decided the best thing to do was sleep if she could, so using the oriental exercises that had become a integral part of her life, she tensed and relaxed every muscle. This time, as she was tied, she was awake and had tensed everything to make the bonds as loose as possible when she relaxed. This was much better. She hoped Steve was faring as well. She drifted off to sleep.

When she awoke it was day light and the van was slowing down. Evidently they had driven into a garage or building, because it became semi dark. She was hearing conversations outside asking where they were going to store the cargo. There was a lot of, 'you are kidding'? and 'you Yankees are crazy'. The side sliding door opened and she was dragged out. She was not given a chance to stand and was dragged thru a steel door and dropped on the floor. In a few minutes she felt Steve practically dropped on her. "Okay you two, don't go anywhere, we will be right back," She slowly opened her eyes all the way.

Reece wiggled and moved herself around until she could see Steve. But he was sort of in a sack. "Steve?" she whispered. She heard a grunt.

Wiggling on over to where she could get her teeth on the sack she began to pull. She had it about half off when the door opened. "Ah, playing 'who is in the sack?' I see," said the voice. "Let me help you," and the man pulled the sack off. Reececup tried not to show the shock when she saw it was not Steve. 'Great, he got away,' she thought.

"Okay you two, I have a few questions. These are simple and I would advise that you answer them. Why, you may ask. Well, because all I am going to do is ask them. If you don't answer, it is no skin off my nose. But if you do not answer, the professionals with all the gear to make you talk will be here in a few hours, and that will not be fun, believe me. So, young man, who do you work for?" at that he ripped the tape off the kids mouth. He immediately started crying. The questioner was taken aback. He did not know what to make of this.

"Shut up, and tell me who you work for, you act like a kid, we know better."

"I-I-I don't know what you are t-talking about. I am not s-supposed to be in jail at all. I just had a joint on me when they picked me up, I have been locked up for over a year," He sniffed. "Who are you and why am I tied up and what the heck did you do to me? That hurt worse than I have ever hurt in my life. Let me see a lawyer or something, this is crazy." the boy blubbered.

"Still going to play games, huh? If you thought the stun gun hurt, you just wait, that will be a picnic."

The boy broke down into a fit of crying. He could not believe what was happening. "Is this a nightmare?" he bawled.

"Forget It, I will leave you for the professionals. "YOU," indicating Reececup, "Who do you work for?"

"Sir, I never got a job. I never got a chance to work for anyone. Me and my brother came into town to look for work and this policeman took us before a Judge. The Judge put us in jail until he could check with our folks in West Virginia. If you will call Judge Black, he will clear this up?" Reece said sniffling. "Tell me, what is going on?"

"I'll tell you what is going on. For the past couple nights we have seen you and Romeo here, talking to the two fake guards and calling to someone on a radio. The trick is up young lady, you have been had. So drop the fake innocent story and answer me."

"You must have me mixed up with someone else. I have no idea what you are talking about," Reece said, meekly.

"Okay sweetheart, just remember, I tried. You will remain locked up here, the walls are solid block and that is a steel door. There are plenty of armed men outside, so leaving here without permission is absolutely impossible. We are not cruel; someone will come in and release you and you will be fed. You will have to work out your own privacy with the one commode over there. As you can see you are in an old mill bathroom. So relax, and if you want to talk knock on the door, but only if you are ready to answer my questions." Without waiting for any response he left. Reececup noted he wore camo's and spit shined boots.

"W-what is going on? Why are we here? Do you have any idea?" the boy blurted out.

The door was opening again, so Reececup said nothing. Without a word a guard released them and left.

Knowing that the room might be bugged, Reececup was careful, "I think they have us mixed up with someone else. It is probably a mistake and they will figure it out soon."

"I sure hope so. I wonder where we are, and we must have rode a thousand miles. I ain't ever rode that long," he said.

Reece walked around the walls, looking for bugs and cameras, she spotted none. She started around the room again, this time in detail. There were no bugs or cameras. Quietly, she tried to explain what might be happening. She did not mention Steve or actually what they were doing. She made friends with the kid and told him if a chance came to get out of here to follow her lead. The kid was street wise and since he was no longer tied up, was getting some of that street smart attitude, 'fight 'em'. "But what can a girl do?" he asked.

Without answering, Reece walked away from him. Instantly, she went airborne and did a hundred eighty degree turn just barely missing his head, but he felt the power of the wind. She followed up with a chop to a two by eight board that was leaning up against the wall, it split. Immediately, in the air again this time using her foot, she broke the split board and landed lightly on her feet. She picked up two pieces and handed them to him as he stood dumbstruck. "Who are you? Wonder Woman?" he asked in amazement?

"No sweetheart, just someone who wants out of here as much as you do, now will you follow me?"

"You bet, through fire, you are so cool!"

"Well, we don't want anyone else to know I am cool, okay? That is our secret."

Reece sat down and began to formulate a rough plan.

Chapter 23
Prudent Kidnappings

It was almost five thirty in the morning when all the detainees were secured. S'gar called Tuck and Buddy into the small office. "Boys, I want a few Aces in the hole. I know you have always done whatever I've asked without question, but this time I am asking you to break the law big time. So, please think it over before you answer. You could lose your license and possibly go to jail. I don't have much time, but give it some thought. What I want is to own Judge Black, Tim Kelly and Officer West. I also want to have at least one high profile card from 'Call it Secure's deck'. Matt and Luke are already set to handle that one. So, I am asking you, up front, to kidnap two officers of the law and a CEO. I know they are crooked but it is still kidnapping. I know you understand what I am saying, right?"

"Sure, you are asking will we do it, yeah, with no hesitation. We know where they live; I think we can handle it," Tuck answered for both, Buddy nodded his agreement.

"If I was younger I would love to go on this one. I think you two can do it also, but I would like for you to have at least one more man. Got any suggestions?"

"I will give Woody a shout. I am not sure how he will feel about it, but I will ask."

"Good, I was thinking of him, but hated to suggest it. Your driver will be Corey. He can lend a lot of muscle, if needed. He has become my 'all round guy'."

Tuck moved quickly to a phone and dialed Woody, who answered on the first ring. Tuck quickly went over what they needed without much detail. "I have been sitting here having my early morning coffee and wondering what was going on. I am dressed and ready. Where can I meet you?" They arranged a spot at a public parking lot.

Soon, with the three in the back of the Limo, Corey was headed for the Judge's house first. He lived in a large colonial style house with a circular drive. At about seven fifteen they were in front of the house.

Woody and Tuck had donned thin stocking masks. They laughed as Buddy slipped on a life-like mask of a very pretty blonde. It looked very realistic. There was a paper dickey that looked like a dress, "Okay, quit drooling, let's do it just as planned," Buddy said in a matter of fact tone.

They moved silently. Buddy to the door, the others on each side. At Buddy's nod, Woody rang the bell. Buddy positioned himself as he had many times before. From the peep hole, he looked like a beautiful woman with a stretch in the back ground having a driver standing by an open door. It had worked at least ten times, the perfect ruse. Tuck was holding the ornate storm door open. The Judge opened the door smiling, but the smile quickly altered into a look of confusion as the lady immediately grasped his bath robe by the lapels and pulled him forward. Woody hit him with the stun gun, Tuck caught him and pushed him to Woody. Seconds later he was over Woody's shoulder in a fireman's carry headed for the limo. Buddy, wearing rubber gloves, closed the door and ran to the limo. Corey drove off; the whole evolution was less than three minutes. The judge was taped and tied before the limo was out of site of his house. The judge was dazed, he could hear, but could not see nor talk. What he heard was, "One down with two to go. We are gonna get you some company Judge. Then, we are gonna give you a taste of jail without due process."

The process was much easier at West's house. His comfortable home was in a rural setting. They knew if they were forced to, they would go in after him. This time Tuck carried a dart gun under his belt in case it was needed. Woody had a taser available inside his coat in addition to the stun gun. The precautions were taken because they were approaching a seasoned street-wise officer. This whole scenario depended on his libido kicking in at the sight of the blonde. But nothing varied; it worked as it always had. West considered himself the ladies' man. The blonde at his door caused him to lose all caution. The evolution was the same. Buddy had counted on it. Men didn't see detail when they saw a beautiful, wealthy lady coming to them; at the time, reason did not matter, SHE was there.

They had saved Kelly for last. Kelly's wife jogged with the neighbor's wife from eight thirty until nine thirty. Kelly left for work around nine. Corey parked up the street and everyone donned the silk stocking masks that distorted the facial features. Corey moved when he saw Kelly head for his car. As Kelly reached his car the limo got his attention as the door window slowly opened. Corey was out of the driver's seat and headed down his side of the limo opposite Kelly. From inside the dark cavernous limo he heard, "Mr. Kelly, we need to talk. As he moved closer Corey hit him with his taser. Buddy pushed the door open and Corey caught Kelly and, for anyone viewing, it would appear as if the man has slipped and Corey helped him inside. Corey picked up the keys to the car and handed them to Tuck as Tuck headed for Kelly's car. The limo followed Tuck. Tuck dropped the car at a large mall and returned to the limo.

With their cargo secured they headed for MVA headquarters. Since both Black and West lived alone there was no problem with a spouse. Later today someone would call to tell Kelly's wife that he was called out of town. MVA would place calls to work sites explaining everyone's absence. The limo glided into a garage area as the door rose then closed after them. The new detainees were put on the cargo elevator and it dropped three floors to the cell area. These cells were the best money could produce. This area was used by the school for mock interrogations. It was perfect because it was basically the real thing, sound proof and impossible to escape from. The guests got separate cells. They had TV's with no controls and the screens could not be reached from any cells. Their legs and feet were freed but not the arms or masks. The tape was removed from their mouths. All the threats, pleading and profanity fell on deaf ears, they were not answered. The crew noted that Matt and Luke had already delivered their cargo.

They would all be monitored by camera for their entire stay. "Shut up and listen," said Buddy, "You will find some coffee delivered in a few minutes. You will figure how to locate it, spill it and it will not be replaced." Leaving their quarry, the team headed to S'gar's office to report.

****

Matt took the Hummer and parked it away from the security company office. Luke drove the blue company car to its usual parking spot. Then together they moved to the office. The Corporal of the Guard was snoozing as they slipped in the door. Luke smiled; he took his weapon and eased it against the sleeping guard's ear. "Wake up sleeping beauty, your relief is here and you haven't even made coffee."

Slowly the guard raised his head, the barrel did not move from his ear. "What time do we expect the boss in?" asked Matt.

"Oh seven thirty, b-but you aren't supposed to be here."

"How do you know?"

"Tex and Bull were taking care of you, what happened?" He was coming awake.

"I guess they forgot," said Luke, "But we are here to relieve you, is that all right?"

"S-sure can I go home then?"

"Well, not just yet, don't you usually make coffee and straighten up the office or something?" asked Matt. He and Luke enjoyed this kind of fun. "You had better get to it."

"Sure, if I can have some room."

Luke quickly done a pat down and removed a Ka-Bar combat knife from his boot, it was his only weapon. "Go ahead, but please don't try anything cute, we really don't want to hurt you."

The guard outweighed the guys taunting him by fifty pounds, now he grinned, as Luke holstered his weapon. The guard had just made a big mistake, an amateur one. He had telegraphed a macho statement, that says, 'I'm gonna show you something cute when I have the chance'. He proceeded to prepare the coffee and switch on the pot. He was making an apparent reach for the broom as he got close to Matt. As quickly as he could he reached for Matt's arm. The idea was to spin him into an arm lock, and use Matt as a shield and retrieve the obvious pistol from Matt's shoulder holster. However, as he reached, Matt was no longer there, he had slid back in a fluid motion and chopped down on the guard's arms with such force the guard thought one was broken. Before the guard could recover, he again felt a gun barrel in his ear, this time it was Matt's. The little laugh he heard was from Luke as he said, "That was close Matt, you are getting slow."

Rubbing his arm the guard said, "You guys are good. 'Bout Tex and Bull, where are they?"

Matt just smiled and motioned for the guard to head to the uniform supply room. Matt and Luke secured the guy; he was not going to make any alarm. Before leaving him they explained, in precise terms, that he should look for another job. IF he did not, like Tex and Bull, 'you won't be around for the Second Coming'. They let him come to his own conclusions.

They went back into the office to wait for the coffee to brew. Luke would greet the security boss. Luke had practiced the 'loose cannon' profile and they knew unpredictability was a very good tool. They chatted about the situation and how losing Reececup was very much their responsibility for being lax. Both of them were going to make up for that in spades. Being bested was something they appreciated, but did not handle well. They did a lot of speculating and brain storming to make good use of their down time. At seven thirty the Jaguar pulled in. Luke, still in uniform, lay his head on the desk with his gun in his hand. Matt stepped out of sight.

Luke did not move as an angry boss approached, the boss picked up a heavy book and slammed it down on the desk. At first Luke did not move, knowing this would disconcert anyone. Counting three, Luke came up smiling and pointing an obviously silenced gun at a stunned man, "Good morning sir, would you like a cup of coffee while we talk?"

"What is going on here, this is not your post, and you are not even on duty! Hand me that gun."

"Wow," said Matt stepping into view, armed also, "This guy is good!"

"Forget the coffee, John; we don't need to chat here. I checked your calendar, you have nothing until fifteen hundred. I left a message on the guy's answering machine cancelling it. But here is something I have wanted to do since we first saw your greedy, smug face," as Matt spoke he produced his taser.

"You have my attention, you don't have to use that," John's eyes never left the taser. He was obviously preparing his body to try to dodge. With his full attention on Matt, he did not see Luke as he launched his taser that caught him in the side. John immediately went down with a loud groan.

"Funny, it works every time, Matt," said Luke. "We only have about ten minutes before Paula shows up, let's move." Luke began to secure John while Matt went to retrieve the Hummer.

Luke taped the pre printed notes on the door. One saying the office would be closed until further notice. The other note was to Paula asking her to check her desk. At her desk he had left instructions for her to release the guard and they both were to talk to no one. There was also an apology explaining that 'Call it Secure' was finished and would probably be closed permanently.

They drove to MVA headquarters, arriving just minutes before the other team. Without any fan fare they locked John in a cell, leaving his hands tied behind him and his eyes taped. They headed for S'gar's office to report and get updated.

In a few minutes Tuck, Buddy and Woody came in. They all explained what had happened in detail, so they would all be up to date.

S'gar called Ben in, "Have two of our students cover their faces and go down and take some coffee. Release the detainees' hands using wire cutters, not a knife. Have the eye cover removed also. Speak only to give the necessary orders. Do not enter the actual cells. Have the work done by one while the other observes. In the control room, start the execution movies to condition them for our interrogations. Come on back as soon as you can."

"One other thing you guys do not know. Early this morning after Sticky checked out the Gibson place. I asked him to wait a little while and check to see if the security alarms were actually off as Billy had said. They cruised into the yard out by the helo and back without tripping any alarms. With this knowledge, I alerted our senior class here at the school, of a field exercise and by 0500 Ben accompanied them to visit Mr. Gibson. Needless to say ten men in combat gear and armed to the teeth made an impression. After a thorough questioning, he delivered basically the following message. "A deeply buried group had their eye on his operation. We feel that militia groups are legal, patriotic and law abiding. Gib was informed he is walking on the edge aiding in the unlawful kidnappings. As I suspected he is pretty straight. Ben feels like he was just used and was enjoying the money without checking where it came from. The best news is that there is a new militia forming in your home town. There is a good possibility that the vans were headed there. Everything points to that. We will know more as the day progresses."

Tuck spoke up, "maybe we had better head in that direction, or at least tell the van drivers to get closer."

"I have already instructed the vans to be driven south as far as the Yeager Airport area near Charleston, West Virginia, and," said S'gar," that will put them within 3 to 4 hours of Mt. Bell. As for us who remain here, MVA has a charter plane waiting with a flight plan for a small airport in Gastonia, just off Union Road. WE will depart if we have a good indication that our Reececup is there. We will leave this place in the good hands of Ben, Dallas, Corey and Woody."

"Gentlemen, I would really like to go along," said Woody. "I haven't felt so alive in years."

"As the head of MVA you don't know how good that makes me feel, Woody. But, I will not endanger your pension, not to mention the other aspects involved. No, I want you to retire with Anna Mae, fish and enjoy life. Later, I would love to spend some time with you fishing. I haven't taken the time to fish since my last extended visit around Mt. Bell. While there, I would go down to the Catawba and do some night fishing for mine and Satan's meals."

"Satan?" queried Woody.

"Long story, Satan was my dog. Anyway, I want you to be here in case we need your investigative skills here in Pittsburgh. We are taking most of our resources with us if we leave. Right now, most of what we are doing is waiting. It will be a long few hours.

There was a lot of discussion as to who to interrogate first. "Our studies have shown us that a subject needs to watch at least two solid hours of the execution film. The film is cuts of actual executions from all over the world. After two hours, even though a subject doesn't really believe they will be executed, there is always that little nagging doubt. So far, in our experience with real life interrogations, death has been the best motivator to use. Here at the school we have learned that is unfortunately not true with the East and Middle East cultures. There death is not a BAD thing. In that case water-boarding is the only way to get answers. So in a couple hours I would like to talk to Mr. Tim Kelly first.

****

Dallas had been in contact with a couple attorneys in Mt. Bell with whom he had business dealings at the time S'gar donated some land for a museum or park. They were searching whatever public records would reveal concerning the ACME mill, and making inquiries as to the present occupants. He learned right away that the ACME was out of the textile business. All equipment had been removed and sold overseas or as scrap metal. It was presently a huge cavernous shell except for the former mill's offices. The importance of the job was explained by Dallas and that he expected to pay a premium for the information.

He already had been successful in getting addresses and phone numbers of retired Police Chief Johnny Harris and of the General contractor Mark David. Dallas had a call into both of them. John was playing golf. Mark was on a job site and would return his call in a little bit. Dallas smiled at the term, wondering how long a little bit was down south. Dallas had once met both men that he was trying to get in touch with, and that was a strange day. That was the day he agreed to go down and be an escort for four kids as they actually toured S'gars digs. At the time S'gar was known as Rags. Could it have been that long ago? 'My my, how time flies' he thought.

V. Jane buzzed Ben, "Ben, your call is being returned by Mark David. He is on line one."

"Hey Mark, thanks for returning my call. I am calling to see if I can ask a favor."

"Most everybody does, I will do what I can, but time is favors like time is money."

"I understand that. We met many years ago over behind what you know as the Eagle. I represented a man you knew as Rags."

"Oh yeah, boy do I remember that well, I thought I recognized that name, Dallas. We have a town near here called Dallas. Sure Dallas, forget what I said about money. What can I do for you? But first how is the old boy doing, Rags?"

"Oh, he is doing great. The information I need is for him by the way. I need some drawings of good information on the ACME mill."

"The ACME is in North Mt. Bell. She is shut down, Dallas. I drive by every once in awhile. But I know a couple folks in County Plans, Permits, etc. If they have done any renovating in the last couple years, they will have plans. When you need this?"

"Today, of course, if I needed it tomorrow I would have called tomorrow. Isn't that the way the line goes?" said Dallas laughing. "But seriously Mark, it could be a matter of life and death, but I am not sure."

"Oh, it is that kind of favor?" Mark remembered that Rags had been deep in the Agency at the same time he was. "Is something cooking in Mt. Bell, Dallas?"

"You know I cannot say Mark, but you know there is always that possibility."

"I will drive to Gastonia immediately, Dallas. Tell Rags hello for me. But didn't I hear Sticky say he had changed his name to something silly like Cigar?" asked Mark.

"Yes Mark, he is now called Esgar, spelled S'gar, and thanks. By the way, Sticky and the kid J. Leon are down there somewhere now. Thanks." Mark signed off and headed for his truck smiling and thinking, 'what can be happening in good old Mt. Bell'?

****

The cell area was prepared for the interrogation. Woody watched with the others as Tim Kelly was moved from a cell to a chair and hand cuffed in place. The next thing that occurred took Woody and all the detainees by surprise. He heard the words 'clear the bars' and immediately a shield of some type dropped in front of all cells. Leaving only the center area with Mr. Kelly sitting there, shocked. On command, the lights came on blinding Tim Kelly and leaving him feeling vulnerable; of course Woody recognized this procedure. It was illegal for law enforcement, but used by the underworld, CIA and FBI when privacy was required. Silently, S'gar took a seat behind the lights. He said nothing for two long minutes.

"Mr. Kelly, it seems that you have taken a very valuable article of mine, and I want her back."

"I have no idea what you mean," Kelly answered, arrogantly.

"There are some things you do not know. You missed one of our people and took an innocent kid, mistake number two. The biggest mistake was taking a sweet young lady who was only doing her job. That was mistake number one. Now listen and listen very carefully. You are at best, going to jail. That is your best option. There your wife can visit and bring you cookies. If you are fortunate, they will put you in a minimum security farm. I will give you a hint of the other option. You will never eat one of your wife's cookies again, and worse you will never see her again. Am I getting thru to you?"

"To start with, I want to call my lawyer, you cannot do this. Second, I am going to sue you for every penny you have. Is that clear enough, crap head?" Immediately after finishing the sentence, Tim Kelly screamed.

"Oh, I see you noticed you are in an electric chair. Good, and I despise being called names. Now, Mr. Tim Kelly, CEO of the Lighthouse Eight Corporation, if I have your attention, let me try to point out your position here. At one time you had thirty million dollars in an account in the Cayman Islands. Notice, I said you HAD. That account now has five hundred dollars in it. The bank maintenance fees will eat that up in a month, it will be zero. Just this morning five hundred thousand dollars was placed in your account by an undisclosed Mafia Family in New Jersey. In a few weeks the FBI will be looking into your affairs. You can be around to answer questions, or just disappear. Personally, we do not care. We have twenty-nine and a half million dollars of your money to spend fighting crime. Now, would you like to be a state's witness against whoever set you up in this, including Judge Black and Officer West who, by the way, are your cell mates, or do you want to wait to see if they will sell you out? I do not want an answer yet. What I do want is to confirm my agent's status. Did you send my agent and an innocent kid to North Carolina early this morning, yes or no?"

"You can go to h...." Tim Kelly once again screamed.

After Kelly settled down from the jolt S'gar continued, "That was only 10,000 volts, little current. Do you know what kills with electricity Tim? It is the current. If I had added twenty amps to that you would be fried. WE have actually gotten to four amps before the subject expired. I am going to let you feel two amps just for the fun of it. If you live I will throw you back in the cell until later. I am through with you for now, give it to him."

"No wait. Yes, we sent them to North Carolina. But if you keep this up you will never see them again."

"I think we will. Let me read you the names of the people who will disappear if our young lady is terminated, as you hint. Are you listening? Guess who number one is, Tim Kelly, Judge Black, Officer West, John Day..... ," S'gar completed the list. You see I am very attached to that young lady. She is like the daughter I never had. Mr. Kelly, look around you when you are returned to that cell. Do you think we are kidding?"

"This thing goes higher than you know, we are protected," Kelly said with little conviction.

"Before the day is out your protection will still be elsewhere scratching their heads. By the end of the day we will know everything you know, everything Judge Black and the rest of your friends here know. Do you think you are dealing with a street gang? You have no idea how high we reach, nor what our powers are. Now, to return to my immediate concern, you said, 'I may never see them again'. Oh, but I think we will and very soon, we have the old ACME mill covered at this very minute."

In the observation room three guys said 'Yes', they knew by the body language S'gar had said the magic word ACME. The conversation ended and everything was returned to its normal state. The team headed back to S'gar's office.

"Well, what do you think?" asked S'gar.

"Reececup is in that old mill, I am sure of it," said Woody. Everyone else nodded in agreement. "The body English was unmistakable. When you said the word ACME he lit up."

They prepared for a change of command to Mt. Bell and started formulating a tentative rescue plan. They knew Sticky and J were doing the same. They could compare ideas in Mt. Bell. In the mean time, Ben was coordinating with the team in Mt. Bell. Using the info they had already transmitted, he started the vans south. Next stop will be Mt Bell, North Carolina their old home town.

Chapter 24
The MVA goes after Its Own

The closest place for a command post was the VFW building not far away from the ACME on Cason St. Sticky knew P.W. Bentley who was the commander. The post could always use the rental money. No one would be in the building until the pinto bean and cornbread supper which was five days off. Mark David had brought in the floor plans for the one story building. The vans had arrived and were unloaded. The scanner was kept inside one of the vans. For power they used an inverter hooked to an extra twelve volt battery. Using this configuration they would not need the noisy generator. J went with the van and parked it just off the street as close to the ACME as possible.

One of the troops got out and started working with the jack, finally he raised the van. He popped the hub cap and tried to loosen the nuts, the tire turned. He kept trying; giving the appearance of being inept at changing a tire. While inside, the scanner was started hoping Reececup had her magnet with her. If she didn't have the stronger pocket magnet, J was eager to see if at least a reading of her magnetic necklace would show up. Five minutes of scans, nothing. J explained it must acclimate itself to the building. You should see some bodies, moving or sitting, soon if anyone is in there.

"Got something," the operator said, "See here in the corner, overlaying it on the plans, it shows the body is near the main entrance. Now, here is another, it is warming to the building." Five more minutes and they were locating exact areas where most of the activity was. But no magnet blips. J was becoming apprehensive thinking, 'if she is there it should have shown by now'.

"Wait, what is this? YES, we have a strong magnet right here! Okay, let's overlay that on the drawings. She is in a large bathroom, only one way in," the operator was saying.

J was ecstatic. 'Hold on sweet heart we are coming'. "Monitor that blip and make sure it moves. Let me know as soon as you can tell."

"Yeah, there it is, not much, but she moved. She is still with us." J called out to the guy outside to go ahead and put the spare on. During that time they marked all body locations and charted the moving ones. After the survey, the van was driven around the block and back to the VFW building. It was now past mid afternoon. Much had happened since midnight. In fourteen hours, by overlapping resources, as usual the MVA was accomplishing the near impossible without appearing to be in a hurry. In their latest communication with Ben, he told them that the remainder of the team was headed for the airport.

****

Back in Pittsburgh, the remainder of the mobile unit was on the move. To avoid delay in the afternoon traffic they were using a helicopter taxi to the airport. If all went as planned they would land in Gastonia at about 6 PM. Everyone knew that speed and shock were needed in any kidnapping case. S'gar was puzzled that the bad guys had not contacted them. Up until now all their points of contact had remained silent. The radio remained with Josh and his technical team. He had the bag phone numbers along with the plane frequencies. S'gar wanted some movement from the other side.

The transition was speedy and smooth. The Helicopter landed very near the corporate jet. The crew was on the ground ducking their heads and running toward the plane. The jet was fired and sitting with the brakes on. The crew, consisting of Matt, Luke, Tuck, Buddy and S'gar were aboard and the bird was taxiing seconds after the helicopter was airborne. With an immediate clearance they were underway in less than ninety seconds. Everyone was buckling in as they shot down the, seldom used, short runway. Next stop would be the Gastonia Municipal Airport.

"Fifteen minutes out, S'gar," the pilot announced, and, just then, Matt's phone rang. He handed the bulky bag phone to S'gar.

"Yes?" S'gar had quickly attached a suction cup mike to the phone and hit the record button on the small micro cassette recorder.

"Are you missing a couple packages?" said the voice.

"Yes, where are they?" asked S'gar.

"I am sure you don't expect me to answer that. If you expect to see them alive and well you will listen carefully," a pause and S'gar could tell he was talking to someone with the mouth piece covered. "Okay, I am told that Judge Black is missing, would you know anything about that?"

"I might, if we can work a trade, I can have him at the Lighthouse facility in an hour," said S'gar.

"You misunderstand. The judge is expendable. I don't care what you do with him, as a matter of fact; it would save me a lot of money if he was out of the equation. He is getting old, senile and greedy. Now, to your instructions; you will turn over everything you have stolen or learned. You will give me the name and location of your organization. For this I will move your people out of the country and keep them alive for one year. You will receive a call monthly to ensure I am keeping my end of the bargain. When I have covered all my bases, I will release them. It may be less. I said a year, that is on the outside."

"There is only one problem with that. I am missing only one small package. It is an important package, but not irreplaceable. The other package you have is an inmate of the Lighthouse taken by mistake and in haste. He has no idea why you have him, and he certainly does not know us," pausing for affect. "By the way, I want to speak to my missing property to make sure you actually have her."

"Then, you are a little concerned about what I do with her, n'est pas?"

"Certainly, I am not without feeling as you seem to be about Judge Black, I wish no harm to come to her."

"Well, since you do not have anything to bargain with, I see no reason to humor you. Do you?"

"Okay, let's try Officer West, can I negotiate for his soul?" asked S'gar.

"Not on your life, I hate crooked cops. If a cop will turn on his own, I will use him and throw him to the dogs. You wouldn't happen to have anymore broken puzzle pieces would you?"

"As a matter of fact I do, six more pieces as a matter of fact, but first, does Tim Kelly ring a bell?"

"You are bluffing; Tim is out of town on business, his wife called his secretary mid morning, good try."

"Oh, he is out of town all right, he is with Judge Black and Officer West. Would you like to speak with him?"

"Most certainly, put him on."

"Put my lady on the phone and I will. On second thought call me back in an hour and we will talk." S'gar hung up without ceremony.

Buddy had stepped inside the cabin area to tell the pilot not to make any announcements until the call was over. When he saw S'gar hang up he walked back and told everyone to buckle up that the pilot was making his approach. The landing was smooth. The Pilot taxied up to a hanger where the MVA van was waiting. Another smooth transition and they were on their way. The pilot would refuel and relax in the pilots lounge or in the plane. He was on hold for twenty four hours. The driver had been instructed to give the late arrivals an around the area tour of the ACME mill. And let them know that Reececup has been spotted inside. Within Twenty-five minutes they were all together at the VFW Building.

Greetings were short. This team knew time was of the essence. "J, you and Sticky have been 'boots on the ground' longer than the rest of us. What is your take and what do you suggest?" Someone handed S'gar a cup of coffee as he finished. The VFW had a giant coffee pot and the troops kept it going.

"Sticky has been in contact with Tuck's brother- in- law. Good guy, retired Green Beret. He knows what is happening around Mt. Bell. He has turned into some kind of local hero and entertainer. He says the word is that this is going to be the headquarters for a new militia group. The step is temporary because this building is scheduled for razing next year. I guess the mill owners want to make enough to pay the taxes before it goes. Anyway, the militia has a meeting scheduled for tonight, nineteen hundred to twenty one thirty. Vernon says they don't hang around after the meeting; most of them need to get home because they work tomorrow. So, we figure to hit them hard about twenty-two thirty."

"How many do you think will be inside?" asked Tuck.

"Today it has been about eight. They are all proud of their side arms and carry them; you know how that is, we all like our weapons."

Sticky added, "We thought about twenty-two twenty-five a couple of guys would have a little Donnybrook outside the front door. Our van, with a driver carrying three guys out of sight in the back, will pull in and slide to a stop. The driver will jump out to meet the second vehicle, a car. It will slide in on the right. Van driver will meet the new driver on the side away from the road but in front of the door, yelling something like, you was with my wife, sucker, you are dead meat."

J finished the scenario, "I don't think the red blooded boys of the militia will want to miss a good fight. We should get at least two of them.

We hope to cut the odds immediately, the more the merrier. There is no serious cover at the back so we will have to 'injun up' on them back there. The good news is, there is not much of a view that way either. We have spotted no cameras or security instruments. They have only been in possession of this building three weeks. We will have three teams. Able team will cause the diversion, disarm and secure their guys and enter from the front. Baker team will plant the explosives on two rear doors early and blow them at twenty-two thirty. Our plans are to have the front clear, everyone in when the rear explosives start. For added confusion they will set off charges at two more locations around the building. Charlie team has a lot of fireworks. They will be prepared during the time the meeting is going on. They will detonate them immediately after Baker teams explosives complete."

"Why the fireworks?" asked Buddy.

"Sticky's idea, and a good one, I think. There aren't many residences around, but there are a few. They will be curious about the bangs. By the time they look out, the fireworks will draw all eyes away from the ACME. It will be a short show. We just don't want any citizens calling the local or county police."

"I haven't heard about extractions," said S'gar, "Who is handling that?"

"Baker team will have two drivers. We rented a twelve passenger van to go along with our cargo van. Of course we will close up shop at the VFW and all our equipment will be packed, we will be prepared to bug out. When the action starts, both vans will immediately pull into the loading dock at the rear. The drivers will be prepared to assist or take on passengers."

"A couple of boys have made a little trip to the edge of the woods behind the ACME. They left the scanner running so we know where the bodies are. Here is the output overlaid on the building plans," J pointed out the set up.

"Do you know if the treasurer is still here?" asked S'gar.

"Negative, we do not know. But we figure, if we see him, he would need a ride back to Pittsburgh, right?" laughed J.

Matt's phone rang, and he handed it over to S'gar, who took out the mini recorder, attached the suction cup mike and punched record, "Yes?"

"Okay, I really hate to lose old Tim, but he is expendable, so we are back to your people," stated the caller.

"Let me speak to my agent," S'gar said evenly, as if asking for a glass of water, "Or is she not available?"

"Not so fast, right now she is predisposed. In just a little while she will be telling us all we want to know."

"Reading in between the lines, that means you do not have her, right? You cannot eyeball her can you?" asked S'gar.

"To tell you the truth commodore, she and her partner are down the hall locked in a rest room that has been converted to a holding cell. Right now, we are located in another part of the world. One you don't even know that exists. So keep your powder dry and I will call you back after our official interrogation. I figure that should be by eleven tonight. I'll call you." S'gar heard the click of disconnect.

All eyes had been on the scanner output, one form had been moving around an office as the conversation took place. Now it stopped. They watched it move down the hall to where Reececup and the kid were being held. The form stayed there just a minute and walked back to the office. "Bingo," said Buddy, "I am wondering if the treasurer isn't the top dog, what do you think?"

"A very good possibility," said Tuck, "A very good possibility."

"Our man Sticky, future politician, is well liked around here. He has an appointment with Chief Jessie in just a little while. Being close to a metropolitan area like Charlotte, crime is spilling over into his fair town and he doesn't like it one bit. The chief is putting in a lot of hours, for a small town; he has actually arrested an associate of a serial killer here in Mt. Bell. Right now his biggest problem is a burglary of the local National Guard building. They took a load of AK's, ammo and a couple rocket launchers. He has several leads but nothing firm. Sticky is meeting him for dinner at Sammy's down town, to talk to him."

"Why don't we invite him in?" asked Luke.

The explanation was short. "If anything big comes out of this, any or all of us would be witnesses. The MVA doesn't have time for that right now. We have some big fish to fry in Pittsburgh."

The team had studied this in detail. Timing each move, and if things went perfect, they needed twelve to fifteen minutes from bang to bug-out. Sticky was going to try to persuade Chief Jessie to clear North

Mt. Bell of patrol cars from twenty-two fifteen to twenty-two fifty. They were hoping to lean on his generosity, offering a possible kidnap victim from Pittsburgh and maybe a couple stolen vans. The tag numbers on the vans were run as soon as they were able to get them and the tags were stolen, so very likely the vans were too. Everyone had agreed that leaving the teenager here would open the dance with Lighthouse Eight Incorporated. They would have a hard time explaining how one of their inmates ended up in North Carolina and they had not reported him missing. A lot hinged on the chief's faith in Sticky and his subsequent cooperation.

Sticky headed for his appointment about the same time the troops were beginning to arrive for the Militia meeting. At the VFW, face paint and camo's were being readied to don, and weapons being checked. The VFW Building was policed and squared away. The scanner would be used until everyone was in position. The receiver would be the last thing dismounted and loaded. The drivers would do that. Buddy spoke up, "S'gar, which van will you be in when the Donny-brook starts?"

"Funny you should ask, friend, because I will be right beside you on Baker team awaiting your orders," S'gar said, smiling.

"But Boss, you can't do that. I mean.. What I mean is, well sir, your age for goodness sake," stammered Tuck.

S'gar laughed this time, "This amazes me, I thought I had surrounded myself with the best in the business. I was under the impression I had chosen sharp analytical minds. Let's try something simple, analyze that sentence you just tried to make. The leading word was Boss. That means I plan to be there to see Reececup, and if necessary kick the butts of the fools that thought she was theirs. Is that clear enough?"

"Sure, but I just thought…"

"I work out daily. I am a medical doctor and a surgeon. But I went thru the same SEAL training some of you did. I will not be an anchor. If I had one small doubt, I would not go. The success of this mission is top priority, I would remove anyone, even me, if I felt the individual was not ready. Now, are we all okay with that?" Everyone nodded.

"Definitely, glad to have you aboard, sir," laughed Tuck.

"Hey, I am watching Reececup. She must be nervous, she is moving around in the cell, look here," said the monitor analyst, "It has been going on for about two minutes."

"Dude, that girl ain't nervous. She is cooler that most men I know. She will stop in about three minutes. That pattern is her karate routine; she is in the habit of using it before every performance or every event. She must know something is up about the interrogation, and she is setting her mind to it, she will be fine," said Steve. Everyone went on about their preparations. Sure enough, in three minutes, the analyst announced she had stopped.

It was twenty one hundred when Sticky returned. "Men, he is going along with it, but he isn't crazy about it. He is protective about his town, and isn't thrilled. He is a sharp investigator himself and he knows I am holding something back. He is a law-and-order cop, and this wrankles him some."

"You did good Sticky, thanks," said S'gar.

"Hey, you guys remember that Harris drove that '34 Ford? Well, guess what James drives, A cherry 1957 Chevy. I think he is as crazy about that car as Harris was his. Of course he doesn't use it during his official time like Johnny did. The town has grown and doesn't smile on that stuff much anymore. He wishes they did." Sticky was filling his cup one last time as he finished. His assignment was driving the big van during Bug-out.

The Militia meeting ended and everyone that had driven up to attend had driven off. Now the troops started getting ready. By fifteen minutes before the first bang time they were all in place. The actors were up near the Abbey ready to drive in for the fake fight. Steve was near the north end of the building. His position was around the corner from the actual door. He would move closer at bang time. He could not actually see the door. It was eerie quiet. From behind him he heard a low but audible whisper, "What in heck are you doing here?" He tensed, ready to attack.

****

Inside, Reececup could tell that there was some sort of large meeting going on in the building. By her estimation it must be night time. The big mouth had been down to tell her to expect company soon, that was a couple hours ago, she estimated. To clear her mind she went through her favorite karate routine again. This time she was taking in every detail of the room. The overhead was like a lot of industrial buildings, it was exposed. The plumbing and heating and air had been run overhead. What she thought was previously out of reach suddenly became a possibility, if the commode would give her the added inches she needed to reach the plumbing pipes. The kid watched in amazement. He was bowled over when she went from the slow exercise to a springing run. Using the edge of the commode as a spring point she launched herself to the overhead plumbing about nine feet up. She then hand walked the pipe over to an opening in a heat duct. At one time there had been a grill over it, but it was long gone. She easily pulled her small frame into the duct.

The two foot diameter duct work was antique stuff, sheet metal but not aluminum. It was no longer used. Evidently when the electric heating system had been installed they left the old supply lines. She felt around and could tell that the duct work angled down at about a 45 degree angle. She could feel an updraft, it smelled of fresh air. 'We couldn't be that lucky', she thought. She backed up past the spot where she entered the duct. Leaning out the hole, she peered into the next room, it was empty. Looking down at the kid staring up at her, she said, "Hand me the smallest piece of the board I broke awhile ago." It took a couple tries but he threw it up so she could catch it. She eased back over to the forty-five degree bend and slid the block down. She heard it slide clear, and hit something at the bottom. It did not sound solid. Back to the hole, she grasped the plumbing pipe and swung down, then dropped to the floor.

"This is what we are going to do. We are going to disappear. Got it?"

"Yeah, but how? I don't think I can reach that pipe." The kid said.

"Did you ever do monkey bars?" Reececup asked.

"Sure, I can do all that stuff, I just can't reach that pipe!"

"That will come later. Right now listen. That pipe is like a slide. Once it passes this wall it slants down to the floor in some kind of store room. I could see around the outside of the pipe where it goes thru the wall. I think it goes outside, I smell fresh night air coming up thru it. I am going to give you a foot up. You are going to get one try at it so we have to make it count. You watched me go up; I used the edge of the commode. I am going to take the commodes place and form a stirrup like this," forming a web with my fingers and holding it down in front of her, "You will step into my hands and push with your other leg. As you push, aided by your momentum, I will launch up to the pipe. You won't have to hand walk the pipe, but you must catch it on the first try. Then you simply swing yourself up into the duct like I did. Can you handle that?" asked Reececup.

"I'm not sure, but I think so."

"There is another option. I have friends. I can go alone, get them and come back for you."

"Not on your life Wonder Woman. I'll take my chances with you."

"Okay, let's get to it," Reece braced against the wall and formed the stirrup. Then she heard the noise approaching. "Okay, we go to plan B."

"What is Plan B?"

Reece paused as she heard them just outside the door, "I am not sure, but follow my lead." As she finished, four men walked in; two in camouflage uniforms and two in suits. The uniforms had a couple suit cases and a sturdy folding table.

Ignoring the two prisoners, one suit said, "Thank you gentle men. Please set up the table and step back out in the hall. Lock the door, and under no circumstances are you to open the door until I give you the word. No matter what you hear, do not come in. Is that clear?"

"Yes sir," they set the table up and left, closing the heavy steel door. They all heard the bolt of the lock set with a snap.

"You people have been very naughty," Reececup cringed, moving away, the kid did likewise, "This can be easy or hard. If you agree I will just ask the questions and you answer, otherwise," as he was talking he had taken some electrical equipment out of one suit case and plugged a transformer into a wall socket. He touched the red and black lead together causing sparks. "By the way don't try to run around this room and try to avoid me. Have you ever been tasered?"

"Yeah, man don't taser me, I was just minding my own business when I was kidnapped. I will tell you anything I can, but don't taser me." The outburst surprised Reececup. This was real; the kid had been tasered when he was kidnapped. He remembered the pain and was scared to death.

The second suit was holding onto his brief case like it contained gold and that he was afraid someone was going to take it. The other suit asked him to plug in another piece of equipment. As he put down a brief case and bent down to plug the second lead into the outlet, everyone was stunned. The scared backward girl all of a sudden became a lethal fighting machine. Springing into the air, she performed the perfect 'Cyclone'. In an airborne three hundred and sixty degree turn she faked with the left foot but connected with the tall suits head with the right heel. It had the force of a small cyclone. The move is aptly called the Cyclone because it is destructive. As she landed, number two suit was standing and reaching inside his coat, Reececup assumed it was for his taser. From the landing she bent her knees and launched herself again. This time she used the 'Scissor Kick'. That move is usually for show and never used against a true opponent. But this was a sitting duck and she wanted to put him out. With the scissor she got him with both feet. She landed as he went down. Then she walked over to the big suit, reached down and with a chopping motion, clipped him on the neck. She returned to number two and did the same. Immediately, she motioned for her partner to help her. For a distraction, she yelled, "**Please** don't do that again, **OH! That hurt!**"

She whispered, "Remove their shoes and socks. Use one sock and put all the stuff from their pockets in it. Save one sock each for a gag. Remove their belts and pants," as she was talking she was looking thru the suitcases. Finding a scalpel, she cut the sleeves off one coat and cut the rest of the coat into strips. Efficiently, she stuffed their mouths and tied the gag in place, and slipped the large part of the sleeve over their head to keep the band and gag in place. She tied their hands and legs like a good bulldogger would do a steer. Together they dragged the victims over to the vertical plumbing and tied their feet to the pipes. Looking around, she took the board she had broken earlier and wedged the door. "We can forget the jump to the pipe," she whispered, as she pointed to the table. They moved it under the opening. Then she really confused the kid. She went over to the commode, turned the water off and disconnected the hand tight supply line. She then flushed the commode. Amazed, the kid watched her remove the tank top. Then using the commode as a lever for itself, she worked it back and forth until she broke the bolts that attached it to the floor. She then laid it over on its side to empty the rest of the water. Some of the water ran over to the two guys who were tied and she felt no remorse as their underwear began to soak up the cold water.

Motioning that they were going to put the commode on the table, the light finally dawned on the kid. Quickly, they placed the commode against the wall on top of the table. Reece replaced the ceramic tank top, and they had a nice set of steps right up to the vent pipe. Placing one of the hard suitcases beside the table, Reece made a sweeping motion, indicating 'after you'. Then she yelled a couple more times trying to sound as if she was in agony, when she really wanted to laugh. With the kid up in the vent shaft, she picked up the brief case, then the socks and climbed up on the table and handed the stuff up. She directed him to slide back away from the wall so she could go first down the pipe. She whispered directions. "I will go first taking the brief case. If you hear three rapid taps do not come down, I will be coming back up. Count to twenty after I go then slide down after me. I'm gone, see you in a minute." He nodded.

****

When the two guards stepped outside in the hall and locked the door they took their posts on either side of the door. When they heard the scuffle, they smiled. Then they heard the yelling and did a mock flinch. Both relaxed. They heard a little movement but not much talking. In a few minutes some more yelling. One guy nodded, all is well. Then things got completely quiet. Hearing the commode flush one guard smiled real big and mimicked holding someone's head in a commode and flushing. The other guy nearly laughed out loud. It was quiet again. For a few minutes they were uneasy but they had orders not to come in under any circumstances. Then they heard some sounds like voices trying to yell through gags. Ah, and again they relaxed and smiled. All was well. Gags would stop all that yelling.

****

At the bottom of the chute was the outside of the building, but there was a heavy grate over it. Reececup's heart sank. She eased her weight against it and it just fell out quietly on the grass. It had been held in place by rusty screws. She quietly eased outside and moved away from the opening, staying on the ground in a prone position. The kid came out and she motioned they were going to crawl across about fifteen feet of mowed grass to the weeds beyond. They began to crawl. Reececup figured they had twenty to thirty minutes and she wanted to get clear so they could run. They needed to find a phone. They needed the MVA. She also knew J and Steve, especially, were very worried.

Chapter 25
Action at the ACME

Lying In his position, tensely anticipating the first bang, Steve heard the whisper, "What the heck are you doing here?"

Steve tensed and instantly was ready to attack to keep someone from blowing the event surprise. His brain said 'familiar', and he rolled to his side and was facing Reececup. A smile raced across his face, "In about a minute I am going to be a hero when I rescue you. **Get back in there!**" He grabbed her and though they were on the ground he gave her a giant hug and she did him. Tears were in their eyes. Over Reece's shoulder, he saw his roommate who was laying there his eyes as big as saucers; this was too much for him.

"I'll get the story later, right now I have to go. In a minute the first bang will go then the flash bangs and we are in. Thank God you are safe, you stay right here."

"You are crazy, I am going in, and I owe these people something." She turned to the kid. "You hold this briefcase and the socks, I'll be back in a few minutes," the kid just nodded he was too blown away to respond. Steve slipped Reececup a roll of duct tape. "This is my weapon?" About that time they heard explosions. Then across the street a fireworks display. The kid figured he must be dreaming. A flash lit up the whole inside of the building and a super bang that vibrated the ground. Steve and Reececup headed for the blown door. Steve was armed; Reececup was too, with a roll of duct tape.

Inside was confusion on the part of the occupants. They were militiamen, but no one had told them that the war was going to begin this soon. The first guys Reececup and Steve ran into were the guards. They were on the deck holding their ears. They had been guarding the door where Reececup had been. "I got them, go!" said Reece. Both guards were trying to recover but it was too late. Reece disarmed them, gave one a karate chop and then taped the other ones hands, then his feet. Last was his

278

mouth. She immediately did the same to the one who was out. She quickly went over the men for other weapons finding only knives, which she kept. Wished them luck and left.

In less than five minutes everything was secure. S'gar saw Reece, acknowledged her, but as every MVA person knew there was a time and place and this was not it. The goal must be reached and depart. The clock was ticking. There would be plenty of time for explanations later. Reececup got J's attention and motioned for him to follow her. She ran down the hall, snapped the lock back, pointed and said, "Two of the really bad guys, I have a kid outside. I'll be right back." She turned and ran down the hall then out through the blown door yelling, "Okay, everything is clear, follow me!" The kid jumped up and followed, carrying the treasures. He and Reececup ran back into the building. J already had the troops moving the two suits to a central area. Of course, they no longer wore suits.

"Okay, do we have anyone important?" asked Buddy.

"Reece says these two are. She also has Steve's stand-in. What will we do with him?" asked J.

Buddy looked at S'gar for guidance. S'gar spoke, "We take the two. Leave the kid as a kidnap victim. Did we determine the senior man, Tuck?"

"Yes sir, this is the Top Sergeant," said Tuck quickly.

"Walk him down the hall and find out who here is from out of town that doesn't belong to this Militia. The rest of you follow the plan," said S'gar, and the evacuation began.

While the confab was taking place the admin crew was busy looking through the office records to see if any papers appeared that connected this group to Lighthouse Eight in Pittsburgh.

Buddy yelled, "Three minutes." It was repeated throughout the building.

The detainees were already secured in the van. Troops were moving out. J and Reececup were briefing the kid on what was going to happen. He smiled when J told him he was in charge until Chief James got there. "Will I see you again Wonder Woman?" the kid asked.

Unable to speak without crying for a few seconds, Reececup hugged the kid and whispered, "I sure hope so partner. You have done a great job. From now on I think your life will start looking up. Now, walk over to the desk at the front door and take your post." The kid was smiling from ear to ear as he walked to the desk and sat down. Reececup waved bye and ran toward the loading docks.

"One minute," Buddy yelled. The admin crew ran out of the office carrying only a couple folders and headed for the loading docks.

"All clear?" Buddy yelled, waited a second and got no response. He waved good bye to the kid, "Good luck son, give the sheriff out regards and thanks." Buddy left on the double.

He jumped in the last van, "All present and accounted for," said Sticky as he headed down the road and toward Gastonia.

"Perfect," said Buddy, "Everyone deserves a bonus for that one. It has been fast and furious since early this morning and now the immediate goal has been reached. He was looking back at J, Steve and Reececup. They were all smiles. Once Sticky turned onto I-85 South, Buddy said, "Now, Reececup explain yourself. If we had known you were going to get the bad guys by yourself, J and Steve could have flown and saved us all a lot of trouble."

"Well, to tell the truth, when you didn't call I got tired of waiting. A girl will wait just so long you know!" Reece retorted. Everyone had a good laugh. After all the congratulations, Reececup related her story.

The van they were in contained the two detainees who as it ended up were the only ones from out of town. The Top Sergeant had never been happy about holding prisoners and being ordered around by 'out of town' civilians. He voluntarily cooperated with Tuck, even to having his hands and feet secured with nylon tie-wraps.

The other two vans headed North on I-77. They would over night for some well deserved rest, then head on to Pittsburgh. There was plenty of room in the charter for the team leaders and their two guests. They drove to a secluded hanger area where the charter was waiting. They boarded, carrying their two guests.

Sticky drove to the small terminal and found the night supervisor. There, he arranged for the supervisor to watch the vehicle until the rental company picked it up. Then, for a fee, he let Sticky have a couple flight suits and drove him back to the hangar area. Once Sticky was aboard, the team released and suited up each visitor. They were then seated and secured into their seats with heads still covered. Tuck was about to remove the hastily made hoods when Reececup asked, "May I do the honors?" Tuck smiled and nodded.

Leaning close to the largest guy, the one who had been the 'mouth' she said, "Now, this can be easy or hard, sweetheart, if you would like for me to remove the sock from your mouth just nod." The man nodded meekly.

Reece pulled the mask up just enough to remove the band holding the sock in his mouth, "I didn't mean to hurt you, but you gave a girl no choice, threatening me with those electrodes. Now, do not speak, it isn't time yet." She pulled the sock from his mouth.

"You little b…" that ended in a scream as Reece pinched a nerve in his neck.

"Now.. Now.. mouth, I said DO NOT SPEAK." she placed a piece of duct tape over his mouth. "I think that should do it. Thank you for your cooperation." She went thru the same procedure with the smaller guy with no problems. Every one took their seats, and the charter climbed into the night sky, leaving the Gaston County area of North Carolina behind. The crew was laughing and joking about what the Chief would say when he found the whole crew bound and gagged with a teenager in charge. Soon the talk tapered off and they leaned back to enjoy an hour or so of deserved rest.

****

Chief Jessie J. was sitting in his '57 Chevy. He was on call twenty four hours a day, so this was not his normal hours. He should be home settled in with a book or watching an old Clint Eastwood movie. Many law enforcement officers still liked the Clint line, 'Go ahead. Make my day'. Earlier this evening a friend, Sticky, had leaned on him. It happens a lot in a job like his, but usually it is something small and, if he can, he will accommodate. He had missed some important family functions in the past while speaking to the Boy Scouts or some civic group. He had agreed to keep the troops out of North Mt. Bell and especially around the ACME. It was not a secret that a Militia was forming. There was a possibility some of his men would or had joined. A lot of folk in this country feel they might have to defend their freedom and wanted to be ready. He understood that and even agreed with a lot of their rhetoric. He had made up his mind he would not make an issue of the group unless pushed. Tonight, He had promised Sticky thirty-five minutes and those thirty five were about up. He wished he had never agreed to this, but Sticky was a solid citizen. He was headed to Raleigh, or so the political rumor-mill had it. It cannot be something illegal he kept telling himself.

Over his radio, he notified every unit to converge on the ACME, time was up. Sticky was not getting one extra minute. He put the Chevy in gear and burned a little rubber himself. He stuck his magnetic light on top and floored the '57. It was less than a mile. He was the first to arrive in front of the office. 'What in the world is this?' Inside the glass door was a kid looking out at his car. It was quiet as a mouse. He heard the squad cars coming so he got out, his weapon down at his side.

As he approached the door the kid opened it, "I was expecting the Chief of Police, do you know him?"

"I am Chief Jessie James son. Step outside for a minute."

"You don't look like a police chief, where is your uniform?" asked the kid.

"I am the chief, who are you and what are you doing here?"

"I'm Leroy Maifield, sir. I was kidnapped in Pittsburgh from the Lighthouse jail for kids and brought here along with Wonder Woman."

'Oh Lord, thought the chief, this must be an escapee from a mental home'. The other cars arrived. "Hey Joe, tell Tommy to pull his squad car around back and check the rear, have Sandy talk to the kid and see if she can make any sense out of him, then you come with me. Let's get inside."

At first, they saw nothing unusual inside, other than no adults were around. 'What has Sticky done to me?' thought the chief. Then they saw their first militiaman, then another until they located and loosed twelve very upset men. Jessie had them in one room under guard until he could make sense out of this. It was plain he was not going to be home early again tonight.

One of the officers approached the chief and said, you need to see this. He led the chief to the room where Reececup had been held. "This room looks mighty curious. That water is fairly fresh where the commode was ripped off. Something strange has happened here."

With his pen, the chief flipped one of the black suitcases open. "Ah, what would anyone need with illegal interrogating equipment. Find me someone who knows about this room."

The officer returned in just a minute with two men. They told about two men from out of town and with Yankee accents, wearing suits, coming into this room. We were told just to do whatever they asked us to do. We brought these cases in and set up that table. We assumed it was to interrogate a girl and a boy who were put in the room earlier in the day. He said that he, the guard, had locked the door. "They were inside and we heard some yells and muffled talk, but we were told not to open the door under any circumstance, so we didn't. They were secured inside when the flash bangs went off. I would swear that it was that same girl who we had locked inside that taped us up, and she did not come out of this room," he had just noticed the commode was on the table. "Hey who ripped out the commode?" asked the shocked militiaman.

'Wonder Woman', said Jessie to himself, "Take these guys back and bring me the kid," he said to the deputy, "And pass the word, no one leaves this building until I say so. Also, if anyone goes to the latrine a guard goes with him. This is looking more and more like a crime scene." While waiting, the chief wandered next door. Before he entered he noticed a door in the hall that had evidently been jarred loose when the back door was blown off. Using the butt of his flashlight he pushed it open, then shined his light inside. 'This looks awfully suspicious,' he thought as his light revealed a couple rocket launchers and three large cases that had AK47 stamped on them. An officer, with the kid, was approaching. "Take him in that room and wait for me." Then the chief called down the hallway, "Tommy, bring me the senior militiaman on duty."

Entering the room again, he knelt down by the kid and asked, "Is this the room you were held in?"

"Yes sir."

"Were you hurt or molested in anyway?"

"No sir, but we were threatened. One of the men was going to taser me again."

"Again? Had you been tasered before?"

"Yes sir, and it hurts worse than anything in this world. They did it to me when I was kidnapped in Pittsburgh. Where am I now, you people talk funny?"

Laughing the chief said, "Well son, you sound funny to us. But why did they kidnap you?"

"I don't know, but it was a mistake, they meant to get Wonder Woman's partner. I have thought about it a lot, I asked him to change beds with me so I would not be close to the window, so when they came in they got me instead of him." As the boy finished talking, a man was escorted into the room.

"Chief this is the local Top Sergeant. Sgt Smith."

"Excuse me son," the chief said to the boy. "Sergeant Smith were you interrogating two minors in this room?"

"No Chief, I ain't crazy. All I have done was follow orders. The CO told me to allow some folks from up north to use the facilities for a couple days. They were renting the space and it was going to help pay our rent. I saw them bring a couple people in, but I did not know they were minors. I provided storage space and a desk." Looking around for the first time himself, he asked to no one in particular, "What in the name of common sense have they done to our latrine?"

"Before I go any further Sarg, have you armed the militia yet? I mean does the militia own any weapons of its own?"

"No chief, true to militia standards, each man furnishes his own weapon and ammo. Just like the early militia, we have a rich heritage. I know this looks bad, but this is all a mistake. The CO will straighten it out tomorrow."

"Step out into the hall with me Top Sergeant," they stepped outside and the chief lead him down to the broken door, 'What do you store in this room, Sergeant?"

"I have no idea, Chief. I have never been inside. The CO uses that area for his own storage. We have plenty of room in this old mill. We can spare one room, what of it?"

"Look inside sergeant, and the chief put the flash light on some of the contents," as a military man the sergeant knew exactly what it was and he backed off. His mind was racing, every militia man knew of the armory break-in and what was taken.

"What I said is true Chief, but I had better not say anymore without seeing a lawyer."

"Good choice Sergeant," then to the officer, "Tommy, make everyone comfortable, but use extreme caution. This is a crime scene, these men are not necessarily criminals, but they have been rubbing shoulders with some." The chief went back into the interrogating room. "Okay, my first question is, how did you know the girl was Wonder Woman?"

Leroy was street smart. He knew the chief doubted his word. "Let me ask you something chief, if we moved that table, could you jump up to that vent pipe?"

"No son, I don't think I could, did she do that?"

"Yes sir, she did. Before the dudes came in she had already jumped up there to find out if we could go that way. She decided we could. But the men came before she could get me up there. Those men didn't know she was Wonder Woman. They thought she was scared of them. After the door was locked one of them threatened me with a taser. Then he made some sparks with two wires. Well, she didn't like that. She went airborne, was spinning around in the air kicking, chopping and everything. When she came down to the floor, both them grown men were out cold. She told me to take their shoes off, use a sock to put their pocket stuff in and she stuffed the other socks in their mouths. She ripped up their coat, took the sleeves and put them over their head so they couldn't see and used the rest of the strips to tie them up. She ripped the commode up. I put the table where she said to put it, then we put the commode on top. She was cool as a cucumber. She made one of those movie moves, swept her arm down and up and said 'after you', and we left. She was a whirlwind that is how I know she was really Wonder Woman. No regular person could so that, could they?"

The chief smiled, ruffled up the boy's hair and said, "No son they couldn't. I really believe you have met Wonder Woman. You will have to tell that story and more, do you mind?"

"Heck no, this has been more fun than I ever had. I was put in jail for nothing. Now I am glad I was. She said I could tell about the men who were here too."

Okay, let's go up front. We have a lot to do."

It was a rough but rewarding night for the chief and his department. Sticky had done him a favor in a roundabout way. He would treat Sticky as an informant and protect his identity. The thirty five minutes that it had cost, was well worth the results. The arms deal was his bust. The kidnapping was turned over to the FBI. Like many nights before, Chief Jessie would get no sleep. That was just another one of the hazards that went with the job title of Chief. Representatives of the County police, SBI and FBI were in and out. Then, first thing in the morning, there was the local reporter L. Thomas, from the Banner, as well as reporters from the Gazette and the Observer. Foremost in his thoughts was that the stolen weapons had been recovered on his watch. They weren't in the hands of some local terrorists. Good detective work would turn up evidence. He was almost sure finger prints would show up, they would find the prime suspects. Someone would be charged and then it was out of his hands.

He still smiled when he thought of Wonder Woman, and he wondered if she would consider a job with the Mt. Bell Police Department. Sticky is connected with some slick outfit. To do that type of work in less than thirty minutes and be gone, shows team work 'good luck you guys, where ever you are. I'd bet Pittsburgh or on their way'.

Chapter 26
The Judge is Judged

The entire team was assembled, following the success at the ACME. This was Pittsburgh plus ten days. Extra chairs were brought in to S'gar's office. Of course there was a tray piled high with sticky buns and gallons of coffee. The technical folk had not had time to eat well, much less chat with friends who were on assignment in other areas of the event. Now, before the meeting, they were exchanging high fives, shaking hands and exchanging bear hugs on occasion. Woody stood back in awe, thinking, I remember this from the force as well as the agency. Camaraderie is the same throughout the world when a team has accomplished a goal. This one certainly had, in spades.

S'gar headed to the head of the table as the group started to settle down and take seats as the boss spoke. "We have had a very successful event. Our goals have been met. The bad guys will be punished and every kid who has been sent to the Lighthouse Eight Corporation facilities will have their case reviewed by an impartial panel. That is going on as we are gathered here. This meeting is a detour from our regular event closing mainly because we have never used this many troops on one event. I want to thank, especially, Ben and Dallas who helped coordinate this endeavor. I never pictured it picking up the speed it did. The last twenty-four hours were too fast for one man to handle and delegate. Ben and Dallas kept their cool and helped this old man control an urge to destroy. That was caused because I did not require enough protection for the undercover agents. No shaking your heads, I know it worked out. But we were successful mainly because of luck, aided by good detection and study. I know we can use luck, but I always planned it the other way with good detective work and thorough study, then accept any luck as a bonus." He picked up a stack of envelopes. "As I call off a name please let me know where you are by standing or waving. I know most of you, but my friends have expanded their agencies and brought in some new faces." S'gar called off names and walked to the person, shook their hand and handed them the envelope. He had started with the last hired and was working his way up to the most senior.

"One of our members has a new name, Wonder Woman. She was trained to survive, and she did. She didn't sit and wait for us to come for her. In spite of being saddled with a young boy, she planned an escape and worked her plan. She fought her way out without our help. Freeing not only her young charge and herself, but thanks to her astute observations she grabbed a wealth of evidence in one briefcase. Her thoughtfulness in preserving the belongings of the two suspects further nailed the cases. The briefcase belonged to the mastermind of this whole ungodly project. It boggles my mind that a man who engineered a project of this magnitude would then carry all the plans, names, and information that could expose his project. This is beyond my comprehension."

S'gar put his arm around Reececup, "The kid who was kidnapped in Steve's place witnessed Reece leap to the ceiling to find a way out of the building. Then he watched as she took out two grown men, secure them and then led him to safety. When the local police interviewed the boy, he swore that he had been in a lock-up with Wonder Woman. After his testimony the Police Chief agreed."

Steve came to his feet and yelled, "Hear, Hear!" everyone stood and applauded. Reececup turned red.

She held her hands up as if to surrender. When the room quieted she said, "Thank you S'gar, but most everyone here could have done the same," then turning to face the crowd, "But as for the rest of you, if I hear anymore about this later you will see Wonder Woman in action, especially you Steve!" she and everyone had a belly laugh.

"Okay, let's finish this role call. Woody," S'gar walked over to where Woody was seated. "For you that do not know, this is Tuck's friend Woody, formally of the FBI. I want to take a minute to thank this real member of law enforcement who took a gamble and ran the ball for us. He has also agreed to return to help anytime we need him. He has added one disclaimer; that is if Anna Mae will allow it. They plan to fish a lot, and he is going to follow one of his greatest passions, cooking. Thanks Woody, you also get a bonus." Woody made an effort to turn the envelope down, but S'gar would have none of it. "I learned something from some twelve year old boys a long time ago. They were called 'The Three and a half

Musketeers'. Their code was, 'Share and share alike'. All these bonuses are the same."

The rest of the envelopes were given out, short accolades given and they all stood to stretch and get more coffee. They all milled around enjoying the idea of relaxing instead of the stress of an ongoing event.

****

The meeting continued with S'gar explaining the unknown factors and the results of the event. "I know you all would like to know the results of the event. In a phone conversation with the head of the Lighthouse group I was trying to appear to be bargaining for Reececup's life. I tried trading Judge Black and Officer West. Both were turned down flat, along with a lot of derogatory comments. I was recording the conversation. I also offered Tim Kelley, the CEO. That fazed him a little but he finally said Kelly was also expendable. To shorten this some, you can imagine how our guests felt when they heard the recorded conversation."

After a short pause he continued, "Once we had everyone on the same page, I called in the FBI. I gave them all the evidence we had accumulated. Dallas handled the legal end. The agent in charge told me he would call when they had decided who was going to be arraigned. I explained to the agent in charge that all the men had been on vacation. When I got the names I could tell them when the men would return home. Buddy, Tuck & J delivered them to their residences. There an agent was waiting to take them into custody for kidnapping."

"With the mountains of evidence, statements and testimony, the FBI will not need any of us. Only one man will receive immunity and that is Officer West. He has lost his fortune but will be allowed to retire on a normal pension. Judge Black and Tim Kelly have agreed to testify against Terry J Booker the Treasurer of Lighthouse Eight. He was the brains behind the whole scheme. For this testimony their sentences will be no less than twelve years and no more than eighteen. The Bureau is sure most of the others involved will cop a plea. The only trial will be that of Terry J Booker."

"I am near the end, stay with me. There was a rumor that some bodies were buried in the fields. That was not the case. Our foot soldiers and techno guys were able to trace all the missing kids. There are no bodies buried, the story was a red herring to keep the inmates in line. We were all glad it did not go that far. I have tried to give you a Reader's Digest version. Are there any questions?"

"I have one for J" said Steve. "Now, when I work with Wonder Woman, do I have to say, sir?" He ducked as Reece swung playfully at his head.

"What do you think Wonder Woman?" said J.

"Only when he is spoken to and then, in case you haven't noticed, I am not one of the boys. It is Mam, to you." she said laughing.

"I heard a rumor that Sticky was being promoted to the North Carolina Department of Transportation. Anything to that?" someone asked.

"I will field that," said Ben. "A friend of mine in Raleigh called to let me know that John Morse aka Sticky was being appointed as first assistant to the NCDOT. Congrats Sticky." There was another round of clapping.

"What is next with the MVA?" asked Josh.

S'gar stood, smiling sheepishly, "I know I don't look it but I am a senior and a bachelor. I made a mistake in my life and never made room for a lady. Well, now in the autumn of my life I have found one. One I love and she for some reason loves me. The story goes back to my tenure at Duke. I dated this lady a couple times, but work was too important. I lost her to a friend. She has been a widow for a few years now. One of our events brought us in contact and we have stayed in contact. As you can guess I have paid little attention to her in the last few weeks. That is about to change. Dallas has been itching to hold this job and I am going to let him have it. He has assured me his assistants can run Wiley Industries in his place. So, I am taking a sabbatical, to see If I can woo a woman in the autumn. Wish me luck!" That was greeted with whistles, way to go, atta boy, you go man, clapping and more. S'gar was waving thanks and giving the thumbs up. He pointed to Dallas.

Dallas stood, walked over to the head of the table, smiled and hugged S'gar. Then he turned to speak to the group, "Nothing is in the works for the near future. Everyone will go back to their own occupations and businesses. All events will be approved by S'gar, but for your information, there was a time as a young lawyer working for S'gar's father I wasn't sure the son would live to find a lady. A very few of us here can remember that this man, who has dedicated his life to do so much good and has spent millions helping some of the down trodden in this nation. That few of us can remember there was a time when he was considered a bum and called Rags." Dallas motioned for everyone to stand, and then concluded, "S'gar, I salute you, **There is no better man**."

And Finally............

Sticky in fact was promoted to the NCDOT and doing a great job.

J returned to Colorado his business and to his love on a ranch.

Tuck and Buddy merged their investigative companies and expanded worldwide.

Dallas reorganized the upper layer of the MVA, installing Ben and Corey directly under him and they handled the everyday operations, including a part of the school. S'gar had seen the potential in Corey, telling Dallas, 'there is intelligence in him that needs to come out'. Corey loved the driving part that he had filled for many years. He had hid his intelligence behind the wheel. Now, that was out, he would no longer drive, except when teaching the driving course to agents from all over the world.

It appears Josh will head his own company.

Steve and Reececup are being encouraged to form a company if they want it. It is a possibility.

The young man Phil was released and was met by his friend Harold. The MVA took a special interest in these boys to ensure a future.

Paula was offered a chance to go to school in Pittsburgh or relocate; she chose relocation and moved to Texas, of all places. She was given an allotment until she found work. She had some distant kin in the area and learned to really love Texas. After Pittsburgh, she gained an appreciation and love of country roads.

Woody's pastor joined the army as a Chaplain and had a stellar career.

And Woody? He and Anna Mae are busy fishing. In their spare time they cook and entertain seniors in upstate New York.

And S'gar did pursue and woo the lady!

Continue to read an excerpt from the book,
'Why Not Forever'

Why Not Forever?
Excerpt from a great book on marriage.
Why Not Forever
By Jack Darnell

September 22, 1956

Chapter 1

Marriage is a good thing.

Marriage with the right person for the right reasons brings true happiness. It is disappointing to see a young couple separate who just a few months before were all starry eyed and so 'in love'. It only took a few months for the glow to go. What happened? In my humble opinion the two never became one. That is a mystical statement. It is only understood by those who

have truly experienced it. How can one know this? First of all you need to read this book (wink).

Many reasons for these separations are not mystical. To be honest many marriages are entered into on the basis of having a place to call home, or sex alone. Ideally I think a couple should refrain from sex until marriage. Sex is going to be a huge part of this union, so you need to discuss it with someone you know and respect. We learned that too late. There was a lot of unnecessary trial and error but we made it through it. Just a small amount of good advice and knowledge would have helped immensely. We, as a nation of adults, **have not been** good parents at educating our young people of the wonders (and dangers) of sex, in the past. I berate myself still, because I did not talk seriously with my sons. My mind told me that they knew more about sex than I did at their age. Older folk cannot understand the openness of the youth of today. Yet with all the openness there is still a lot of misinformation. The young still do not know the wonders of the two becoming one.

When the minister/Rabbi/Priest or Notary says: 'you two are one'. What they are really saying is: 'The two of you will become ONE'.

It is a mystery, but one that needs to be unraveled. It is one that needs to be fathomed. It is so important your very life and well being depends on it. You need to spend some quiet time thinking about it. You will never fully understand the mystery, but you TWO can enjoy this mystery as ONE. You will become half a person on your own. I know folks that after divorce are like a fish out of water. That is because they are only half a person now. They have given the other half to someone and are too stubborn to admit it. The freedom they

Why Not Forever?

pictured is not there after the divorce. When facing some crisis in their marriage, they began to picture being free from responsibilities. They imagined the wild parties and the super sex. What they experienced was self gratification and a lot of loneliness, but not happiness.

Marriage is the joining of two lives that truly become one. This should be a wonderful learning experience, turn it into that. Marriage is the best thing this world has to offer for the right two people.

That statement brings up one of this life's favorite old statements: There is a mate out there that God has created for you. Oh, it feels that way when you have chosen that special someone. But in reality, in the majority of cases, we create our own 'angel'. In my life there was one or two girls that I thought could be the one. I am sure in Sherry's case there were boys who 'could' have been the one.

But when I saw Sherry I was struck. But it was one of those cases where I felt she could never be mine. And in reality, she admits, I was not in her mind. I was not even considered as a possibility. So much so, that when my name came up she said, 'Who?"

When we finally did get together we clicked. She was my angel, she was the one. I set my mind to make her mine. Now a psychologist might be able to explain that, but as a sixteen year old boy I just knew I had to have this girl. After a couple dates I think she started thinking seriously about this young kid. We were in the same school. I was a grade behind her. Sherry was from a working family. She took a job in her sophomore year. She had the afternoon off from school to work in a hosiery mill. So, during her senior year, when she left school at noon to go to work, I felt obligated to walk her to work thus skipping my

Why Not Forever?

afternoon classes. I was in Belmont High School. They had what was called a detention hall. You gained hours in detention in many ways, one was skipping school. I set a pretty good record skipping school to walk my new love to work. I also skipped detention hall, so I got hours added for that. I was a pretty good candidate for delinquent of the year. At sixteen, I was not looking good for a 'catch' for Sherry. But she too had fallen in love.

With all the negatives she knew there was something in this boy she wanted. There were no negatives on her side (that I knew of) so I kept pursuing. The only reason I am covering this ground is to let you know that even though things look bad on the surface, they can still work out, but it is not ideal. My point? Not many folks would consider this a match made in heaven. Not many folks would give a marriage between these two much chance of succeeding. I finally beat that detention hall thing, I quit school. I joined the United States Marine Corps. After boot camp at Parris Island (known as Pleasure Island to Marines) I made it home every chance I could get. Still chasing the same girl, I was in love.

It is sort of a practice for young marines to spend the weekends and evenings at the 'Slop-chute', a USMC tag for the Enlisted Club. I went several times. I still was not old enough to drink real beer but I could be served what was called '3.2', a weak beer. I had a friend, R.D. Fletcher, from Pennsylvania. He was like me young and in love with a girl named Marian. Many evenings Dallas and I would sit and talk about our girls. He thought Marian was the best looking, but I knew Sherry was. We were in the same duty section, and were on four section duty. Meaning we were allowed liberty during the same periods. Four section duty meant we had to stay aboard the base ever fourth night and every fourth weekend. When the liberty

Why Not Forever?

weekends rolled around Dal hitch hiked to Pennsylvania to see Marian and I drove to Belmont to see Sherry. Dallas and I became close friends. Today Dallas and Marian, Sherry and I are still married. Together we have been married over one hundred years. To be clear here, we were a little different than most of our comrades. Of course He & I thought we were God's gift, but neither Dallas nor I could have been classified as 'skirt chasers'. These two Marines were in love with two girls. One girl in North Carolina and the other in Pennsylvania, and no one else mattered.

Now in marriage the male is the dominating partner. At least we think so. I am convinced most marriages stay together because the woman allows us to think that. I was a smoker, Sherry was not. Whether she ever thought she could change me I do not know. It was many years, but I did quit smoking. Dallas was a smoker, Marion was not. Dallas still is. I brought that up for one reason, if there is something about the prospective partner you really do not like, do not marry planning to change him or her. Be ready to accept them as they are or set your sights elsewhere. The person may change, but it is not likely.

Understand in the beginning we do not change another person to fit our mold. People do change, but it is usually at their own pace and when they want to. It might appear to work on the outside, but you can create a pot that will come to a boil. Studies have shown that a woman who marries an abusive man hoping to change him ends up being abused. Alcohol abuse is the same. If a man continues to get 'drunk' on dates, find a way to distance yourself, this is not your knight in shining armor. Forget him.

To summarize, you create your angel, you fall head over heels, the Lord may be up there shaking his head wondering
Why Not Forever?
why he lets you live on His planet, you act so dumb. But He knows you have been smitten by the most powerful drive in the universe, LOVE with an overriding desire for sex. He just hopes the one you are smitten by feels the same as you. You see, He knows there are many rough rows to plow that lie ahead of you two. And unless you two actually become ONE the marriage will never survive.

For the marriage to survive the man must love the woman even more than he loves himself. The woman must love the man more than she loves herself. You must WANT to take her pain when she is sick.

She must want to shoulder your pain (without belittling you) when you miss the promotion. For the marriage to succeed you must hold each other tight when trouble comes rather than push the other away. When the two bodies embrace they become one sharing the trouble and pain. You squeeze and hold tight, until you know you are in this as ONE.

If you can't accept all the scars, moles and irritating habits you had better not try marriage. It is most likely that you will never change the person.

****

'Why Not Forever' is a great book for anyone planning to be married. It is a good gift especially to newlyweds since it covers areas we don't like to discuss. It is a book of advice on parenting, sex and in-laws.

The pages also include some thoughts to seniors who are looking for happiness in marriage in the autumn of their lives.

www.ingramcontent.com/pod-product-compliance
Lightning Source LLC
Chambersburg PA
CBHW060537180626
46817CB00002B/615